IN THE PINES

MARIAH STILLBROOK

Welcome to the coven!

Mariah Stillbrook

cJm

Published in the United States by Creative James Media.

IN THE PINES. Copyright © 2023 by Mariah Stillbrook. All rights reserved. Printed in the United States of America. For information, address Creative James Media, 9150 Fort Smallwood Road, Pasadena, MD 21122.

www.creativejamesmedia.com

978-1-956183-50-4 (trade paperback)

First U.S. Edition 2023

For Mom and Gina.

Arianna

The answers, along with the wicked and the not so wicked, the prisoners of invocation—they have always been in the pines. It is one of the reasons our family has ended up surrounded by them in every life, these familiar souls who have come back time after time. Unlearned, out of sync, they are meant to see what others do not. It is all there for whoever takes the time to see it, along the lines of these wise trees, their bark like the deeply set wrinkles of the ancestors our family has lost over the years.

Then again, if my daughters had been able to see their truths as I have always seen them or held the sort of wisdom these trees are akin to, then there would be no story to tell. And that, dearest witches, would be unfortunate. A story is quite like another lifeform; it is its own energy. I would hate for any life to be kept in the dark, and that is saying a lot, for I have lived many, many lives.

The night it began, in this particular lifetime, my familiar, Mr. Jackel, was sitting next to my foot. Had any stranger stumbled upon the two of us, they may have very well confused him for a statue. He was still because I was still. His feline energy aligned with mine, his neck erect, as he listened to the howls inside what my daughter Olivia always referred to as the folds. Though his eyes were centered before him, they weren't looking at any particular ghost or goblin—he, as well as I, was only searching. Searching for what we could feel but could not see.

I'd turned on the dim lamp from the porch to witness the snowflakes falling to the forest floor, as big and sparkly as winter fey. The snow grew heavier and the wind began to howl. I could no longer see the pines, for the forest was a blur of white streaks painted over the black canvas of night. The recent blizzard had caused night to fall early, but in the case of this family, darkness, like an oversized cape, had fallen over our coven years ago.

My sister Lana, my husband Ron, and I built this forest retreat before our children were born. We built it with only our wands, and in the case of my non-magical husband, his bare hands. We called it Sage Brook because of what grew next to the creek that ran through the property. The retreat was usually closed this time of year. We shut down just after Yule and reopened after Imbolc, the first day of February. According to an old Gaelic tradition, the Queen of Winter would decide on that day whether she desired to have a longer winter. Winter would be extended if the day was sunny because she could go out and gather more firewood to stay warm, but if it was gray and cold then spring would come early. But Imbolc hadn't yet arrived, so even if it had been gray on the first day of February, the retreat would still be vacant. The only souls, besides us, taking residence in the forest on this night were those who came without bodies.

"What is it you are searching for, Arianna?" Lana asked. I didn't need to feel her hot breath on my neck to know she was standing just behind me.

I brought my hand up to the glass pane embedded into the

door, feeling the chill from the blistering wind kiss my warm hand from the other side. Without turning, I replied in a wispy voice. "There's more than one storm brewing out there. Wherever *it* is, it's about ready to show itself."

It was a curse that plagued our family. One small misstep in a lifetime, buried by so much dirt it could fill a crater. A curse that came for us in each new life, stealing the lives of witches. As I stood there, the stench of rotting flesh surrounded by ocean water filled my senses, and I knew it was only moments before the curse struck us yet again.

I turned and faced my slightly younger sister. Nine months apart. Our mother had always said we'd wanted to be twins but that Lana had missed the first train. She'd returned to the kitchen table, her hands clasped around a steaming mug of tea, two empty shooters of whiskey next to it. Next to her, my husband Ron sat behind a newspaper to which he was only pretending to pay attention. He may not have had a magical bone in his body, but it didn't take a witch to know that today had been marked for a curse. It was in the air—I'd known from the second I woke up that morning. So had he and so had Lana.

"Have you heard back from Olivia?" Lana asked, her stony features firmly pressed into their places of rest.

"She texted me back," I said of my oldest daughter. "She said that she's down with a cold. She didn't seem to be aware that anything was off."

Lana scoffed. "Her awareness is not especially one to be trusted these days."

I sealed my lips together before retorting. "When one is haunted, it doesn't matter how far they look in the other direction, the haunter will always find them. My Olivia may have run, but she cannot hide, and I very much believe she knows this as well. Her time in hiding is coming to an end."

Ron looked from me to Lana, before folding up his paper

and placing it over the table's surface. "Well, I'm starvin' waitin' for whatever it is that's out there to show itself to us. How about I make us somethin' to eat?"

My husband never got the chance to tell us what he had in mind to make for dinner. He didn't have a chance to even scoot his chair back . . . to take the last swig of coffee from his mug. For in that moment, the shrillest scream I'd ever heard in this life shook every cabinet, every glass pane, every chair, every book—every last lingering spell in this house, and I knew immediately whose lungs that scream had come from.

A small cry escaped my lips as Ron gripped the table and Lana sat straight up, the back of her neck matching my familiar's.

"Ellie," was all she said.

I jerked my head to the side, waiting for more—to hear my youngest daughter cry out to me yet again. When she didn't, it took me but a half second to sprint from where I stood next to the glass door to the scrying bowl I kept charged under the skylight in the living room. Mostly, I waited to see my lost grandson's face in that watered reflection, but at that very moment all I wanted to see was *her*. And I didn't mean Ellie.

"Rowena . . ." I whispered our curser's name so softly that my loved ones wouldn't be able to hear. My voice was saturated with a hatred meant to draw her out, for that is what she fed upon—hate and fear. Pain. And that name she used— it was but a disguise.

The water rippled inside the bowl, but no face appeared. No shadow. Just an indulgent snicker.

"Nice trick, witch. But do you think one little zap from your spell can keep me away? She lies alone on the closet floor, your Ellie . . . She lies without air . . ."

"You deceive me," I said back to the invisible monster, my teeth clenched, my hand coming up to meet the necklace strung around my neck—the lock I'd kept in place from the moment I made these charms for myself and my daughters. It had warmed. The spell was in action.

The water continued to ripple as the whispered cackle persevered. *"If I'm not mistaken, you were warned that there would be consequences when you messed with your family's curse. The game has changed, as have the rules. I will have a witch today, Arianna. It is up to you who I lay my hands on. Ellie is weak. Your spell will only last so long to protect her life."*

The rippling water stilled, and just like that she was gone. *It* . . . it was gone.

When I finally turned around, I found Ron and Lana staring at me. In my husband's hand, his phone. "Ellie's not answering," he said.

Of course she wasn't. That scream had been real. That vile energy had my child's life in its rotted-out hands.

I started to say something, but Lana beat me to it.

"Your lock, Arianna—it has turned red."

I stared down at the little charm. One of three formed into my hands after locking words with the goddess so many years ago, in the lake that stood just outside this home. The charms were part of a protection spell, or at least that's what I'd told my girls.

"Never take these off, my little witches," I'd said to my daughters so very long ago. Ellie had been five and Olivia, ten. "If you ever need me, the necklaces will know, and my magic will keep you safe." I'd clasped a key around each of their necks, and we'd danced under the marrying tree and watched as the snow fell over our shoulders in August.

My daughters didn't know then, nor did they know now —all grown up—that it was never a protection spell. It was a spell I'd created under a shower of stars to end a curse plaguing our family for ages. A curse only I knew the origins of because only I could see as clearly into our past lives as my sister Lana could see into the future, as Ellie could create magic from the strings of her violin, and as Olivia could communicate with spirits.

I knew the origins of she who called herself Rowena, and I knew why she came back to us in every life, plucking witches from our family tree like pine needles from skinny branches. I knew why my two daughters fell away from each other in each life, even hated one another. I knew why Ellie struggled with love, and why Olivia always gave up and danced in any direction other than where she was supposed to be. I knew all these things and I was sick of them. So I created a spell. When Rowena was ready to strike at any one of us, when the time was right, then the truth of her identity would finally come out.

The spell wasn't foolproof; Olivia's son's disappearance early in his life was proof of that, and my goddess warned me that there would be consequences for breaking into such dark magic. But in every new life I was their mother, and in every new life I had to watch them make the same mistakes over and over. I had had enough.

Before walking back into the kitchen, I looked past my sister and husband. As I reached for my coat and car keys, I whispered softly, "It has Ellie. I must go to the city. I have to—"

"It? Who or what is *it*? Who has Ellie?" Lana questioned.

Only myself and my Olivia knew Rowena's name.

"Arianna—" Ron started, a crack to his voice.

I squared myself with him, placing my hands over his shoulders. "We've spoken about this. We knew this day was in the cards."

"What are you talking about?" Lana's eyes, almost accusatory, landed on my husband. "What has she told you that she hasn't told her own blood?" When neither of us answered, she pleaded in a very unconventional way for her.

"At least let me come with you. It is ten degrees out there and the plows won't come out until tomorrow."

"I must go on my own."

"This is stupid, Sister."

"No Lana, this is a trade." Somehow, I knew that's exactly what this was.

There was nothing but silence in the house in the moments that followed my speech, just the sound of the wind howling out of doors. Finally, Ron pulled me in closer so I could feel his heart beating against my own. "Be careful," he whispered into my ear.

The skin over my face tightened. Several lifetimes I'd spent with this man, loving him more in every new body I lived in, and now I wasn't entirely sure when I would see him again. If ever. "I love you so, my heart." Pulling away, I studied him. "I think it's time you get that extra guest room back in order." He raised his eyebrows in question. "Olivia will need a place to stay when she returns."

He lowered his chin and nodded softly.

"Olivia?" Lana questioned from where she stood, off to the side like a disheveled coatrack.

Biting down over my lip, I stiffened my jaw so I would not cry. Rowena may not have been showing herself, but that didn't mean she wasn't purring over my shoulder, waiting for me to break—to quit what I had started all those years ago when I messed with her curse.

"Broom Head," Lana said, calling me by the name my upsetting hair had earned me when we were just kids. For the first time in our lives I saw a hint of moisture in my sister's eyes. "The magic coming from your necklace—it's not emanating protection. That was never your spell's intention, was it?"

I blinked but said nothing. Secrets were not something Lana and I kept from one another, but for what I'd started under those falling stars to manifest, I had to let all the elements unravel on their own. It was the only way.

"I have to go," I said. And after one last kiss over my husband's cheek and one last glance at my sister, I took the door handle in my hand and said to them both before walking out into the storm, "Take care of Sage Brook . . . and watch over my girls."

Mr. Jackel's fierce meow was the last thing I heard before the wind slapped my face, and the howls from the spirits I could not see as easily as my first born cried for me to turn around.

My necklace continued to glow a vibrant red as I drove through the snow-packed roads. It took me an hour to get to the highway, and another thirty minutes to get anywhere near Denver, but I was never destined to get to Ellie. I knew, the second I saw the ghostly figure of a witch, with long straggly dark hair down to her backside, her black dress drenched in the ocean water that she drowned me in the first time—I knew that for Ellie to regain the air she'd lost, it would have to be taken from my lungs.

All I saw before the crash was that same wicked grin I'd seen so many lives ago. The vile expression was painted over the canvas of a witch I'd known when she'd been happy . . . before she'd known pain, and before pain made her body into a monster.

Her song was the last thing I heard after my car slid across the highway and crunched against the guard rail. A song that could chill its listeners to the bone. A shiver ran down my spine as the image of a forest full of pines filled in around the snowflakes. Her words ringing in my head as the car fell from the bridge down into the street below.

Her laughter faded away into the recesses of my mind. And then my spirit left my body. Mostly.

OLIVIA

Six Months Later

When I was a little girl, I asked my mother if evil was born evil, just as we were born witches, or as my father was born without magic. She returned my question with one of her own. "What do *you* think, my Olivia?"

I told her I didn't know, that's why I was asking her. She told me the answer was already inside me; everything I needed to know was coded in my bones. It wasn't a lot of help. Even still, I would've given my freewill to have her back just long enough so I could ask that question again. Because maybe this time, all these years later, she would actually help me find the answer I was seeking. But she wasn't here with me, and she wasn't there with them. She was gone, and not even the truest psychic of our family, my aunt Lana, could tell us where she was.

The lost coast had been my refuge for many years, but even someone like me—a person who had a habit of finding consolation in sanctioning herself away from everyone who she had ever loved or loved her. Even I knew that my time alone was coming to an end.

It was palpable, the chill of separation hanging in the air. One so cutting that I didn't have to be on the other side of this window to know that she—*it*—was out there. That it had been waiting for me like a starved creature of the sea since the moment I was born into this life; waiting for just the right moment to show itself to me. Saliva dripping down its rotted out, graying chin, in anticipation of finally tasting my flesh. When I thought of Rowena, I thought of gnarled hands, like the twisted knots of an ancient tree, atrophied in a claw-like maneuver—poised and ready to unravel just so she could claim my neck. I'd closed the veil years ago, holding my breath of any spirits, not just hers, but just because I couldn't see her didn't mean she wasn't there . . . that she wasn't floating on the other side of this window, looking in. Just because I had *chosen* not to see her didn't mean that she couldn't see me.

It wasn't especially kosher to call them ghosts because that wasn't what all of them were. In truth, there are many variations of spirit, and many folds may or may not keep them in place. Some spirits are manmade: unfortunately those spiritual types do not usually come in the benevolent variety. Others may be imprints of a soul that has moved on, a recording of an identity that plays over and over; these imprints are often responsible for 'hauntings.' Some are lost, some are cursed, and others are travelers. Many of them are spirits who are between lives, spirits who may come and go as they please; they are often referred to as spirit guides. As far as other things out of sight—angels and demons—I wasn't raised to believe in them as far as most theologies describe them. We were raised to believe that there is good and evil in the world, period. Spirits, just like people, come in dark and light.

Even though I was brought up to respect each individual spirit, I've still always found it easier to call all the spirits who flock in my direction ghosts; and as far as Rowena, regardless of what I believe and don't, I decided long ago that she *was* a demon.

The front door slammed shut, causing the smallest of vibrations to work themselves through the house to where I was standing. Not even a half minute later I watched as Maddie, my last visible child, stalked past my office window. She had just turned sixteen; and was good at acting like it. Why couldn't just one thing be easy?

I lifted a pale hand up to the windowpane as she glanced haughtily in my direction, her sharp eyes like seeds being spit from the mouth of a bitter soldier. The pads of my fingers just barely touching the window, I exhaled a breath filled with the sensation of dry sand as my daughter strutted past the old lighthouse, just past my property line, and her back disappeared down the breaks and to the edge of the California lost coast.

I pressed my lips together, the lump in my throat bobbing up and down as a familiar fear settled over me like the hands of a gentle demon. The lack of control that I couldn't handle, would shake me down to my bare bones and cause Rowena to take notice. I had no choice, I needed to vent, to talk to someone, and there was no one *alive* who could help me.

I took a deep breath, held it, then let it out slowly as I followed the instructions given to me by my mother when I was just a small girl. Her voice haunted my thoughts. "You can shut them out, my Olivia, whenever you need. When the spirits get too plentiful, simply build a barrier around yourself and tell them they aren't welcome to visit during that time. When you are ready to communicate with them again, let out the air you've kept cooped up in your chest—as it *will* be cooped up—for your gift, little witch, is made up of spirit talk. As soon as the barrier is down, they will be able to find you again."

My mother's voice drifted back into the shadows as I did what she'd instructed me to do so very long ago. I allowed the barrier I'd kept built around myself (for a much longer time than she'd ever advised me to do) to slowly crumble away. When that invisible cape fell from my shoulders, I heard *his* voice. He was my mentor, a friend to me when I had no one else. When I walked away from my old life and into the lost coast, *he* was the only one who I'd confided to about my magic.

"Hello Olivia."

A shudder of a breath fell from my lips. "Hello Gerald."

"It's been some time now."

It had been two years since I'd last slipped the veil.

I suddenly felt like fire ants were crawling inside my veins. In attempt to occupy my shaky hands, I reached for the pen occupying space on the windowsill. I gripped it firmly between my forefingers and thumbs. It was the way I had used to hold my wand.

I turned from the gray sky, looming over the black waters crashing down over the lost coast and faced Gerald.

"I would ask why you've suddenly opened yourself up after so long, but I think the answer is plain to see. You've fear in your heart, Olivia."

My words were hostile as I choked out what I could no longer turn from. "I am being chastised."

His lips were as cherry red as I remembered them, his beard white and trim. He posed his question as if he already knew the name of she who was most likely floating outside my office window. "By whom?"

"You know by whom. I swear, my family's curse is stalking

me—taking bits of my life away so little at a time that it makes every day all that more excruciating. She—*it* is, like, *breathing* down my neck."

I took small, hesitant steps towards the chair opposing the one Gerald sat in. Normally the seat he was in was mine, and the one I was currently sulking down into was reserved for my patients. But just now, I was the patient. Gerald was no longer living in the physical sense, but he was the only psychotherapist I trusted.

He gestured to the window with his chin. "You and Maddie fought—she stalked off. What was it about?"

"I didn't open the veil so we could talk about my shitty parenting."

He realigned his gaze with mine. "No, you called on me because of your ghost. But to deal with the past, we must first figure out what's going on with your present. Now tell me, what have you and Maddie been arguing about?"

My shoulders hunched forward of their own accord, and I glared down at the pen in my hand. When I spoke, I retorted like a stubborn adolescent in starvation mode when confronted with the question as to why he or she was refusing to eat. "Let's not pretend like you don't already know."

Gerald crossed one leg over the other while pressing a pale white finger into his chin. "She's asked you to return home with her. She, like most everyone in your family, doesn't understand why you've not come home during this dreadful time."

My pupils were like the pointed ends of sharpened daggers. "I *did* go home. When my mother was first taken to the hospital—I returned."

"For a heartbeat."

"Long enough to see their unforgiving faces all staring back at me."

"Is that why you didn't stay?"

"No." I softened my voice and raised my hand to gently touch the key hanging around my neck. *It was warm*. Ignoring the strange occurrence, I continued. "I went back to humor my aunt. She had it in her head that the charms our mother gave to us when we were little could unlock her heart . . . that my mother wasn't in a coma at all but was stuck in some sort of spell. But just as I thought, nothing happened when Ellie and I stuck our keys into our mother's lock. She remained as still and cold in the seconds that followed as she'd been when I'd first walked into her hospital room." With my tongue coated in vinegar, I chirped, "It was driving in a blizzard and wrecking her car that earned her that coma—not a spell."

Gerald strummed the same finger he'd cupped around his chin over his lips, and his eyes narrowed on me as though he didn't quite buy my last statement. "Why did your aunt believe your mother's coma was part of a spell?"

I shrugged my shoulders. "I don't know." Staring relentlessly back at him, I replied, "I didn't stay long enough to ask."

He bobbed his head shortly and curtly, then added, "And Ellie? How did she react to your short and abrupt arrival?"

I sucked in a ragged breath. "She didn't say a word."

He reacted with a guarded chuckle. "Well then, that's out of character, isn't it?"

Staring down at the pen in my hand but seeing instead the anger in my sister's spirit I'd seen that day—the rage, I replied, "She didn't have to say anything. She didn't have to speak for me to understand that she wished more than anything that *I* was the one in that coma instead of our mom."

Gerald lowered his hand into his lap and dug deeper. "Since we're on the subject of your sister—"

"Don't." I knew what he was going to say. He brought this up every time.

"Olivia," he stated in a parental tone, "you always say that you don't blame her for what happened to Tha—"

"Don't say his name."

He gingerly closed his mouth and nodded his head before going on. "You are adamant that you are not angry with Ellie for what happened to your son—"

"She wasn't the one who did this to him."

And just like that, the memory returned to me. The one where Ellie ran into my room when we were just little girls. The light inside her had been visible—her skin all a glow. And in her little balled up fist, a bit of notebook paper.

We'd been encouraged to write our own spells. It was like poetry, our mother and aunt said time after time. We were never allowed to work them until they'd been approved, but that particular spell my sister wrote, it never got the chance for approval; for I knew with just one look down into her sloppy, childish handwriting, that this spell could never ever see fruition.

She'd called it The Whispering Wind. Once the words had been recited and the magic taken hold, she or he who was in the throes of the spell would be sucked into the elements and only be able to communicate with the world via earth, wind, water, or fire. Ellie saw it as a whole other way to experience life. Inexperience showed in the spell's creation.

"Don't destroy it, Olivia, *please*! It's a dance that never ends! How beautiful would this be!"

"No Ellie," I'd retorted, holding the piece of paper away from her outstretched hands. "Don't you see, the way you've written this, you wouldn't ever be able to come back. Mom and Dad would be really sad. *I'd* be really sad."

She shot me an angry look that I would learn to know very well, then crossed her arms over her little chest before storming from my room. I folded up the piece of paper and stuck it between the folds of my spell book. It had been the biggest mistake of my life, not destroying it. All I'd had to do was burn it. Why hadn't I?

"Ellie was just a child when she wrote that spell," I said to Gerald.

"Ellie was not the one who cursed your son, we know who that was. But it *was* her spell, and if she hadn't ever created it—"

"She was too young to understand the implications of such magic."

"Yes, but does that change the way you feel? If she hadn't ever formed your son's words, he might still be here instead of lost to the wind. On some level, do you think you *do* blame her? That *that* is why you ran away? Because you couldn't stand to look at her?"

Once more I allowed my surroundings to turn to black, returning to the day my world shook and burned to the ground. I'd woken in the arms of my husband. Tyler was the other half of my heart's beat. I'd spent the morning with Maddie in the gardens, picking tomatoes and peppers for making tacos that night. Thaden was upstairs in his room with his new little playmate—he called her his invisible friend, but I knew she was more than that. My son had not only inherited my magic, unlike his twin sister, but he had also inherited my gift.

I wasn't nervous. I had done for my son what my mother did for me. I allowed him to get to know the spirits who would be flocking to his side for all his living years; and if he got too invested, or felt too crowded, then I would show him how to cut them off, just as my mother had shown to me.

But I *should* have been nervous. That day, I should have checked in on him earlier.

I'd waited until Maddie was plopped on a pillow on the floor, the sound of her favorite afternoon television show blaring into the living room, to go upstairs and see what my son was up to.

I can still remember the chill that found my skin that hot summer day—the humidity that licked my nose with the scent of rot inside of incoming ocean tides.

As I climbed the steps to my son's bedroom, I recalled what my mother had told me when I was a little girl. "*Our family is plagued by a curse, Olivia. It's you she's truly after, but she will hurt you by hurting all of us. She will take from you all your love if you let her. I beg of you, my Olivia, don't let her. No matter what happens, don't let her burn away your heart.*"

The putrid scent only grew stronger, and as I took the stairs by twos to get to my son's room quicker, a terrifying thought crossed my mind. Thaden's playmate. He'd said she was a little girl . . . that she was once a witch, too.

"No, it couldn't be," I'd muttered to myself, as the realization of what could've been conspiring took hold in my mind. Could it have been the devil in disguise this whole time? My very own demon dressed as an innocent friend to pluck her first victim in this life. "Thaden!" I'd yelled, running into his room. But I knew as soon as I got there that I'd been too late.

All that was left inside the four light blue walls was the scent of my ghost, a fading laughter, and the piece of notebook paper I'd stolen from Ellie when she was a little girl. Rowena— this demon—had gained my son's trust, then given him a spell that would take him away from me forever. Taken him into a fold so deep that I could never be sure whether he was still alive.

How was I supposed to keep it together after that? Per my mother's request, how was I supposed to keep from letting this terrible creature, who cursed our family lifetime after lifetime, from burning away my soul?

I continued twirling the pen between my fingers as though

it was my wand. Sometimes I missed the feel of the real thing. The heaviness of the magic inside the wood. Returning to Gerald's question—did I blame Ellie for my son's too early departure from this world? I continued to study the pen as I answered him.

"No, I don't blame my sister. I ran away from my home because I just couldn't be there anymore. It was never Ellie's fault. If anything, it was my fault for not getting rid of the spell in the first place. But how was I to know that *she*, that *that thing* would find it and use it against me so many years later?"

"Exactly." Gerald turned his cheek to the side. "How were you supposed to know? You couldn't have. Which brings me around to my next question. Why do you continue to punish yourself? You don't blame Ellie. Regardless of whether you've told her that or not." A dig from my former colleague. "You understand that it was and is this evil entity behind all your pain. So why do you walk down into that reef every day and sit on those jagged black rocks, staring into the ocean as if you wish it would swallow you up? Why, Olivia, do you keep yourself secluded here—miles away from everyone who loves you?"

Insolence found me once more. "People move away from their families every day. What I've done is nothing unusual."

He raised his brows. "Oh? Is it normal for a wife and mother just to leave her family with nothing but her wand and the clothes on her back? Is it *acceptable* for that mother to drive until she hits the coast, and then begin forming an entirely new life for herself? For what has it been—eight years now?" I scowled. "And is it customary, for an individual such as yourself—bound by magic to her husband, unable to divorce or see other people, or witches, without the taboo that will find each new relationship—to just pretend that the bond between you, your husband, and your goddess does not exist? *That*, you say, is completely fine. People do this every day?"

A wave of my sister's temperament raged through my chest and I clenched the pen tightly in my right fist, warding away the urge to tell Gerald to fuck off. Instead, I held it in, causing the room to shake violently as though a quake of the earth had found us.

Once it had settled, Gerald readjusted himself in his seat. "Right. I see bottling up that magic of yours is working out well."

"You don't have to be sarcastic. I know there are repercussions. And I also don't appreciate you coloring me in such distaste. I didn't *desert* my family."

He shook his head back and forth innocently. "I've only stated the true events of your past and present. You chose this not only for you, Olivia, but for your family—extended and intermediate. You chose to leave your husband, and now every relationship you or he attempts will inevitably fail."

"That's not necessarily true."

"Oh really? So, your magical union with Tyler was a special one? You and the goddess made a tailored pact?" He waited for me to give his sarcastic question an answer. He was alluding to the fact that witches married a little differently than the non-magical. And even though Tyler wasn't a witch, we were still bound by magic. It wasn't something that could easily be undone. When I didn't react, Gerald continued. "Tell me, what happened with that fellow you saw a few years ago? The, uh, psychology professor. I believe you met him at my funeral."

I had laid my hands flat over the pen on my lap, and as I answered him, I chose to look away. "I ended it."

"Because . . ."

I let out an exasperated breath. "Because his most recent research began to get skewed. I had an inkling that it might have had something to do with the two of us being together."

I allowed my eyes to roll back in Gerald's direction. He had the vaguest of smirks on his face.

"And what was he was trying to put into print? You'll have to remind me; I just can't ever remember."

From the ornery grin quivering along the fine lines of his face, I knew very well that he remembered. "I don't think I need to resurface this upset."

"Oh, but I disagree."

"Fine! His study on schizophrenia developed towards that of sheep. He theorized these mentally impaired animals could be cured. He ran them through a shallow river on a twelve-hour loop on the third evening after a new moon."

"*And . . .*"

"And he began to grow fur below his knees. And his toes may have started forming into hooves."

He tried. He really did try not to laugh, but it was only seconds later that Gerald shook in his seat with a hand clenched over his mouth.

"Oh! I'm so very sorry, Olivia, but I just can't get enough of that one!"

I replied haughtily under my breath, "This isn't very professional, Gerald."

"Sorry." He continued to chuckle, plucking a ghostly tear from under his faded blue eyes. "Oh, I just love a good dark comedy; don't get much of that on this side. And at least he's back to normal, now, hey?"

"Yes. It's all better now," I said through clenched teeth.

Once he'd settled, his lips twitching ever so slightly in the aftershocks of the humorous episode, he placed his attention over me once more. "I'm only trying to get you to understand. This is why Maddie is angry, why Tyler is angry."

"I wouldn't know if Tyler was angry," I muttered.

"Exactly, because you haven't spoken to the man verbally since the day you left. These emails you communicate through so that you can deal your daughter back and forth, these are but mechanical movements."

"I get it," I stated.

"Good, then let's return to your fight with Maddie. Tell me what happened."

I began to reinstate the fact that he already knew, but then drew back. Taking a deep breath and placing the pen on the arm of the chair, I straightened my posture and looked at my ghostly old friend.

"She tried to coerce me into coming back with her to Colorado tomorrow. It should have been of no surprise to her that I said no, but as soon as I did, she flew off the handle."

"And then what?" Gerald asked.

"She called me selfish."

I waited for his facial expression to change, to justify with a microscopic movement of the brows Maddie's truth, but he didn't. And of course he didn't. He was a good therapist—a good teacher. He'd make me say it out loud.

"She was right," I muttered. "Everything we've been talking about, you and I, it all points to my self-serving lifestyle."

"Yes well, though there may be attributes of truth in there, we both know it is the pain in your heart that has kept you here—not because you don't want to be with your family."

"They are reminders of what used to be," I whispered.

"And Maddie is his twin."

My gaze rose to meet his, but I did not answer.

After a sorrowful moment, Gerald rearranged his legs and moved on. "Does Maddie know of your ghost?"

Hesitant to say the name out loud, because I felt like it drew her closer, I did so only for clarification. "Rowena?"

He nodded.

"Just because Maddie was born without magic does not mean she hasn't been warned." However, I was the only one besides my mother who knew the entity's name. The only other one who knew *why* Rowena detested us . . . or me rather. The rest of the family knew that we were slaves to a curse.

"But your demon only takes witches," Gerald said in an inquisitive manner.

"So far. It doesn't mean Rowena wouldn't stoop so low as to steal my only other child."

"I see." The answer seemed hesitant.

Questioning his wavering demeanor, I asked, "What is it?"

He looked up at me before wrinkling his forehead. "Oh Olivia." I frowned back at him in confusion of his informal address. Grasping his chin with his hand, he stared at me wholly. "It is not for me to say this to you, but your timing of lifting that veil of yours is impeccable. I daresay it must be your witch's intuition."

Leaning slightly forward, I asked, "What are you talking about?"

He sighed, dropping his hand back down to meet the other. "Olivia, while I was living, I thought of you very much as the daughter I never had. You came to me eight years ago raw and unnerved. You laid out your truths for me to hear and showed me what you really were. You came to me a patient." He paused. "Do you know why I trained you to become the therapist you are today?"

"Because your cancer was terminal, and you wanted someone you trusted to take over your practice. You told me I had the eyes of that person."

"That was just something I said to make you feel needed. I made you into a therapist because I could see from the second you sat down in my office that you were haunted. That you were someone who couldn't be told what to do or how to let go—that you needed to learn this on your own." He stilled, taking a deep breath before returning to his thoughts. "Whether or not it is the goddess light inside your heart, you have a natural tendency when it comes to helping others, and perhaps this is why your gift lays in seeing spirits. You know how to help others move on. When I chose to help you become what you are today, I did so because of these attributes, but also because I hoped that at some point you would be able to apply what you saw in others to yourself. To take your own advice."

I hesitated. "You make it sound as if I failed you."

"No." His faded eyes sharpened. "Some things just take more time. However, time is something I fear you may no longer have."

I jerked my head to the side. "What are trying to say, Gerald?"

He cleared his throat before responding. "You know that I try very hard to keep what I hear from the other side quiet, just as I know that when it is time for you to speak about certain things you will. But I happen to know you're working against a clock that has recently been wound, and I cannot in good conscious leave this one on the table."

"Wh—What do you mean?"

"Your sister, Ellie, her life was nearly taken the day your mother got into her accident."

"Yes," I affirmed. "It is why she was driving to her, she sensed that Ellie was in trouble."

"When you saw Ellie at the hospital the day you returned for that half second—you saw the marks around her neck, yes?"

I turned my gaze to the wall. It was shameful. Yes, I had seen the proof of my sister's assault, but anyone who had ever met my sister wouldn't believe that she was a victim of any sort of abuse. If anything, she was the giver! With her too vibrant personality, her snippy comebacks. She was impulsive, cutting. The word selfish even came to mind when I thought of my sister. But apparently, even the most unbreakable of stones could be scratched. Her alcoholic wife, whom I had never met —for Ellie had been engaged to her high school sweetheart, Derek, when I left—had nearly strangled her to death in a fit of drunken rage. I knew that much because Maddie had told me.

When I saw Ellie that day in my mother's hospital room, I looked away before I could *really* see her. I looked away from her pain, and her willingness to bleed before others. I knew how much she was hurting, but who was I to stand before her and ask for forgiveness? I'd already dug myself into this hole and I had no will to fly myself out.

Gerald's voice cut into my pulsating thoughts. "You do know, Olivia, that it was Rowena who came for your sister that day."

My gaze shot back to his immediately.

"What? No, it was Joe."

"It was Joe's body, but it wasn't Ellie's wife who came for her."

"H—How do you know this?"

"Spirits talk," was all he said.

I sat there quietly for a moment, trying to piece together my next words with a quivering jaw. "But that's—it's impossible. If Rowena had her claws around my sister's neck she would not have let go. Once she tastes blood, she can't help but drain the vessel."

"Not if the rules have been altered."

"What are you talking about?"

Gerald held my gaze for a moment before leaning forward, placing his elbows on his knees. "Did you happen to notice that day in the hospital anything different about Ellie, other than the marks around her neck?"

I paused, and my gaze hardened over his as I tried to place what he might've been alluding to. I pictured my sister, draped over the other side of our mother, her eyes dry but red. The

24

bruising of her neck all different shades, but predominantly yellow and brown. And her necklace, the bronze-colored charm, the necklaces our mother had given us when we were little girls—never to be taken off for they were wards against evil—it had changed.

"Her key was purple." The words drifted from my mouth in realization. "I—I guess I never thought much on it because there was so much going on that day, and I—I just wanted—"

"You just wanted to leave," he finished for me.

"Yes." Suddenly I realized that Gerald was no longer 'shrinking' me. "Wait a second. Where are you going with this? What did you mean a little while ago when you said I'm working against a clock that has recently been wound? That the rules have been altered."

As I looked at him, a heaviness set in as though I was being filled with sand.

"You should listen to your daughter, Olivia. You should go home."

I wrinkled my forehead; my heart was beating in my ears. "Are you trying to tell me—"

"Your sister's life was spared on the same day your mother's soul ascended from her body. Your mother's lock was red, your sister's key purple. *Think about it, Olivia.*"

"Are you insinuating that what my Aunt Lana said had merit? That my mother was inside some sort of spell? That she still is?"

"Did you ever really buy that protection spell your mother worked over the two of you with those keys of yours?"

"Why wouldn't I have?"

"You gave up your magic. You became a different person— protection was the last thing you wanted, because the pain in your heart was so palpable. Yet you never have taken *that* off." He pointed to my necklace. "Look down, Olivia. The tides have brought Rowena in, and she will not rest until at least

25

one soul is forever taken. Until more than one light is permanently put out. It wants what it couldn't have the first time."

My mouth twisted as I tried to form my words around what I needed to say—what I needed to ask. I turned from Gerald to the wall, sucking in my cheeks and biting down so hard I could nearly taste blood.

"What it couldn't have the first time? My mom insisted that Rowena was after revenge, because of what I—" When I faced the chair I commonly resided in, it was empty. Gerald had gone.

"Shit," I cursed, suddenly realizing how cold the air in the room had become. Even though spirits brought with them a change in temperature, this wasn't the case. It was the emptiness that had chilled the air.

Look down, *Olivia*, Gerald had said.

A short breath escaped my lungs and I lowered my chin down to my chest, lifting the key charm which had warmed not so long ago, into my hands.

I looked up at the vacant chair and whispered to him as if he was still there, "Why is it blue?"

ELLIE

I woke up to shame.

A slow invisible drill was screwing a jagged piece of metal into my skull. My mouth was dry but rank with the scent of red wine, and dry heaves were already on the way. There were two and a half empty bottles of wine staring back at me from the kitchen counter. Bile crept up my throat just at the sight of them. The cabin inside my family's retreat—my chosen place of enduring my marital separation—was small. There was no room for the regret that hung in the air like a thick, muggy fog.

Derek's lifeless hand lay over my stomach. Immediately, my mind was filled with a procession of curse words. Then again, what is the proper reaction to waking up naked next to your ex-fiancé after a wine binge? I sure as hell wasn't spitting out rainbows.

My phone vibrated against the wood floor in intermediate cadences. Dread immediately sank into my rotten gut the second I caught sight of Joe's name flashing across the small screen. Careful not to wake Derek, I began to untangle my naked limbs from his, then grabbed for scraps of clothing from the floor. I kicked at the silver spoon with Joe's hair tied around its shaft then crawled down to the naked floorboards.

If my head hadn't hurt so badly, I would've been shaking it at myself.

Joe and I were separated, but neither of us wanted our marriage to be over. It was a time for reflection—not screwing other people. Then again, this all happened because I decided she was partaking in casual sexual encounters . . . Or was that just me jumping the gun?

Jesus, why the fuck was I so impulsive? *Why the fuck had I meddled inside her head?* If I hadn't screwed around with taboo witchcraft, then I might not have sunk to such drastic measures. I mean, I could be a real douche bag, but screwing Derek—

"Oh god, Ellie," I muttered, choking down the urge to yack. "You've really done it this time."

A brand-new apology stared back at me from my phone, a request to allow me to hear her out. I sighed and my head rolled backwards of its own accord. All I'd wanted to do the night before was a spell of intention in my shitty little cabin. *Goddamn it.*

I shifted my gaze to the table where my wasted spell ingredients laid scattered like torn up pieces of canvas from the hands of an artist betrayed by their own mind. Bayberry and acorns, collected for good fortune—ha! —now lay like victims of a recent terrorist bombing. Dandelion root, clovers, and amber incense from my Aunt Lana's stash, for protection and positive energy—strewn over the table like drowned victims washed up on a beach. It was all wasted now, of course. Covered in shame and vengeance. All because of that one reckless text from my wife.

I think you should move on. You deserve better than me.

It was just so unnerving! And so like Joe to send me

something like that just when shit was looking like it might be turning around.

We'd been separated since that nightmare of a day. Since she'd gotten so bloody tossed that she couldn't even tell when she wasn't herself anymore—when she'd let that cursed bitch wear her skin like a fucking wetsuit. Because of her I almost died, and because of her my mother, the one witch I needed more than anyone in my life, was stuck in a hospital bed, and goddess only knew if her soul was with her.

The problem was, I loved Josephine Redvine. I loved her in a way that could only be described as unearthly. Maybe I couldn't remember our past lives like my mother, but I could remember Joe. From the second I looked into her golden-brown eyes, a warmth trickled down deep inside that made me feel both home and as if I was going to be sick. It was that feeling that helped me overlook the storm kicking into action as soon as she started drinking again, just a year after our wedding. And it was that same feeling that kept me from leaving when she didn't stop.

That incident in our loft that day, when she, or that thing inside her, strangled me to the ground, it had changed her. She was awake. She'd literally told me a week prior that she hadn't had a drink for months. After everything—the loss of my nephew to our family's curse (which I constantly felt responsible for), my sister's desertion, my mother's coma, and my wife's shitty disease—I was actually beginning to trust again. Then she sent me that fucking text. I could've skinned her. One would think to not piss off a witch, but apparently, I married the one person dumb enough to fight against that stereotype.

What did she think I was going to do when I got that text? *You deserve better than me.* She had to have known I would freak out.

Sure, she didn't know that I had a tracker I'd made

from a spoon that had once rested over one of the crisp red and black tablecloths in her restaurant, or that once I whispered a few sorted words while I held it, her hair hugging its silver shaft, that it would allow me to dive into her body. It's not like it's super shady witchcraft—a tracker wouldn't allow me to possess her—not like she didn't know what *that* felt like. With my magical homemade device, I was given the opportunity to look out from her eyes and see that she was clearly in a bar, an opened beer under her alcoholic face, and that there was a busty, red-headed *see you next Tuesday* writing down her name and number on a napkin meant for *my wife*. The spell also allowed me to hear *Jody* tell my wife to call her—that their meeting was of no coincidence.

Of course I'd been pissed. How then Derek had gotten here . . . well, I could only assume from the empty wine bottles.

"Really mature, Ellie," I muttered to myself.

I stared back down at Joe's recent plea and cringed.

I didn't mean what I said last night—it was a mistake. Can we please meet in person today? We really need to talk.

Trying to ignore the smell of lingering sex in the pint-sized cabin, I typed four letters and a question mark.

Jody?

She responded right away.

I have no idea how you got her name but trust me when I say she's nothing. Please Ellie, give me a chance to explain.

I ran my sandpaper tongue over my leathery lips. Technically I had no right to be angry anymore; if she had cheated, well then, the playing field had been evened out. But I *was* angry.

Again, she begged.

Please . . . come to the city today, to the restaurant.

The sheets over Derek's ass moved, his shaggy brown hair

moving with his head as he made a waking noise. I kind of wanted to run out before he woke up.

I held my breath and typed.

What time?

Her response was immediate.

Noon.

I checked the time on the left corner of my phone's display. It was nine. At least that wouldn't give me very much time to overthink things.

Okay.

I exhaled.

Thank you, Ellie. I miss you like crazy—I really do.

Christ.

I'll see you at noon.

"And fuck if I don't miss you, too," I muttered.

I set the phone on the ground just as I heard scratching coming from the other side of the door. I scooted over and wrapped my fingers around the unlocked doorknob. I pulled it open, allowing Biscuit, my big gray wolf, to saunter in. She ran directly over to Derek and sniffed him, licking his face like a pup before coming back and performing a nosedive directly into my lap.

"Hey," Derek said as he came back to life; his voice was like a spinal tap.

I squinted painfully, and without matching his groggy gaze, said, "So . . . that happened."

The grin on his face evaporated as soon as he saw the regret hanging down over my shoulders like a ritual cape. Before questioning me further, he looked over at the silver spoon I'd kicked across the room.

"You do some skinny-dipping last night, Strings?"

Strings. He'd been calling me that since I fell in love with him at first sight back in the tenth grade.

"Word is you play a mean violin," he'd said, after sitting

down next to me in our high school band room. Choir practice had just let out and everyone was filtering out from the room. In that moment it felt like we were the only two people who existed in the whole wide world.

"Oh? And who tells you that?" I'd questioned, my stomach purring from some kind of recognition of his soul.

"The same people who say that you're a witch."

"Yeah well," I'd snorted, "everyone says that."

We'd been raised to be who we wanted. Things had changed, we didn't have to hide in the shadows as we'd had to in previous lives. And let's face it, nobody believed we were for real anyway, so what was the harm in owning who we were.

"So, what do you say? Wanna play in my band? I think we could rock."

I'd looked him in the eyes and said so easily that one would have thought I'd rehearsed the line, "You know I'll break your heart, right?"

He'd stared down into his hands, a small smirk appearing in the corner of his mouth. "Yeah. It wouldn't be the first time."

I furrowed my brow at Derek as he sat over the bed we'd rolled around on together all night. I cringed at the thought of it, and at the part where I'm pretty sure I had loved it, then I cringed again at the pain in my skull from the severe dehydration.

"It's called a tracker, Der," I retorted in response to his initial statement. "And yes, I snooped around on my wife, but it wasn't for nothing."

He shot me a judgmental look, which I scoffed at. I knew what he thought of those things, that they were invasive. What the hell did I care—fuck privacy. It's not like I was the first witch to make one, and we couldn't manipulate the person. The spell only allowed the seeker to see and hear what the chosen she or he was saying, and or doing. I suppose one could accuse the magic of being slightly stalker-ish, but then again that someone probably wouldn't understand what it was like to lose a loved one to spirits. And I don't mean ghosts. I think as her wife, I deserved to know if Joe was drinking again.

"Whatever, Der," I said when he hadn't uttered a single word. "She started it."

"You sound like you're five, Ellie."

I growled, causing Biscuit to whine. "She sent me one of those pitiful self-destructive texts. She told me I would be better off without her."

He stared back at me with bloodshot eyes. If there was one person in this stupid world who could make me feel like the twat I was, it was this guy. Some days I wished he hated me more for skipping out on what we had and marrying Joe instead. Derek had never given me a lick of shit . . . which in hindsight was a little weird, but I wasn't about to argue with him. It wasn't like I didn't love him anymore, I just loved him differently. He wasn't Joe. That's all.

"Look, I saw her in a bar with another woman, okay. Some bitch named Jody was giving her her number. I freaked out. I texted her and told her she had two options—that she could either finish her suicide off quickly, or take Jody home and be done with it, because I sure was. Then I guess I started drinking." My gaze rose to the empty wine bottles. "And apparently called you."

With his mouth partway open, he flicked his tongue over his back molars.

"I'm sorry!" I exclaimed, a rise in temperature coming over me that had nothing to do with my hangover.

"When I got here, you said it was over between you two."

"I said I was sorry," I muttered. This was the problem with the non-magical, they believed far too easily. Witches were jaded, more careful with our beloved selves . . . or maybe that was just me.

Derek licked his lips and looked towards the wall. "That's about right, isn't it?" There was a crack in his voice, the same one he'd had when I'd told him that I'd fallen in love with his best friend from grade school. The friend he'd introduced me to on my twenty-fourth birthday, which had just happened to be at Spiked—Joe's restaurant. She'd just moved back to the city to open it up after a three-month stint in rehab.

"You don't deserve this from me, Der." Christ, now I sounded like *her*. "I mean, I shouldn't have called you."

He half-heartedly reached for his pants, pulling a bottle of mint drops from the front pocket and depositing some on his tongue. He'd been carrying the same mint drops since the day I'd first met him. "Don't sweat it," he muttered.

Fumbling with one of Biscuit's ears, I said over his last remark, "You've just gotta think I'm so stupid for loving her still."

"You can't help who you love, Ellie."

His words stung.

After a few more moments of pure, unadulterated discomfort, he stood up and started dressing himself. Pulling his shirt over his head, an old Wicked Incantations T-shirt, he paused and stared down at me. "Let's just keep last night between the two of us, yeah. She doesn't need to know."

I clicked my tongue, while visibly tracing the lame logo on his T-shirt. I couldn't believe he still wore that thing. We'd made, like, fifty of them when we still thought we had a shot. But the agent who came to hear us that last night our band played didn't sign us—he signed me. Kickstarting one hell of a successful career and leaving my band members left to cough on the trail of pixie dust I left behind. Another reason for Derek to hate me.

I grimaced. "Why are you always so nice to me?"

He grinned in that way of his that made me feel feral inside. "Because I'm a narcissist."

I frowned. "That's a wicked dumb answer, and it doesn't make any sense."

He just winked. "Maybe yes, maybe no. Hey, in other not so related news, I've been meaning to tell you, Cindy Bernstein is getting married. Do you remember her?"

"Uh, no, I don't think so." I contorted my face. What a quick lane change that was.

"We went to high school with her. She was, like, a freshman when you were a sophomore. She was always hanging off to the side." He stalled, waiting for me to remember, but all I could muster was to give my shoulders the slightest of shakes. The only thing I retained from those days was that ugly maroon sweater Derek used to wear over his tan corduroys. That scroungy look of his had always gotten to the root of me. Still did apparently. "Anyway, she's getting married and contacted me. She wants to know if we can all get together and play at her wedding. She knows about your mom and that you've had to cancel your *tour*— "

The way he said the word, I knew it was a dig.

Whatever. I may have gotten signed, but karma still found me. I'd lost a sister. I married someone who could never love me as much as her self-hatred. My mom was in a coma that I felt heavily responsible for. And I was currently living in a shitty one room cabin with a toilet in the fucking shower. There was an unremovable glitch in the cleaning spell that had been administered and sometimes these cabins rearranged themselves; needless to say, it wasn't always in good favor. Oh, and lest we not forget my new waitressing gig because we'd just lost another server at The Dewdrop, the retreat's shop slash restaurant by the road.

"—anyway, she really wants us to play," he finished.

His words were not registering. I just stared at him like he'd lost his mind.

"So far everyone's in, except you. What do you think?"

Biscuit yawned and kicked her feet up in the air, her belly shifting under my hand as she wiggled her back along the floor like a worm.

"Um, I don't know," I finally answered. "This chic—Cindy—she seriously wants an old high school band to play at her wedding?"

Derek gave me a piercing look. "We were more than a high school band, Elle. And come on, it could be cool. We haven't played in years. Candy and Leo have already said they're in."

"You're shitting me." When he didn't offer a reaction, I said, "A wedding, really? Our music isn't really, like, wedding music."

Derek sounded like Dave Gahan from Depeche Mode and Candy could wail like Janice. It was kind of a bizarre request for such an event.

He shrugged his shoulders. "Come on, you could use the distraction."

"Christ, I don't know, Der. Are you guys gonna do it either way?"

"Probably, but you know it's really you she wants. The rest of us don't have music videos."

And another jab. I couldn't help it if what I had to offer was more savory. Back when I got signed there weren't any other dancing rock violinists.

"Can I think about it?"

"Sure." His keys dangled from his right hand. "*So*, I guess I'll call you later."

"Yeah, okay." I couldn't bring myself to stand up.

He nodded his head uncomfortably and started for the door. Aware of his departure, Biscuit immediately stood and wagged her tail, crying softly as she laid her snout into his hand. She was my familiar, but she loved Derek because I loved Derek. Even though I loved him differently now he would always have a place in my heart.

"Bye, B," he said, ruffling her furry head.

"Hey." I smiled weakly. "I'm sorry . . . again."

"Don't be," he said, returning the smile. I covered my mouth to imprison the foul belch that was trying to escape. It was singed at the edges with the leftover stink of fermented grapes. "I'm not." And then he left.

I WORE tight black capris and an even tighter tank top—my tits looked great. They were a tad on the small side, but they were perky as hell, and my ass had just the right amount of curve to make up for it. My shirt matched the streak of hot pink I'd painted in my hair earlier in the summer, and my freshly chopped, bouncy yellow locks covered up the appearance of my hangover. I looked hot as hell, which was the plan. I wanted my wife to drool, I wanted her to feel as bad as possible about whatever had happened the night before, and about that fucking text. We'd worry about my infidelity later.

Also, my new feather, inked in by my cousin Patrick, was healing nicely on my arm and I wanted to show it off. I had a feather for every moment in my life worth remembering, good or bad. They were mixed in amongst the rest of my tatts. At this point I'd lost count.

Patrick laced his tattoo ink with more than color, and this new image represented strength. As soon as it was drawn into my skin, I felt stronger. I liked to think that if my sister ever got her shit together that the two of us could get matching feathers, but the longer she stayed away, that daydream became less and less of a reality. If her own mother's health couldn't thaw her heart, then what could? I gave up on her the day of my wedding. I mean it was stupid of me, thinking she might at least come back for that.

It was my dad who'd had to tell me to stop looking over

my shoulder that day, just before he walked me over the forest floor to where Joe was waiting next to my Aunt Lana and Biscuit; my wolf decorated with a string of flowers around her neck, and the ceremonial broom laid before their feet.

"She's not comin', Elle." His words had stung like a fierce pixie snagging a bite of flesh.

"I know," I'd finally said. "I just thought . . . maybe."

She hadn't come back for my wedding, but she *had* returned for a hot second when my mother was admitted to the hospital. It was so brief that I barely had a chance to take note of her snooty new 'look.' She was a *doctor* now—a psychopath, or excuse me, a psychotherapist; but Maddie once told me that she never actually went to Berkley like the certificate on her wall says she did, that she only used her magic for the last time to spin herself a new title for her new life. Whatever. All I know is that she looked so dumb when I saw her in the hospital. Stiff cheeks, tan *pleated* pants, and fucking penny loafers—who really wore that shit anyway? I knew she'd long since buried her wand, but there was still a stick of some sort stuck up her ass.

She showed up for long enough to try and unlock my mother's heart. It didn't work, and why would it? For it to work, you had to believe in magic; and V wasn't a witch anymore, not really. Still, at least she humored us and attempted to stick her golden charm into my mother's red lock, but the fact that both my mother's charm and mine had changed color and hers hadn't, it just seemed to highlight the matter that she had no spark left. She checked out as soon as the necklaces failed us, and she hadn't been back to visit our mother since. Bitch.

"Skank," I verbalized aloud, just at the thought of the prissy imposter who had dared to pass herself off as my sister. The V I knew didn't need to wear *loafers*, cause her feet were so calloused from running in the woods at night that shoes bothered her. And her hair—which had been slicked back and straightened—should have been as frizzy as my poor soulless mother's.

I wiped my sweaty palms on my pants and trekked on to find Lana. Not far from the shop by the road there was a creek that ran down through the property. My Aunt Lana utilized the clearing next to it to hold Zumba classes every Tuesday and Thursday.

It was a small class, but she had a few regulars. Zelda, who lived in the area, a 63-year-old retired schoolteacher. Betty, a 58-year-old woman, whose husband had recently passed. And last but not least, Minnie. An older German lady who baked everything under the moon and stars. She had her own delivery service. She'd baked my wedding cake, cinnamon and lavender.

There were usually a few stragglers from the surrounding area who had heard of the gathering, and then of course anyone who was staying in the retreat was welcome to join. As I strolled around the lake, I saw that there were six total in attendance for the day.

"Oh hello, Minnie," Lana said to the older lady as she joined the group. "And don't forget your goddess bracelet." She wrapped a red band around the woman's wrist.

"Oh, sank you," Minnie said in a heavy German accent, grabbing Lana's free hand in hers and shaking it affectionately. "I svear zis band gives me extra energy. I should have it in zee kitchen." She chuckled, before joining her friends off to the side.

I came up alongside my aunt and crossed my arms over my chest. The two of us stared at the assorted group of older women, and the one young woman who was staying in one of the cabins, looking sorely out of place.

"Still spelling them into shape, I see."

"Whatever gets their hearts working," Lana replied.

"Oh Ellie, hello!" Betty hollered, waving her arm at me, her arm fat jiggling. "Will you join us today?"

"Sorry, I have a thang in the city—next time!"

"I'll hold you to it!" she threatened, with her finger in the air.

Lana, sizing me up, ventured to spout out the obvious. "You reek of sour grapes and mistakes."

I stared down at my shoes, black high-top sneakers with hot pink laces, and then looked over my shoulder. I had a hunch that she already knew of my little one-night stand. She was fairly psychic.

"Did you see Derek's truck, then?"

"Biscuit was crying. I started walking over to your cabin when he pulled up; he hadn't even opened your front door all the way when your hand reached out and yanked him inside."

I stuck my thumbs into the waistband of my pants, squinting as I looked out into the distance. "I feel terrible if that makes up for anything."

"Good. You should feel bad."

I didn't need my mother to shame me, I had her sister to do it for her.

"I don't think it's cheating if you've already slept with the person."

Ignoring my comment, she said, "You're going to see her, aren't you? Right now. Josephine."

"Yes."

"Are you going to tell her?"

"No way. It would only hurt her."

Her iron gaze didn't budge from inside mine for a full minute. Finally, she laid a finger gingerly over the new feather on my arm and nodded. "Just remember your strength, Wichahpi. Waiting for someone so close to your heart to heal is not easy. But you cannot force it, she must do this at her own pace, and you must be patient."

40

Aunt Lana was always addressing us by the names gifted to us from our grandmother. Our nana had been full Sioux, while my grandfather had been half German and half Swiss and had a head of wool—genes that resulted in a chemistry experiment that had gone haywire on my mother's head, earning her the nickname Broom Head from Lana, who had miraculously received a beautiful mane of thick, dark hair. My name, Wichahpi, meant star. My sister's, Wachiwi, meant dancing girl—which seemed like it should be mine because I was a dancer, but then again it made sense cause V was always dancing away from her life.

"I will," I replied to Lana's insistence that I remain patient. "I'll try and visit Mom while I'm out. Do you need me to take anything to her room?"

"No. I will go see her later this week. I have other things to tend to this afternoon."

"Okay." I nodded, then walked away.

"Wichahpi."

I glanced back at her.

"You *will* be back in time to help at the restaurant tonight?"

"Of course," I said, giving her a strange look. "Why wouldn't I?"

"Just making sure." Her expression was set as it usually was, straight and narrow. But as I walked towards my car, I thought I sensed that Lana had been hiding something. She'd been acting kind of strange the last few days.

Lana was always the first to know when a shit storm was about to hit. Getting into my car, I tried not to overthink it. I had my own disaster to sort out.

OLIVIA

The day I left Sage Brook I never intended that I wouldn't return. I had three worked over dollar bills in the overalls I wore that day, no shoes, and no plan. I simply stumbled out from the forest and into my old beat-up station wagon and drove away. I literally had nothing but the clothes on my back, except I was born a witch, so I *did* have my wand, and that bit of willow got me from there to this place where I finally ended my journey. This place had black sand, black water, and rocks as jagged as the knife that had been used to gut me.

When I first pulled up to the California lost coast, I knew I'd been here before in a different body. It smelt of the past; but the longer I looked out into the distant waves, the more I realized I was no longer concerned with what was behind me in any life. That hurt too much. What I needed was a fresh start. A new person to be. And she, as I quickly realized, didn't need magic. For the magic our goddess mother, Diana, had 'gifted' me with had given me nothing but pain. In the end, what good was it to be a descendant of a goddess if one was too damaged to share that gift? It didn't take me long to cut the cord between myself and the spirit world either, because even though I had driven for miles and miles, spirits couldn't be hidden from. Especially one in particular.

She, Rowena, would find me. This would happen when she was ready to take her next victim. From an early age my mother informed me that this ghost from my past would return and show me her full form before taking the life of a witch close to me. It's how it always was in every past life, and until she was burned, it was how it always would be. The thing was, though, she never did show herself . . . not more so than a blink of one of her eyes in a glass ball, or a rain puddle. Anything worth a scry. When she took my son, there was no warning.

When I ran away from Sage Brook, I still had not seen Rowena. Not fully. It wasn't until I heard her breathing next to me, once I'd taken possession of the property at the lost coast, that I decided to shut down the communication between myself and the spirits who flocked to me like moths to a flame. Rowena's breaths were so loud I could hear them over the sound of my house going up over the gravestones of ancient trees. I pounced on her as soon as the scent of her grew so close that rot and sulfur became unbearable.

"You can't have any more of them," I said to her. "If you cannot find me, then you cannot find my family."

I believed that they would all be safe if I couldn't see her. Even though she'd still managed to get to my son without showing herself to me, I clung to this conviction.

Against my threat I heard her whisper.

"*In the pines, Olivia. In the pines.*"

It was the first time I'd heard her voice. Her guttural articulation cut through me like a jagged knife. Just before my guard was completely up, just before I closed the connection between myself and all spirits, an ice-cold hand wrapped around my wrist, leaving me with one final warning before fading back into the ocean mist.

"*I can still find them . . . and I will always be near.*"

To this day I carry the chill of her touch.

My connection to the other world was closed, but she remained around me like a reaper, stalking every angle of my life—waiting for the right moment. I ignored her invisible presence. I rebuilt my life and moved into my new home, and once I had everything I needed to get started, I hid my wand away.

And I never looked back.

I wanted nothing more than to remain in my state of ignorance for the life I left back in Colorado, but recent events could no longer be ignored. Gerald's voice haunted me in a way his ghost never had. *The tides have brought her in, and she will not rest until at least one soul is forever taken.*

Without showing herself to me, she'd come for Ellie. *The rules have been altered,* Gerald had said. Still, my sister was alive, so Rowena had failed, which meant she was most likely now fueled by an even darker, hungrier rage. And somehow my mother was tied up amid all of this, though for the life of me I could not understand how. Either way, no one was safe—especially not my daughter. True, Rowena only took witches, but she'd already broken the rules once, if not twice in this lifetime. It seemed she was creating a new game to play, and whether or not I liked it, I was going to have to fight her.

Presently, I walked across the grass towards the edge of the coast, blinking to adjust to the brightness of the gray skies hovering over the black waters. Since I hadn't seen her since she'd gone down there, I had to assume that Maddie was still down in the reef; and with the mists hanging over the ocean—like a ghostly hand coming in with the tide to take the skin of those in its path and leave only bones—I could not have her exposed. Not for another second.

I hugged my sweater tighter around my body as I marched over the thick, long grass, towards the breaks that looked out over the reef. As I grew closer, the wail of my familiar caught my attention, and I watched as Delila—my owl—fell from the sky to a bit of driftwood.

As I came to the cliff's edge, I stumbled over a rock and cursed. I teetered near the steep wooden stairs that led into the reef and looked down to where my daughter was balancing over a rock, a crab dangling from the end of a stick. I sighed softly. She would inevitably ask to have the stick filled with magic.

Ever since she was a little girl, Maddie always picked up sticks and asked any witch within range to have them charged, but magic wands didn't just work like that. They attached to the magic in the witch just as much as they did to the energy in the wand itself. Having just one component of anything ensured that something wouldn't work properly—magic was no different.

"Maddie Jean!" I cried over the cliff's edge. "Would you please come up here now?"

She glanced over her shoulder, just enough so that I could see the defiance living in her soul. She was still punishing me—scratch that, she was *always* punishing me.

Releasing another sigh, I took a step down onto the first stair. "I'm not messing around, Mad! The sky is getting darker, we're in for a storm!"

Before I could assess my daughter's blatant disregard, a low gurgle erupted from around me, like that of a soft percussion growing into a deeper resonating rhythm that one always seems to feel at the very bottom of his or her heart. Wherever it is the blood pools.

"Did you forget to close something, witch . . ."

I crammed my eyes shut and swallowed my fear. "No."

I looked down at the necklace in my hand. The sapphire-colored key. I had intentionally left the veil open. As much as I hated the idea of facing this evil crone, I had to know if what Gerald had told me was true. I had to know if Rowena was behind my mother's coma. Of course, I *had* hoped to get my daughter out of the ocean before this wretched hag found me. As I stood there, the stench of death surrounding me, Delila hooted in what I knew to be upset.

"Witchy, witchy, little foe, are you ready for what be in stow?"

I balled my hands into fists, watching as Maddie bent down and allowed the crab to crawl back into the water. She was so exposed. I wanted only to reach down and grab her.

I hissed back at my ghost through clenched teeth. "What do you want?"

Her laughter continued to swirl around my head.

"*To play.*"

"You're sick," I barked back.

"*At least I know what I am.*"

The fear I was trying to suppress quickly transformed into rage. "What do you know of my mother's coma?"

She replied with more seedy laughter, and four sharp words. "*Tick tock, tick tock.*"

My jaw tightened, and I said, "You twisted bitch, you tried to kill my sister."

"*Did I?*"

Maddie was taking her time balancing from one rock to another as she made her way back to the wooden stairs that led up the steep coastal edge. Growing impatient with my daughter's lack of urgency, I replied hastily to Rowena, "It wasn't a question."

A slow hiss entered my ear canal, and I could feel and smell her sulfuric breath as it brushed against my cheek.

"*Arianna has used her last save.*"

I sucked in a quick breath.

"Who are you talking to?" Maddie questioned from below, a scowl printed onto her face.

Ignoring her, I turned my head to the side and scoffed at the still transparent ghost. "What do you mean by that?"

I was given no answer. Instead, as though an atmospheric pressure was pressing down directly upon me, I felt the weight of the demon—her stench. In another half second, she was gone.

I took a moment, assessing the world around me. Other than a few traveling spirits who were lurking by my house, (word must have spread quickly that I had taken down my guard) there were no remnants of my ghost.

While Delila hooted mercilessly I pulled the wrap around my shoulders tighter and stepped away from the stairs. With my gaze centered over my owl, I whispered in her direction, "Where has she gone?"

"In the pines, Olivia."

The necklace in my hand grew nearly so hot that it was untouchable, and my heart grew heavy in my chest. Turning back around to face the breaks, I stared at my daughter. Her copper-colored irises had been filled in by darkness.

Resisting the bile that was rising in my throat, I dropped my hands by my sides, pumping them as though I was getting ready to step into a fighting ring. An eruption of wings fluttered behind me, and I didn't have to turn around to see that Delila had gone.

"Get out of her," I demanded of the ghost.

The bit of beechwood Maddie had been holding below was still in her hands, and the demon was holding it now as though it was a wand, between her forefingers and thumbs, just as I would. Was she mocking me?

A smile twisted along the lines of Maddie's lips, then Rowena opened my daughter's mouth and began to sing. The lyrics were both familiar and haunting. I hadn't listened to them since I was a teenager. Nirvana's "Where Did You Sleep Last Night." Except coming from her mouth, it wasn't just haunting—something about how she sang it turned my stomach into knots.

"Stop!" I screeched, my hands coming up to cover my ears.

The demon cocked Maddie's head to the side. "What is it, Olivia? I thought you and Ellie used to love that song."

I dug my fingertips into my skull, dragging them down my skin. The world around where I stood was coming in and out of focus and somewhere, far away and much too close were the buried screams of a woman. "What are you trying to do, Rowena? I'm right here—if you want to take somebody, take me!"

She clicked her tongue, tapping the stick against Maddie's palm. Then very seriously looked up at me. "That wouldn't be any fun, though. So why would I do that?"

The fist that had been clenched around my magic for years, began to lift. I may have been a shitty mother, an absent parent, but I loved my children, alive or no. Hell hath no fury like a witch scorned.

Taking a step forward, I didn't stutter when I spoke next. "Leave my daughter alone."

The blackened eyes of the demonic lunatic inside of my daughter drifted downwards. Maddie's lips pressed together, and a slow hum burned into my ears. That blasted song. She kept focusing on the same lyrics again and again.

"The pines, Rowena. What pines? What are you playing at?"

"She shivers . . . she suffers . . . she waits not to be found."

My lips quivered. "Who?" Was she talking about my mother?

I received no more answers. No more anything. Instead, Rowena, still in charge of my daughter's body, smirked at me as Maddie's feet lifted from the ground as though there were strings attached to her shoulders, lifting her into the air; and as my heart flooded with beats, the sound of them deafening in my ears, I ran for her as the demon floated Maddie over the edge of the cliff.

"NO!" I screeched, clawing at the air. The ghostly visitors who had made their way to my home were now by my side— pulling at my elbows as if they could physically hold me back from giving Rowena what she wanted. More death. They had about as good of a grasp on me as I did over Maddie. "I told you to take me! *Take me*, Rowena! Leave my child alone!"

"And I already told you," she sang, "that would be no fun for me."

"Why are you doing this? Why me? Why *my* family?"

My daughter's body was now balancing dangerously over the edge of the breaks with nothing but sharp rocks below.

Rowena settled her expression into a serious one as she asked, "Hasn't Arianna told you?"

I could barely breathe, let alone form the words to answer her. "Told me what? That you haunt my family in every life we live—that you kill anyone and everyone *I* love!"

In an excruciatingly calm way, she replied, "Yes, of course. But hasn't she told you why?"

My toes were sticking out over the cliff. If I hinged forward at all I would be dead. Staring directly across into the black eyes of the beast, I answered her. "I killed you."

She only blinked.

"You went bad, Rowena. You turned, not only against your magic, but against your coven."

"You don't remember," she sang.

"No, that curse was unfortunately only granted to my mother. But she told me what you did. How you somehow allowed anger to turn you, and how you became a murderer of witches. I *had* to kill you; you gave me no choice!"

The sound of the waves crashing down below, the

impending fog rolling in, the wind sending curses past my cheeks, streaked with salt water—all of it seemed to have been put into slow motion as I stood there, full of rage and powerless against this demon as she held my daughter's life in her tainted, dead hands. Eight words were all I was afforded in the two seconds that followed.

"You were the one who let me in."

And then it all happened at once. There was a fluttering of feathers, the sensation of a stick being forced into my hand, and the sound of my own screams as my daughter's body fell; but then I just as quickly lunged forward, standing on air and pointing my bit of willow down at her body just before it was about to make contact with the jagged rocks below.

Maddie, now in possession of her own body, stared up at me with wide eyes and a gaping mouth as I floated over her like the witch I once was. And before she could utter a single word, before I could make out the laughter that seemed to be drifting back into the fog, I used my wand to lift her back up to the cliff and set her down before landing back on solid earth myself.

Hunched over her, the willow branch still clenched in my fist, I wrapped my arms around my daughter and squeezed her with all my might.

"What—just—happened?" she asked, the inflection in her voice somewhere between broody teen and someone who had just seen a ghost. Someone who wasn't used to seeing ghosts that is. As it was, we were currently surrounded by about five spirits who had come over to check out the unusual commotion.

Refusing her a direct answer, I pulled away so I could examine her, and make sure there were no more remnants of Rowena living inside her. "You—You took a dive. I didn't think I was going to be able to sav—"

"Cut the shit, Mom," she said, laying a hand over my arm

and staring down at the wand I hadn't held for eight whole years now. Her gaze directed at the tool, she spoke over anything I tried to say. "She found you, didn't she? Your ghost."

I waited a second to reply. "Yes."

Maddie swallowed hard. "How did you get your wand in time?"

There was a quiet and understated hoot over by where my familiar had taken residence back over the large piece of driftwood.

"Delila."

Because she was the only other one who could find it.

Maddie nodded, and I could practically see her heart beating through her T-shirt. "Did she show herself to you?"

My chest was still heaving as I stared over my daughter's shoulders at the most recent spirit to join our circle. She was just as I'd always imagined her. Her dress was long and black, soaked by salt water. Her skin was the color of an oyster, and her hair was drenched and unruly.

"Maddie, you're not going home tomorrow. You're leaving today."

"What—why?"

I shook my head. "There's no time. We have to go *now*."

"We?"

I slowly let go of my daughter as the ghostly woman in black smirked at me.

"Yes, both of us. I am not willing to let you out of my sight. And your grandmother—she's in no coma."

For the first time in a long time, my daughter was silent. Only after a few moments had passed was it that she repeated herself. "Mom, you didn't answer me a second ago. Did your ghost—did she show herself to you?"

Rowena lifted her chin to me before turning away and surrendering her form to the mist. "You could say that."

ELLIE

The last day that Joe and I were together everything unraveled around me so quickly that it ended as soon as it began. We'd been fighting for days on end, and this time she'd left for three days without the courtesy of telling me where she was. While she binged on liquor and hung out with drunken souls as harrowed as her own—so that she could find sympathy from people who only knew how to be broken—I sat in silence. Every cell of my body on fire.

Though nothing had ever possessed Joe to the point of trying to *murder* me before that very special day, I'd witnessed wicked spirits attempt to try her on like a sweater during moments of weakness. On more than one occasion she'd had enough to drink that a presence that didn't belong to her made itself comfy in her bones for just long enough to salivate in my direction.

I'd warned her that bad spirits were drawn to witches. That what they really desired was *my* skin to sit in, to have *my* powers at their nasty disposal. What better way to get to me than to take the body of someone close to me who was too weak and too inebriated to even know they were being possessed.

"Whatever Elle," she'd said just days before the incident, "you're just making shit up because you can't deal. There's nothing wrong with me having a few drinks. The restaurant is stressful—"

"Enough with the excuses!" I'd yelled back. "What's the point of living if all you're going to do every day is try to escape? You know what, you're right—I can't deal, and I shouldn't have to. Not right now. Just get out—just go. I've got a tour to prepare for and I can't practice with you drinking yourself into a stupor and staring at the wall like you can't wait for it to fall over you. What's so wrong with our life anyway? Why are you like this?"

She'd stared back at me with hardened eyes, but at least at the time they were hers. "It's so easy for you, isn't Ellie? Easy to point at me and call me a drunk. Everything's always been easy for you. You and your magical life. You can make pink flames appear from the music you play for fuck's sake. You can snap your fingers and make it rain, and you can hold your mother's hand and *feel* that she loves you. Guess what, princess, I never had that."

"You do now. Our souls are bound by magic; my family is your family. And are you kidding me, Joe—you think my life has been sunshine and rainbows this whole time? My family's cursed!"

"Yeah well, maybe I'm just part of that curse."

"Get out," I'd repeated. "Get the fuck out of here right now."

And since she'd loved to stonewall, she did just what I said. She left.

So, there I'd been, stewing, for days. I couldn't breathe, and it physically hurt to be awake. I just wanted it over. Sure, Joe and I had been married in a witch's union, and my sister and Tyler were proof that that union couldn't be undone, but I would've rather lived the rest of my days alone than be a slave to Joe's drinking. And then she walked into the front door of our apartment with a face made of plaster and an expression that could have very well belonged to the devil. I was too upset with her to witness the true glint of evil residing in her; I was too raw to notice that my wife still hadn't come home. All I saw was that I didn't have to get close to know her breath reeked of gin.

All it took was one look in her direction and something inside me snapped.

"I'm done, Joe," I'd stated, and I'd meant it. Years of watching her slowly kill herself had finally broken me down. I couldn't watch it anymore. "I want out of this marriage."

I didn't wait for her to retort, instead I turned and ran up the stairs of our loft before that endless darkness that she'd invoked had a chance to try and stop me. So quickly did I run from her that day that I completely forgot to reach for the handful of salt to block my path. It was something I usually did when we fought. Salt barriers protected one from that which intended to do one harm. It bothered me that the salt had always stopped her.

I ran right past it that day, though, and I didn't stop until I reached the very back of our walk-in closet. All I'd wanted was to curl up in the dark and be alone, to cover my ears from the tantrum that was ensuing below; but I'd failed to protect myself as I usually did when I ran from my partner while she was at her worst, and this one mistake nearly cost me my life.

The stench of rotting flesh crawling up around my shoulders first caused me to look up. The moisture in the air that reeked of saltwater. Through the tears clouding my vision I saw Joe salivating down in my direction as though I was dessert. Her aura was filled in by something sinister. I realized it wasn't Joe sharing that space with me. A shiver came over my body as I watched her mouth turn into a grin. It was followed by a deep, throaty laugh that had never belonged to my wife.

I walked my hands up the wall and inched my way up so that I was facing her.

"Evil sorceress . . . unchained wreckage . . . your soul I shall keep." The words that came from her mouth bounced off my chest like spit fire. Then she, *or it*, changed its tone. Trying to sound like Joe, it pressed out a single word. It slithered from her mouth like the head of a serpent. "Princess . . ."

"Who are you?" I asked, as my chest filled with wet, prickly air. As I stood there so visibly weak, I knew just then that I'd made more than one mistake that day. Not only had I forgotten to throw down the salt, but my wand was still resting right where I'd left it on the kitchen island.

"You are as pathetic as you were the first time I laid eyes on you. Ella . . ."

My voice quivered like a violin string being played by a shaky hand. "My *name* is Ellie."

This creature, this demon—she grinned back at me. I remained still, trying to appear tough and unafraid, but none of that mattered. Whatever this thing was that had a hold of Joe, it was old, and it was hungry. As her elbow came up against my chest, shoving me against the wall, I did my best not to panic. That was until her hand replaced her arm and crept up to my throat.

Her mouth screwed up into one of the nastiest grins I'd ever seen, and her spirit filled with a brazen excitement. I couldn't help but scream. I knew it was a mistake, that she enjoyed every last second of that shrill noise that exited my lungs, but I couldn't help it. What this was, whoever this was, she had come to take me to hell.

Just before she released her hold over my airway—just before my body hit the floor—my necklace burned with the heat of the sun and my mother's words filled my head: "*I've taken this first punch for you, my little witch. You must go back now and help to keep the curse from finishing what it's already started. You must help her see . . .*"

I don't know how long I was out, but when I started to move again, after waking up alone in the cold, dark closet, my neck sore and red from where Joe's grip had held me against the wall, I felt as though shards of glass were raining down all over me. The last thing on my mind were my mother's bizarre words. Or the fact that my necklace had burned so hot that it had left a mark against my already bruised skin.

Downstairs everything was in disarray. Pots, pans, lamps, books, glasses—my violin—all of it smashed or shattered. I was too shaken to think about what to do next, about the fact that I had almost died.

I'd mechanically pulled my phone from the floor when I saw the missed calls. One from my mom, worried, a message that she was on her way, and a second from my father. But I never finished listening to that second voicemail, because the phone fell from my hand back to the floor before he'd finished talking. Then Derek barged through the unlocked door and caught me, just as my body was about to join my phone and all the other things Joe had trashed.

"What happened?" was all he had said, not alluding to how or why he was there. I was in too much shock to question the timing of it all.

"Joe . . . she tried to suffocate me." I left out the part about how it wasn't Joe. I wasn't ready to deal with what had just happened. It didn't change the fact that she'd let it in. That this was all her fault. "It's . . . it's over. And my mom." I was crying so hard I could barely talk. "She was coming for me— she knew I was in trouble. She slid off the highway. It's bad. Derek, it's *so* bad."

He picked me up and helped me gather my things, because I wasn't returning to the loft. Not after that.

"Come on, let's get you to the hospital," he said. "To your mom."

After that I stayed with Derek for a couple weeks before moving out to Sage Brook. It just made sense. Since my mom was gone, they needed help running the place. I never did ask Derek how he'd known I was in trouble, but I guess it didn't really matter. He saved me. That was all I needed to know.

Now, all these months later, I still didn't know what to do about my marriage. Standing at the back entrance to Spiked, my hangover wrapped around me like a weighted blanket, I slammed my car door while puffing out my cheeks. It was the first time I'd been back to Joe's restaurant since we'd parted ways, but that didn't make it any less habitual—standing at the back of the restaurant, visually tracing every brick in the wall as if I'd just been there. It was also familiar in a sickening way because I couldn't help but wonder how many more times I would walk through that back door as her wife.

"Hey you," she said as soon as I entered. She took my elbow and a gentle spark of electricity surged through my body. We looked at one another for a second before I turned away, afraid she'd see the previous night's events in the blacks of my eyes. It was only in that moment that I realized the true heaviness of what I'd done with Derek . . . that Joe had only looked guilty from where I'd spied on her with the tracker, whereas I truly was.

With my voice raised about an octave too high, I asked, "Is it busy?"

"Bumpin'." She turned and yelled at one of her chefs to take over her station. Joe was a petite woman, light brown skin littered with freckles, red hair that she kept dyed black—but her voice had base.

"Maybe I should come back later," I offered, watching

knives moving at lightning-fast speed over every surface of the stainless-steel kitchen.

"Fuck that. I made us lunch. Bean burgers with curry ketchup, your favorite."

"Right," I muttered.

I wiped a bead of sweat from my brow as she ushered us over to the corner booth she usually reserved for VIPs. As she slid a decorated plate under my nose, I compulsively picked up a fry and shoved it into my mouth. Before I could swallow, I improvised with a conversation starter to cover up the overwhelming shade of guilt I'd worn in place of blush for our lunch date.

"When are you gonna try out for one of those reality cooking shows?" I stuffed another fry into my mouth as if the action was a nervous tick. It wasn't a silly question; Spiked had recently been platformed by one of those reality shows that features crazy sick places to eat.

She dipped her chin and suffered a dry chuckle, ladling some ketchup over her burger with a steak knife. "I've thought about it, but I've been so busy helping Tyler get the new restaurant in order. I wanna make sure things are good to go before I try to start competing with your fame."

Tyler started working at The Dewdrop back before he'd even met Olivia, before the two of them got married and made their home in Sage Brook. Over the years he'd really grown as a chef, and it only took a little time under Joe and her instruction for him to blossom. Currently we were funding just a little under half of his new restaurant that was being set up just outside the city. Just because my sister had ditched her husband didn't mean we didn't still take care of each other in this family.

I swallowed a large bite of food. "I thought you were Tyler's *silent* partner."

Joe shrugged her shoulders. "I will be soon enough. It's

just a lot of work getting it going. Have you been by to see it yet?"

I shook my head, taking a very unladylike bite from my burger. "Not yet."

"Maybe we could go sometime. He's got this whole farm to table theme going on, and he rented out some of the land to this yarn lady who raises alpacas." Curling her lips into a smile —as if all was good and our marriage was happy—she added, "There are fainting goats on the property. It's kinda fun to freak them out."

I chuckled, swallowing my most recent bite as I pretended for just a second that it *was* okay to smile back. The warm food gently landed in my hollow, rotten gut.

For a while we ate in silence. Our eyes danced uncomfortably over the table, each of us afraid to look at the other for too long. Eventually, I had to say something.

Slicing away the murky sentence that immediately came to my brain—the one where I cornered Joe about how many Jody's there had been since I'd been slumming it in the shitty cabin in the woods, I decided to take things in a more agreeable direction. "So . . . we have some shit to discuss."

Joe swallowed her food and wiped the edge of her lips with her napkin. "Yeah, we do. Look Elle, I don't know how you got into my head last night, which by the way, it seems to me that witch or no, privacy is still something that should be respected. But just so you know, Jody is just—"

"Ugh. Can we please just table anything that has to do with her. I really can't even fathom the mention of her name." I pushed around my unused fork. "Besides, we've all made mistakes."

"But Elle, it's not what you think."

My gaze shot up to hers. "Is she in the past or the present?"

"Neither."

"Then shut it down," I warned. "I came here to talk, but not about her."

Joe balled up the cloth napkin in her hands before setting it next to her plate. "Okay . . . fair enough." She slid a hand through her faux hawk and released a ragged breath. "I'm sorry about what I said last night—that text. I didn't mean it."

"You never do."

She heaved a sigh. "I admit, it was a weak moment. It's not like those are just never going to happen, but you've got to understand that I've been trying really hard. I seriously feel like I am truly embracing my sobriety."

"That's not what it looked like last night."

"Ellie—just—I didn't drink the beer okay! I ordered it, but I didn't drink it." She held my gaze for a stiff moment, and I held hers. "Look, *I'm trying*, and I know you're scared to move forward because of how I used to be, but I've changed. And I think it's time we start discussing, you know, maybe putting things back together."

I gawked at her. "You're kidding me, right?"

She had the audacity to look surprised. "No, I'm not. I realize you've got a lot going on with your mom and helping at the retreat, but you don't need to be living there to do those things."

I laid my palms flat on the table and leaned in over my plate. "Joe, I saw you last night, *in a bar*. You know I can't be with you if you're still drinking."

"I told you I didn't drink it! And it was a restaurant not a bar!"

"Bullshit."

"Fuck it. I can't tell you I've changed. You won't believe me."

"I wish I could say you were wrong."

She scoffed, making a fist and staring down at it. "Ellie, I need some help from you here. I need to know what I can do

60

to make you look at me differently. It's been six months. I miss you like crazy, and our place is, like, *haunted* with your anger. I hate being there, and I won't even go upstairs anymore because of all that fucking scratching coming from the closet."

My gaze shot up from where I'd let it fall to the table. Scratching?

Blind to my reaction, she hammered on. "I just don't see how you continuing to punish me is making any of this any better."

"Babe, I'm not punishing you—you have to know that." I waited for some sort of recognition that she knew that. When the lines of her forehead softened, I said, "You know what I need. I need to know that you're sober . . . that what happened won't ever happen again."

Dropping her hands down into her lap and scooting forward, she brought her voice so low that it was barely audible. "You know that wasn't me that day. Ellie, you *know*— you must know. I would never hurt you. There was something in my skin. You must believe me. Something, like, *jumped* me."

My head was already aching from my hangover, but suddenly I was near positive that it was going to explode. As I sat there staring at her, the whole thing came undone in my mind once more. A blur of stars and the lack of air, my necklace burning and then me waking up on the floor . . . alone.

"Joe, here's the thing, you made the choice to get plastered that day. If you hadn't, then none of that would have happened. I mean, how am I supposed to just let what happened go when you just left me there? When you just left me there to die." Even though I knew it wasn't her who had left me there.

Scratching . . . she was hearing scratching coming from the closet door.

Joe had turned her head to the side and covered her mouth with her thumb; it was obvious she was saturated with self-hatred. "I'm not that person. I'm not." She was repeating the words as if they could undo her actions.

Reaching across the table, I pulled her hand down from her face. She looked at me, her pain was tangible.

"I believe you aren't that person, but how many times did I warn you that unleashing yourself so carelessly opens you up to *things* out of your control? Even if it wasn't really you who—"

"It wasn't."

I waited a beat or two before picking back up to where I was. "Even if it wasn't, you allowed yourself to let it in. I need to be sure that whatever happens with us, that you won't permit yourself to become that vulnerable ever again. It's not just you it effects."

At that Joe started rambling. "It won't happen ever again, I promise! We—We can move out of the loft, start somewhere fresh. We can live outside the city! Some place where Biscuit can have all the space she wants." I started to shake my head, but she just gripped my hand tighter. "Come on, Ellie, I know you don't belong in the city. Your skin needs to shine against the moon light. We could live off a lake, just like Sage Brook. Maybe we can even talk about, you know, starting a family."

I rolled my eyes, pulling my hand away from hers. If we weren't fighting about her drinking, then we were butting heads about this blasted kid thing. "Joe, we've been over this. Who is going to give us a kid? You're a train wreck and we are both gone all the time—"

"I'll stay home more! And we don't have to adopt. I can carry. I know you've already said that it would be too hard on you and the baby with all your touring and—"

"Oh my god, Joe!" I clamped my hands around my skull. "I can't believe you are even bringing this up right now. We are so far from where you are drowning in the middle of the goddamn ocean! Having a kid isn't going to just magically solve all our problems. You can't give it the life you never had if you can't keep the shake from your hands."

I took a deep breath and stared into the kitchen, letting the hustle of her chefs distract me.

"You're right."

I turned and looked at her. That was probably the fastest I'd ever seen her cave.

"So, I guess it's up to me to get us back to shore, huh."

"Yeah," I said, "it kinda is."

"Okay."

That was all that was left to say.

After that she walked me out to my car. I felt a little bad, putting all the weight over her shoulders, seeing as my pores stunk of wine and I may still have had Derek's scent on me from the night before. Regardless, she really did have a lot to prove to me before I could just move back in with her. It wasn't just about the drinking; it was her lack of control. She'd let down her guard and let herself get possessed by something evil. As far as I was concerned, that was nearly unforgivable.

"Are you going by the loft at all?" she asked, bravely tracing a finger over my new feather.

I chucked my bag into the passenger seat, trying to bury the truth that my skin tingled from her touch—that I wanted more. "I wasn't planning on it. Why?" I knew why.

She removed her finger from my arm, backing up against my car and crossing her arms over her chest. "It's been long enough, don't you think? Ellie, if you want me to move forward, you have to start forgiving me."

This was her subtle way of begging.

"I guess there's a few things I could stand to pick up."

She nodded her head, staring at her feet.

"So, I'll just hear from you when I hear from you?" she asked.

"Yeah."

I started to get into the car, but she reached for my arm again, stopping me.

"Ellie." There was a hitch in her voice.

I looked away, knowing there were tears in production. Joe never cried.

"I miss you, too," I said, before pulling away from her and folding myself into the car.

ELLIE

T'd returned to the beginning of the end, and it was heavy. Climbing the stairs to our loft felt like returning to a past life.

As I pulled on the strength from my new inked in feather, I touched my necklace, thinking of my mom. It wasn't until later that night in the hospital, after my near-death experience, that Derek had pointed to my little key and cocked a brow. At some point it had turned purple, and if I had to guess, the change had most likely happened when I'd heard my mother's voice. *I've taken this first punch for you . . .*

It was entirely possible that it was my family's stupid curse that had been coming for me that day in the closet, and that my mother had somehow stopped it from taking me; but who had been inside Joe, I wasn't sure. I didn't think it was the same thing that was scratching on our closet door, leaving her to feel haunted. Whatever had been inside my wife wasn't something that thrived on party tricks. Whatever, *who*ever, had possessed Joe that day had roots. It smelled of rot and sea water, and the way it looked at me—I knew this wasn't the first time it had tortured my soul.

Ella. The way it had said that name. That thing knew me from a previous life, and that thing had killed me before. I was sure of it.

When I got to the front door of our loft I just stood there, a rancid sensation filling the pit in my stomach. I laid my hand over the brass doorknob; it was scratched and worn from age. Then, before I could change my mind, I unlocked the door and flung it open. Immediately, I was right back in the heart of that day.

Before I left the loft the day that Joe, or Joe's body, attacked me—after Derek had already stepped out into the hallway—I'd turned around to face the mess that Joe had left for me. The only thing coursing through my veins was rage. Anger at what she'd done to our marriage, my trust, my ability to love, and my mother's accident that never would've happened if she hadn't been so reckless.

As I stood there, those feelings grabbed a hold of me between the place where dark and light live. I raised my wand and brought it down again, utilizing magic without having to utter a single word. I made damn sure that Joe wouldn't be able to pick any of that shit back up. No matter how hard she tried.

But now, standing there and seeing everything all over again—I just wanted it gone. Lifting my wand, I waved it in the direction of my old practice nook and swept all the clutter into the corner. It was still a mess, but at least Joe could pick it up.

Having cleared a path, I picked up a random chunk of my old violin and made my way slowly through the loft. There were heaps of jeans and T-shirts piling up over our furniture, and Joe's shoes were scattered all over the floor. She had moved all her clothing and other things downstairs. She wasn't kidding when she'd said she hadn't gone back into the closet, and with good reason if what I suspected was true.

It had to be a fairly newborn ass bag living in that closet, and those could be just as shitty as the ancient ones. Full of themselves and super cocky, but this also made it easier to get rid of them. They were so sure of themselves that they didn't often keep their guards up.

I slid the purse from my shoulder and looked up the windy stairs that led to our bedroom, clearing my senses, and focusing on the disturbance. I felt every particle of energy vibrating within range. Though it wasn't the foul beast in the closet that had taken over my wife that dreaded day, there definitely was something up there. I hadn't wanted to freak Joe out, so I'd kept it to myself what I'd assumed was living in our loft.

I dropped my bag to the floor, taking each step carefully until I reached the landing. I had a small altar set up across from our bed, and inside I always kept hand rolled sage amongst other supplies. While I'd been living in the loft, I'd had to routinely sweep the living quarters to protect us from things of this nature because of Joe's consistent drunken negativity. It sure hadn't taken very long for one of them to form together after I left; it was probably just biding its time.

With my attention fixed to the closet door, I grabbed a thick sage stick, a bottle of cedar oil, and held out my wand—a flame was already at the end as though it was a giant matchstick. After I was properly armed, I stood before the door, deep breaths entering and exiting my nostrils as I concentrated on the light inside my heart.

I'd never been afraid of these things, but I knew this energy would try and get inside me. I could already visualize it, drooling inside that closet, craving the body my soul was residing in, and the goddess light attached to it. Malevolent energies wanted witches, they wanted us more than anything in the world. Sure, they could create their own sorcery, but what we were born with was far more powerful. In the wrong hands, witch magic could be the deadliest force in the world. Showing weakness at this point would be suicide. Behind that door was residue from mine and Joe's soul; it was leftover junk from that god-awful day, and most likely the days that followed. A mass that had formed itself into a new entity.

I rolled back my shoulders, elongated my neck, then took a deep breath before I reached out and swung open the closet door. I showed the black cloud no emotion when it turned from its corner and hissed. It took the nasty energy only half a second to lunge for me.

"Out!" I screeched. "In the name of the Goddess Diana, I cast you away!"

Unable to get past the sage, it shoved at me, like a large bully cornering a small child in a desolate hallway. But I stood strong, statuesque, holding the smudge stick out like a sword and making large circles of billowing smoke.

"Unhappy energies are not welcome in this place! Any*thing,* any*one* who wishes those who live here harm must leave now!"

The black fog rammed into the smoking sage. Tendrils from the dark cloud attempted to wrap themselves around it, but my light was fierce and had been born of a goddess who was billions of years old. I was an unbreakable force.

"What's wrong, princess?" It was using Joe's voice, because these things, as they grew stronger, could show themselves however they wanted. They could reach into your mind and pull at details no one else would ever know. Joe's words fell around my shoulders like hail spitting down from a black cloud. This evil piece of shit was trying to crack me like an egg. "Don't I make you happy? No one is ever good enough for you!"

"Away!" I yelled, keeping my features still, careful not to show any emotion.

"Aw—wait. What is that I hear?" it hissed. "The wind . . . it whispers."

"You fucking ass bag—"

"If it wasn't for your spell your sister's son would still be here. *She* would still be here." The cloud backed away, shaking as it laughed. "Everything you touch dies!" I clenched the things in my hands tighter. "Your mother's spell shouldn't have saved you. Rowena should've been able to put you out of your misery!"

I cocked my head to the side. "Rowena?"

Its laughter was deep and throaty . . . evil.

"Don't worry, princess, she isn't through with you. She'll have all of you soon enough. She's hungry, and your mother's soul—I bet it's tasty."

Don't let it get to you, Ellie, I coached myself. This is what these things did, they got to the root of whoever they wanted to feed from. I had no choice but to be strong. Disregarding the strange things it was saying, I concentrated harder, focusing on growing more fire at the end of the smudge stick —creating more smoke. Utilizing all my strength, I built a force field between the ass bag and me, and when I spoke, I did so fiercely.

These were the words that had been instilled into my sister and me from a very young age. "As dust you will fall and die away, my light is more powerful than you on any given day!"

The smoky formation paused, as if it were considering my threat. Then, agonizingly slowly, it shifted its form, and as it did, I had to force myself not to cringe.

"Ellie . . ." it whispered. Thin red lips, moving inside the outline of a small head with short, pixie-like hair. The frame of the woman I loved. As it floated before me, the likeness split in half—forming not only into the likeness of Joe, but of Derek as well.

"You harbor feelings for both . . . which one will it be?"

The two imposters hissed. "She loves me, he loves me not. He loves me, she loves me not."

I gritted my teeth, my stomach twisting. "I cast you out!" I shouted, dropping my hands down by my sides and releasing the force field.

The entity formed back into a black fog and immediately charged at me, but I was prepared for it, hitting it with a cloud of concentrated smoke. It fumbled and fought as though it'd just been caught by a web of rope; as it struggled, I pulled out the cedar oil and sprinkled it in the air, watching as it floated in the space before me as though there was no such thing as gravity.

The beast was growing weaker, but it continued to fight. As it watched me turn the oil into a fine mist, it failed to contain its fear—its energy pulsating as it worked anxiously to smuggle itself free.

"Let me in, Ellie! Between my darkness and your magic, we could rule!"

"I said you are not welcome! Be gone!" I backed away as soon as I yelled the last words, and as I did the fine mist of cedar I'd created shot into the entity like thousands of tiny bullets.

After another minute, all that was left of the nasty energy were the last of its screams as it died away. I grabbed a broom and swept up the fine layer of black dust covering the floor.

"Good riddance," I said, as I flushed the remains down the toilet. I had not been expecting it to be that big.

My mom had always called these unfortunate creations Freddies. I had to assume the name came from somebody in her past who she didn't care for all that much. Perhaps an ex. All I knew or cared about was that they were energies, bad ones. Most everyone had them lurking around in their homes or workspaces, but as witches, we could see and hear them. It was our job to sweep them away when they got out of control.

They were leftovers from emotional pain or extreme anger —fear. If they weren't dealt with, they could become very dangerous. A lot of people who thought their houses were haunted simply had a buildup of negative energy and it was feeding from them. Freddies were like mold spores; once they were unleashed, they quickly grew out of control. They even had the ability to possess people. All they needed was an invitation, or someone too weak or too blinded to fight them off. Freddies were bad, really bad.

I decided to smudge the rest of the loft when all was said and done. After something like that it was never a bad idea to do a little extra 'cleaning.' When I was finished, I ran back upstairs and rummaged through my drawers, grabbing a few things I'd been missing. Just as I was about to close the dresser, however, I noticed something I had completely forgotten about. Slowly, I leaned down and retrieved a stack of cards wrapped inside a blue, tasseled scarf. V's tarot cards. I'd completely forgotten I had them.

We'd boxed up her stuff when it looked like she really wasn't coming back, but there were just some things that were too precious to throw away. Her cards had been one of those things. Before she tossed her gift to the ocean, my sister had been a master of divination; besides her crystal ball, the tarot had been her eyes.

I dropped down to my knees and held the deck against my chest. I wanted to unravel the scarf and shuffle the cards, feel my sister's energy in them before she changed, but that sort of thing wasn't done. Without permission, it wasn't okay to touch another witch's deck, even if that witch had lost herself somewhere along the way.

My drifting thoughts were suddenly cut off by the sound of our land line ringing down below. Dropping the tarot cards into my bag I walked downstairs and gathered the rest of my things, preparing to leave before the answering machine picked up. I was afraid it was Joe, and I didn't have anything else to say to her. No one else had the number for that line— we only had that phone because it was super rad. This orange rotary number that hung on the wall just like my mom had used to have in the kitchen.

I was halfway out the door when I heard the beep.

"Hey Joe, it's me, Jody."

I immediately turned around and hissed, sounding eerily similar to the thing I'd just murdered in the upstairs closet.

"Listen, I was thinking about last night and I really wanted to give you a shout. I just can't let you go, not like that. Call me crazy, but it had to be the stars aligning that brought us together." She chuckled, and my jaw tightened. "Anyway, call me, okay. Bye."

Mother fucker.

"Bitch," I said out loud.

I stood there for I don't know how long, just staring at the machine.

My face grew hotter by the second. My dry mouth and heavy head were suddenly washed away as if I'd never had a hangover in the first place, and before I knew what I was doing I'd dropped my things to the floor and was running back upstairs to my bed stand, to where I kept my small bowl of salt.

As soon as I had what I needed, I marched back downstairs as though I'd been reprogrammed for an entirely new mission. I made my way through the house and grabbed my things, throwing them out the front door, and then I turned back around to face the loft. Without even a second's hesitation, I threw the salt up in the air as I recited the only words going through my mind. Then I walked out, slamming the door behind me.

ELLIE

When I returned to my shitty cabin, I was so pissed that I couldn't see straight. Biscuit paced as I threw junk around, shouting at the walls. I'd picked my cell phone up several times to call Joe and scream at her but decided against it every time. There was no need for that, she'd feel my wrath soon enough.

Just—how could she? How could she sit there eating her burger and play as if the night before had been nothing at all? I couldn't get that wicked bitch's voice out of my head.

"Snatch face!" I screeched, picturing myself wringing Jody's stupid neck.

I was supposed to go over to The Dewdrop and sling glasses of Pinot Noir and Chardonnay in an hour. I needed to calm down before I went in there. At this rate I was bound to set fire to someone's hair just by looking at them.

"Wichahpi?"

I paused from my charade of curse words and turned around. My front door was wide open and my aunt was on the stoop. Her familiar, Puddin, was cuddled into her arms.

"Oh . . . hey," I huffed. I reached for a sheet of paper, a

melody I'd been working on scrawled across it, and childishly tossed it across the room.

"Bad timing?"

"No, everything's just peachy." I shot her a fake smile.

"Can I come in?"

"Sure." I flopped down into a chair and looked up at her, winded. "What's up?"

"How was your mom?"

"Shit." I rubbed at my forehead. "I had a really bad afternoon. I forgot to stop by."

"So, it did not go all that well with Josephine?"

"I *so* don't want to talk about it."

"No matter. We will be going to visit your mother tomorrow anyway."

"Fine," I said, sizing Lana up. There was still something off about her, but I couldn't be sure what it was. "What's going on?"

"Nothing."

She was lying. I could sense the truth of whatever she had seen or was anticipating—it was on the tip of her tongue. Something big was about to hit us.

"I have to take Minnie to the doctor. She needs to get her eyes dilated and I told her I would drive her. I shouldn't be gone too long but I need you to watch Puddin for me, make sure she doesn't freak out the guests."

I narrowed my eyes. She was as cool as could be. Her perfect long black locks falling around her bare shoulders—the hair my mom had always wanted but couldn't have. Lana's skin glistened with a midsummer's glow, but her motivating force was dark.

"What the hell, Lana? Are you going to tell me what's going on, or what?"

"Just take Puddin," she said impatiently, walking over and dropping the small creature into my arms. The little fur ball purred like a cat against my chest. "I'll be back in a couple hours." As she was walking out the door, she paused. "Just remember to stay present. Yes?"

Without giving me the opportunity to react, she strolled right out the door, and before I could even sit up, I heard her truck backing out of the driveway.

An hour later I was behind the counter, helping my cousin Patrick prep for dinner. We were a quaint establishment, but we managed to fill our tables a few times a day. Our guests tended to eat all their meals with us, and the surrounding neighbors came by regularly because our food was fresh, and our drinks were strong. Plus, it was rumored that you could see witches flying over the tree line during a full moon.

"Dude, what was wrong with your mom earlier?" I asked Patrick, pouring myself a cup of coffee and leaning back against the counter.

"I dunno, I didn't see her. Why? Was she doing that thing where she gets weird?"

"Yeah."

He shrugged his shoulders. "Something's in the wind. She never says though."

"That's just great," I scoffed, taking a sip from my coffee. "As if this family hasn't been through enough already. And on that note, have you ever heard the name Rowena before?"

"Uh, I don't know. Should I have?"

"No . . . probably not." The Freddie had probably been messing with me.

"Shit. This is feta."

"So," I said, staring down at the cheese he'd pulled out.

"I'm making steak with gorgonzola sauce tonight." He slammed down his fist.

"So, change it." I signaled to the wand sticking out from his back pocket.

"No way, it never tastes right when I do that. I need run to the store. Can you handle the kitchen for an hour?"

"Sure," I said, unenthusiastically. "I can make burnt toast if anyone orders anything."

"You're such a brat, Ellie."

I wrinkled my nose and sipped my coffee.

Patrick paused on his way out and leaned down to the only patron we had at the moment, a young woman typing on her laptop at a table for one. I rolled my eyes as he whispered something into her ear. She was attractive. Tan skin, blonde hair, thick black reading glasses. Patrick would inevitably try to sleep with her before she checked out.

It had already been a long day, and my hangover was still bringing me down on top of it. I just wanted to go back to my cabin and close the shades, turn off my mind and make reality go away; but I was only afforded about ten minutes of pure unadulterated silence before I heard the freak out.

"Oh my god! Oh my god, *how did that get in here*!!"

Alarmed, I jumped away from the wall, and as I did, I noticed that the baby gate between the kitchen and bar area had fallen.

"Whoops," I said, unaffected by the disturbance. Relaxing my shoulders, I set my coffee down and made my way over to where the blonde woman was shrieking and staring down at her feet in terror.

"What do I do?" She was panicking, her hands up in the air and her body frozen.

"My bad. I was supposed to keep her in the back." I reached down and cupped a hand around Puddin's face. "She was just trying to nestle, she's a cuddler. Don't worry, she doesn't spray unless provoked." I could tell the woman thought I was stoned or something.

Unable to relax, she transformed her horror into a most perplexing expression. "That—that is your pet?"

"No, this is my Aunt Lana's. Her name's Puddin, but don't worry, she's as sweet as can be."

"But it's a skunk. That's *got* to be against health code."

I pulled Puddin into my chest and began to argue that the familiar's spray was probably less offensive than this lady's perfume but was cut off before I ever got the chance.

"Witches don't choose their familiars." I froze. That voice . . . How dare that voice enter this establishment. "But don't worry, Puddin has never been anything but a loving and caring creature. She won't bother you."

I came back up to my feet and hesitantly turned around, my hand over the skunk's head as though I was shielding the creature from evil.

Baring my teeth, I said, "What are you doing here, V?"

Her eyes were stone cold. In them I could see waves crashing against heavy, jagged rocks. Or was that just how her heartbeats sounded nowadays?

Repeating myself, I continued to question her. "V? Why are you here?"

With her lips knitted tightly together, she paused before speaking. "To save our mother."

OLIVIA

Ellie had been calling me V ever since she was a little girl.
When she first started talking Olivia flowed through
her mouth like a bag of marbles, so she started calling
me by the one letter she could pronounce clearly. Nowadays,
though, I think she referred to me as V because it was short for
vagina. Either way, I couldn't have known what to expect
upon my return, nor what I would have done if the roles had
been switched; but I know my sister's first reaction was not
what I had expected.

"What's up with the fucking headband?" She scowled; her
eyes pinned on the hard-plastic band I had placed over my
ironed-out locks. I'd hoped it would keep the oncoming frizz
at bay.

I ignored her, turning my attention to the poor woman
who had the misfortune of witnessing my homecoming. She
was surrounded by spirits, a couple of them with wings.
Judging by the laptop and stream of consciousness she'd been
typing, I had to presume that most of these energies had been
writers in their past life—their arrival connected to
inspiration. Either that or a longing for lost words to have a

place in the physical world. One of them seemed adamant that the writer hear him; even over the disturbance created by my existence he was crouched down beside her ear, whispering frantically.

"Don't listen to the witches, listen to me. Listen, girly. I've got the secret twist you've been needing for the plot to thicken." Upon catching my gaze, he flinched, jumping up and pointing a stretched out, translucent knobby finger in my direction. "Leave us, witch! She needs her privacy to create my masterpiece!"

I rolled my eyes and excused myself from both Ellie and the young woman, stalking off towards the kitchen. After the shitty 'conversation' I'd had over the phone with Tyler's sous chef about our daughter—because goddess forbid she be allowed to stay with me at the retreat when it was Tyler's turn to take her, and goddess forbid my husband tell me that himself—I was *not* in the mood to be berated by my sister. As I walked away, Ellie's energy followed close behind, like a bomb about to detonate. All it made me want to do was to irritate her further by exuding a calm demeanor.

"V? Why are you here?" Puddin was still clamped against her chest.

"Absolutely nothing has changed," I observed, ignoring her question while cocking my head around the corner to where my office had used to be, right next to my mother's.

I'd overseen events when I'd worked here. It had been my idea to start hosting weddings at the retreat—who knew they would grow to such popularity. Then again, the rumors surrounding this place had caused it to become a tourist attraction. In fact, I bet that writer over there had come specifically because of the many artists who had become famous after visiting our forest destination.

"V? *Hello*?"

I pushed past Ellie and her continued digs at my arrival,

taking in the lost scents of the shop that had used to be just as much my home as the house I'd lived in down the road. This was where I'd grown up and always thought my kids would grow up too.

My sister's anger transformed into a low gurgle as she seethed in my direction. "This is so you, V. You come home after eight years, and instead of talking to your sister, you look around for the nearest ghost to chat up."

"I'm not looking for ghosts," I retorted.

"Then why don't you turn and face me, you coward?"

The muscles in my upper back stiffened. Lowering my suitcase to the kitchen floor, I took a very deep breath before squaring my shoulders with hers.

"Ellie," I began, but she cut me off before I had a chance to go on. Before I had a chance to tell her there was nothing I could do or say to make this situation run smoothly.

She sneered. "What the fuck are you wearing?"

I looked down at my clothes. "Slacks and a shirt." Then, narrowing my eyes on her, I returned the crude remark. "What are *you* wearing?" She looked like more of a punk than usual.

Ignoring my jab, she retorted, "You look like a moron. Seriously, what's up with the plastic headband? We stopped wearing those when we were five."

I slicked a hand down over my ratty locks; I'd inherited our mother's broom head. I'd hoped it would calm down now that I was away from the coast, but there was a slight humidity to the air, even here. "I like headbands, is that all right with you?"

"Nothing about you is *all right* with me right now, V." Ellie sat Puddin down on the floor and put up the baby gate so the animal couldn't run out and scare our guest again. Then she laid her hands on her hips, cocked her head to the side, and jutted out her chin. Carbon copy of Maddie and her adolescent attitude, except Ellie was thirty-two. "You can't just come waltzing in here in your—those things on your legs—"

"Slacks." I raised an eyebrow.

"With your stupid slacks and dress shirt—and what the shit is on your feet?"

"They're penny loafers. I find them very comfortable."

"Ew."

"Look, *Ellie*, some of us have professional careers and need to dress the part—"

"Oh whatever, you don't even own a diploma from a community college. You gained your 'experience' from a ghost. Maddie told me all about it."

I took a deep breath and pumped my hands down by my sides. "Listen, you have every right to hate me—"

"Damn right I do."

I continued to shake out my hands, wringing them out in front of my stomach. "I would hate me, too. I can't undo what I've done, but the truth is that I'm not here to try and make you love me again. I'm here for Mom."

She made an annoyed sound in the back of her throat and her gaze fell to rest over my hands. "What the hell are you doing? Are you trying to stun me into forgetting that you're a big, beige wearing, deserter? Cause it's not gonna work. There's not a spell powerful enough to do that."

There weren't enough meditation exercises in the world to try and make this intervention bearable. Still, I worked on taking rhythmic breaths in and out of my nose, just like Gerald had shown me. "I'm using a technique to calm myself, because being here is not easy for me. And no, I would never stun you—I hardly even practice magic any longer." Other than rescuing my daughter from evil that was.

Ellie's face contorted into an expression one might wear after eating mushy Brussel sprouts. "But you're a witch, your energy is made from magic."

I finished shaking out my hands and reached for my

suitcase. "I would appreciate it if we could speak about all this later. I would like nothing more than a shower."

I hadn't even had a chance to breathe yet. From the second Rowena had walked away it had been one long stride of packing, spinning a little bit more of my rusty magic to get Maddie and I booked on the soonest plane out of there, and wrestling with Tyler's stubborn ass via whoever he could persuade to talk to me instead of him. I was drained, dirty, and my head hurt.

Repeating my words back to me, Ellie said mockingly, "You would like nothing more than a shower? *Are you fucking kidding me?* You know what—no."

I tucked my chin. "Excuse me?"

Shaking her head, Ellie puckered her lips, and lunged forward so quickly I didn't have a chance to defend my being. "This shit" –-she plucked the plastic band from my head— "has got to go."

"Hey!" I said, reaching up and smoothing out my hair. "What'd you do that for?"

"I can't look at you with this stupid shit in your hair. The V I knew wore ripped jeans and Birkenstocks, and her hair was curly because she never blow-dried it." She backed up and waved a hand over my body. "This person is not my sister. Ironed hair, *slacks*—and what are those earrings—pearls?"

"People change, Ellie."

"You haven't changed, you've reinvented yourself into some sort of Martha Stewart looking—whatever, you look dumb."

"All right, that's enough. Look, I know you're upset and you have a lot going on right now, with Mom and Joe—"

"Fuck off, you've never even met my wife."

"Really nice, Ellie. Great educated vocabulary you have there. You know what, I'm gonna go. I'll be back when you can talk like a grown up."

She began to retort but the sound of footsteps interrupted her, followed almost immediately by my cousin Patrick's voice.

"Hey, I just remembered I stowed the gorgonzola in the other fridge, so I didn't need to go out after all—*oh shit.*" I turned around just in time to find him with a look of horror plastered on his face. Recovering quickly, he slapped on a silly grin. "Hey there, cuz."

"Hi Patrick," I said as casually as I could.

"Uh, long time no see, I guess." He pulled me into his chest, patting my back a little too hard. I could hear him mouthing 'what the fuck' to my sister.

I pulled away and bent down to gather my suitcase. Ellie had her arms crossed over her chest, still clenching her fingers around my headband, and Patrick was staring from her to me and back to her again. I needed to go somewhere and catch my breath before I could continue with this reunion. I'd come here to speak with my Aunt Lana about what had gone down earlier in the day. Not to get harassed by Ellie.

"I know Lana is living in my old house, but she doesn't seem to be home. Is Dad around? I was hoping to stay with him while I'm here."

Ellie refused to respond, and the way she was grinding her teeth together as she faced me was getting creepy. Thankfully, Patrick stepped in.

Wrapping a hand around my shoulders, he ushered me out of the kitchen. "Yeah, Ronno's home. I'll walk ya over."

"Thanks," I said, glancing back at Ellie. "I'll come back after I get settled. Maybe we can talk over dinner, or a glass of wine. Er, that is if you still drink. I know Joe is recovering."

She twisted her mouth to the side and snapped my headband in half.

Okay, I deserved that. "We'll talk later."

WHEN I WALKED UP, my father was sitting on the front porch with a glass of iced tea. He didn't flinch or even blink twice when he saw me. Judging from the empty glass next to him on the table and the empty shooter of whiskey, he had been warned of my arrival.

Picking up the empty glass and sniffing it after a less than affectionate embrace, I asked, "Where's Lana?"

"Had to go out," he answered, leaning back on his heels and stuffing his hands into the pockets of his trousers. "She'll be back for dinner, I 'spose. Where's Maddie?"

I wasn't shocked at all that this was how my father had taken to my abrupt arrival. Even if he hadn't been prepped by Lana, this is how he would react. He was a quiet man, contemplative. Then again, he'd been surrounded by witches for more than half his life now. In the end, it's all about survival.

"I dropped her off at her and Tyler's *apartment*." The emphasis over apartment was so he would understand that Maddie and Tyler's new living arrangements were news to me. Up until quite recently, as far as I had known they were still living *here*, in the house he and I had built together. "Did you know they were building a house next to that new restaurant of his?"

He dug a toothpick from his pocket and bit down over it, continuing to rock back and forth on his heels. "Um hm."

"I see." It was all I could say.

He looked down at his feet, nodded, then reached for my suitcase. "Yep, well, let's get ya settled."

I stared at his back before following him inside, trying to assess how much he wished I was a different person in that moment. I wasn't the one he'd wished had come home.

As soon as I stepped foot inside, the familiar scent of the house nearly knocked me down. Incense, dried acorns, cherry tobacco, and old books . . . magic. She wasn't dead, but I could already feel my mother's ghost haunting the walls.

"Dad, don't you want to know why I'm here?" I asked.

He was already heading up the stairs. "I know why yer here."

"Oh really—why's that?"

"Yer mother." He paused from where he was standing on the fourth step and looked down at me. "She's been waitin'. That brief stint of yours a few months back, you showin' yer face for that short moment of time—that wasn't it. This is it."

"What do you mean by that?" I asked. But he didn't seem to hear me. If he did, he pretended as though he hadn't.

I remained planted just in front of the stairs, listening to his footsteps moving around on the second floor. Eventually I made my way towards the living room, scoping out what my mother had done to the place over the past eight years. It wasn't all that different, but there were subtle changes that seemed a lot bigger in the grand scheme of things.

"I thought Mom didn't want a television in here," I said as soon as my father had come back downstairs, my gaze fixed over a sixty-inch flat screen in the corner of the room.

"She changed 'er mind. Maddie got 'er into one of those video games with dragons and such, so we got ourselves a small picture for in here, but then she decided it wasn't big enough." He chuckled. "Yer mother. Any who, we stuck that in our bedroom and got this one here so she can play her Skyrim, or whatever it is. She plays a wood elf, or something of that nature."

I snickered at the idea of my small, gray-haired mother, sitting cross-legged in front of that giant flat screen playing video games.

"We got some new furniture, too. I like that chair over there." He lifted a finger and pointed to an oversized brown recliner. Corduroy. It was sort of awful.

"It's nice," I said.

It was quiet for a few more seconds. The silence was nearly unbearable. It wasn't worth waiting for him to tell me that I was an asshole, that I left my husband and the one child I had left, because he wasn't going to. But that didn't mean he wasn't thinking it.

"How have you been, Dad?"

His hands back in his pockets, his bite occupied by the toothpick, my father simply continued to stare straight ahead, nodding. "Dinner's at six."

He turned and made his way back to the front porch.

"Dinner?" I asked, causing him to pause.

"Yep. Reckon you wanna see yer aunt. Her and I have a dinner date at the restaurant at six. The word is Patrick is cookin' up some steak. He's been gettin' real fancy after working with Tyler. That husband of yers has been doing some radical things in the kitchen—workin' with that Joe. Betcha that new place of his is gonna be a real hit."

"You know, Dad, he's not really, like, my husband anymore."

Again, he turned and settled his gaze so that it was directly in front of him. One sharp chin dip. "Yep. See ya at six."

OLIVIA

An hour later I hadn't moved but a few feet. Enough to sit on the couch and stare at my father through the glass door. He hadn't been cold to me, but that was only because my father would always have a warm heart. He was a fisherman, and he'd easily spent half his life in his waders, standing amidst the rapids of the river, alone with his thoughts and whatever else he welcomed. Sometimes I wondered if he had a sixth sense of his own.

What was he thinking? I wondered, watching as he sipped his tea. As he filled his pipe and smoked it. Bits of the familiar cherry tobacco smell were inside these walls, evidence that he'd been smoking inside while my mother had been away. If it was any other father, I would have believed that he was thinking nothing but negative thoughts about me. But this man, no. As I studied him, fully aware that he could feel my gaze, I gathered this much—he wasn't thinking about me at all. He was thinking about my mom, and whether I could help her. He would worry about his feelings for me after all was said and done.

Eventually, I made my way upstairs long enough to shower

and sift through the medley of clothing I'd picked out. It *was* all beige and beige-like colors. I'm not sure when I'd transitioned from hippie earth child to fifty-year-old librarian, but I most definitely had. Whatever, Ellie could suck it. I had to be professional for my patients, and it didn't matter where I got my training. I was a good therapist, dammit. Hell, I'd been shrinking spirits left and right since I was a little girl. After all, someone had to send them back to where they came from. The living weren't that different.

I ended up fixing myself back up into an outfit nearly identical to what I'd been wearing earlier, before I headed back down the stairs in search of my father. It was about five minutes till six, so I'd supposed he would be waiting for me by the door; but when I got downstairs he wasn't yet there, so I stood patiently in the living area and waited.

As the seconds ticked by, I lowered my gaze to the small black bowl of water lying on the nearest table. There was a light reflecting from it from the skylight directly above. *Smart place to stow your bowl, Mom,* I thought. Having it under the break in the ceiling meant it could be continually cleansed by the moon.

When he'd first gone, my son, I'd filled our house with bowls of water, searching for signs of him in every reflection. It was never him who came to the surface—never *his* eyes who I saw staring back at me—taunting me. It was only ever Rowena. After a while I could no longer take it and threw all the bowls away.

As I continued to stare into the little black bowl, the water inside it began to ripple. I immediately gasped, leaning in to see what was manifesting—as a tear in my heart, that had only been somewhat sealed back together by loose stitching, began to reopen. I held my breath as I stared into my mother's bowl. After all this time, would I finally be afforded a glimpse at the son I'd lost? Proof that he still existed. But whether it was him or my ghost, I wasn't destined to know. For just then a set of footsteps coming down the stairs caused the ripples to even out, and the pair of eyes that were just beginning to stare back at me faded away.

My dad appeared at the bottom of the steps. "Wouldn't touch that. That's yer mom's crying bowl. She said to make sure I keep it filled with water, and never move it."

"It's a scrying bowl," I corrected. My words drifted away as I said the next part. "And she probably didn't want it moved because she wasn't ready to give up on him."

My confession, that I *had* given up on Thaden, hung in the air like an unmovable fog.

"Right," my father said, so obviously trying to move out from the awkward occurrence. "Er, well, you hungry?"

"Famished," I lied. My appetite had vanished the moment that beast had possessed my daughter.

"All right . . . well, let's go."

"After you," I signaled.

He paused only to pick up an old, faded hat from the kitchen table and fit it around his head. He didn't speak again until we were halfway around the lake, The Dewdrop in the near distance.

"Yer sister's probably working tonight. Have you talked to her yet?"

I chirped a short and unsweet, "Yes."

"How'd that go?"

"As well as could be expected."

"Yep," was all he said.

"Dad." My voice sounded more like a little girl than I had intended. "I appreciate you letting me stay with you."

"This is your home, Olivia."

After that he said nothing else, and neither did I. When we got to The Dewdrop, he held the door open for me and nodded his head at an elderly couple sitting in the corner. I scanned the space as I followed him to a table in the opposite corner and let him pull a chair out for me. I was surprised at how many people were there for dinner.

"It's gotten popular here," I noted, scooting my chair into the table.

My dad just smiled; his gaze directed at the table instead of me.

We'd only been sat for about a minute when Ellie arrived by our sides. As soon he saw her, my father's demeanor changed—as if a fresh breeze had just wafted into a stuffy room.

"Hey Daddy," she said, leaning down and kissing him on the cheek. Ellie had never called our father 'daddy' in our entire lives. She was laying it on thick. "Do you want the steak?"

"Do I want the steak?" He chuckled. "Course I do. What's he got fer sides tonight?"

"It already comes with a salad," she said, shutting down the option of French fries before he could use our mother's absence as an excuse to eat junk food. I may have been gone for eight years, but I could tell that some things never changed. "You want a beer with dinner?"

"Yeah, that sounds good. And bring an iced tea with a shot of whiskey for yer aunt. She should be here any minute."

Ellie nodded, then turned and faced me; as she did her expression fell cold. "What do you want?"

I blinked twice. "A chilled glass of Chardonnay would be nice, and I would like to see the menu if that's okay."

She grumbled something under her breath as she turned back towards the bar. When she returned with our drinks, she slapped a menu in front of me so hard my frizzy hair blew to the sides. She'd killed my only headband—my one savior against the torment of my inherited broom head.

"Thanks," I muttered. Once she was gone, I stared across the table at my father. "Well, she's still Ellie, isn't she?"

"She'll come around." He took a long pull from his beer.

I shook my head and looked down at the menu. All the dishes were still named after the people in our family: Ellie's Maple Mac-N-Cheese, Ron's Pistachio Crusted Trout . . . Tyler's Coconut Gumbo. This one was new, however— Olivia's Lame Duck.

"So, Maddie's been talking non-stop about the new restaurant. Sounds like Tyler's come a long way from his sous chef days here at the shop."

"Yep."

I held my stare over my father, at his refusal to look back at me. "And it also sounds like he has Joe to thank for how far he's come."

He grabbed his utensils and slid the napkin off from around them. "He's been workin' real hard opening that new kitchen. He deserves everything he's got comin'." Then with a quick glance up at me, his right eye narrowed just slightly, and he added, "But even with all of everything he's got goin' on, he still manages to make it out here and help Patrick from time to time."

Mother fucking dig.

I set down my menu and laid my hands flat over it. "I'm really sorry, Dad. I never meant to hurt anybody by staying away for so long. You know that it was always about me, right? Not any of you."

He cleared his throat and looked over at the bar.

When he didn't offer a retort, I sat back in my chair and asked, "Is Tyler planning on being here this weekend?"

He shrugged his shoulders. "I wouldn't know. Lana is the one who deals with the shop schedule."

Plucking invisible darts from my skin from my father's passive target practice, I was about to ask when exactly my aunt had moved into my old house when a shadow fell over the table. A second later, there was a voice to match.

"Tyler and Maddie aren't coming this weekend; and to answer your question I've been in your house—*my* house now —for three years, as it made more sense for Tyler and Maddie to live in the city after he started working for Josephine."

A rush of cool air wafted over my sticky shoulders just at the sound of my aunt's voice, and I exhaled her name as I slid my chair away from the table.

"Wachiwi, I saw you coming," she whispered into my ear as soon as I wrapped my arms around her. There was so much magic in her soul. "And I know why."

I pulled gently away and studied her. I remember thinking when I was a child that her face must be made of stone. She was a natural beauty, but rough around the edges—a lot like Ellie. When she smiled, all of her smiled, but the rest of the time her face rested in the same neutral position. I used to think it was because Patrick's father left when he was only six, but as I got older, I realized this was just how she was.

"You know of my ghost . . ."

A line formed between her brows. "I only know a dark force has driven you home, and that you worry it is here for your mother. But you seem to know much more than I." Her attention shifted to my father, who was staring up at the two of us with interest. Returning to me, she added, "But right now is not the time for such talk."

My hand over her shoulder, I started to argue. "But Lana—"

Her voice firm, she replied as she cut me off, "Tomorrow."

I cinched my lips tight, allowing my hand to drift back down by my side. Eventually I took my seat back, just as Lana and my father exchanged a brief and friendly nod. I knew that my aunt was psychic enough to understand that we were up against a ticking clock, and that if she was okay waiting until tomorrow to dive into our family's un-retractable curse, that I should trust her . . . but she wasn't the one who could see ghosts. She wasn't the one who had watched Rowena step foot inside her daughter and attempt to take Maddie's last breath from her. Then again, I knew better than to fight against her. Lana's word was, quite often, final.

The dinner conversation was about as uncomfortable as I imagined it would be. My father continued to speak to anyone who bothered to address him, as long as it wasn't me, and my aunt acted as though everything was fine.

Eventually Ellie returned with our food, and she was in good spirits until she came to my side of the table. Delivering the steak dinners Lana and my father had ordered, she chirped happily in the waitress persona she'd temporarily picked up, until she came around to me—at which point she growled.

"Here's your fucking salad and soup," she grimaced, all but dropping the food into my lap.

"Ellie Jean," my father scolded gruffly.

"Sorry Pops, just slipped out." She made a face and walked back to the bar where she placed her head in her hands and glared at me.

Trying my best not to give her the satisfaction of a scowl, I creased my napkin over my lap, and without looking up, grumbled to Lana, "How did you manage to get Ellie behind the counter anyway?"

My aunt answered, just as she placed a large chunk of steak into her mouth, "She offered. Dia, our full-time waitress and barista quit a few weeks ago." She raised her eyebrows, waiting for me to show some kind of name recognition.

I cleared my throat. "You mean the woman Tyler was seeing?"

Maddie always made a point of telling me the names of each and every woman who Tyler had attempted to date. Nothing ever worked out; I tried not to believe it was because of our witch's union. Because that would mean I truly was an asshole. But deep down I knew it was.

"Yes," Lana stated, chewing her food like a cow gnawing on a mouthful of grass. "Dia left and we were short staffed, so Ellie volunteered to help out more than she already was."

More than she already was—gross. What she was was a little kiss ass. She was always good at kissing up and getting what she wanted. Her career was proof of that.

Trying to muffle the annoyed thoughts churning in my head, I attempted to remind them that the *star* of the family wasn't all that perfect either. "I imagine she could use the distraction right now." I flattened out the napkin that was already over my thighs, and continued, feeling as the strings I'd tied so tight around my being started to come undone. "Sounds like her world has fallen apart. And wasn't she supposed to be in Japan right now?"

I couldn't get Maddie's screeching voice out of my head from when she'd called to tell me that her *way famous aunt* was going to be headed out on a worldwide tour. Ugh.

Lana stopped mid-chew, staring at me as if I was growing horns. "So, you *do* know about their dispute? Her's and Joe's."

My gut wrenched as I stared back at my stony aunt. "Yes. Maddie told me."

"I was just wondering," Lana continued, speaking right over me, "because you didn't seem to take notice of the bruises around your sister's neck when you stopped by the hospital six months ago."

My hands became fists.

Without looking up from his plate, my father mumbled as he sawed through his steak with a giant knife. "When you hear things from a child's mouth, you hear only as much as the child's brain can process."

I laid my hands flat on the table and stared at my father. "What are you saying? That I don't know the half of it? I understand perfectly. Ellie dumped the man who loved her more than air for a woman who loves the drink more than breathing."

My father only wrinkled his forehead.

Frustrated by both his and Lana's expressions, I continued to argue, "My daughter is very good at giving me details. Maddie is a lot older on the inside than she is on the outside."

"There's reason for that," Lana said.

I took a deep breath and stared down at my lentil soup, and because I didn't know what to say next—other than a lot of words my sister was good at—I pulled the spoon to my mouth and was about to take a bite; but just then the spoon bent in half and all the brown liquid splashed onto my lap.

"Shit," I cursed, sitting back in my chair and looking down at my legs. Most of the soup landed on the napkin, but some of it had splattered onto my pants. I stared at the spoon in its unnatural shape and then looked up at my sister, who was now wearing one of the wickedest grins I'd ever seen, and I'd seen a few.

"Oops," she mouthed.

"You all right, there?" my dad asked, wiping his mouth with his napkin while looking from me to my sister.

"Yeah," I grumbled, wadding up my napkin and trying to wipe away some of the mess. Out of the corner of my eye I saw my father shaking his head at Ellie. How mighty wide of him to school her for being mean, his precious baby who was putting the family business first only because her life was shit.

After that, I decided to set aside the soup, and instead I grabbed my fork and pulled the salad in front of me; but as soon as I was about to dig into the beautiful fresh greens Patrick had arranged, my plate cracked and the lettuce turned into a bunch of slimy seaweed—a snail crawling out of it.

"Dammit, Ellie," my dad growled once more. "Let your sister eat her meal!"

"It's okay, Dad," I said, shoving my plate carefully away. "I wasn't really hungry anyway." Ellie pushed away from the bar she'd been resting against and headed to the other side, her back to us.

"You know, some people really like seaweed," Lana said, tapping my broken plate with her fork. "Maybe you should try it." I couldn't tell if she was messing with me, but I think she was serious.

"No, really. I think I'm good," I replied shortly. This reunion was everything I'd imagined and so much more. And they wondered why I hadn't ever wanted to come back. "Excuse me for a minute." I pushed away from the table. "I need to speak with my sister."

Laying my dirty napkin over my ruined dinner and ignoring my father's eye roll, I stood. I knew Ellie could feel me coming. We'd been connected our whole lives . . . until I ended our bond by running away. But as I pulled around to the other side of the bar, facing her, she pretended I wasn't there.

"So what?" I began, flattening out my hands over the bar. "Are you just going to ignore me forever?"

She refused to look up as she cleaned the spots from a wine glass. "Well, I figure you had your turn, so why can't I have mine? Besides, I'm not what you're here for, remember?"

"Ellie—"

She threw the wine glass into the sink and it instantly broke into a hundred pieces. The muffled sounds of people chatting at their tables stopped, and I knew everyone was staring at us. Ellie, however, was not fazed by this in the least.

"No! Don't you come in here and ask *me* why I'm not speaking to *you*! I've had a bad day! You picked a lousy time to waltz in here and try to sew things back together."

"I didn't choose this day," I spat out quietly. "If I had my way, I wouldn't have come back at all." I bit my top lip; I hadn't meant to say that. If it was possible my sister looked even more angry, more hurt. "Look, this isn't about you or me. This is about—"

"Mom," she finished for me. Her eyes were rock hard. "Sure. Don't worry, I never suspected you came back to say that you were sorry for all the years you ignored us. All the years you pretended I didn't exist. Cause why bother having a sister, right? Someone to help you braid your hair at your wedding, or to give a toast. Or when shit gets real, and your home turns against you—when life has its arm up against your neck and you can't breathe anymore, and all you can think is, 'This is it. I'm dying, alone, right now.' Who needs a sister then, right?"

She wiped her nose with the back of her hand, then pulled a stick from where it had been tucked into the back of her high-top sneaker and pointed it at the broken glass. It turned to sand then slid down the drain.

"Ellie, I didn't know . . ."

"There's a lot of things you didn't know." Pain flowed from her like light from a star. "I gotta help Patrick clean up back there. You have a good night with Dad."

I watched her back as she walked away. There was a metallic taste in my mouth as scalding tears trickled up to my eyelids like spilt milk readying to fall over a countertop.

Suddenly all my anger towards her, Rowena—this whole day—faded. I was left with only a sickness in my gut, and I couldn't stand the idea of myself. I was standing in a pile of shame and I had to move out of it as soon as possible.

I retrieved my hands from where they were suctioned over the bar and shook them out, as if I could release the disease of shame from my body. I then tucked a piece of stray hair behind my ear and walked up to the table I'd been sitting at with my dad and Lana. Lacing my fingers together in front of my stomach, I leaned over the two of them. "I'm really tired. Would you mind terribly if I went back to the house?"

"Of course not," my father said. "There's some food in the fridge back home if ya get hungry later, otherwise I'll see ya when I see ya."

"Thank you, Dad. We can try to catch up again tomorrow night."

He nodded and looked back down at his plate.

Attempting to pull myself out of the mound of degradation that had surfaced around my ankles, I returned my gaze to Lana. "So, should I just knock on your door in the morning, then? I would like to go see my mother first thing."

She was still shoveling food into her mouth as though she hadn't fed for days. "Sure, but not before ten. I sleep till at least nine. Ellie should be ready by then. I usually hear her music playing in the forest as I wake."

"Ellie's going?"

"Yes, we will all go," she said matter-of-factly.

I was too tired to argue. "Okay," I said, and then turned and walked out into the night. There was a slight chill in the air, and the smallest of winds picked up around me as I walked briskly back towards my parent's home. If I hadn't been so upset, I may have taken comfort in the way the wind felt, so soft against my skin, like that of a loved one's embrace.

ELLIE

That stupid—mmmmm. The nerve! To come back after all this time and stand next to me as if she belonged in this coven. The fury bubbling from my gut up to my stiff jaw grew kinkier—feistier even, than our mother's hair. All I wanted to do was scream, shout, and throw things. After I'd helped Patrick clean up the kitchen I'd stomped back to my cabin, pausing only to allow Biscuit to come running in from the woods, and then I proceeded to scream, shout, and throw things.

"Whore!" I screeched, kicking over a chair. Then grabbing my phone from where I'd left it on the counter, I continued to rage. "You stupid, beige wearing, piece of—piece of shit!"

The room was nearly spinning. After several heated moments, my temperature much higher than it should've been, my breath erratic, I plopped down on the bed. Biscuit followed my lead, resting her head on my lap. It was only after I'd calmed down that I noticed I had several missed calls from both Joe and Derek.

The snarl on my face curved into an evil grin. Joe had tried to go home.

I leaned back into my pillow and dialed Derek's number. As I did I dug out the remote for the stereo from where I was lying, aiming it at the old CD player in the corner. Soon enough the sound of my own music poured out into the cabin as I fell back into the bed, instantly calming my anxiety.

Derek picked up after only three rings. "Ellie?"

"Hey."

"What the fuck, dude?"

"What?" I asked innocently.

"Seriously? Salt. That's such a juvenile move."

I curled a piece of pink hair around my finger. "Oh whatever. She deserved it. Did she tell you about her little friend?"

"Yeah actually. Or at least what I could make out through her hysterics. Joe's here."

I sat up. "What?"

"She needed someone to talk to, Elle."

"And she had to find you? She has tons of other friends, and there's always *Jody*."

"Yeah, Ellie, you need to let up on that."

My face flushed as blood rushed back up into my cheeks. I truly believed that I could spew fire through the phone line if I tried hard enough. "Don't speak to me like *I'm* the one in the wrong here. I'm the victim in all of this, Der."

There was a pause on his end, and I could tell he was finding a private place to talk away from Jody's girlfriend. "All I'm saying is that she isn't the only one who has made mistakes, and maybe writing 'Go fuck yourself' on the floor in salt that won't let her pass, is being a little harsh."

I bit my tongue, waiting a full ten seconds to reply.

"But that stupid Jody left a *message* on the answering machine!"

"Ellie," he lowered his voice so that it was no more than a whisper, "you and I had sex last night. Three times."

Three times? Wow, no wonder my thighs were sore. I shook my head. "That doesn't matter. What she did was—"

"Nothing," he finished for me. "Listen, I don't know the whole story about this woman, but Joe just got here and she's a mess. From what I can make out it's all a misunderstanding."

He paused, then continued when I said nothing in return. "Listen, I need to go. She's out there sobbing on my couch."

"Derek!" I yelled. "You can't be her friend more than mine right now!"

"Ellie, I love you, but you can be a real asshole sometimes. You hold grudges for far too long. And yeah, she fucked up, big time—but it's been half a year. She's trying to put it behind her. You mean more to me than the world, but that woman out there is alone and she needs someone to let her cry on their shoulder, too. You aren't the only one who is hurting. If you want to talk, call me tomorrow. We can do lunch in the city or something."

And then he hung up.

I just laid there with my mouth open, staring at the phone as if it was his face.

"The nerve." My wolf grunted and dug her nose deeper in between my leg and the bed. Petting her furry head, I said to my familiar, "Why did today even happen?"

I was about to turn off the lights and go to bed early when I heard a rapping on my door.

"Dammit," I cursed, stumbling back onto my feet and carelessly swinging the door open. "What?"

"Easy there, Wichahpi."

I sighed. "What is it, Lana?" I asked, dropping my arm from the door frame. I grabbed the chair I'd thrown down just a few moments ago and set it back on its legs, flopping down onto it.

My aunt walked in and backed up against the wall, casually crossing her arms over her chest.

"Rough day?"

"You could say that."

"You need to cleanse yourself. Anger is not a good quality for a witch to dwell upon. It turns us quickly."

"I know. I'm sorry—it's just—I mean *V's here*. She's here and I'm just supposed to go with it."

"I know," Lana said, letting down her guard briefly. "It isn't fair, but it's life. We must remind ourselves that she did what she did because it hurt so much to breathe that she couldn't stand it. You can understand this, can't you?"

I took a deep breath and turned my head away. "Who can't?" Then cranking my neck back to look at Lana, I pointed a finger out my door. "But that person is *not* my sister. She walks around like she's got a goddamn rod holding her up . . . I've never seen anyone so stiff."

The corners of Lana's lips twitched slightly as though she was struggling not to smile. "People change, Wichahpi."

"I get that, but she didn't change, she just covered up who she was. Who she is."

"I'm not asking you to like her right now, but we need to try and be civil. She didn't come back because she had a change of heart. I can sense it, something dark has entered her life, and because we are all connected, it will soon infiltrate all our worlds if we do not stop it."

I glanced down at my fingernails, the black nail polish I'd applied a week ago needed to be touched up badly. "You know something you're not telling me. I know V is back here because of my mom. Spill it, what's this got to do with her?"

"Everything." She pointed to the necklace around my neck. "Your keys are meant to unlock something other than your mother's heart. It was never a protection spell, that much I can tell you."

I furrowed my brows, grasping the charm around my neck. "What do you mean? Of course it was a protection spell.

If it hadn't been for this necklace, then Joe" –-or whoever that was— "well, she would have suffocated me to death."

"The necklace saved your life, but that was because your mother knew the time would come when *you* would need her help. Those keys aren't finished, not yet."

I shook my head. "I don't understand."

"There is an order to all things magic."

I sat up a little straighter in my chair. "I'm not following you."

Lana moved away from the wall and sat in the chair across from me.

"Your mother continually told me how she'd seen us all living the same lives over and over again. How terrible it was to have to see the ones she loved constantly battling the same struggles, making the same mistakes. She said we were slaves to a curse."

"I know, death follows us. But she never alluded to—"

"She knew more than she was letting on. She told me a long time ago; that she wasn't going to watch the same things happen all over again, not in this life." She stared at my necklace. "She placed a spell over those charms—and I don't know how or why, but it was because she was trying to end a curse that she was afraid to mention out loud."

"Lana," I started, then stopped myself, trying to navigate through my thoughts. "If she knew the reason we were all cursed, then why wouldn't she have warned us?"

"I don't know, but I have a feeling your sister knows something that maybe we don't. You and Olivia need to bury your grievances, at least for now, because every night for the past week I've dreamt of a showering of lights from far up above, and under those lights stands your mother's spirit—as it slips away into darkness."

My heart skipped a beat. "A showering of lights. You mean like the Enrapture?"

The Enrapture was a meteor shower that happened every thirty years.

"Yes." A simple word with a complicated foundation.

"Lana, the Enrapture is scheduled for the first week of August."

"I know. The dream is a message. We have one month to figure out how to use these keys around your necks, and if we don't succeed in time, your mother's heart will lock us out and she will die."

My mother's voice echoed in my head. *You must help her see . . .* I still didn't know what it meant, but somehow, I knew my mother's message had everything to do with what Lana was saying.

"And not only will she die," I said, "but the curse will live on."

"Yes, Wichaphi. Now you see the urgency of the situation."

"Shit. Why wouldn't she have told us about this while she was awake? We could've prepared."

Lana leaned to the side and pulled a small flask from her pocket. She took a swig from it, then wiped at her mouth. "Some things are best left unknown until the time is right. If my intuition is correct, the struggle doesn't lie outside of our circle, but within it. To take down darkness we must encircle it with light. A circle inside of a circle."

I strained to understand my aunt's words, and I was still skimming over them when she stood a few minutes later and prepared to leave.

"We will go see Arianna first thing tomorrow. When you wake come to my house. You know the rules."

I nodded. "If I arrive before you're downstairs, start the coffee."

"Good little witch," she said, patting my head.

"Good night, Lana," I said, but she was already out the door.

I sat there for a few more minutes, shuffling mental cards around in my head. I'd already been living each day feeling like a less solid version of myself, and now that my head was even more cluttered, my world had become even more discombobulated. I really wished this day hadn't ever happened.

Before I knew it, I'd jumped to my feet, because I couldn't just sit there any longer—in that cramped and musty cabin.

"Come on, kid," I said to Biscuit. "Let's go for a run."

She jumped off the bed as soon as she heard the word run, and I kicked off my shoes and changed into my running gear. I grabbed my wand and handed it to my familiar, who held it in her mouth like a bone.

With Biscuit's tail wagging like a machine, the two of us exited the cabin and took off for our usual trail. It was dark, but the moon was still bright enough that I didn't need to illuminate our tracks.

We didn't run that far because there was still a dull ache in my head from my waning hangover, but we still flew through the trees long enough to shake off some of our thoughts . . . our worries. When we came back into the clearing Biscuit spit out my wand and dropped it at my feet, running towards my parent's house to the dock that led out into the lake. I'd barely even leaned down to retrieve my wand when I heard the splash, looking up to find that my silly girl had jumped into the cool water.

I laughed at her as she splashed around like a pup, wiping the sweat away from my brow. It was hot, nauseatingly hot, and more humid than it usually was in this part of the country. I didn't stand there long before following in Biscuit's example.

As soon as my skin hit the water my aura was cleansed. My

mind and body surrendered as the moonlight filtered into the reflections of the night. It was like Diana was holding me, whispering into my ears, "Relax daughter, let it go. Remember love, forever and always."

"In perfect love and perfect trust, blessed be," I chanted, as my head emerged from the lake.

I was still wearing my necklace—I never took it off. And as soon as the moon hit it under the water it warmed against my chest. Immediately my skin prickled as illuminating purple rays shot out in all different directions.

"Whoa." I wiped away the excess water from around my eyes and looked down. The charm had turned purple after my mother's accident, but it hadn't ever glowed.

"*It is here that you can help her to open her eyes*," a female voice whispered.

I spun around in the water, searching for the source of the voice, but there was no one.

"*You must be together . . . to help her see. To fall into the fold.*"

"Hello?" I called out quietly.

Nothing. Just the sound of the water bugs buzzing around the lake, and the giggles belonging to the fey from where they were fluttering around in the forest.

Dunking my head under the water one more time, I calmly, but swiftly swam back towards the dock.

"Come on, B," I said, checking over my shoulders, "time to go."

I grabbed my shoes and wand, feeling a set of invisible eyes caressing my glistening skin. It was still bright enough that our surroundings were visible, but I didn't hesitate to send a wave of illumination out from where I stood. Holding out my wand, I sent my light inside it and watched as it poured out from the other end, traveling into the woods. I hastily scanned the trees and shadows between the cabins, but I couldn't see a thing out of the ordinary.

"Losing my mind," I muttered, pulling down my wand and retrieving the light. "Let's go," I repeated to Biscuit. But when I started to move, she didn't. It was then I noticed that she was staring up at my parent's house, a low growl growing deep inside her throat.

My hand gripped tighter around my wand, and I walked back over to her.

"What is it?" I asked, but she refused to remove her gaze. Her growl was still so low I could barely hear it, but deep enough that I could feel it in my bones.

Laying my free hand over her wet head, I stood in line with her, cranking my neck to look up at the side of the house. Instantly my heart fell.

"V?"

Biscuit's growl turned into a small bark.

"Shhh," I shushed her, not wanting to wake the guests in their cabins.

I held my wand up, shining a yellow light at the window. V was standing there, staring down at the spot where I'd been swimming in the lake. But there was something wrong with her eyes; it was like she was hypnotized.

"Ah shit," I said, as my shoulders relaxed. "She's just sleepwalking."

I forgot she did that. It used to creep me out when I was little, waking up to see my sister at the end of my bed, holding my feet. I used to call it walking with the ghosts, since she could see them and all.

I pulled my wand down again and patted Biscuit's head. "Come on, she'll find her way back to her bed." I started back for my cabin, but I had only walked about ten steps when I realized my wolf had still not moved. Turning back around, I shouted softly to her, "Come on, B." But she was stubborn, her low growl turning into a small yelp. "What the hell?" I muttered, starting to walk back over so I could lead her away, but once more I found myself coming to a halt.

On my way back to Biscuit I'd looked up one more time, but the person standing at the window was no longer my sister. I froze under the moonlight, the pendant around my neck not just warming, but beginning to get uncomfortably hot.

I tried to back away; but suddenly forgot how to move my feet. The woman—a pale-faced ghost with ratty black hair and eyes to match, wearing a long black dress soaked to the bone, cloaking her thin shoulders—continued to stare down at me. Her mouth began to move and the voice I'd heard while in the lake echoed into my ears.

"*They are in the pines, Ellie. The answers are there where they have always been . . . inside the fold. You must take her back to the beginning . . .*"

A chill ran down my spine and I reached for my wolf. "B-Biscuit. Time to go—for real now," I stammered. This time my familiar listened.

Holding my wand in the air as though it was a sword, Biscuit and I turned away from the window and made our way briskly back towards our cabin. As soon as we got back inside and locked the door, I looked at my guardian. "And that is why we are glad we can't see ghosts."

I jumped into my bed and pulled the covers over my head like a little girl, wishing so badly that either Joe or Derek was with me so I wouldn't have to be alone. But I didn't have to look over to see that Biscuit wasn't lying down. I knew she wouldn't sleep that night; she was already perched by the door, her neck erect and her muscles tensed. If that ghost tried to come in here, she would have to pass through my familiar first.

OLIVIA

I woke early, to a headache that hinted of a migraine coming. I'd slept straight through the night but felt like I hadn't slept. Coming up to my elbows I noted that the bedroom door, which I'd closed the night before, was open, and scattered all over the floor were the remnants of an opened bag of flour and an emptied packet of chocolate chips.

"Dammit," I cursed, flopping back down, and laying a hand over my clammy forehead.

I hadn't slept walked a day since I had moved away from the forest, and all it took was one bloody night. From the looks of things, I'd been wanting chocolate chip cookies. My kids and I had often made them together, but with—oh yep, there it was. Oatmeal, ground into the carpet. Great.

Before getting up and dealing with the clean-up, I addressed my beeping phone. It was Maddie.

How's it going? Have you gone to see Grandma yet?

Today. Are you still wearing the pendant?

It was a protection spell I'd hastily made from one of my old necklaces—a real protection spell, unlike whatever it was my mother had made for Ellie and me.

Yes Mom.

Good. And did you sleep inside of the protection circle like I told you to?

I could practically hear her sighing.

Yes.

Good. Don't forget to close it just like I taught you, and make sure you do it every night.

I know. I will. I told you not to worry—I will be fine.

You keep saying that Mad, but Rowena was inside you just a day ago.

Just trust me, okay. All she can do is scare you. Have you seen Ellie yet?

The mere mention of my sister caused me to scrunch up my nose. I couldn't get that pained look on her face from the night before out of my head. It was all but etched into my psyche like the tattoos covering every inch of her porcelain skin.

It's complicated.

I thought about it for a moment longer, then typed:

I think I have some mending to do. When is your dad going to let you come out here?

I don't know. He's really busy and says he needs my help.

Right. Not that he wasn't seriously busy, but keeping Maddie away was more of a war game tactic than anything else.

I'll text him again and try to relay the urgency of having you by my side.

Your ghost can't hurt me. I'll be okay.

My ghost isn't playing by the rules this time, Mad.

Trust me, Mom.

I could almost see my daughter's expression. Occasionally, she came at me with these phrases that made me wonder how it was she wasn't a witch. And every now and again I could've sworn she *did* have magic . . . just not the same kind as the rest of us.

Just be careful, please.

Fine. So, by the way, Joe's moving in with Dad and me for a little while—don't tell Ellie.

I furrowed my brow. That was weird.

Okay.

I thought about asking why, but the truth of the matter was that I didn't even know Joe. Her and my sister's relationship was completely foreign to me, and as much as it pained me to say it—if I saw Joe walking down the street, I wouldn't have the vaguest idea who she was.

After chatting with my daughter, I sent a quick text to Tyler, again stating that it was imperative Maddie be with me while I was here. When I didn't receive a response—and I knew he had to have his phone with him every second of the day since he was getting ready to open a restaurant—I sent another message. This time I pleaded with him to at least make sure our daughter didn't leave his sight.

Eventually I got myself up and around, managing to clean up my mess from my sleep walking incident, and tied my frizzy hair back into a bun. I was too tired to try and unwrinkle it with the flat iron.

When I finally made it downstairs, I found a note that read, "Gone fishing."

"Who's dancing away now?" I muttered, pitching the note into the trash and glancing at the half empty pot of coffee. It was nearly see through.

Yuck. My father brewed coffee to the state of dirty water. I needed something with the consistency of wet sand; and one glance into the fridge, revealing nothing but a lot of fish, I quickly decided that I would be going out for breakfast.

I barely touched one foot to the ground once I got outside when a swoosh of moisture wrapped around my face like saran wrap. Since when had there been moisture in the mountains? Good thing I'd sprung for wearing my work-out capris and a tank top. Slacks and long sleeves were not going to work for this trip. I wiped away an immediate bead of sweat from my brow and headed out on foot for The Dewdrop.

I continued over the gravel path, undeterred. This time of day there were often guests out and about, either taking toys out onto the lake or enjoying a casual stroll. I didn't feel like chatting or answering the common question of whether I was *one of them*—one of the witches who was rumored to live here in the forest.

I was getting closer to the smell of sweet dough rising and ground espresso when something to my left sought my attention. My gaze immediately darted that way, towards the trees, and to the sound of crunching pinecones followed shortly by a small bark.

"Biscuit?" I called out hesitantly.

I had yet to see my sister's familiar, but when he or she barked again I knew it couldn't be her. This was more like that of a pup.

"Hello?" I called out cautiously.

A small rustling of leaves ensued, followed by a soft, girlish laughter and tiny feet running after another set of even smaller feet . . . or paws.

It was probably just the child of one of our guests playing around.

"Okay you, be careful in those woods! We've been known to house wolves in there! And skunks!"

I shook my head, exhaling a light-hearted chuckle, and continued to the shop.

My stomach growled hungrily as I reached for the flimsy wooden storm door and flung it open, drenched suddenly in the smell of sausages, cinnamon rolls, and coffee. I nearly had to wipe my mouth of saliva as I dropped down into one of the stools before the bar and looked up at the waitress to place my order.

"Hey," she said to me, throwing a towel over her shoulder and reaching for a menu. "How's it goin'? Care for some coffee?"

"Yes," I said, pushing the menu back towards her. "Large. And one of Patty's famous cinnamon rolls if you don't mind."

"You got it," she replied, pausing to look at me as she pulled away the unused menu. "Hey, I recognize your face. You're *Olivia*, right? Tyler's ex-wife." The way she said my name—it signaled instant distaste.

My blood sugar was too low to put in the energy needed to scowl, and there was no point in correcting the part about ex. "Yeah," was all I said.

Her eyes fixed uncomfortably into mine. Cool. She must've been good friends with Ellie.

I patted the counter and stood back up. "I think I'm going to take my stuff out onto the porch if that's okay. I'd like to eat outside."

Raising her brows, she said a little too quickly, "No problem."

After doctoring up my coffee with a bit of cream and honey and inspecting my cinnamon roll for poison, I retreated to the front porch where Delila was waiting for me, perched on one of the chairs as though she was an ornament. Curled up on the ground next to her was my mother's cat, Mr. Jackel. I nearly fell to my knees at the sight of him. My heart fluttered with the knowledge that my mother's familiar was alive and well, and a breath of fresh air entered my lungs.

Carefully placing my breakfast on one of the tables, I bent down and lifted him up. "Hey there, bud. You have no idea how good it is to see you."

As soon as he was in my arms, I experienced an immediate connection with my mother. I pulled him into my chest and sat down at the table, petting his head, and letting him swoon. As I held him and took a ravished bite of the breakfast roll—cinnamon and butter melting against my tongue and sending happy impulses into my brain—a small child holding a puppy materialized in the chair opposite me.

I paused mid-chew, staring across at her impish little face, before checking to see that no one else was around.

"Hello," I said, washing it down with a sip of the finest arabica brew in the state, if not the world.

The little girl smiled.

I nodded to the creature in her arms. "Is that your dog?"

She shook her head, and her dimples grew deeper into her cheeks.

"He's not yours?"

"She's not a dog," she repeated in the cutest little voice.

Mr. Jackel purred. I petted his head, looking closer at the spirit animal in the little apparition's arms. "Oh," I said, a gentle smile on my face. "She's a wolf pup."

The girl nodded.

"My sister has a wolf, too. Her name is Biscuit."

"I know," she answered.

"Are you the one who was playing in the woods back there just a little while ago?"

She nodded; her smile so big I was worried it would jump off her face.

"Were you following me?"

She squirmed giddily in her seat. "You can see me. Nobody else has yet."

I sipped from my coffee and set the mug back down. "What's your name?"

"Lillette."

Mr. Jackel purred again and I laid my hand over his head. "That's a very pretty name. How long have you been here, Lillette?"

"Not long." It was like she was in on her own little joke.

I started to ask her whether she was just visiting or what she was up to—because she definitely seemed up to something, but just then I was suddenly interrupted by a growl. When I turned my head, I found myself face to face with Biscuit. Her fur was sticking up on the back of her neck, just like Ellie's would be if it was her sitting before me instead of her proxy, and her teeth were bared.

"Seriously?" I asked the wolf.

She barked, as if in answer. When I returned my attention to the little girl, she was gone.

"Thanks B," I muttered, taking a rather un-lady-like bite from my roll. "She was the only one who hasn't looked at me with disdain in their eyes since my return." She barked again.

All in all, I was actually very surprised that I hadn't seen more spirits in the forest. I was still wide open and didn't plan on closing the gap any time soon—not with a monster that smelled like shit lurking around every corner of my life. Keep your enemies close. And truthfully, it felt better to have the veil loose. When it was closed, I found myself more constricted than usual.

The spirit world had been part of my own ever since I was a little girl. The way I saw it was like this: the world I lived in was an envelope. All one had to do was slip their hand inside and they could touch the other realms; but it was also like there were envelopes inside of envelopes, and it was possible that if one kept digging, that they could find where they were currently residing deep inside another fold. It wasn't something many people could understand, sometimes even witches were confused by it. To me it always made perfect sense.

This place, however, this retreat—spirits flocked to it in all shapes and sizes. Sometimes even bringing entire realms, or past scenes—memories—with them. It was the magic, I believed, that caused everything to be so much thicker. That little spirit, she wasn't like the others. Her glow had been different. I would venture to say that she wasn't on her way out . . . but she didn't seem to be a traveler or a drifter either. I was a tad upset that I hadn't been able to speak with her longer.

The sound of gravel spitting stole the attention from my thoughts as Patrick pulled speedily into a vacant spot. He threw on his chef's jacket and jumped out of the car, a lit cigarette dangling from his lips.

"Looks like you're late!" I hollered to him as he neared.

He winked. "I had to take last night's date home this morning." Scouting out the gathering around me, he gestured to the animals while putting out his cigarette. "What's all this? Having a familiar reunion?"

"Looks like it," I said with a mouth full of sweet roll. "Hey, who's that waitress in there? Are her and Ellie really tight?"

He glanced through one of the windows before smirking down at me. "No, not really. That's Mona."

I scoffed, rolling my eyes and taking another sip from my brew. "Well, that explains that."

Mona and Tyler had dated for about a year, but they'd broken up quite a while ago. Maddie had told me all about it, of course. Apparently, Mona had started contracting some sort of rare condition that made her hiccup all the time, which was only annoying until she started coughing up insects. So that sort of put a damper on things. I'd gotten a few unhappy texts from Tyler about that one, but what was I supposed to do? I would have gladly divorced him if I could. Unfortunately, the sort of ceremony we'd had couldn't be undone, and as Rowena's ghost was proof of, curses, or magical binds, weren't all that easy to break.

Patrick, seemingly not in a hurry to head into the kitchen,

flopped down into the seat where the spirit girl had been sitting. Curling his lips into a wicked smile, he asked, "She give you any shit?"

"No, but she sure as hell didn't try to hide her discontent."

"Yeah, well . . ." He let his words drift away. "Shit, it's like humid, right?"

"Yeah." I ripped away part of my roll and stuck it in my mouth, careful not to let my mom's cat get any. She'd kill me if I fed her familiar sugar. She'd curse me from her coma. "Was it not like this at your place?"

He shook his head. "Nope."

That was weird, he only lived a few miles away.

Next to me, Biscuit continued to growl, and I somehow just knew that she was romanticizing the idea of piercing my skin with her fangs.

Nodding in the wolf's direction, Patrick asked, "What's her problem?"

"Me. Ellie hates me, so Biscuit hates me."

"Right." He dug into his pocket and pulled out his cigarettes, holding them out to me in offering.

I shook my head. "No thanks." I'd used to indulge now and again, but I hadn't had a cigarette in so long that it would probably just make me sick.

Patrick lit up and exhaled the smoke through his nostrils. "Give her time. When it comes to Ellie, everything hits harder."

"Yeah, I know. On that note—I'm really sorry I just left like that, Patty."

He took another drag off his cigarette. "Right. But, uh, V, what happens after all this? If you can sort out Arianna and all that? You just gonna run off again?"

I pulled my coffee into my chest and squinted out into the forest. "Truth?"

"Always."

"I haven't thought that far ahead yet. Coming here was on a total whim. I didn't really have a choice."

Out of the corner of my eye I saw him tap his hand on the armchair, causing ashes to fall. "Sure ya did."

"Not really."

He was dissecting me, trying to undo the layers I'd spent years perfecting around my being. "What's really going on, V?"

Searching through the branches for any traces of the little spirit girl, I said almost too softly for him to hear, "I can't talk about it right now." Besides the name of our curse, I didn't even really know.

"I guess that's fair." I couldn't tell if his response was genuine or sarcastic, but I chose to just leave it on the table. "So," he asked after a short while, "you talk to Tyler yet? Like, in person?"

I returned my gaze to his. I'd only eaten part of my roll, but I couldn't finish it. Too much sugar. "No. But I plan to at some point." I waited for him say something else, perhaps clue me in as to what to expect from my husband, because he and Tyler were close. But he simply let the subject drift away. Probably in the same way as Tyler had let me go finally.

Biscuit whimpered in surrender and licked Patrick's knee before shuffling off and away. A second later Mr. Jackel jumped from my lap and followed her into the forest.

"Off they go," I whispered.

Patrick finished his cigarette and put it out. Laying his hands over his pants, he leaned back in his chair and rested his head. "You gotta know Arianna's okay—wherever she's at right now—cause Mr. Jackel is just fine."

"I know." A familiar couldn't leave his or her earthly body until his or her witch passed on. Reminiscing, I said, "You know, I used to sit out here for hours after Thaden was taken."

Patrick's eyes grew wide in attention, probably wickedly

surprised at the mention of my son's name. Before I left, after we'd finally realized he wasn't coming back, I'd refused to let anyone say it out loud. It hurt too much to hear.

"My mom said Delila came to me when I was three, and Biscuit found Ellie when she was only six-months-old. A witch's familiar always comes to them at a young age, but I never ever saw an animal around my son. After he disappeared, I thought, well maybe if I could find his guardian then I would be able to communicate with him through the animal. I sat here every day and stared out into those trees, looking for any signs of him in any animal that I could find, but there was nothing. Eventually I deduced that he was going to evaporate without me ever knowing when or how." I struggled to find my next words. "Without proof of his existence I was forced to believe my son was dead."

"He's not—"

"Don't," I warned, shaking my head. I hadn't seen, heard, or smelled any trace of my son since the day he left us. Just believing that he was around wasn't enough for me. False hope was more dangerous than any dark castor. It was why I didn't dwell on the what ifs.

Patrick bit down over his lip, presumably choking back his next words. After a few moments, he replied, "Nana never told you about how she met Lola, did she?"

"Lola?" I scoffed. Delila made a gurgling sound in the back of her throat before flying away. "That bird *hated* me."

Patrick pulled a hand over his mouth and half coughed half laughed. "She didn't hate you, V," he said, amused. "She just took after our grandmother. She was stiff as hell, and without much of a sense of humor—kinda like this persona you're trying to pull off."

I scowled at him, and pulled apart a piece of my roll, chucking it at his chest.

"All right, all right," he chuckled, throwing up a

surrendering hand. "But the reason I bring her up is because Lola didn't fly down and take a perch on Nana's shoulder until she was, like, thirteen."

I stared at him in disbelief. "Nuh uh."

"Yeah." He lit another cig. "Evidently, they don't always find us right away, or they don't come until the moment is right."

"Are you sure Nana just never saw her? That's a really long time to go without a familiar."

"Positive. Every witch is different. Mom told me once that Balthazar flew into our house one night before I was even born. She thought there was something unusual about the bat, but it didn't make sense until I was two and he flew through my window and slept next to my head. Our familiars have their own spirits too, V. They come from the same place as our souls. But getting here is a journey and we don't always take the same train, otherwise our moms would be twins. It's possible Thaden hadn't met his familiar yet when what happened happened; or he had, but you'd never seen him or her."

I poured over his words. All I could hear was the presence of my son in what he was saying.

"So, you think that he's . . . You really *do* think he's still alive?" Even as I said the words, I knew that I'd just peeled away a protective casing around my heart, around my soul. Vulnerability had found me.

Patrick hesitated. "Yeah. I do."

"*He's not though . . .*"

My chin snapped up in attention. "What was that?"

Patrick frowned. "What?"

"You didn't hear that?"

"Hear what?"

That sickening, vile, voice. *She* was here.

"Um, nothing," I replied, shakily, carefully leaning forward and setting my coffee on the table.

Patrick sat up and tapped the ashes of his cigarette, then asked in his best big brother tone, "You all right?"

"Yeah." I cleared my throat. "It's just a lot right now, you know. And I don't like talking about him. You know that."

"V, you do know that what happened—it wasn't your fault."

"I don't want to talk about this," I repeated.

But *he* did. Leaning in so the elbow of his chef's jacket was over the table, he said, "*He was alone, V. He was practicing shit he shouldn't have been.*"

"He wasn't alone—*she* was with him," I shot back.

"What? Who?"

Rowena. That foul evil skank.

"Nobody," I muttered, looking away.

"Whatever," he remarked, shaking away my comment. "Anyway, our parents always told us that playing with magic was like playing with matches—"

"*He thinks your ignorance did this to your son . . . everyone does. That you should've been there. If you had been with him this wouldn't have happened.*"

"Jesus! Where are you, you nasty bitch!" I exclaimed, my gaze wrapping around every tree, every square inch of what was surrounding us.

"V, what the hell? Are you all right?"

I clenched my jaw, waiting for more, but no more whispers came. Attempting to straighten myself out, I started to retort, "Sorry—"

But suddenly my chest ignited with fire; and as it did, something reached a hand carefully around my neck. I could feel its breath, and its touch instantly darkened me.

Patrick, oblivious to what was happening, went on. "Look V, when Thaden found that spell he knew he was playing with fire. There was a reason we weren't supposed to recite anything alone until we got old enough."

A searing knife cut through my chest, and I clenched up. "Is this your way of saying I was a bad parent before I was a bad parent? Because I wasn't watching my kid when this happened?"

"No—god no. Shit, you're frustrating sometimes." He laid a hand over his forehead and stood up. "All of us miss him. But you can't change fate. His physical life wasn't in the cards this time. In fact, do you remember those things, Olivia? Your cards? Do you remember who you used to be before you let this" --he waved a hand over my body— "whatever person you claim to be now, take you over?"

"Shut up, Patrick." The hatred that was infiltrating my being continued to brew in my gut like rancid goat's milk.

"They used to be your eyes, those cards. You aren't *you* without them—without your magic."

My voice meshed with someone else's, and I growled. "I don't use my magic anymore."

"What the hell?" Patrick leaned down, inspecting who was looking back at him. After a pensive moment, he very slowly pulled a long hickory stick from where it was hiding, tucked into his sock.

"Hey—Hey V. Look at me."

I wanted to take a hold of him by his neck, squeeze it. I could already feel the pleasure of his life in my hands . . .

"V!" He pointed to his eyes. "Look here, kid. You got me?"

I furrowed my brow at him. What was he doing?

Then there was a flash of purple, an angry bout of shouting in my head, and an instant feeling like I'd just been set free. I blinked a couple of times, realizing that Patrick's wand was pointed directly at my forehead.

"What just happened?" I asked.

Pulling it away, he leaned down and perused my pupils. "You had a fucking lunatic on your back, that's what just happened."

"What?"

"Don't worry," Patrick said, sticking his wand back where it belonged. "It's gone. For now." Exhaling his most recent drag, he pointed his cigarette down at me and returned to his agenda as though the possession was nothing more than a bee he'd had to shoo away. "This is what I'm talking about—you gotta get over all this. You're inviting shit into your body just by being this way. We've had enough of that shit in this family."

Unlike him, I wasn't keen on simply skimming over the mad occurrence. That *thing* had just infiltrated me. In all my years I'd never allowed anything to get inside of me. Rowena wasn't just messing around—she was just getting started.

Meanwhile, Patrick was still ranting. I shook my head at the ground, rubbing at the back of my neck. "I get it. That's enough, you can stop."

"It's the truth."

"Enough, I said!" I was way too overstimulated. "Jesus Patty, just—thanks for getting that thing off me, but don't you have to go cook something for Christ's sakes."

He didn't respond right away, instead he just hovered in front of the door, scrutinizing my entire being. Taking a few more drags, he put out his cigarette. "When you gonna stop dancing, girl? Ain't those legs tired yet?"

Before I could utter another word, he pushed open the door and disappeared into the cafe. That was that. So far, my homecoming was going as smoothly as a road paved out of broken glass.

A second later Ellie walked up, a subdued look on her face. "Sup yo? You and Patrick have a fight or something?"

"I'm not the most popular kid in school right now, that's for sure," I said, before I reached for my coffee and chugged it.

Ellie rocked back and forth on her toes, but thankfully didn't feel the need to press further in about the argument. Sizing up my workout clothes, she smirked. "Whatevs, at least you're not dressed like a Bible salesman today. I'm going over to Lana's, you coming?"

I brought my hands together in front of my stomach and began to wring them. "Yeah. Let's get out of here."

After that the two of us walked towards my old house, a soft wind clinging to my side, urging us forward. In the background, darkness—biding its time.

OLIVIA

Taking that first step into my old house had been like putting a toe into a body of water filled with electric eels. To get to where I was going, I had no choice but to wade through. And no matter how I directed my footing, a shocking current was eventually going to find me.

The house was very quiet, and it no longer felt like mine. Still, there were ghosts in every corner. I couldn't see them, but I could feel them. The sound of broomstick fights in the far end of the living room, pans moving around in the kitchen as Tyler cooked—plants hanging from the ceiling—the herbs I'd used in my remedies. All of it was still there, just not in the present.

"Is she still sleeping, you think?" I asked of our aunt.

"Probably," Ellie answered. "She stays up all night staring at the stars. She'll get moving soon." She automatically reached for the coffee pot and set it up, just as Puddin padded groggily across the kitchen floor. "You want something more to eat? I think I'm going to make some eggs."

I leaned down and petted the skunk's head as she overexaggerated a yawn. "Yeah, I could still eat. I went to bed without dinner." I made a face.

Ellie chuckled. "That's too bad." She bent down and pulled a pan from under the stove, then dug through the fridge for ingredients. "*But*, as Mom would say, it's a new day, witches." She paused and shot me a look. "So let's act like it."

Was she serious? When she made no mention of retrieving the comment, I simply nodded my head, then looked down at the ground. I thought about saying something back, but decided it was best to leave her kind offer on the table. Releasing my hands from where they were massaging Puddin, I stood and stuck them at my sides, taking a casual stroll through the kitchen into the living room.

Lana had an altar set up where our television had used to sit, where my two little ones used to lay on their stomachs and watch *The Nightmare Before Christmas* over and over, until I thought Jack Skellington was literally going to walk right out of that screen with his long, skinny legs. My fireplace, where the four of us used to roast hot dogs and marshmallows during the winter, was now full of candles; and the mantle, which I had covered in family pictures, was now lined in Native American artifacts.

I gripped my hands tightly together and turned, my attention landing where my own altar had once stood. My table was still there, but my things had been mostly replaced. The purple runner I'd laid over it was still present, but instead of my goddess statue of Diana, there were now four five pointed stars. In the middle of them, still untouched after all this time, was my crystal ball. Just where I'd left it.

I gasped at the sight of it, and as soon as it felt me, whispers filled the area around the ball—not like the twisted visitor I'd just had attach itself to me—but like a hundred lovely voices, softly caressing my shoulders with their messages from far, far away. I grew closer, my hands reaching for the ball as though it was an old friend.

"Hello there," I whispered, reaching out to slip the blue cloth away from where it protected the energy of the crystal. Immediately a pair of eyes inside the ball centered over mine, and with a magic stronger than that of a tsunami, I was pulled into the folds of the manifestation before I had even a second to react.

———

ONCE INSIDE, *she was waiting for me.* Who she was, or *what* she was, I couldn't yet define. All I knew was that it was cool inside this place . . . weightless.

"Come to me, child," a female voice whispered into my ears, and for a moment I wondered if this was my mother.

Faint, soft droplets of moisture fell onto my skin. Whoever this was, she was trying to manipulate me into a calm, meditative state.

"Who are you?" I turned in circles, trying to associate some sort of recognition. "Where am I?"

The mist separated and I stared ahead, out into Lana's living room. I was inside the ball.

The mist falling over my shoulders thickened so that it took away my window. I turned back around, searching for a body to match the voice of the entity who had brought me here.

"Hello?"

The mist began to mix with an easterly wind; and as it did it whirled around my body faster and harder, leaving my cheeks feeling as if they were being rubbed raw. Through the chaos, a translucent hand reached through the fog, towards my face, cradling my head into its palm like I was a distant love affair.

"In order to sift through the smoke, you must stop trying to decide if and when you are going to put out the fire. My child, it is going to burn either way, so why keep fighting it? If you must dance, dance along with the flames, not away from them."

I shook my head at the voice, arguing with the howling wind. "I've come this far! Why would you assume I would dance away from this now?"

Without answering me directly, she said, "Take it upon yourself to be the change. Do not rush into madness because of fear."

"I *have* taken it upon myself. I'm here, aren't I?"

"You reacted, and that is why you are here. What is needed now is your action."

"But I—"

"Your fire has been reignited. Your magic. This heat in your chest, the billowing smoke is already drifting into *its* nostrils; its appetite is growing."

"It?"

"You know of whom I speak."

"Rowena . . ."

The wind continued to howl.

"I—I know all this!" I shouted. "Tell me something I don't know—like how to kill her!"

Why would anything be that easy?

"This is just the beginning," said the voice. "It is important during these hours that you be weary of imposters."

"What does *that* mean?" When she didn't answer, I asked in a softer voice, "Who are you?" I reached up and felt for the hand attached to my face. Something about the touch was familiar . . . but it wasn't my mother, that much I could be sure of.

"You already have all the answers. You always have."

"No—I don't. I am the one the ghost is angry with, so why is she after my mother? Why has she taken *her* spirit?"

"How do you know she is after her, or that your mother's spirit is in peril?"

"No witch would find themselves in a coma like that, not unless it was a spell." It was a truth I think I'd always known.

Through the thickness, through the fog, I thought I saw a woman smile. "You must trust what you feel in your heart, Olivia. Listen to the sound of your beats. You will find what you once lost. You will be able to end this."

I paused, taking in her words, the wind still blowing around my face, my body. "I don't understand! What are you saying!"

The hand on my face pulled away and the wind blew in another direction.

"We used to dance amongst the flames, together. The planet was ours . . . the moon our mother. It was our true home. But then the darkness took it from us—made it so we couldn't return. Remember this, child. Remember where it all began. You already know."

And then it was over.

———

THE ROOM FELL SILENT, and I came to hunched over the ball like an old crone.

Ellie's voice immediately brought me back from my reverie. "V? Yo V?"

I turned my head in my sister's direction. She had a spatula in one hand and a glass of orange juice in the other.

"You look like you just saw a ghost." She snickered. "I swear that wasn't a joke." I wasn't registering what she was saying. The blue handkerchief was still clutched tightly in my hand as I tried to put together what I had just experienced.

"Seriously though, you okay?" she asked when I hadn't muttered a single word.

Blinking a few times, I readjusted myself to my surroundings, then cleared my throat before carefully placing the handkerchief back over the crystal ball. Not even noon and I'd already been possessed and caressed. I couldn't imagine what my hair would look like now if I hadn't been smart enough to tie it back.

"Yeah, uh, thank you," I replied. "I just, um." I shook my head and pasted a fake smile on my face. Then, realizing my sister could see right through me, I let a nervous laugh escape from my lips and said, "The ball has been waiting for me."

"Yeah, it appears so." Ellie placed the juice in my hand. "Drink this, you've lost your color."

I accepted the juice and fell into the nearest chair, at which point she shuffled back into the kitchen. Taking a long sip from the juice, I let the sugar settle into my system. As it did the dizziness began to subside, but it didn't manage to help my throbbing head; it was beginning to pound even harder than before.

Several seconds passed before I realized how hot my necklace had become. Setting down the glass, I leaned forward and felt for the charm hanging around my neck.

Ellie poked her head back out. "Everything okay?"

"Yeah," I began. "It's just that it's, uh, blue now." I held up the key.

Ellie nodded. "When did it happen?"

"Yesterday."

She lingered for a moment longer, and I could tell her thoughts were churning, but instead of adding anything she marched back to the stove and tended to her eggs. Still trying to decipher what had just happened inside my ball, I looked back to the table it sat upon.

"What are the stars for? The ones on that table?"

"They're trackers. There's one for you, me, Patrick, and Mom."

"Trackers," I repeated the word. I'd almost forgotten about those. A tracker was an enchanted object used to find someone; it put the witch directly into the person of whomever they were tracking. I'd never really used them. I mean, my mom had done it for Thaden when he'd first gone, but the results had come back inconclusive. "Wait," I asked, sitting up straighter, "has Lana tried to use that to find Mom?"

"Of course she has," Ellie said, as if offended. "It's the first thing we tried after the accident. But all Lana has been able to see are falling stars."

"Falling stars," I repeated. The hairs on the back of my neck stood straight up. "She's in transition then."

Ellie continued to hold the spatula in the air like it was her wand. "What did you just say?"

"Don't you remember when Mom used to put us to sleep at night? She told us to wander as far into the stars as we wanted, but we had to wake up before they began to fall."

"Oh shit," Ellie said. "Because if they started to fall that meant we were going home, and we weren't supposed to go there until this life was over."

Our mother had explained it to us many times. As witches, we could divide our spirits into pieces. It was because of this advantage that we were able to return to our favorite place of existence in between each life. With each new incarnation, our spirits split. Half our soul taking residence in our new body, while the other half hung back. When our lives were over, the other part of ourselves would come and get us, taking us back home.

I stared harder at my sister. "What if she went home?"

There was something eerie in that thought, and it made me think of the words from whatever spirit guide had found me just now. *The planet was ours . . . the moon our mother. Remember this, child. Remember where it all began.*

"What did she call it?" Ellie asked, referencing the place our mother used to speak to us about when we were little girls. A sphere surrounded by winged creatures—the spirits who inhabited the bodies of our familiars. It was the place where our souls first met and brought down the moon that filled us with the light to make us into witches. Our mother was the only one of us who could remember it, because she could see into the past.

The sound of the stairs creaking broke the silence between Ellie and I, and Lana appeared before us.

"Latharia," said our aunt. "And if this is where she is, then she is safe . . . for the moment. She must have left the tiniest bit of herself in that body of hers."

"What are you saying, and what do you mean that she's safe for the moment?" Ellie questioned.

My next words were but a whisper, and I could tell from the look on my aunt's face that she understood. Thinking about what Gerald had told me just yesterday, and what I already intuitively knew, I said, "Because if we don't act in time, more than one witch's light will forever go out. It will not matter where she is when it happens." I knew just then that it was time—time to lay it all out. I took a deep breath, rolled my shoulders forward, and said, "Okay witches, there's something we need to discuss. The curse belonging to our family has a name, and the reason she's after us—well, it's all because of me."

OLIVIA

Time is a human notion—that's what my mother always used to say. Latharia was the beginning of all things, the in between, and would one day be the ending, but how to define the end of something from the beginning of another was nearly impossible. Her words made sense, somehow, but it was still jarring that my mother was in a realm that even I couldn't see. Even if time was only something we entertained in these bodies, we were still against a clock; and after the conversation the three of us had just had, I now understood how dire the consequences of that ticking clock were.

I'd now admitted to my aunt and sister that I'd known about Rowena since I was a little girl, and that for whatever reason my mother had told me it was important that we keep her identity to ourselves until the time was right. Until I saw Rowena in her full form—and that I'd finally seen her fully for the first time the day before. I told both Lana and Ellie the truth, that she was on a mission of revenge. That I had wronged her in a past life, and to say the least, she wasn't dealing with it very well.

Lana had then gone on to tell me about what she had 'seen' most recently. As she stated her premonition of my mother's passing, I'd felt more than ill. Gerald's loose definition of a ticking clock had now been explained. The Enrapture. That was when our time was up. And when those lights fell, if we still hadn't slayed Rowena, then it wouldn't matter where my mother was. She could be taken—her soul extinguished by darkness.

"Your mother tried to stop the ghost," Lana said during our talk. "She knew the consequences, but she did not care. When you mess with a curse, you do not walk away unscathed." The meaning in her words had been darkly ominous. It made me wonder—even if our mother survived this, would she be the same?

Ellie, who had been silently staring at my necklace from across the table, had added, "She drew down the stars . . . not the moon."

"What?" I'd asked.

"I saw it when she placed the charm around my neck for the first time. I saw our mother in the water, pulling on the stars. I heard Diana's voice, warning her that if she tampered with a curse, she would find herself inside one of her own making, and I heard her say she did not care. The stars fell and the charms appeared in her hands. She did not use the moon for her spell—she used the meteor shower because it was more powerful. If you think about it, the spell always had an expiration date of thirty years, because the magic would only last until the stars fell again." She'd paused before returning her attention to me. "Didn't you see it when she put that necklace around your neck?"

"I don't remember seeing that," I'd said quite seriously. "I was so young."

"But I was younger."

Lana, her gaze floating back and forth between the two of

us, had simply laid her hand over the table. "There is reason for everything, Wichahpi. You were destined to see what you saw, and your sister was either blocked, or was not to see it."

Ignoring their exchange, I just stared at Ellie. "How come you never mentioned that before?"

She just shrugged, causing the tattooed feather on her shoulder to look like an earring. "I don't know. I guess I never thought much on it before now."

Shortly after the breakfast conversation that had shaken the world, the three of us piled into Lana's old truck and headed to Denver. It was a 1985 white and red Chevy pickup, and as we drove to the city, all three of us packed into the front seat with our heads bobbing up and down, I thought I was going to be sick.

"You know, I would've been more than happy to drive," I said for the second time, letting my head fall against the passenger side window. I had used my wand to rent a fairly spacious black Cadillac SUV for an unlimited amount of time, this nausea could have been avoided.

"I always drive," Lana said flatly.

I scrunched up my nose, knowing full well that Lana's way was never to be argued. I'd already begun to experience a dizzying headache; now I had car sickness and racing thoughts to add to the menagerie.

My mind was still reeling when Ellie chirped up. "What exactly are we expecting to happen when we get to Mom? I mean, do you think this time is going to be any different just because V is here?"

"We can't know until we get there," Lana replied.

I fingered my blue charm. "We could try to insert the keys into her lock again now that they've all changed color." I turned my head slightly to the left. "Hey Elle, does yours ever get warm?"

She looked first at me, then down at my necklace.

"Yes. Does yours?"

"Yeah, but only sometimes. It first happened yesterday, just before I saw Rowena."

Ellie fidgeted uncomfortably. It was becoming a pattern . . . every time I said my ghost's name, she wiggled.

I hadn't mentioned to either of them about how Gerald had told me that it hadn't been Joe who'd tried to strangle my sister to death all those months back, but I had a feeling Ellie knew the truth. She might not have known Rowena's name up until this day, but she'd known her near death experience hadn't been by the true hands of her wife. Ellie was a brick, though. If she didn't want to talk about it, then she wasn't going to.

Lana's gaze was tuned to the road, but when neither Ellie nor I said anything else about our necklaces, she prompted, "The heat is either because the magic is being woven, still, around the enchantment, or because it is warning you of something that could potentially be dangerous. Either way, young witches, do not disregard the burning of any spell."

I looked to Ellie; she was still refusing to move her eyes from the road.

———

WHEN WE GOT to the hospital, I followed Ellie and Lana as they easily maneuvered through the hallways and elevators. This place that I had come to only once, and for only a few heartbeats, had become like a second home to them.

I *hated* hospitals. The smell, the lighting, the spirits—so many confused souls. But the second I saw my mother again, I decided that I hated hospitals even more.

"Oh my goddess." The words fell from my mouth before my next breath.

I froze at the end of her bed. The last time I'd seen her

she'd at least still had some pigment left in her skin. Now the only color surrounding her was the red lock strewn around her pale, gray neck.

Our family had been back and forth as to whether to keep her in the hospital. She'd been rushed there after the accident by the ambulance, but it wouldn't have been that difficult to get her out of there, not when most of us carried wands. Still, without a total assurance that she was spellbound, and not just in a coma, we each agreed that it would be best to leave her there. At least for the time being.

The first thing Ellie and I did was try to reinsert our keys into our mother's lock, but just as the first time, nothing happened.

"I didn't think so," Lana said, turning back towards the door and locking it shut with one flick of her wand. "It didn't feel right. The timing is possibly off."

"Well the timing better figure itself out," I replied, as Ellie pulled out her wand and turned it into a hairbrush.

As Lana began lighting floating candles with the end of her wand and turning my mother's hospital room into a magical circle, Ellie attempted to brush through my mother's kinky hair.

"She always said, even witches have bad hair days," Ellie said.

"Yeah, she did," I agreed, patting the knot I'd made with my own straw hair at the back of my head.

"Let's just hope that her hair is the only thing our spells can't manipulate," Lana muttered. She had already gotten to work, stirring herbs and oils into a purse-sized cauldron, and as she chanted quietly over the mixture, she dipped her fingers into the spell and drizzled it over my mother's entire body. Working clockwise, she started from the feet and worked her way up to her head. She repeated the process three times.

Dipping my nose into the cauldron, I noted a familiar

herb. Ingredients had always kind of been my thing. "Vervain. You're trying to remove a binding?"

Lana remained steady, continuing with her ritual. "I am trying to reach her in any way I can. She left me with nothing to go on, Wachiwi."

"Right," I muttered.

I'd asked my mother only once why I couldn't talk about Rowena to anyone else in the family. She'd just stared at me and said, with a face as stony as her sister's, "It is your mess to clean up. Why alert them to what has been spilled if they don't have the equipment to clear the stain?"

"Perhaps she doesn't want us to reach her," I said, as Lana continued to drizzle the ingredients around my mother's body.

Her insistence was palpable. "She made this spell in secret, who is to say what she wanted and what she didn't want. I only know that we must keep trying."

I nodded in agreement then turned to Ellie, who had stopped brushing through my mother's hair. "Have you all tried this before?"

"Every time," she answered.

"And what happens when it doesn't work?"

She shrugged, letting my question linger in the air unanswered as she turned the hairbrush back into her wand with one flick of the wrist. After that the lights above our heads flickered, and my mother's body glowed.

Lana immediately pulled at my elbow, cautioning me to take a step back with her so that we were standing just in bounds of the circle she'd created.

"What's happening?" I asked, my voice slightly unsteady.

"Just wait," Ellie responded flatly, standing apart from the chair and backing away.

My mother's bed shook and a blue light manifested over her body.

"Goddess, it's working. I mean, *something's* happening." My thoughts began to churn—maybe she *did* want us to try and make contact. Maybe she was willing to help me clean up this mess after all.

The light began to take form, beginning to twist into a cyclone. "The triangle of power," I whispered. "It's working, it's forcing her energy—"

"*Just* wait," Ellie repeated, sounding bored.

The blue light continued to grow, and the lights began flickering. The entire room seemed alive.

Lana was incredibly calm, standing perfectly still, as though she was a cardiovascular surgeon watching the monitor after piecing her patient's heart back together. "Come on, Broom Head," she whispered softly. "Give me something, come *on*."

But just when it seemed the blue cyclone was about to drop down into my mother's heart, lightning began to strike near the ceiling, and as quickly as the spell had manifested, it all went away. The lights returned to normal, the bed and fixtures stopped shaking, and the room fell more silent than it had been when we first entered.

"Damn," Lana cursed silently, immediately walking forward and gathering her things back into her purse. She took the small cauldron and threw the rest of its contents into the air, letting them evaporate into nothing before walking in widdershins three times. Just like that, the circle was closed.

"Now what?" Ellie said, dropping back into her chair and staring at our mother's face.

"What just happened?" I asked, feeling very scattered all the sudden.

Lana simply continued to clean up any evidence of magic. "Whatever spell she used, or curse that rebounded upon her, it was *and is* powerful; she isn't coming back until the magic has finished its course."

I scanned the room and my jaw set tighter together. "Why couldn't she have just told me what I was supposed to do? Why did she make me keep all these secrets? She knew about Rowena! She knew everything but just told me the barest of details—why?" I reached down and grabbed my mother's feet, they were cold. "Why couldn't you just tell me what to do when this day came?"

Lana walked up behind me and laid a hand over my shoulder. "A circle inside a circle is needed to rid this darkness. Does this make sense to you?"

Letting go of my mother, I turned and faced her sister. "No. Neither does a witch who turns bad and kills all of those in her coven, but apparently that's what Rowena did, and I decided to kill her for it."

Lana continued to stare at me for a moment, in that way of hers that took her into your soul. When next I looked down, she was handing me a sage stick wrapped in rose petals.

"What's this for?"

Lana's flat expression didn't budge. "Wachiwi, do not act like you do not know what it is. You are a witch; it would be best for everyone if you stopped pretending you are not."

Hesitantly, I accepted the sage, then watched as she passed another one just like it to Ellie.

"We are going to clean this room, protect your mother against the shadows, and then tonight we are going to ask Diana for answers. This is all we can do."

"Of course," I muttered softly, my aunt's verbal jab about my magical dismissal stabbing me in the gut. I truly didn't feel very much like a witch. So far all I'd done since I'd returned was manage to conjure up a lot of ghastly energy.

I pulled out my wand, and I was about to heat the end of the bundled herbs with the fire from my chest when a shadow flickered in the corner; from it the same snake-like voice that had possessed me earlier that day. And then she began to sing.

140

A chill ran down my spine, pausing around my rib cage as though it was preparing to reach for my heart. I froze.

"*Olivia.*"

"Stop it," I muttered to the wretched ghost, bringing the palms of my hands up against my throbbing head.

Both Lana and Ellie gave one another furtive looks.

"V?" Ellie asked, concern lining the edges of her voice.

Electricity ran through my body as I shivered to the screams of a woman begging to be laid to rest. What was this madness? A sick laughter followed the lyrics sung only to me, and I looked down to find that there were streaks on the floor. Wet streaks made from a thick, heavy dress saturated in salt water.

"Wachiwi?" My aunt's voice rang in my ear.

Through gritted teeth, I said, "She's here."

Lana's expression remained as stone. "I hear it . . ."

"Me too," echoed Ellie.

"It is your Rowena?" asked Lana.

"Yes."

She readied to say something back, but before she could, her eyes filled in with white clouds, and when next she did speak, it wasn't her voice—it was my mother's. "It cannot harm you if you keep the fear from your heart. It can only try to sway. You, Olivia, are the one who chooses which direction to dance. The true ghost is with you all. She will have been given enough magic from my spell to hold back the one you must burn . . . if you stay strong."

My necklace had grown uncomfortably hot, and light streamed out of it like a star. One quick glance towards Ellie's and my mother's, and I could tell that theirs were burning as well.

Several moments passed as Ellie and I stood still as stone, waiting for Lana's eyes to return to normal. Lana was a medium. It was not the first time we had seen our aunt get taken over by someone else's spirit, but it was the first time our mother had been the one to speak through her.

"Arianna," Lana muttered, once she'd finally come back into her own.

"Mom." Ellie whispered. "Was that really her?"

"Yes," Lana said, "but it was not her in the present. It was like a note she'd tucked away inside this spell—only to be read if needed."

"But what did she mean by that?" I questioned, focused on the last of our mother's words.

Lana turned towards me. "Who is the true ghost, Wachiwi?"

There was only one ghost I knew of in this curse. "Rowena. It was Rowena I killed. Rowena is the one who is out for revenge."

"Are you sure about that?" my aunt questioned.

Unsure of how to answer her, I leaned down and touched the wet floor. As soon as it moistened against my skin my head twitched unnaturally to the side. Sickness enveloped me, like the rot of the spirit who had left it there was entering my body for the second time that day. My finger turned gray, seaweed hung from it, and there was an amused growl echoing in the back of my head—so guttural that I could've sworn it was a man's laughter. And then it left me.

"Wachiwi?" My aunt laid her hand over my shoulder once more. "Whatever this is, do not let your mother's sacrifice go to waste. Do not let this sickness invade you."

At her instruction, I came back to and quickly wiped my hand on my pants. When I looked at my finger again, it was clean and dry.

As I continued to inspect my finger, I said, "I don't know what she meant about the true ghost, but I do understand what she was trying to say. This thing that curses us in every life—it cannot hurt us—not today. Not unless I allow it to."

Then, inhaling a deep breath, letting oxygen pour over the small fire in my chest, the flames inside me roared. I stood, the end of my sage stick beginning to burn as I said to whoever it was haunting me, "Begone darkness. You can't have my mother; you can't have any of us. Not this time."

As the smoke filled the room, from not just my stick, but from those of Lana and Ellie's, the warning my guide had issued that morning inside my crystal ball began to ring through my throbbing head, repeatedly. Beware of imposters.

ELLIE

To say it had been one hell of a morning would have been an understatement. It was all I could do to wrap my head around everything V had told us about Rowena and how this repellent ghost fit into our family's curse. It was pretty bad ass that my sister had taken out a witch killer back in the day, or past life, or whatever, but the vengeance that remained was so uncool.

In the blink of an eye, I'd connected the spirit boards between my sister's description of her haunter and the ghost I'd seen the night before. It's just that something didn't quite fit . . . If I wasn't mistaken, the Rowena *I'd* heard the night before seemed to be encouraging me to *help* my sister, not the other way around. And there was also the matter of its eyes; that ghost (from what I could tell) didn't share the same eyes as the ones I'd been staring at inside my wife that day Joe's arm came up against my airway.

Still, I'd met Rowena. I was sure of it.

It made the message our mother sent us just an hour ago all that more intriguing. *The true ghost is with you all—she will*

*have been given enough magic from my spell to hold back the one
you must burn.*

If I was aware of anything, it was this: I now knew the name
and backstory (or as much of her story as V could remember)
of the bitch who had tried to kill me. But that didn't fix things.
If anything, everything had gotten more complicated; if that
wasn't enough to stress out about, now Derek wanted to meet
over food so we could discuss my attitude towards Joe.

My attitude. As if. I didn't have time for this shit.

The kid at the cash register waved me forward and I
moseyed over to place our order.

"*Whoa*," he said. His eyes were glazed over and I was
pretty sure he was stoned. Still, as soon as he laid eyes on me,
they grew. "Dude, aren't you that chic? That violinist?"

"Cha brah, I play some strings," I retorted, mocking his
stoner vibe. This wasn't unusual; I got noticed a lot. I was kind
of famous. It had been awhile, though, since I'd been
slummin' it in the forest. "I'll have—"

"Your performance on the MTV Music Awards last year
was, like, so cool."

"Thanks. So I'll take two—"

"I'm so sorry, but could I like—" He pulled his phone up
next to his ear and gave it a little shake.

I held back the urge to sigh and smiled instead. "Go for it,
man."

"Righteous," he said, as he pushed his chest over the
counter and maneuvered his head back around to get the selfie
of the two into his social media instrument. Three clicks later
and my fan was appeased.

I nodded after he thanked me and tried a third time to
place my order. "Two brown rice bowls with tofu, all the
veggies, and the hottest, sweetest sauce you got."

"For sure," he said as he typed my order into the touch

screen. As he did, he asked, "So you've been off scene for a bit, huh."

"Yeah. Got some shit to tend to."

"Cool." He bobbed his head. "Have you ever thought of rocking it out with a band? I mean, your sound is rockin', but like, meshed with, like, voices and shit—that could be seriously hazardous. Like, in a good way."

I didn't even blink. "Right. A band. Yeah, that'd be cool."

His chin bounced up and down, and he said, "Yeah dude. So, anything to drink?"

I tried to keep from rolling my eyes, and as I did I accidentally spied the bottle of Saki on display, but considering what had happened last time Derek and I were together, I decided alcohol was a bad idea.

"Just two iced teas please."

"Righteous. She drinks iced tea," he said, shaking his head in awe.

"Yep, she drinks tea."

After I'd finished ordering, I grabbed my number and found a table. I'd just started unwrapping my chopsticks when Derek slid into the seat across from me. He nodded in place of a greeting and grabbed for his tea before uttering a single word.

"Sup?" I asked.

"Just another day in paradise. How's Arianna?"

"Same."

"And your sister? She still hanging out?"

I shrugged. I'd already filled him in on my sister's arrival. "She hasn't run off yet. I think she's willing to try to be a human again for the sake of our mother."

"You mean she's going to try to be a witch."

I smirked. "Yeah, but I can tell she's still on the fence."

"She always is," he muttered.

"What?"

"Nothing." He tapped his hands on the tabletop—a musician's habit. "What'd you order us?"

"Same thing we always get." We were both vegetarians.

He nodded, his lids halfway over his eyes.

"So, what's up?" I asked. He was so obviously keeping his gaze trained anywhere but at me.

I scoffed because I knew this game. It was *my* game. He was giving me the cold shoulder but doing it in such a way that I had to dig the dirt out from around him to see that he was doing it.

I dropped my chopsticks and laid my hands over the table. "Yo, you just gonna ignore me? You're the one who wanted to meet up so we could talk."

He stopped fidgeting and stared at me. "Okay, fine. I'm pissed at you."

I made an annoyed sound in the back of my throat and leaned back. The server came around and dropped off our food.

Pinching a piece of tofu between my chopsticks, I asked, "Why?"

He looked at me like I was crazy. "What do you mean, why?"

"Is this about Joe, or what happened the other night?"

"Both!"

Instead of reaching for the gun and firing back, I shoveled a bite of broccoli and rice into my mouth. After I swallowed, I took a huge swig from my tea—stalling while I contemplated his retort. Finally I said the only thing my crowded head would allow me to. "Yeah . . . Well, I guess you can be mad about—you know—but Joe's and my business is our own."

"Not when she comes over all broken up and shit because of something *you did*. She's my friend, too, you know."

I sneered at him. "I'm aware." They'd been friends since the second grade. I couldn't tell if that had made our broken engagement easier or worse for him. "Here's an idea, how about *you* go over to the loft and reverse the spell. I know you know how."

I'd used the salt barrier on him a few times back when we were dating, but eventually he'd gone and figured out how to reverse it. I'd questioned him about being able to tamper with my magic—seeing as he wasn't a witch—but he always shook my questions away like they were hornets.

Barking back, he retorted, "You can't treat her like you treat me, it's not fair."

"And it's fair to you? Look, Der, I'm sorry for the way shit turned out, but I was the one who tried to let you go. You wouldn't go. And I didn't force you to come over the other night, to come to my side like a goddamned familiar. You're a big boy, you could've said no."

I regretted the comparison right away; it might have been a tad harsh.

Derek smiled and laughed sinisterly to himself. Then, shaking his head and looking in the other direction, he muttered two words. "Jesus Ellie."

"Sorry." Word vomit was kind of my thing.

"Look," he said, returning his attention to me, "that thing that happened with us the other night, you wanna say it was just sex—fine. It was just sex. But when it comes to Joe . . ." His words drifted away and he bit the inside of his cheek. "You know, I've listened to you cry about how much you've missed your sister for years. About how if she would only accept that certain things can't be undone, she would have a chance to live the rest of her life. Joe is *trying.*"

"Is she though? I saw her in a bar. You *know* I can't let her back in my life until she quits drinking."

"I understand that. She's made some seriously ill mistakes, and believe me, no one is more worried about your well-being than me. I would kill her if anything happened to you."

"So why are you backing her right now?"

There was an irksome and somewhat defeated look in his eyes. "Because *you* chose *her*."

"Dammit Derek." I dropped my chopsticks into the bowl and pushed it away.

"What? What do you want me to say, Ellie?"

"I don't know," I replied, rubbing my sweaty palms against my legs.

"Look, Joe's far from perfect and she knows it. So am I, so are you. She says she's done drinking, and I believe her. I think it's time you begin to cut her a little slack."

"She obviously didn't tell you about Jody."

He laid his hands flat on the table. "Actually, she did."

"So then how can you defend her?"

"That's something the two of you need to discuss, but believe me when I say it's nothing."

A dry laugh escaped my lips. "It seems like a lot more than nothing to me."

"Do you really think you should be throwing stones right now?" He wrinkled his forehead.

I looked away.

"Just try to ease up on her. She can't even go home. It might help if you just cleaned up the mess."

I reached for my tea. "I have a lot of shit to deal with right now—like actual life and death. Sweeping away a bit of salt isn't high up on my list of priorities."

"Either way, sort that shit out."

"Whatever. You know what—fine."

"Fine," he repeated, grabbing his chopsticks and taking a bite from his food.

This was how we communicated . . . always. It didn't help that we were both Libras.

The tension between us slowly leveled out, and as it did Derek's energy shifted so that it was a little less jagged.

"So, what else is up?" he asked. "You look tired."

I stirred the ice in my tea around with my straw. "I didn't sleep very well. I saw a ghost last night."

"What?"

I rubbed my forehead, attempting to iron out the wrinkles. "Yeah, it was the strangest thing . . ."

I dug into the shithole my sister had opened ages ago. I skimped on the deepest levels—about how this all began lifetimes ago. I focused on this life, and about how my sister was haunted by a vengeful ghost. I told him how I'd looked up after my swim the night before to find V standing there, only to be replaced by a ghost. That I now had a name to go with the face.

After I threw down my shovel, Derek's face immediately fell. "Did you tell Lana and Olivia about what you saw?"

"Not a chance. I didn't want to freak them out. They'll think she's stalking me or something."

"Yeah," he exploded. "Cause she probably is!"

I sat up straighter, all the people at neighboring tables suddenly staring in our direction. Cupping a hand around part of my face, trying to shield away the audience we'd just made, I retorted quietly, "It's all right, Derek. It's not me she's after. V said she's here for our mom." Never mind that she already tried to kill me and all that other stuff about her possessing Maddie and nearly killing my niece.

Nevertheless, Derek's face turned bright red. Shaking it wildly, he leaned into me. "Ellie, she is dangerous. That is not just your average ghost, all right. That is a spirit of a witch who is uber pissed off—"

"She can't hurt us!" I spit out. Lowering my shoulders, I hunched forward in my seat and lowered my voice. "Look, something just happened back in my mom's hospital room, and even though it wasn't one hundred percent clear I—I think it was my mom trying to say that part of this spell she weaved, that it's, like, protecting us from getting hurt. At least while the spell is in action . . . and if V can stay strong."

Derek deviated his jaw. Whatever he was thinking in that stubborn ass head of his, he kept it to himself. Instead of arguing with me any further, he simply said, "Just promise me you'll tell your family what you saw, okay? Don't go acting all badass witch—you have no idea what you're dealing with. That thing's already killed you once, it'll do it again."

That thing? Wait . . . what? "Did I tell you that part?" I was pretty sure I hadn't mentioned anything about her killing us in past lives.

Derek stared me down, and for a moment I couldn't tell whether he wanted to smother me or was trying to distract me.

"Just be smart, okay," he retorted, deserting the topic before glancing at his phone and checking the time. "Shit, I have to get back."

There was no way I was just going to let him get up and go; I was still too frazzled. "What do you mean that *thing* has already killed me once?"

He took another bite from his food before responding. "Your family's curse," he said as though it couldn't be clearer. "It's death that stalks you guys, right?"

"Yeah."

"So, it's killed you before, in past lives—the ghost, or whatever the hell it is."

I turned my cheek to the side in question. Something was off.

Whether or not he was as nervous as the beads of sweat accruing over his forehead said he was, he quickly disregarded any mention of my suspicions as he shoveled a few more bites of food into his mouth, his Adam's Apple moving up and down like a giant lever as he swallowed everything in one huge bite. When he had bypassed choking on the food, he pulled at his tea through the straw and said, "I really gotta go. So, practice next weekend for that wedding gig. You in or what?"

I set aside the questions piling up in my head and let out an exasperated breath. I'd forgotten all about that stupid gig. I tried to find an excuse on the fly but couldn't come up with anything other than working at the restaurant. However, Derek knew I could get out of that if I really wanted to. I was sort of notorious for doing whatever I wanted.

"Ah, what the hell," I succumbed.

"Cool."

He took one last swig from his tea, stood, then leaned down and kissed my cheek (because we never ended on a bad note; it was, like, an impossible thing for us). He started walking away, but I quickly stopped him by reaching for his leg.

"What's up?" he asked, retracting his steps.

"I don't get it, Der. Why are you fighting for Joe and me to get back together when you never even fought for the two of us?" When I looked back at the night Joe and I first met, it was almost like he was bringing me to her—depositing me into her arms.

His eyes softened.

I reached for his hand and grappled his fingers into a knot with my own. "I can't pretend anymore that I don't feel anything for you—I still love you, Derek. I know you love me, too. It's like a whole other curse, you know. Like if I take Joe back, I'll always miss you, and if you and I try to get back together, I'll always miss her. And then I wonder sometimes— if you had fought for us, would I have stayed with you?"

Derek fell to a squat, brushing a stray piece of hair away from where it had fallen into my face. "I'd already fought and lost."

I puckered my lips, readying to question his statement,

but he didn't give me the chance. "She needs you, Ellie. You two need each other."

My heart broke just a little. "What if it's too hard to be with her?"

He sighed, pressing his lips together, and for a second I thought he might be entertaining that possibility. His next words were nothing I would've ever expected. "It's just one life, Elle. Don't make more out of it than it is."

I studied him, the corners of my mouth turning down. "What?"

His head fell forward, and he shook it, laughing softly to himself. When he looked back up, he tapped my lips with his thumb. "I love ya kid, I always will, but I'm not your goddamn familiar, and you're not going to give up on her." Standing, he pointed at my chest. "Do me a favor—don't sleep alone. Keep Biscuit inside with you, promise me. I'll see you a week from Saturday night for practice, come to my place at eight."

"That's it?" After I'd just poured my heart into his slippery little guitar playing hands. *Come to my place at eight*," I said, paraphrasing his nonsense.

"That's it." He stood, stuffed his hands into his pockets and walked away.

OLIVIA

A claw clenched its talons into the back of my head—digging into my skull. The dull, achy pain I'd woken with had only worsened as the day went on. It was why I'd been looking forward to slipping into the guest room at my parent's house and taking a nap before we searched the moon for more answers later that night. But that was just my ignorance setting in. I had eight years of desertion hanging over my shoulders, and no matter how forgiving it was that they were putting on, my family wasn't about to let me get away with it.

Weddings had always been taken care of primarily by me and my mother; when I left, out of nowhere, my mother took on the entire ordeal by herself. When she got into her accident, Lana and my father shut down the venue for any events, due to family crisis. But as Lana had said on our drive home that day, events, especially weddings, brought in more money than they knew what to do with; and considering my mother's hospital bills, even with a few wand strokes to minimize the damage, they really had no choice but to reopen the bookings. Lana had only posted the news on the retreat's website that they would be reopening to events again two weeks ago, but already she'd been bombarded with phone calls.

"I hate them," she said, pulling into the retreat's long driveway, her bony knuckles white from clutching the steering wheel so tightly. "It doesn't matter if they are witches or not, I despise the human bride. Not to mention I'm already drowning in all the other things I need to do to make this place tick."

"I thought you guys would've hired a consultant by now," I said, rubbing at my temples.

"We spoke about it, but we were handling everything just fine before your mother's accident. If it wasn't for these damn weddings—I just can't do it all."

"Don't look at me," Ellie said as Lana parked the truck, all our heads lurching forward then back again. It was the first time my sister had muttered a single word since we'd picked her up after lunch. "I've already got myself involved in a wedding thing, and I don't even want to do that. Plus, I've got my manager breathing down my neck. He wants to know when I'm 'coming out of hiding.'"

"No, no, Wichahpi, I would never ask you to do that. You've already done so much."

It wasn't until I'd gotten out of the car and was praising the solid ground under my feet that I realized they were both staring at me.

"Right. Well, I guess I could help. I'm assuming it's all the same as it used to be."

"That would be really great," Lana said, nodding appreciatively as she began running up the steps to my old house. "I think the first bride will be here in thirty minutes— oh! That's probably her." She pointed to a small white sedan pulling in next to the shop. A second later a halo of blonde hair popped out, along with an arm full of binders.

And that was how I found myself running through a train

of overexcited brides for the remainder of the afternoon, while forced to try and ignore the ever-present claw reaching further into my brain with every passing second. It was not an easy feat; each bride squealing in delight. The last one was easily the worst.

"Oh my god, I have, like, been wanting to get married here since I was, like, sixteen!" she shrieked.

"That was, what, three years ago?" I asked dryly. Luckily, she thought I was being witty.

"You are fun*ny.*" She said funny like the word was made of bubble gum.

When I took her to the marrying tree, located deep into the forest—the same tree my mother had termed our very own tree of life because its roots were as prominent as its branches —the bride, Jessi was her name, frowned.

Looking around the forest, at the large number of trees grouped together like a choir, she said, "It's kind of crowded. I didn't think it looked this crowded on the website. Is it crowded?"

"Not as crowded as your energy," I muttered, too soft for her to hear. Raising my eyebrows and replacing my hardened expression with a jolly smile, I said, "The forest makes room when it's time."

"Huh?"

"It will be spaced out," I stated clearly. "You won't have to worry about a thing. Now, have you given any thought to which package you'll be choosing?"

She sat down on a log and crossed her long pale legs, flipping open the binder she'd arrived with.

"Well, Peter and I were trying to decide between the Princess or the Faery Tale Package."

"In your case, I think the Princess Package would be more suitable," I replied, rubbing out the wrinkles in my forehead. All I wanted to do was grab an ice pack and lay down.

"Hang on," she said, running her finger under the description of the Faery Tale package in the packet she'd brought with her. "We were curious about this one. I mean, there's a disclaimer involved, which is sort of weird."

My hand had somehow found itself wrapped around my wand, which stuck out from the back of my pants. I wanted so badly to turn her into a raccoon, but that sort of thing was frowned upon in the community.

"If you decide to get married by one of our officiants then you have to sign a legal disclaimer in the event that your energy doesn't bind, or in the event that it does and you ever try to separate."

"What?"

I pulled my wand out and stroked it. "If you choose that package, you are allowing an actual witch to reach for the light of our goddess and then fuse it with the energy radiating from your soul, and that of your betrothed. If the union is meant to be, then the light will merge before dispersing back into your bodies, at which point you are bound together in this life permanently. If the union is not meant to be, the goddess's light will extract itself and you will not be bound. But you see, we would still have to charge you, so that's the reason for the disclaimer. That and the curse that will find you if your energies are bound and you try to divorce later, and believe me, that curse is no treat."

Jessi's jaw unhinged and she looked at me like I'd lost my mind. Without questioning my explanation, her attention drifted to my wand. "Why are you petting a stick?"

"Oh," I said, lifting the piece of willow. "This is so you don't end up making a giant mistake." I directed the end of it at her chest and focused my intent. Her expression was only wild with excitement for a mere second, as a bright pink stream shot through her body—but it was over quickly enough.

I tucked my wand back into my pocket and raised a hand to rest back over my forehead—which seemed to be pulsating —then held out a hand and helped her up from the log. "So, you've decided on the Princess Package, then."

"Um, yes," she said, getting to her feet; she appeared slightly dazed. I was a little rusty, I may have unintentionally hit her a bit harder than I should've. "I think that's best. I'm really only marrying Peter because I want to get married so badly, and he was the first to ask. We aren't meant to be . . . we'll probably be divorced within a year." She paused, looking around the forest. "It's funny, I don't remember coming out here."

"Yeah well, we've been drowning you in details. You're probably just tired. We'll have Mona make you an iced coffee back at the café." I continued to hold her arm as we exited the woods.

Looking over her shoulders, she repeated, "It's kind of crowded, isn't it?"

I closed my eyes and bared my teeth. "I assure you, Jessi, on your wedding day, everything will be perfect."

After she was gone, I exhaled an exhausted breath and marched into Lana's office, dropping off three fairly large deposits.

Her brows raised in appreciation. "Thank you, Wachiwi. This was very helpful."

"You're welcome," I muttered. "Now, if you don't mind, I need to get some aspirin and lay down before we attempt to do anything under the moon tonight."

"Uh, Wachiwi."

"What?" I asked, turning back around to face her.

"I couldn't help but notice that our last bride left with a raccoon tail. You don't know anything about that, do you?"

"Nope. Not a thing." I started for the door again.

"Wachiwi."

I flipped around once more. "It'll be gone by nighttime. I just couldn't help it."

Lana's lips twitched, and I could tell she was trying not to laugh. "Try to help it from now on, okay."

"Sure," I said, however unconvincingly.

"And aspirin is not going to make that headache of yours dull." She pulled open her drawer and retrieved a large pink pill. "Toss this in some water; it will help with the dizziness. Your blood needs to get used to having magic flowing in it once more."

"Thanks," I said, accepting the pill. "I'll see you tonight."

"Yes, get some rest, young witch."

When I got back to my parent's house, it was empty. I had to assume my father was fishing, since that was usually the story. Wasting no further time, I reached for a glass of water and dropped the pill inside. Immediately the water fizzled and bubbled.

I brought it up to my nose and gave it a good sniff. "Faery potion," I said softly to myself.

I hadn't ever had it, but I had gone into the woods with my mother when I was a little girl to barter licorice for the ingredients we used to make it. It was a valuable potion because its effects depended solely on he or she who was consuming it. Once you drank it, it fixed whatever was ailing you. In my case, it was an overdose of magic in my blood after not allowing my heart to pump it for so very long.

"Bottoms up," I said, then downed the drink in one swallow. It tasted like chocolate chip cookies with a hefty amount of oatmeal.

Moments later, I was crashed out on the couch. Not even a dragon would have been able to wake me from that slumber.

I woke hours later to the sound of laughter coming from the television and looked up to find my father watching old reruns of M.A.S.H. He was tucked into his terrible chair with a T.V. tray in front of him. The room reeked of fish and instant mashed potatoes.

"What time is it?" I asked, sitting up groggily.

"Almost ten," he answered, taking a bite of trout. "Yer damn owl's been pecking at the window for an hour now. Appreciate it if you told her to stop it."

I turned and found Delila perched outside the window. Her yellow eyes were pointed directly at me.

"Shit, I was supposed to meet Ellie and Lana," I cursed, pulling out my phone and finding that the battery had died. "Did Ellie call?"

"Yep. Told her you were taking a Jack Daniels nap. She was pretty irritated."

I crammed my feet into my tennis shoes and scowled at him. "I was *not* drunk. Why didn't you wake me up?"

He shrugged away my question and retorted with a mouthful of fish, "Seemed pretty out to me."

"Whatever," I muttered. "I'll be back later."

"I'll be here," he grunted, taking another bite of food.

I jumped out the door, wand in hand, and practically flew towards The Dewdrop. Almost as if she could sense something that even I couldn't see, Delila swooped down beside me and flew along my side.

ELLIE HARDLY GAVE me a second look when I barged into the shop. As I stood there, chest heaving, she threw a rag somewhere into the kitchen.

"Sorry," I muttered.

"What the hell, V? Lana's probably pissed."

"I took a potion. Is it too late?"

She walked out from behind the bar and flicked her wand at the lights. Once the shop was coated in darkness, she swung open the door and waited for me to follow so she could lock up. "I dunno, I haven't heard from her. I had a couple from one of the cabins who I couldn't get to leave. I had to hit them with a sleep spell. All I know is that we were supposed to meet her an hour ago."

Trucking after Ellie, who had already started for a path inside the trees, I asked, "So you haven't spoken with Lana since we got back?"

"No," she retorted shortly.

"Any idea what her plan is?"

"Nope. All we can do is try things. It's what we've been doing from the beginning of this nightmare."

"Right. So, did you talk to your manager yet?" I panted as I tried to keep up with Ellie's giant strides. She'd been nothing but active since she popped out of our mother's womb, and she was in incredible shape. Her chiseled legs put my toothpicks to shame.

"No."

Huffing, I noted carefully, "You were quiet on the ride home today. Did you have a good lunch with Derek?"

She pointed her wand at a branch; it snapped in half and fell to the ground so we could pass through easily. "It was fine."

"Just fine?" I gasped for breath, stumbling to a halt as Ellie turned swiftly around and pierced me with her eyes.

"Look V, I'm trying not to hate you, but if you want this to work, I need you to shut the hell up. Do we understand each other?"

Nodding my head, I retorted, "Sure."

A low growl escaped her lips before she turned back around and climbed up a rock.

"Guess it didn't go all that well then," I muttered.

She flipped back around and pointed her wand at my face. "What was that?"

"Nothing."

She mumbled a few curse words under her breath and started back on the path.

"Just, uh, know that you can talk to me, alright, sis. I know things are kinda messy for you right now."

I tripped over a pinecone, and she chose not to respond. That was fine, at least she wasn't shooting fireworks at my head.

We'd almost reached our destination when our aunt appeared before us. She had a bag slung over her shoulders, most likely full of ritual tools, and her expression, as it most always was, was flat.

"Sorry we're late—" Ellie started to say.

"No matter, it's not the night."

Ellie and I looked from our aunt back to each other.

"What do you mean?" I asked, completely winded.

Lana squinted up through the various pine and cedar trees. "Not the night. The moon does not want to be drawn upon."

Ellie threw her hands up in the air with an irksome look on her face. "Really? It's not like we're on a restricted time frame or anything?"

"Patience, Wichahpi," Lana replied. "It's not never, just not tonight." And with that she walked between us, heading back to her house.

Ellie and I looked at one another. "Now what?" I asked.

She turned and started back. "We go home."

MY DAD HAD FALLEN asleep in his chair by the time I walked back into the house. His tray was off to the side and the television was still blaring. Not wanting to wake him, I turned down the volume and took his dirty plate to the kitchen, washing it off and placing it in the dishwasher.

I stared listlessly into the fridge for a little while, trying to find something to fill my empty stomach, but there wasn't much to choose from. Settling for a piece of cheese stuck between two pieces of bread and some pickles, I ate it then slowly ventured back upstairs.

It wasn't until I caught a glimpse of myself in a hallway mirror on the way to my room that I realized I'd run out of the house so quickly earlier, that I'd forgotten to tie my hair back; and now, to say that my hair had totally frizzed, would have been the understatement of the century. I looked like a burnt marshmallow.

Holding my wand near my head, I concentrated as blue sparks flew from the end; but instead of my dark brown locks laying down, they crinkled up against my ears even more. "What the actual fuck?" I whimpered. How, just *how* could it be this bad? My mother had been right, there really were some things that even magic couldn't fix.

I attempted to run my fingers through it, but the crusty, tangled locks only fought harder against me.

"This is *so* not okay," I said, marching directly for the bathroom inside my parent's bedroom.

It was a commonly known fact amongst the females in our family that my mother had a large stash of hair products in her vanity cabinet. The old Olivia hadn't really cared about what her hair looked like, but even back then my hair had never turned this wicked. I blamed the recent humidity. It seemed even more damp out here in the forest than it ever did next to the lost coast.

I sifted through the bottles quickly, in case my father woke up and wandered in. At least fifteen products were taking up space in my mother's side of the cabinet.

I picked up each bottle and studied the label, shaking each

one to see which had been only slightly used. In the end I found three that were halfway empty, leading me to believe she'd favored those ones. Grabbing them, I started to stand, but just as quickly knelt back down at the sight of something pink.

"Oh my god," I said, a hand coming up to cover my mouth. A tiny laugh escaped my lips, and a small trickling tear fell from my left eye.

I laid my wand next to the three bottles I meant to take with me and pulled out two giant pink curlers. There wasn't a childhood memory I could think of that didn't include me starting my day without running into my mother—these atrocities perched on the top of her head. She'd always said that they were the only things that ever worked to tame her frizz. She would wear them directly on top of her head so that when she released her hair it would smooth down over her kinky locks, shielding the layers of hay that laid underneath.

I chuckled a little, pulling at a gray hair tangled around one of the curlers. "Oh Mom," I sighed, my eyes continuing to water, "I'm so sorry I ran away. If you come home, I will never leave again." I stared down at them for a little longer, feeling like a piece of her was with me. "These old things . . . the secrets they must hold from knowing you for so long." And that was when I got the idea.

Gathering my wand and the anti-frizz solutions into my arms, I took the curlers, left my parent's room, and walked back down the hall to where I was staying. Unloading the bottles, I gripped my wand fiercely in my left hand as I placed the curlers under the moonlight on the windowsill.

"Diana," I said, calling on my goddess for the first time in years. It felt strange, but familiar. Pointing my wand at the curlers, connecting their energy with mine, I stated firmly, "Heartbeat heartbeat, hear me now as two bodies become one.

I will not stray, instead I will but pray. I wish I may, I wish I might, to become my mother this very night."

A faint blue stream of light shot out from my wand and enveloped the curlers—my hand full of static. Within seconds the spell activated, and as quickly as the light had flown from my wand, it retracted, leaving only enough energy in the curlers to weave in the folds of magic.

When I could tell they were ready, I laid down my wand and gingerly picked the curlers back up. The moon streaming in from the window was the only light, but it was plenty enough to see that my new trackers were ready and fully operational. I hesitated only for a second, but my mother must have been waiting for me, because as soon as they were against my chest, a warmth ran down over my body, up through my hands and fingers, and into my heart. I turned off all my other senses, shutting down the reality of where I stood in the physical world and concentrating on the other side. As I did this, I felt it happen. I traveled.

I'd assumed, because of what Ellie had told me earlier that day, that I would find myself floating amongst falling stars, but that was not what I saw. Perhaps I did for a split second, like when you blink and see a black stain over the sunlight, or the veins of your eyes—but it didn't last long.

What I did see when I finally reawakened into my mother's spirit, was a campfire under the night sky, and my nose was filled with the scent of the ocean. Every breath I took was fresher than the last, and every vein in this body I was inhabiting was alive with magic.

There were drums beating, bells ringing, and sand kicked up into my lap as feet pounded into the beach. Women and men, wrapped in colorful scarves, ankles strewn with bells and jewels, were dancing in circles around a fire.

I let out a warm breath and felt my hands reach up and tug at the shawl around my shoulders. I looked down to find I was sitting on a log, and as I did, someone touched me softly on the shoulder.

"Arianna? Are you okay?" It was a male voice.

I turned my head to the right and found myself in the face of someone who seemed oddly familiar, a pair of silver wings cascading down his backside. The entire place, I realized, was a memory of a place I'd once been.

And then it came to me . . . this was the birthplace of all witches. This was Latharia.

"Oh," the man next to me said. He nodded his head as a causal smile lined his face. "We are not alone anymore. They've found you."

"Who are you?" I asked, my mother's voice echoing though my head. Normally trackers only allowed a witch to see through someone else's eyes, but once again, I could tell that my mother had been expecting me, for she was allowing me to speak through her.

"Arianna calls me Jackel. Who am I speaking with?"

"Olivia," I said, in awe.

The man's eyes widened, and I could've sworn I saw them twinkle. He took a deep breath and let it out slowly. "Oh my." He reached over and took my hand in his. "It's been a very long time, Olivia. Welcome home, if only for this breath under the moonlight. Welcome home, sister."

I blacked out after that, but when I woke the next morning I was tucked into my bed, and when I went to relieve myself in the bathroom, I looked in the mirror to find the two pink curlers like a crown on my head. When I took them out, my hair fell in straightened planks, smoothing over the kinky locks beneath them.

ELLIE

A week went by without any more news from Lana about our next course of action. V hadn't had any more communication with that wretched ghost Rowena, and I hadn't either, but my tortured sister *had* come across an unchartered vision. She'd created a tracker that had allowed her to communicate through our mother, from where she was 'vacationing' in Latharia.

V couldn't remember the entire vision, and she hadn't been able to visit again after that first time, but that didn't mean she hadn't gained some interesting perspective. She was positive that it had been Mr. Jackel who she'd been speaking with, and he made it sound like it had been a *very* long time since V had been 'home.' That information alone had caused Lana to temporarily set down her whiskey.

"But Mom said we go home after every life," I argued when the subject had first been brought up. "You must have misunderstood the cat man."

"No," V had insisted. "There was something about how he looked at me, like *I* was a ghost. I just don't understand."

"Well, it *is* something," Lana had said, biting the tip of her finger and walking away.

So, there was that. But with less than three weeks left until the Enrapture, it felt an awful lot like we were about to lose this battle, along with our mother *and* her soul.

I hadn't had to worry about getting my shift covered at the restaurant for band practice because Lana had persuaded Tyler to let Maddie start working at The Dewdrop as a waitress. And it had taken Lana doing that because he was *not* team Olivia. When he finally gave in to reason, Maddie's new summer job took care of two things. One, my sister could stop Facetiming and texting her child every five seconds to check on her, and two, I could hand over my apron. Let's face it, I was a terrible server.

It was Maddie's first shift, and I, along with the rest of my nosy family, had been more than a little curious as to how the reunion between Tyler and V was going to play out when he dropped Mad off at the shop. The last time they'd seen each other was forever ago. As soon as we heard a car pulling up the driveway, Lana, Patrick, my dad, and I all walked casually out from our hiding places and waited for the show; but as it turned out, there was nothing to see. At least as far as my sister was concerned.

"Joe?" I asked when she popped her head out of the car. Maddie had barely nodded my way before jumping out and disappearing into the shop. "What are you doing? Where's Tyler?" I ignored the fact that my family had now found a new source of entertainment.

"What's it look like I'm doing? I gave the kid a lift. And he's busy. You know how the restaurant business is."

"Oh . . . right. Well, thanks for dropping her off."

"Yeah," Joe replied, chewing the inside of her cheek while looking towards the lake. She was still pissed about the salt jab, but whatever, maybe she shouldn't have tried to make such good friends with *Jody*. "Tyler said something about it being 'safer' for her here." Her icy stare drifted back to meet mine. "Is everything okay?" I think maybe she really wanted to know, but anyone standing there would have said otherwise.

"It will be," was all I said.

"Right." She looked like she was challenging me.

I chose to say nothing back.

After another few uncomfortable moments, she patted the top of the car and prepared to fold herself back into the driver's seat. "All right, well, talk to you later, I guess."

I was already choking on the dust made from her spinning tires by the time I reacted. It wasn't until I said the words, "Yeah, okay," that I realized I'd been holding my breath. After that, I was happier than ever to go to band practice, even if it was with the band who I'd deserted for fame.

Cindy Bernstein had emailed me earlier in the week, thanking me for agreeing to play with the group again; she'd said she'd heard about my mom and would've understood if I'd bailed. I'd responded with a simple, 'you're welcome.' I thought that was easier than pretending to know who she was.

Forty-five minutes later, and two hours early, I pulled up to the house Derek and I had shared once upon a relationship. The garage door was open and he was inside getting set up when I walked in.

"Sup, strings?"

"Hey."

"You're early."

"I needed to escape."

He smirked, standing up from the amp he'd been plugging in. He tossed me a beer and I took a seat.

"I went over to the loft and fixed your salt tantrum," he said.

Pulling out the striped arm sleeve I wore when I played, I replied, "Cool. One less thing I have to worry about."

Derek wiped some sweat from his forehead and took a pull from his beer. He was wearing loose jeans and an old green T-shirt that fit him well. I could define his chest muscles from where his sweat had pulled the shirt closer to them.

"How are you able to do that anyway?" I asked.

It was already building up in the space between us, like a mist making it hard to breathe. Sexual tension. Perhaps it was always there, the attraction we shared, but now that we had ripped our clothes off in front of one another again, the elephant in the room was exposed.

Taking a seat on the amp, he asked, "Do what?"

"You know, sweep away my salt."

A very fine-tuned grin inched itself onto his face. "First of all, a salt barrier is to be used to ward away your enemies—not to piss someone off because they brought you a chocolate malt instead of a strawberry milkshake."

"I only did that once, and I was, like, sixteen."

Derek continued to smirk. "Secondly, I believe that if you know someone well enough you can easily undo them. And a spell, is after all, only a part of you."

"But undoing a spell requires magic of your own."

"Aren't you the one who used to tell me that anyone could possess magic if only they believed in it hard enough?"

"Well yeah, but—to undo a witch's *actual* spell . . . That's a little different."

He stood, and his smell lingered in the unbreathable mist before smacking me in the face. I tried to ignore the urge to reach up and pull him down to me as he turned and made for the door to the kitchen.

"Don't overthink it, kid. I'm gonna jump in the shower real quick. Why don't you tune up. We can start before they get here."

"Fine," I replied, chugging my beer in a violent attempt to tame the infidelity trying to weasel its way out of me once more. When I pulled the bottle back down, the beer foamed out from the top, and as I pulled it away from my instrument it got all over my shirt.

"Shit," I muttered, looking down at the mess.

I set my violin down and stormed inside, heading immediately for the kitchen sink to clean myself up. When I was done, I leaned back against the counter, relishing in the air-conditioned room before heading back out into the stuffy garage.

I listened to the water running in the shower a few opened doors away, and as I tried not to think of Derek all wet and naked, my powers of observation veered towards a picture hanging on the fridge of Derek's parents. Welcoming the distraction, I inched over to it and pulled it away to get a closer look.

Derek's parents moved to Chile before I'd ever met them, leaving him to stay with his grandma, but I'd Skyped with them plenty of times over the years. They were pretty chill. I felt like a real dick when we broke up. I loved them like family.

That was something I'd given up being with Joe—she had no parents or anyone else for that matter. Her mother died from an overdose of sleeping pills when she was a child, and her father of liver failure when she was twenty-one. She used to say it ran in the family, her illness. I never thought that was anything but a shoddy excuse. Not to mention that it made me feel like shit; because I was supposed to be her family now, and apparently, I wasn't worth staying sober for.

I reached for a magnet and began putting the picture back where I found it, but the snapshot slipped between my fingers and fell to the ground. As I bent down to get it, I noticed there was writing on the back. Glancing over my shoulder to ensure I was still alone, I lifted the picture back up and began to read.

Hey Der,

This is us at Cerro San Cristóbal. Foggy as usual, but per your request we bottled as much as we could! As for your E.O.C. I've had trouble getting my hands on it lately. I know it is difficult to find in your part of the country, but you may have to begin finding these things on your own. Either that or give up the act. Seems like a lot of work to me, but what do I know, I'm just your mother.

All right, love, hope all is well. Come visit soon and give Biscuit kisses from us.

Cheers and blessings,
Mom and Dad

Bottled fog? That was witch speak. And E.O.C., what the hell was that? It sounded like a spell ingredient.

I peeked into the hallway, listening to ensure the water was still running. Upon confirmation, I quickly stuck the picture back on the fridge and tiptoed towards Derek's room, pausing for just a second in front of the bathroom. Steam poured out into the hall.

"Just in case," I muttered, swirling a bit of it around my shoulders via my wand. I whispered an enchantment and utilized the mist to make myself invisible before stepping into the bedroom we'd used to share.

It was still the same, minus the altar I'd kept next to my side of the bed; other than that, he hadn't changed a damn thing. It was even the same comforter. An old navy blue one we'd found at a JCPenney's after drinking too many margaritas after a show we did in our early twenties. Just a few months before the band broke up.

Our drummer, Leo, and guitar slash female vocal, Candy, who had been hot and heavy ever since the tenth grade, got in a raging fight on the same night we'd picked for a gig where a certain agent was listening. We'd been told beforehand that he'd been considering our sound. To this day I still don't know if it was the fight that threw off our mojo, or if it was a last-minute decision on Howard Lamae's part, but after the show he expressed that all he wanted was me.

I knew the band was let down, but we'd been working towards getting signed for years, and it felt like that night was our last opportunity. It was either take hold and fly solo or die with the band. In the end, the band told me not to let the opportunity slip between the violin strings, so I took it. Things sort of unraveled from there. The band separated, as did Candy and Leo. All that was left was Derek and I, well, until Joe came around.

Very quietly, I rummaged through Derek's drawers, pushing past boxers, socks, shirts and pants. I wasn't sure what I was looking for—I'd never used either of those things Derek's mom had written about. But if he had spell ingredients, I would find that very interesting, considering he wasn't a witch.

"Bottled fog," I mused aloud. "What in the world?"

Many witches used enchanted fog on non-magical folk to mess with their memories if they saw something they weren't supposed to see. It's possible he was collecting it for me, but if that was why his mother sent it to him, why wouldn't I have ever seen it? Not to mention that she would have to be a witch to bottle it. And E.O.C.—I hadn't the faintest idea what that was.

The water shut off and I heard footsteps walking down the hall. Cursing softly under my breath, I quietly closed the drawer and backed off into a corner, trying not to breathe too loudly.

Derek sauntered into the bedroom with a towel wrapped around his waist; he was singing Beck softly to himself. His singing faded to a low hum as he took a drink from his beer and dropped his towel to the floor.

My eyes widened and I took a step back, accidentally

bumping into his bedside table. The lamp teetered. I managed to steady it before it fell, but the commotion was enough to cause him to freeze and turn towards the corner where I was hiding—full frontal.

I immediately clapped a hand over my mouth so I wouldn't screech or laugh.

Derek was still, his gaze flitting from the table back up to where I was now cowering, trying not to move. The problem with using mist to turn invisible was that if one looked hard enough, they could see the form of your body glistening in the light. I just had to pray that the room was dark enough. Eventually, he turned back around and began getting dressed, singing that old song all over again.

I waited until he made his way out of the room and into the hallway to move. I needed to stay closely behind him so I could get back outside before he found me out. Luckily, he dove back into the bathroom to hang up his towel, and that's when I jetted for the kitchen and slipped out the door into the garage before he could catch me.

Whispering the counter spell under my breath, I removed the invisibility, and the mist I'd pulled from the steamy shower evaporated into thin air. A second later I heard the doorknob turn and I jumped for my violin, throwing it up under my chin.

"Hey," Derek said, stepping down from the kitchen and holding out my beer. "Left this inside." His eyebrows raised and his lips curved up slightly at the edges.

"Oh! Thanks," I said, reaching for it. "I was, uh, I just went in there to wash my hands real quick." I pulled at my wet shirt. "Spilled some."

"Whatever." He continued to smirk. "So, I was thinking we could jam out on a few of our old songs, and then maybe work through a couple new ones."

"New ones?"

"Yeah. Come on, Elle, just cause we broke up doesn't mean I stopped writing."

"Broke up? You mean the band?"

"Yeah," was all he said.

We left it at that.

———

EVENTUALLY CANDY and Leo showed up, and after a short reunion we had a decent practice. In fact, the longer we played, the better it sounded. So good, I couldn't believe our career together hadn't ever made it. My solo act seemed so dimly lit in comparison.

After about three hours I set down my violin and reached for a slice of cheese pizza.

"Damn it, man. We sound better than we used to," Leo said, placing his drumsticks over one of his drums. He wiped his face off with a red handkerchief. "Way better than those assholes I've been touring with for the past six years."

"Eh, they're not all that bad," Candy said, shooting a look in my direction that said otherwise.

"You're in another band?" I asked with my mouth full.

"Yeah, it's called the Whorish Devils," Candy said, choking on her beer as she said the name.

"No, it's not!" I exclaimed.

"Sadly," --Leo smirked in Candy's direction— "it is. Didn't know you were following us, kitten."

"I accidentally caught a live show during the worst date of my life." She turned to me. "If you and Joe don't make it, don't let your friends try to set you up. I swear I went on more shitty dates after that divorce than I knew existed, and my split didn't even come with a witch's curse."

"Speaking of, how is Mark?" I asked. I'd been in her wedding, but I knew it wasn't going to work—he was a dentist, and her name was Candy. It just wasn't meant to be.

"He's all right, and he's a good father, I'll give him that. Speaking of," --she pulled out her phone and checked the time— "I really should be going. He was out of town so I had to get a sitter and I told her I'd be home by eleven."

"Lame," Derek griped. "I thought we were just getting started. The neighbors haven't even called the cops yet."

"Shit," Leo retorted. "I think your neighbors are too scared of the two of you's to call the cops. You're the only ones with ink on your skin on this block, not to mention the wolf you keep in the backyard half the time. I always said you two were out of your element to buy in this neighborhood. I mean, when it was the two of yours . . . now it's just you, Derek. I mean—"

"It's cool, Leo," Derek said, stopping him from sticking his foot further into his mouth.

"On that note" --Candy raised her eyebrows in Leo's direction— "how about you give me a ride home on that bike of yours. I took an Uber so I could drink excessively." She threw back the rest of her beer. "*And* I think I've safely accomplished my goal. I'm ready to do something stupid."

"No way! You guys can't go yet," I pleaded.

Leo started making his way out from the garage, wrapping a hand around Candy's shoulders. "Meh, it's time to call it for the night. Anyone spoken to Cindy lately?"

"I did," I said. "Over email. She's pretty stoked to have us."

"I heard from a friend of a friend that she just got sacked from Poor Richard's Records," Candy added. "Just before her wedding too—super lame."

I hunkered down.

"Hey," Leo said. "Isn't that the label we wanted to get

signed by?" He jerked a thumb in my direction. "The one you signed with."

My cheeks turned the color of my pink hair.

Derek scooted up behind me on the amp I was using as a chair and wrapped a hand around my shoulder. "The one *we* told her to sign with, you mean," he said.

Leo frowned.

"Yeah, that's the one." I still felt like an asshole. "But I've switched labels like three times since then. That's weird that Cindy worked there." I tried to say it like I knew who she was.

"Not really, she was always into music," Candy corrected. "She tried to be our 'band manager' like a zillion times when we were kids."

Leo pulled out his keys and shuffled them around in his hand. "Not like she could sign us now. Ellie made sure that would never happen for us."

"Hey!" I started to sit up but Derek pulled me back down. "I resent that! You guys were the ones who told me to do it."

"Yeah, but we didn't think you actually would," Leo countered.

I stared from him to Candy, who chose to redirect her attention to her spiky black heels.

"Then why did you tell me to?"

"You would've done it either way," Leo muttered.

Candy brought her tattooed shoulders up by her ears. "Any who, this is getting kind of heated." Piercing Leo's eyes with her own, she said, "That was a long time ago—we've gotten over it, right?" She'd always been the peacemaker.

Leo shook his head and stared down at the floor. After a bit he muttered, "Whatever you say, kitten. It was just Ellie being Ellie, right. She's always after number one, always has been."

"Leo, what the fuck?" I started to jump up, but Derek pulled me down again. "That's so not true—"

"Come on, Ellie. It is too, and you know it."

"Really guys?" Candy said, getting between us. "What's done is done. We all have our own lives now. Let's just enjoy playing together again, all right." She tugged at Leo's arm. "If you drop this, I'll let you take me out for ice-cream."

"Ice-cream?" He gave her a funny look.

"I told you I wanted to do something stupid tonight. It's been a long week."

Leo's demeanor instantly changed. "Yeah okay. I'd be down for that."

"Cool, let's go," she said, as she pulled him out into the driveway towards his bike. "See you guys next week."

"See ya," Derek said with a wave, then snorted to himself before leaning in and whispering into my ear. "That used to be our code word for sex."

I snapped my head in his direction. "What?"

He nodded his head, still chuckling as Candy swung her leg over Leo's bike and hugged his waist. Derek's eyes were pretty glazed over. He was more than buzzed.

Suddenly my anger was replaced by intrigue. "So, they're going to go have—"

"Sex."

"No shit. What the hell, they're both single, right."

"Yeah." Derek draped a heavy hand over my leg. "And they were pretty damn good together back when they were a thing."

I took a deep breath and looked down at his hand over my bare thigh. This was no longer the same guy who I'd been talking to a week ago; the rational one who had told me that Joe needed me. This version was drunk, high on our sound, and seemed to be feeling that same sexual tension that I had been battling on and off all night. Joe looked to be the furthest thing from his mind.

Trying to diffuse the sensations festering down under, I asked a burning question. "Do you feel the same way as Leo? That I screwed you guys over when I signed with Howard?"

"That was a long time ago, Ellie."

I stared down at his chin. His breath was hot against my face. Humid.

"You didn't answer my question."

"What do you want me to say?" he asked, a tear in his voice that only surfaced when he was getting intimate.

"Derek—"

"Ellie, shut up." His hand came up behind my neck, and he pulled my lips to his.

Within seconds we were tangled together and he was carrying me into the house. As he fumbled his way through the hallway my back smashed against a portrait, and I caught it with my wand before it crashed to the floor.

"Nice one, strings," he said, his tongue wrangled up in mine.

"Thanks," I replied, squeezing my legs harder around him.

Before I knew what was happening, he threw me down onto his bed, onto the blue comforter, and his shirt was being pulled over his head. He was on top of my body before I could even imagine digging out the rational from where it hid under sexual desire. The scent of Old Spice body wash filled my nostrils, and with my eyes closed, it could have been ten years ago. Back when there had been no such thing as Joe. When it had just been me and Derek . . . in sync. No distractions.

His penis swelled against my crotch, and I groaned. I rubbed up against him as he reached his hands up my thighs. His fingers slipped inside me and I gasped, my own fingers fumbling to unbutton his jeans. The only thing I was aware of was that I needed him inside me. All of him.

"Ellie . . . I want you."

"I want you, too."

His lips left mine, tracing my jaw down to my neck.

"I told you that you still loved me," I whispered.

"Of course I do," he said, as his hand pulled at my bra.

"So, is this you taking back everything you said the other day?"

"What do you mean?" His breath was thick.

"When you said you weren't going to fight for me. That Joe needed me."

His lips stilled from where they hovered over my nipple, and a pained look washed over his face.

"Derek?" I asked, my fingers wrapped around chunks of his hair.

"Goddammit," he whispered, and in one excruciating breath he pulled away from me. He retreated to the side of the bed, leaving me sorely rejected and half naked. After a long, uncomfortable minute, he said, "I can't do this."

I wiped my hands down my face. "If this isn't right, then why do we keep finding ourselves in this situation?"

He didn't answer.

"Derek?"

"You're only with me because you're mad at her—because you think she cheated on you."

I sat up. "That's not true. I just told you the other day that I still love you. There are real feelings here. And—And somedays I wonder—" I paused, almost afraid to admit it out loud, "—if the only reason I'm scared to leave Joe for you is because of the curse that would inevitably find us. It weighs over me, Derek. That maybe I made a huge mistake in marrying her."

Shaking his head, he spoke over me. "We wouldn't be cursed. There's a way out of it. You must find yourself with someone you've been bound to before in another life." I frowned, but before I could add anything, he said, "But it wouldn't matter. The feelings you have for her are deeper. The only real reason this happened between us in the first place was because you were mad at her. If you knew the truth, everything would change." His eyes sharpened and he looked as though he was intrinsically torn. Pounding a fist over his knee, he sputtered to himself, "I told myself a long time ago I wouldn't do this anymore. It's not fair to either of you."

I pulled my shirt back into place and crawled towards him. The arousal that had been so very intense just seconds before, now dimmed like a dying light bulb. "Do what? What's not fair?"

I placed my hand over his shoulder and he looked at me, his energy was immediately beginning to feel more sober. "Ellie, Jody's from AA."

My heart sank. "What?"

He ran a hand through his hair and repeated himself. "She's from a meeting. That's how Joe knows her. Joe was having a bad day and found herself at the bar inside that Chilis a few doors down from Spiked. Jody was there and recognized her and stopped her from taking that first drink. That woman only wanted to help Joe. This whole thing between us—it was a mistake. I should've told you the second I heard, but—I didn't. Ellie, I'm just so—"

"Wait," I gulped, swallowing shards of glass. "Are you serious?"

"Yes."

"Shit." I fell back against the headboard, hitting the back of my head against it repeatedly. "Shit, shit, shit."

"I'm so sorry."

"Shit!" Not hearing his apology, I continued to freak out. "Why didn't she tell me?"

"She said she tried, but you wouldn't listen. She was going to try and explain again after you'd calmed down, but in typical Ellie fashion it's taken you awhile. In your defense you've had a lot on your mind."

"Shit." I could say nothing else.

Derek stood up and reached for his shirt. "I think it's best if we just pretend none of this ever happened. Just go back to the way things were."

"Right." I nodded my head, my eyes flitting back and forth. I couldn't look at him, not directly—because he was completely and irrevocably right.

I still loved him, that hadn't been a lie, but I loved her too. I knew the second I saw Josephine Redvine that she was supposed to be my wife. As much as I'd always felt like Derek and I were in sync, I hadn't ever gotten that striking truth from just looking at him.

I'd really messed this up. This whole time I'd been deranged because I thought she was cheating on me, when in reality *I* had been the one filling our marriage with disloyalty.

I didn't speak again until he was practically out the door. "Hey Der." He turned and looked at me. "I'm sorry I did this to you."

"Did what?" He grimaced as he tried to hide his pain, his defeat.

"I don't know . . . gave you hope."

He shook his head before walking away. "No. I'm sorry I did this to you."

I frowned, unsure of what his last words were supposed to mean.

I sat there for a long while. When I finally stood up, I brushed our near sexual encounter away from my body and made my way back outside to find Derek sitting on a bar stool, fingering his guitar strings with his head down. He didn't acknowledge me at first, seemingly lost in his melody; but when I went to put my violin away, he placed a hand over my wrist.

"Hey." He nodded to the instrument in my hand. "Just the two of us, for just a little longer?"

I didn't hesitate. "Sure."

I took a seat across from him and carefully placed the violin under my chin. A second later I began to play. The only interruption to our strings was Derek's voice—his song, his bleeding heart.

It was after one in the morning by the time I decided to call it quits. Derek walked me out to my car, opening the door and watching as I got in.

"Thanks," I said, "for telling me the truth."

He nodded.

I squeezed the steering wheel and looked out the windshield. "Hey Der."

"Yeah."

"There's only one person I know in this whole world who is as accepting of fate as you are." I paused, considering my next words. "My mom could see the past, therefore, she understood the workings of the future, of the present. That was what helped her gain perspective and accept the things she couldn't change."

His gaze drifted to my necklace. "Not always."

"Huh?"

It almost looked like he had more to say, but he stopped himself before mentioning something he might regret. "It's not always a gift to understand the workings of the universe. It can often feel like a curse."

His words struck a nerve, and as he said them, all I could think about was what he could be hiding from me? What was behind all those bottles of fog?

As witches, we can tap into the energies of those around us. We get into the habit of doing this from a young age. Call it a survival tactic from when the world was a way less accepting place and witches had to be more careful of who they shared themselves with. Tapping into someone's soul allows us to decipher whether this is a 'safe' person to be around, and it also tells us whether someone is a witch.

I tapped Derek the moment I met him. Not because I was being nosy, but because I recognized those eyes of his. My gift lies in music, not in seeing the future like Lana, or the past like my mom. When I saw Derek for the first time, I had a memory of the past, and not the past as it refers to this lifetime.

When I'd tapped into Derek's aura, I saw snowflakes falling to the ground, and an ironic feeling of warmth as it touched me in places I'd never realized existed. But as far as the spark I experienced while tapping into a witch's energy, there hadn't been one.

I pointed a shaky finger at him. "You're hiding something from me."

He smirked, leaning in over the driver's door. "Go home, Ellie. You've got a lot to do before the sky sheds its light, *and* more band practice on top of it."

I licked my lips and took a long, deep breath through my nose. Ultimately, I decided he was right. I had a lot to do, and whatever he was up to—because he *was* up to something—now wasn't the time to play detective.

"Got my eyes on you, Der," I said, before buckling up.

"I'm sure you do," he quipped, before he slammed my door shut and backed away.

———

ONCE I GOT BACK to the retreat I was immediately greeted by Biscuit's wet nose. I was about to lead her into our cabin and try to sleep away the fact that Derek and I had almost slept together all over again when I saw a light flickering inside The Dewdrop. Curious, I dropped my things off just inside my cabin door and turned towards the shop, but not before bending down and retrieving my wand from where it was clenched between Biscuit's fangs. It was way late, there was no reason for the lights to still be on.

"Come on, girl," I said to my familiar. "Stay by my side."

Guarded by my wolf, the two of us stalked towards the shop by the road.

OLIVIA

I'd been back home for over a week, and even though I still had fences to mend, things were becoming a bit more manageable. Most things anyway. There was still that one person who was refusing to acknowledge my return.

I'd been mentally preparing myself for that moment when I would first see Tyler again, and the second I realized he'd had Maddie dropped off by Joe instead, something inside my chest tightened.

I tried to hide my disappointment as I wrapped my arms around my daughter's shoulders, the two of us walking into the shop together. "You excited to work, Peaches?"

"*Mom*, could you not call me that in here?" She shrank in my embrace.

"Sorry. It's kind of fun though, right? You know, this is where I met your dad. Patrick hired him as a sous chef and I was waitressing. It was the summer after I graduated high school, and he—"

"I know the story, Mom," she said, before catching sight of Patrick and wriggling out from my arms.

"Right," I whispered, as she ran towards him. "Of course, you do."

I kept my distance for a little while, pretending to keep myself busy with wedding details, but I couldn't help myself. As soon as Patrick settled her down with some side work, I sidled up against the wall across from where she was rolling silverware into napkins.

"So . . . why did Joe bring you out? Was your father just busy, or . . ."

"He's starting up a restaurant, Mom. He's always busy."

"Joe had time to bring you by."

"She's more of a silent partner. Willow Creek is really Dad's solo gig."

It was the first time I'd heard the restaurant's name. I stopped staring at my feet and gave my daughter a skeptical look.

"He named it Willow Creek?"

"Yeah."

"Interesting."

"Not really. He said the name was whistled into his ear from the wind."

Maddie insisted that she could hear Thaden speaking to her. That if I just allowed myself to believe in him, I would be able to hear his voice again too. But all that kind of speak made me feel was mad. It was insulting to think that everybody else could feel his presence, hear his whispers. Everybody but me.

"I see," I said, instead of sparking an argument. "Has everything else been okay? You know—like possessions by evil witch ghosts and—"

"It's fine, Mom. Your ghost hasn't bothered me again."

"Right. Well, I should let you get back to work. I'll see you when you're done tonight."

"Whatever," she muttered, rolling her silverware tightly.

Old soul or not, she was definitely a teenager.

I spent the rest of the day walking around the lake, feeling listless. Much like a child who's bored of her toys and with nothing else to do; except I had a lot to do, it was just that I didn't know where to start. Ellie had gone off to practice with her old band, Lana was busy working in her office, and my father, as usual, was fishing. I had only myself to entertain me. Even the spirits were sparse that day.

Maddie was exhausted after her first waitressing shift, and when she got home she shook her head at the bowl of freshly popped corn I'd set before her, as well as the movie I'd pulled out in anticipation of watching it together.

"I can't keep my eyes open," she argued, slinking towards the stairs. "I'm going to bed."

"But it's Diane Keaton—we love her!"

"Sorry. We can watch it tomorrow, or before you take me back home on Monday."

I raised my eyebrows. "*What do you mean* before I take you back home on Monday?"

"Dad said to tell you he was too busy to come pick me up, and Joe can't that day."

I scrunched up my nose. "No, I mean—what do you mean you're going home? I was under the impression you'd be staying here with me, at least until we get rid of this 'little problem' of ours."

She paused, her hand resting over the banister. For a moment I saw myself in her. A person who just wanted to understand what silence sounded like again—someone who just wanted to shut it all off. "Dad said he could only spare me for the weekend."

"What? I mean—does he not fully understand the wicked reality of our situation here?"

She let out an exasperated breath. "Yes, but he's got a restaurant to open, and our new house is being built—he needs me there. It's not like he's leaving me alone. He's always there."

"But he's not a witch! He can't protect you the way I can!"

She held her stare over mine for a moment. "No, he's not a witch."

Shaking my head in disbelief, I continued, "Then why does he think he can protect you?"

"He understands that I don't need protecting."

"What in the world do you mean by that nonsense?"

Again, she sighed. "Maybe he's not scared of Rowena. *Maybe* he thinks he's already been burned enough by witches that they can't hurt him anymore."

I opened my mouth to retort, but nothing came out. Instead I just stood there, dumb, watching as Maddie pressed her lips together and nodded softly to me before climbing the stairs up to her room. I was still standing there when she padded back down.

Her expression was laced with exhaustion, and with a pair of eyes that shouldn't have belonged to a teenager. "He doesn't *actually* hate you. That's the problem."

I was forced to look away as tears threatened to betray any semblance of strength that I may have had. I pinched the area in between my eyebrows and took a deep breath. When I looked back in the direction of the stairs, Maddie had gone.

"He just *wants* to hate me," I whispered. I slapped my hands over my face, drawing them down as though I could wipe away my identity and reveal a new one. "What am I even doing here?"

As soon as I said it, I heard a splash. The black bowl sitting on the end table—it was rippling.

Hesitantly, I took a step forward, and with a single hand over my chest, I peered into the bowl, knowing full well that what was manifesting in there was one of two things. A spirit guide or my haunter. Up until this point it had been a fairly quiet week. Not a lot of distractions in the way of good or bad spirits.

As soon as I heard it, though, the laughter, deep and sinister—the same taunting voice that I'd heard off and on since this nightmare began—I backed up until my spine hit the glass of the nearest door.

Like a snake, her words slithered through the space around me, penetrating my skin, and slipping into the space between my heartbeats.

"*So says Ezekiel, so I say to you . . . 'I let them become defiled through their gifts—the sacrifice of every firstborn—that I might fill them with horror so they would know that I am the LORD.'*"

My blood ran cold, and I shouted a whisper to the voice echoing into my ears from every corner of the room, "Rowena, I will not cave to your destruction—BE GONE!"

"*Rowena.*" The voice chuckled, so deep that I couldn't decipher whether it sounded more like a man or a woman. "*Rowena, Rowena, Rowena . . . Where is your son? Where oh where has your little boy gone . . . where oh where does he play? In the wind he blows, and the water he waves, but how long before he's flame?*"

"You've already had your fun with him! You stay away from my children from now on. Do you hear me?"

"*I am the wind, and he is the flame . . .*"

"Stay the hell away from my son!"

The voice receded into laughter again, bellowing like a whirlwind around my head. It was pressing on my soul, this foul beast pricking at my skin, and it wanted in. If I couldn't relax—hide my fear—it *was* going to get in.

My throat tightened, and I knew immediately that it had its hand gripped around me. My mom's message had said I had to stay strong. Whatever this thing was, she or it couldn't hurt us if I stood against it like a warrior. The problem was, even if I had the potential to be a soldier, the wounds that had been inflicted into my flesh during this fight ran deep, and I couldn't figure out how to make them stop bleeding.

"He's dead, your son . . . There is no Thaden. Not anymore"

I pulled out my wand and reached out my other hand towards a smudge stick laying over a porcelain dish on one of the end tables. Within seconds it flew across the room and was in my palm. I wrapped my fingers around it and the end caught fire. Holding it up like a torch against the monster, I muttered a spell that filled the house with the smoke.

Immediately the hold over my throat evaporated, and there was a high-pitched squeal, followed by a slow hiss. I'd managed to chuck *it* off me at least, but from the commotion ensuing across the room—a chair jerking onto its side and a lamp rattling off the end table to the floor—I knew it was still in the house.

"You're going to have to do better than that."

I continued to hold up the burning sage as I swung open the door I was backed against, but as soon as the outside air hit me, so did something else. I gasped as the ghost pushed me so hard that I fell through the door onto the porch—the fire at the end of the sage stick burning out.

"You want to play, witchy witch. I'll play."

"Leave me alone!" I screeched.

"Your heart is beating faster. Is that fear, Olivia?"

"Fuck you," I grumbled, before picking myself up off the ground and taking off in any other direction.

The ghost stayed on my tail as I ran barefoot over the gravel road, my wand in my hand like a sword as I ignored the pain in the soles of my feet from the rough surface. The lights were still on in The Dewdrop, so I sprinted faster, not slowing down until I was on the shop's wooden porch. My chest heaving, I aimed my wand at the apparition starting to appear just ten feet from where I stood—the outline of the woman I'd grown to detest. Before she could completely take form, I allowed the fire in my heart to roar as I muttered a spell.

Her energy exploded out into all four corners, and there was another high-pitched shriek. When it was over, I lowered my wand to my side and tried to catch my breath. The jinx wouldn't last for long, but it would keep her disintegrated for long enough that I could regain my strength. My partial sanity.

Patrick was drinking a beer at the bar alone and didn't even turn around when I let the door slam behind me on the way in.

"We're closed up," he shouted over his shoulder.

Winded, and with small cuts now embedded into the soles of my feet, I replied, "I heard if you can turn a spider into a hamster you get free drinks for the rest of the night."

He turned around, his tone changing as soon as he saw it was me. "Hey, V. What are you doing here? Everything all right?"

"Yeah, it's fine." There was only a slight shake to my voice. "Everyone back at the house already fell asleep, and I saw the lights were on, so I thought—"

"Come on over," Patrick said, jumping over the bar and grabbing another beer, sliding it my way as I took a seat.

Condensation ran down the bottle and I waited less than a second to pick it up, draining it in one gulp. Placing the empty bottle on the bar top with unsteady hands, I asked, "You got anything stronger?"

Patrick smirked, then reached for a bottle of tequila. "Wanna talk about it?"

"Not really."

He shook his head and pulled out two shot glasses. "Fine with me." Filling the glasses to the brim, he slid one my way and picked up the other. "What are we drinking to?"

That was the question, wasn't it? Right now, I had way more pitch forks aimed at my head, causing me to *want* to drink than anything to really drink *for*. I needed a distraction is what I needed. Something to take away the fact that I'd almost been made into a puppet by our family's cursor.

I pulled out my wand and studied it. Before long the end came alive with a yellowish spark. "How about a drinking game instead; it *has* been a while since I've slayed a proper dragon."

Patrick peered at me over his shot like an armed outlaw might towards a sheriff with nothing on him but a butter knife. "Why do you wanna torture yourself, V? You know you can't beat the master."

"When's the last time you played?"

"You still had pigtails."

I shot a spark out of my wand, manifesting a tiny knight on a miniature horse. The figure immediately galloped around, as if confused about his whereabouts. He needed a target. "Loser takes a shot."

Patrick's smile grew as he pulled out his wand and held it up in the air. Sparks flew and formed into a green dragon with purple wings, about the size of a thirty-pound dog. As soon as it was spotted the knight pulled out his sword and charged for the beast. Grasping my wand tightly, I flicked it at the horse my knight was riding and scrunched up my nose. A second later, the horse grew wings and flew after the dragon.

"Hey! You can't turn it into a Pegasus," Patrick argued, his wand steadying in the direction of his dragon, flicking it once more, and turning his player invisible.

"Why not?" I asked, directing my knight to follow the scent of the dragon.

"Cause it's my game and I make the rules."

"Well you didn't patent it, did you? And if you can make your dragon invisible, then I can make my knight fly."

That was how we began the first game of Hot Cold Dragon in nearly thirty years; a game Patrick devised when we were kids. The idea was that he or she who played the knight had to catch the invisible dragon before it was too late. If the knight wasn't fast enough, the dragon would burn it up with its fire breath.

Three hours after I'd initiated the challenge, the bottle of tequila was nearly finished and I'd just watched yet another of my knights burn to ash. I don't understand what had gotten into me to make me feel so cocky. I really was a horrible player.

"Slam it down, Olivia!" Patrick yelled, his dragon swirling around his head, victorious yet again.

I squeezed my eyes together and threw down the shot of tequila. "I feel like this game is rigged. I should be able to find you, easy." I hiccupped and warded off a bit of a spin.

Suddenly we were joined by a third voice. "There's a trick to it."

I swerved in my seat, hanging onto the table while trying to center my fuzzy vision over whoever had entered. "Ellie!" Feeling rather loose, I picked up my wand, shooting sparks into the air. "Where'd you come from?" She stood in the doorway, her wand down by her side like a loaded gun. "Come drink with us!" I knew I sounded drunk but I didn't care. "We're playing dragons!"

"I see that," she said, walking gingerly towards our table. She pointed in my direction as she spoke to Patrick. "Did you give her drugs?"

Patrick simply filled a shot glass and handed it to her. "This, here, was her idea. Here go."

Ellie took the shot and pulled up a chair, sitting down as though she carried more than just her body weight with her. She made a face as she swallowed the tequila and sat back in her seat.

"It's past your bedtime, V. Maybe we should get you back to bed before you start yakking."

"No way," I scowled. "So, what is it?"

"What's what?" she asked.

"The trick—to the game."

"Oh right." She set her wand on the table and crossed her legs. "His dragon has irritable bowel syndrome. It shits all over the place and its droppings aren't transparent. Find it in the act and you find the dragon."

As she said it, I looked over and saw Patrick's dragon crouched down on the floor making a mess.

"Gross!" I howled.

"Thanks for outing me, Elle," Patrick grumbled, before he flicked his wand towards the beast causing it to disappear, along with its mess. Game over. "You wanna beer?"

Ellie let out an exasperated breath and nodded her head. "Hit me."

He reached for a cold one by his ankles then tossed her a Corona. "You look a little like V did when she first walked up to the bar tonight. How about you, anything you wanna talk about?"

Ellie tipped back the beer and drank half of it in one draw. "Nope," she answered.

All was quiet after that, the three of us staring down at the table instead of at each other, because for whatever reason the energy in the room had just grown heavy. That was until I heard the pitter patter of soft pup feet padding across the wooden floor. I tried to peer through the dim lighting—the energy streaming from the lightbulbs hammering down was like a sheet of iron—but when I finally did see through the thick heaviness of my alcohol buzz, I saw it was none other than the little spirit girl I'd been seeing off and on all week. Along with her familiar. She walked up to our table and had a seat in the fourth chair as if she was already a part of our little group.

"Hey there," I said.

Ellie leaned in closer to me. "Uh V, who ya talkin' to?"

195

"Lillette," I said, holding out a hand towards her. "We're getting to know one another." Smiling at my little friend, I grabbed my wand and pointed it at the space in front of her nose. A moment later a wooden tulip grew out from the table and turned blue. The child giggled and clapped her hands together.

"Nice, V," Ellie said. "How are we going to explain that to Lana in the morning?"

"It's pretty!" I countered. "And Lillette loves it."

"That's an interesting name." Ellie observed.

"That was her name in her past life. She's said her next name will sound like snowflakes. She knows that cause she's a little witch, aren't ya."

Lillette nodded her head appreciatively.

"All right, well, I'm gonna say that's my cue." Patrick stood, stretched out his arms and yawned. "I'm gonna go crash next to Puddin."

"You want me to straighten you up so you can drive home?" Ellie asked, picking up her wand.

"No thanks," Patrick said, refusing the sobering charm. "I just want to crash out right now." He placed the rest of the beers over the table before moseying out the door.

Ellie shrugged her shoulders before zapping the magic in my direction instead, causing the corners of the room to immediately crease and sharpen at the edges.

"Hey," I said in protest, my speech suddenly less slurred. "Why'd you do that?"

Lillette giggled before fading away, leaving Ellie and I to be on our own.

"Cause you were swaying like a hammock in the wind, and I have already had a night. I don't feel like babysitting."

I stole the beer from in front of her. "Did it not occur to you that I've *had a night* also, and it was kind of nice to be on the other side of things."

"Did it not occur to *you* that your son was taken by an evil bitch disguised as a little spirit girl who claimed to be a witch?"

I froze, my gaze redirecting from my sister's to where Lillette had just been seated.

I thought on it for two seconds before retorting back at Ellie, "Lillette isn't Rowena in disguise—I'm sure of it."

Ellie leaned in over the table. "How can you be sure about anything right now?"

I swallowed hard and decided not to say anything back, because I wasn't really sure what to say.

Ellie scoffed. "Whatever. I'm gonna take my drink and walk Biscuit back to our cabin."

As she stood and headed towards the door, the heaviness of being alone suddenly sped up before me like freshly sharpened knives.

"Ellie, wait!"

She turned and set her witchy eyes on mine. In a desperate maneuver, I pointed to the clock on the wall. "It's uh, it's almost three in the morning."

"And?" On the other side of the door Biscuit was yawning.

"We're nearly upon the witching hour. Mom always said not to walk outside by yourself when the veil is thin, just in case the monsters are out to get you."

Ellie shifted her weight to one leg. "That was because she was trying to scare us into not sneaking out. And besides, any monsters that are out to get us, they're gonna get us no matter what the time."

"Yeah. You're probably right."

"See you tomorrow," she said, starting to turn back around.

"Ellie wait!"

She faced me once more. My heart was beating too fast and I wasn't sure I'd be able to continue breathing if she walked away. "Please don't leave me alone." Her expression softened. "I'm not asking you to feel sorry for me or anything like that. I just, I really don't want to be alone right now. I—I'm not feeling all that strong. Can we just be sisters for a little while? Just long enough to have one more drink together?"

Ellie remained still. She may not have been experiencing a bully of a ghost breathing down her neck, but I knew she was stressed. Just yesterday I'd heard her screaming at her manager over the phone as I walked by her cabin. They wanted her back weeks ago and they were getting pushy. I knew she could use a distraction just as much as I could.

"Come on," she finally said, gesturing to the door, "let's take a walk."

"Yeah?" I asked, hopeful.

"Yeah."

OLIVIA

We ended up at my mother's tree—the marrying tree. The place where we'd been given our key charms, and where my mother liked to make it snow in the middle of summer.

Ellie and I had our backs against the same tree's trunk and were staring up at the stars through the gaps in the branches.

"Hey V."

"Yeah?" I rolled the beer in my hand over my forehead, cooling it off. It was so humid that the summer heat seemed to have tripled.

"Have you ever heard of something called E.O.C.?"

I peeled my sweaty back away from the tree and stared at her. "What in the world has you asking about that?"

Ellie suddenly appeared very unsure of herself, which was completely out of the norm.

"I don't know. I just—I came across some spell work that had that written in there and I wasn't sure what it stood for."

"That's because you can't get it anymore. I mean, I guess if you really wanted it you could find it, but it's incredibly difficult. It was banned in the early 1900's because in order to get it you have to boil a live creature."

Ellie's jaw dropped. "You have to what?"

"Essence of Chameleon. Let's just say it was a sick practice, but the end result was a highly valuable ingredient. I bet you can find it on the black market if you need it bad enough. It's harder in the states, but I'm sure it's out there. I don't understand what you'd need it for unless you're trying to disguise your soul."

Ellie inched forward. "What do you mean *disguise my soul*?"

I shrugged my shoulders. "That's what it's for. It's been a while since I've researched it, but from what I can remember it has only one real purpose; when it's used correctly, it can disguise someone's soul with that of another's."

Ellie's jaw had come back together and she now looked as though she was about to scream. "Disguise one's soul?"

"It doesn't completely change it. If you were to take on mine, for instance, the heart of who you are would still be there, but it would be buffered by my soul. Like whoever was looking at you would have to look through me to see you." I gave her a discerning look. "Elle, what is this really about?"

"I don't suppose bottled fog would have anything to do with any of that?"

"Well yeah, because whoever's soul you are tapping into to copy, you can't really do that without that person knowing. Not unless they are willing to let you . . ." My words drifted away, but I could already see that it was too late. She hadn't come across a curious spell, at least not one of her own. "Does this have something to do with Mom?"

Ellie's lips twitched and she looked like her head might explode. After a moment she contained herself and replied curtly, "No. It's not about Mom at all." She took a draw from her beer and made a face. "This shit got warm fast. Could it be any hotter out here?"

I hinged forward, preparing to dig deeper into this strange inquiry, but I quickly decided against it. Ellie was temperamental and I needed her right now; I needed this time in the woods with my sister. If I pushed her, she was liable to stomp off.

"So," I said after a while, attempting to change the subject. "This thing with Mom is pretty crazy, right?"

Ellie scoffed. "That's one way to put it." Centering her gaze over mine, she asked, "Your spirits, have any of them offered any new advice on how to reach her?"

A chill ran down my spine and I suddenly felt like she was there, my ghost. Like she was standing behind us, staring down at us with those endless dark tunnels she called eyes.

"Uh, no." I coughed softly into my hand. "Not really."

Ellie stared down at the dirt around her ankles. "Have you seen her again, since you got back here?"

"Rowena?" My voice shook as I said the name. Ellie nodded. "*Seen* her—no." Only because I'd blown her up before she could reappear.

"I saw her."

My head popped up. "You what?"

Ellie had pulled out her wand and was drawing stars into the dirt. They lifted from the ground and floated into the night sky like pieces of yellowish, white light.

"I went for a little nighttime swim the same night you returned. When I got out of the lake, she was staring down at me from that big window in Mom and Dad's house."

I opened my mouth but nothing came out. I sorted through visions of the frightening ghost until I finally stammered out the words, "Ellie, why didn't you say anything?"

She dropped her head back and stared at the moon. "I don't know. I didn't want to freak you guys out."

I could have sworn a succubus had found me and was sucking the air from my lungs. "Ellie, you know she's after more than one witch."

"Yeah, I know," was all she said.

Unable to sit still, I stood, wrapping my free hand around my unruly head of frizzy hair.

"We have to tell Lana." It was the only thing I could think to say that made sense. "Showing herself to you, it had to be some kind of message, or warning."

"You know what though," Ellie said, her sudden tranquility slightly overwhelming. "Her showing herself to me —I don't think it was meant as a threat."

"What do you mean?" Of course, it was.

"I don't know." She leaned back against the tree. "The way she looked at me was different from how you described her— she wasn't evil. It makes me wonder about what Mom's message could've meant. Like maybe there really are two of them."

"What?"

Ellie just looked up at me. "You know, like good witch, bad witch. I don't know how to explain it. I just really don't think the ghost I saw that night was bad. I think she was urging me to, like, find something."

"Like what?"

"Answers—fuck, I don't know. Goddess, it's hot."

I reached for a tree branch and hung onto it, balancing myself. I was becoming buzzed again, but not sloppy like I was before. My skin was *so* sticky, and the air was thick as wool. It made all this confusing talk way more suffocating than it already was.

As if reading my mind, Ellie stood and grabbed my hand.

"Come on," she said, beginning to pull me back through the brush.

"What are we doing? We can't just desert this topic. Unless —are we going to Lana's?"

"No way," she said, picking up the pace, causing me to stumble over the twigs and pinecones littering the forest floor as I was dragged behind her. I was positive that my feet—still bare— were bloody as all hell. "You crazy if you think I'm waking that witch up in the middle of the night without a damn good reason."

"I think this is a *damn good reason*."

"And it's nothing we can't save for the morning. But for now, it's hot and humid, and if we're gonna stay up, we're not doing it on dry land."

Letting go of my hand, she sprinted forward through the trees and towards the lake.

"You wanna go swimming!" I cried out, trying to keep up with her sculpted calves as they practically floated over the path.

"You gotta better idea?" she called back to me, not the tiniest bit winded.

"Not really, but—oh, what the hell," I huffed, a branch scraping my arm. As she flew through the forest, I pulled out my wand. "Fine Ellie, but you have another thing coming if you think I'm going to let you leave me in your star dust!"

She stopped and turned around just as I shook out my wand, transforming it into a broomstick, the end sprouted with the weeping leaves of a willow tree.

"Oh, we gonna play that game?" Ellie smiled like a devil as she pulled out her own wand, shaking it into an ebony broom.

"Last one there's a sour toad!" I shouted, jumping on my broom and lifting into the air for the first time in too many years to count.

The humidity smacked my cheeks as I glided over the

trees, Delila circling my shoulders as I sped towards the lake. Luckily for us it was late and there were no wanderers outside. Lana would've had our hides if we'd been seen. Regardless, we dropped down to the dock and dropped our brooms to the ground, standing over the wooden planks with our hands held together like two little girls.

"All right ya old witch, on the count of three," Ellie said, the two of us staring down into the reflection of the moon.

Before we jumped, I looked up at her. Ellie's perfect, gold and pink locks were stuck to the side of her head from the sweat rolling down her face. For a moment I became hypnotized by her portrait, and raw beauty—and then something wonderful happened. I let go of Rowena, if only for that moment, and I squeezed my sister's hand in mine. "I'm so sorry I hurt you, Elle. I'm sorry I missed your wedding. I should've been there for you . . . for everything."

The light over the lake caught the bit of moisture shining in the corner of her eye. "Don't sweat it. I'm sorry for a lot of things, too. Let's wash it off, all right?"

I bobbed my head up and down. "Yeah. On three."

Ellie squeezed my hand tighter, and together we chanted, "One, two, three!"

It was short, but high-pitched enough that I couldn't miss it—the squeal that bellowed over the trees as we jumped from the dock. It rang through my ears only for a second before our bodies collided with the lake's surface, as we dunked ourselves into its refreshing waters. Rowena's disembodied scream, her fit of rage at me for being able to let go of her for the first time in my life went away, and all that remained was the coolness of the lake. As we welcomed its embrace, it cleansed us of any worries or hatreds we had stored in our souls. It was an old sort of magic, but one that never ages.

When we came up for air, Ellie and I saw one another again for only a second.

Immediately my necklace burned hotter than ever before, and when I looked down it was glowing bright blue under the lake's surface. Before I could even take another breath, my arms stiffened and my head jolted back.

An illuminating light made of every color I knew grabbed me by the charm and I looked up to find that the moon had lined its light with ours. Even Ellie's charm was shining like a star. My body became completely paralyzed by this unknown magic, and before I could take another breath, the lake around me disappeared and I materialized into thin air.

———

THE SOUND of seagulls woke me, my vision slowly coming into focus as I came to. After the blurry lines straightened themselves out, I immediately recognized where I was. It was different; my house was gone and the lighthouse over the breaks was absent, but this was definitely the California lost coast.

As I moved towards a commotion down over the breaks, near the reef, I found it was like a dream. I couldn't see or feel my body. Here, I was ominous, spirit-like.

"Cora! Cora!"

The voice was coming from down below. It continued to holler out the name, stalking breathlessly up the hill, until I saw my sister's eyes appear inside the face of another. It was Ellie in a previous life. From the looks of her clothes, it was many, *many* years ago.

As she appeared, so did another familiar witch. One with pale skin and dark irises, but the unruly hair I'd commonly associated with her was wound together in a bun. She walked up to my sister, her hands clasped tightly together in front of her stomach. A piece of black hair fell from the bun into her face.

"Rowena," Ellie said, her expression colored in by pain. "What did you do?"

"Two women shall not lie in the same bed, it is written."

The exhaustion colored around the edges of Ellie's person deepened. The love that had been ripped from her heart shone in the color of her skin . . . it was gray and green, as if her blood had ceased to flow anymore. Slowly, shaking her head, she moved closer to the witch. "Where is Cora, Rowena? What have you done with her?"

Rowena's stare was soulless and cold, and as Ellie grew closer to her, she didn't budge. Not an inch.

"She was your sister!" Ellie screamed, tears beginning to fall down her face in pairs.

"She was no sister of mine."

"In the light, Rowena! We are descendants of Diana! We share the same light—we are sisters and brothers, all of us!" Ellie's chin was quivering, and her nose was beginning to run. "We saved you," she whispered. "When they came for us, Cora and I and Mother, we saved you from their burning stakes and hanging trees. I know you have done everything in your power to make the memory of that night go away, but—"

"Perhaps I was saved so that I may save all of you."

Ellie took a step away. Balling her fists up next to her sides, she looked as if she could fight. "What do you mean *save all of you*?"

"From sin. What happened back there was because of our transgressions, and it will continue to happen until we wash our hands of all this. We have been born of the devil, and the only way to save ourselves is to lay aside our wickedness in the face of the lord."

Ellie was shaking. "You killed her, didn't you?" Rowena said nothing. "I'm not of unsound mind, I know of the rumors being spread of you. This speak you deliver is unlike anything you've ever allowed to pass by your tongue. These are the words of men who fear that which is different, which is unexplained. It is the opposite of faith. You've changed, Rowena—you are not the same soul. Tell me the truth. Did you kill her?"

Rowena's lips, pursed tightly together, came undone only to repeat the words she had first said, "Two women shall not lie together."

A shrill and painful scream escaped Ellie's mouth, her fists came unlocked from where she'd been holding them down against her sides, and she lunged at Rowena—throwing punches against her chest until she was exhausted and fell to the ground.

Rowena, unfazed, simply looked down at Ellie once she was finished. "If I were you, I would stop dancing under the moon. This is your warning, for all that is evil shall be put to rest." And then she turned and walked away, leaving my sister with nothing but pain and heartache.

"I'm so sorry," said a foreign voice from within the fold I was residing.

I fought to stick my hand through the envelope, to pull through into the world in which my sister was shaken down to her core, but I was paralyzed. Before I could analyze the scene any further, the sun beating down over the two of us changed to a moon, and as stars filled in around the sky I gasped for air. We were back.

The first thing I heard was my sister's voice as she whimpered, "Oh my god."

I was floating in the lake, about ten feet away from her.

"What just happened?" I asked, lost in a daze.

"Rowena. She killed—she killed Cora. *Cora was Joe.*" Her gaze aligned with mine. "Where *were* you?"

My arms and legs flailed as I tried to keep my head afloat, as I attempted to rationalize what I'd just experienced. "I was there. I saw everything, but it was like I was a—a ghost."

Ellie looked away before she said very slowly, "That's because you were a ghost. I remember thinking that my sister was gone, and now my lover."

The two of us tread through the water in silence for a few more beats before slowly returning to the dock, but once we crawled onto the wooden slats, we didn't stand up. Not right away.

"If you were dead," said Ellie, "then that means your *spirit* was the one who killed her. It's almost unheard of for a spirit to kill. Once we are whole again with the other half of ourselves, we leave behind struggle and pain. We leave that for the living to work out. It seems unlikely that your ghost would act in vengeance. Are you sure you are the one who killed her?"

I turned my attention to the moon. "I'm positive." Our mother had seen it; she wouldn't tell me I'd killed her if I hadn't.

After a few more moments of silence, I stood, turning to walk back to my parent's house, but before I did, I said, "We have to go back in there." Ellie nodded. "It is under the reflection of the moon that we find our answers."

It was true. That was the reason Rowena had screeched before we dove into that lake. Not because I was gaining my strength back, but because I was stumbling into our mother's spell. We were getting closer. "I'll see you in the morning," I said.

"Good night, sis." Ellie's words were barely more than a whisper.

ELLIE

I'd hardly gotten into my cabin when I felt my heart breaking.

Too much had happened in too little time. Fate wasn't unfolding before me; it was shredding itself and falling over my shoulders like motherfucking confetti. I was tired. So fucking tired. Ever since I'd woken up naked next to Derek I hadn't quite felt right. Like a leech was feeding from my soul. I guess even selfish witches can have a conscience.

Plopping down onto my bed, I pulled out my phone and stared at my wife's last text to me. It was still from that day I'd met her at the restaurant.

I wondered what she was thinking. If she had decided it wasn't worth it. I had made it clear that I wasn't in the mood to forgive.

Why hadn't I just heard her out? Why couldn't I just, for once, have let her take the mic from my hands and sing the song for herself? Was it because I was so used to being on stage alone? Did I really need *all* the attention *all* the time?

"Goddamn it," I muttered, scolding myself as I prepared to type a message to her for the first time in over a week.

Joe, I can't take back any of the things I've said to you, because I meant them all—

I stopped, then erased the sentence and prepared for do over.

Hey, I just wanted to check in. I wanted to apologize for the salt thing . . . it was childish. But you really pissed me off—

Again, I erased what I'd just typed. Biscuit, her head draped over my leg, sighed, and I looked over at her. "Right. You're right."

Joe. This is not the first life in which I've lost you. I can't remember them all, but I know this for a fact. Whether it's been because of this kind of shit that we're dealing with now, or because someone or something has come between us, we've been tortured again and again, and our love has fought to find its way back to us again and again.

This life has been a shit show. I would be lying if I said that I haven't fantasized about having a normal life, apart from a partner who will always suffer from disease. But that's the raw truth of it, just as raw and truthful as my connection with you. Because when we're good, we're better than good, and that feeling is so pure and natural that it's worth trumping all the bad.

I'm writing to you because I need to tell you. You're not the only one who fucked up. I slept with Derek when I thought you were cheating on me.

It was stupid, and reckless, and selfish of me. But it's over. I promise you, Joe, it really is. I will always harbor feelings for him, but you've always been the one. I knew it the first time I saw you . . .

I stopped typing and stared at the ceiling.

"What am I doing?"

Within seconds I was pressing down over the back key, deleting everything frantically. I couldn't send that to her— she couldn't know about Derek and me. It would crush her.

The wind blew open the cabin's storm door, and as it entered my space, it circled around until it came to the single white candle that I had centered over the kitchen table. A second later the wick came alive with flame.

Biscuit casually looked over in the direction of the occurrence, yawning as I pulled my leg out from under her and got up from my bed. The flame danced between lengths as I neared it, and in its energy I became comforted.

"Hey," I said, as I stood before it. It continued to pulse, as if it were speaking back to me. "I'm glad you're here. I could use some company. Did you see us go into the water earlier? I think we might be getting somewhere." Again, the flame answered; he had seen us.

I nodded. But I could only pretend for a half second that the crazy shit V and I had just experienced was the only thing weighing me down. My emotions buckled and I clenched a fist over my chest. A bastard sob escaped my throat.

"I fucked up, you know. With Joe. I feel like my marriage is over and it's my fault. I can be such a stubborn hag. I mean, *I* fucked up this time—that shit's on me. I don't know how to make it better."

The flame danced for a moment longer before going out. As soon as it did a small wind circled my shoulders, embracing me. I closed my eyes, relishing in the love, in the magic. When I reopened them, wind had once more become flame, and the small bit of fire was simply staring back at me.

"Do you think you could stay here tonight?" I asked. It answered by lengthening to a height twice its original size. "Thanks. I just really don't want to be alone."

I put my phone away. What good was it to send her a text? Especially after the shit show of a night I'd had. What I really needed was rest. I would wait to speak to her again until my head was screwed on right. Even though that was never really a thing. I was in a constant state of what the fuck ever. Still, the timing wasn't right. I might've been wrong about quite a few things, but on this particular issue I was sure. And if witches were good at anything, it was deciphering the timing of a thing.

I couldn't stop plucking out the details from the spell our mother weaved, the vision of a life lived in the past that V and I had just experienced. I was up against a wall, but I *was* sure of one thing—timing was exactly what my mother had in mind when she created this spell. That memory was just the beginning. There were more answers in that lake. More truths.

OLIVIA

Monday morning I woke to a stomachache. I knew there was an eighty-five percent chance that I was going to see Tyler, and there was an eighty-five percent chance that I wouldn't. For reasons I couldn't allow myself to accept, I began primping.

I was just finishing up with my usual regimen of hair product therapy, followed by extensive flat ironing, when my phone rang. It wasn't until I looked down at my device to see my assistant's name flashing across the screen that I remembered that I still had another life elsewhere, and a boat load of patients who were awaiting my return.

"Dammit," I muttered. If there was one thing I was sure of, it was that I couldn't be there for them anytime soon. Not in the way they deserved anyway.

When Gerald had first presented me with the idea to take over his practice, I wasn't on board. Ironically, I'd called him crazy. But after thinking it over, I'd decided he was right. I had a new life, I was alone, and I could use a project. I never thought that eight years later I would still be at it, and with a whole new patient list all of my own, no less.

I loved what I did, but I could feel the truth digging into my soul. The 'doctor' persona I'd used to blanket the person I'd used to be wasn't me. Not really. I was good at it, but the reality of the situation remained the same as it did the moment I opened my door for that first patient—as Gerald, visible only to me, stood against the wall and walked me through that first session line by line. The profession was only a temporary thing. A gift from a friend, and something only meant to bring me solace until I was ready to return to my old life, or my real life.

The truth had presented itself and I couldn't allow my mother to become a sacrifice. I couldn't keep dancing away this time . . . it wasn't an option.

I stared at the phone long after the missed call. Eventually, a long, shaky breath escaped my lips and I hit the redial button. Not even a half second later the voice of a young woman answered.

"Denise—hey."

From there I did what I knew I had to do. As soon as it was over, a heaviness lifted from over my shoulders; a load of bricks that I hadn't even realized was weighing me down.

Soon after getting off the phone, my bedroom door creaked open and Maddie peeked in.

"Are you staying here?" she asked, a lift to her voice.

I swung around, the lipstick in my hand held out like a taser. "Maddie Jean, how long have you been standing there?"

"Long enough to catch you getting ready like you're about to go to the prom, and to hear you tell your assistant that she should see about getting a new job."

I leaned back against the vanity. "I was just trying to look out for her best interests."

Maddie lifted her eyebrows and made a face; she wasn't buying any of it. "Right . . . her best interests along with your entire case load from the sounds of it."

Exuding a bit of my Aunt Lana's hardened exterior, I stated simply, "It isn't fair to keep those in need waiting. They will be referred to someone who I trust."

"And your house?"

I looked down at my lipstick, then turned around to face the mirror, drawing a more perfect line around my lips. "I'm not sure yet."

Maddie stilled for a moment before jumping onto my bed. She watched as I continued to pull at my hair and pad my face with more powder and blush. When she decided to speak, she said more respectively than usual, "You know, Dad might not even be there this morning." I paused, but quickly returned to what I was doing, trying to keep a neutral expression. "Are those grandma's clothes?"

I pulled at the blouse I'd plucked from my mother's closet, a loose-fitting pale pink shirt that I thought looked very 'easy going' over the pair of black leggings I'd also stolen from her wardrobe. "I'm not trying to impress anyone. I was just sick of my other things, that's all."

"You look nice," Maddie said, shrugging her shoulders. "I just don't want you to get your hopes up."

I squeezed the tube of lipstick in my fist. "I know he's avoiding me."

"He's not avoiding you," Maddie retorted a little too quickly.

I looked up at her, disapprovingly.

She shrugged her shoulders again. "I already told you, he's just really busy. You can't just exactly expect him to come running as soon as you decide *you* want to talk."

"Who said I wanted to talk?" I chattered back, checking my make-up in the mirror. It was pristine.

"It's okay to feel the way you feel."

Something about my daughter saying those words made me feel exposed. Suddenly my cheeks were on fire, and my wand—resting on the dresser—began to shake. I was done with this conversation.

I flipped around and rolled my shoulders back. "I really don't care. And enough of this, we really should be getting you back."

"Yeah," Maddie answered. "I guess we should."

For a moment we just stood there, trying to look anywhere but at each other, until Maddie's gaze fell to my opened suitcase. It was overflowing with slacks and plain shirts—my penny loafers tossed carelessly into the corner as though they should be ashamed of themselves.

She twisted her lips to the side. "You know, we're not in that much of a rush. If you want, we could stop by the mall. Maybe get you something a little more comfortable to wear; sounds like you might be here for a while longer."

My first reaction was to argue, because that was what I was used to doing with Maddie. Then I realized that she was right . . . and she wasn't fighting with me. In fact, she wanted to spend more time with me.

"Uh yeah," I said, "why not. If I stick around here, I'll just get put to work by Lana."

Maddie smirked. "I saw today's schedule while I was at the shop this morning. She's going to ask you to lead the cake tasting with the brides today."

I only had time to blink before reaching for my purse and tossing the lipstick into it. In one fell swoop I gestured for my daughter to get moving as I signaled for the door.

As my wand flew into my purse, I ushered us away. "Like the house is on fire, Mad! Move!"

"Sweet," Maddie said, stopping to grab her things from her room before we ran out of the house and sped out of the retreat like a couple of cult junkies escaping their false Messiah.

OLIVIA

S hopping with Maddie had never been something I really looked forward to. She was judgy, and more than a little rude about the pieces I usually brought to the register for purchase. I'd become accustomed to flocking to the slacks and mind-numbing rows of white and beige blouses; the kind that made you feel a little sick to touch. I'm not sure why I'd changed my style so drastically. At first, I was just playing the part I'd drawn up for myself . . . the recluse psychotherapist. *She* didn't have a taste for fashion. Eventually, it became part of me, matching how I felt on the inside with my outside. Colorless, and without life.

That wardrobe was nothing if not depressing now. I didn't want to wear any of those things—I didn't even want to look at them. What I wanted was something that could breathe.

As if reading my mind, Maddie pulled away an ankle length, sleeveless summer dress from the rack. It was navy blue and made from several layers of sheer fabric. Around the middle was a gold woven belt.

"Oh wow, that's gorgeous," I cooed, pulling it up to my body. It was so soft that I lost my arms inside it.

"You, like, have to try it on. You would look like Athena wearing that."

I didn't argue with her, in fact, I couldn't get it into the dressing room fast enough. It was brilliant of course, and I bought it—along with eight more outfits Maddie threw over the door while I was occupied in the small cubicle.

I chose to wear the Athena dress out, with a new pair of sandals on my feet to match the golden belt. "We look ravishing, if I do say so myself," I said, as we piled all our bags into the back of my rental car. "And I love that little skirt."

Maddie beamed. "Thanks," she replied, pulling on the jean skirt I had gotten for her, paired under a hot pink tank top. She was Ellie, minus the tattoos. I guess it was good she resembled my sister so much, for it seemed a little crazy to believe that Ellie would ever have kids of her own. Especially in her current separated state. Maddie was like her stand in child.

"I don't know quite how you pulled it off, but you look more and more like your Aunt Ellie than me every day," I muttered.

"I'm not the one who got your eyes."

The statement was short but piercing. I paused from where I held the key next to the ignition, but instead of slamming my fists against the steering wheel or lashing out in a voice that matched Rowena's, I simply looked at her and nodded. It wasn't much, but it was progress. A month ago, I would've bitten off her head and chucked it into the ocean for saying something like that. For reminding me of the child I could no longer see or feel.

"So," I said, after starting the car. "We might as well get some lunch, seeing as we're already way late. Where do you want to eat?"

Maddie scrunched up her face and acted like she was trying really hard to think about it, but I could tell that she already had the name of the restaurant on the tip of her tongue.

"Well, we *are* in Denver."

I raised my eyebrows. "You want to eat at Spiked?"

"Yaaaassss! *And* it would be a good time for you to meet Joe. She should be there."

I bit my lip. I'd been hoping she'd tell me we should go eat at Willow Creek. I knew it wasn't open yet, but I thought perhaps they had enough set up that we could have a menu sampling. Or maybe I was just hoping to see Tyler. Just at the thought of him, I found myself double checking my make-up for the tenth time since we'd left the house.

"Yeah, okay. Let's do it," I caved.

"Sweet," Maddie said, picking up her phone and speed texting.

A few minutes later we were there. Maddie directed me to the back of the building where the employees parked to save us the trouble of trying to park elsewhere.

"Are you sure this is okay?" I asked, worried that I was taking someone's spot.

"Yeah, Dad usually parks here."

"Oh," I retorted a little too quickly.

I threw my purse over my shoulder and trucked slowly behind Maddie, who was practically skipping to the back door. She swung it open and waited for me to join her.

We walked into absolute chaos. The kitchen was alive with some sort of fog, steam, or mist, rolling over the workstations, while knives chopped so quickly it was nearly inconceivable to believe the chefs weren't using magic. Then, suddenly, there was a whirlwind as a small figure in a chef's jacket dove in to give my daughter a giant bear hug.

"You look so cute! Is this new?" the woman exclaimed, tugging at Mad's new skirt.

"Yeah, we just came from shopping. Joe, this is my mom."

Looking up at me, to where I stood ever so awkwardly off to the side, my sister's wife held out a small paw of a hand. "Oh hey, Olivia, nice to meet you."

I smiled plainly, accepting the handshake. *This is her,* I thought. *This tiny little thing nearly strangled my sister to death? Oh yeah, she had to have been possessed.*

"Thank you for addressing me by my first name," I said, holding her hand in mine. "I'm sure you only know me by other, less than conventional names."

Joe smirked. "You're not the only woman to have been scorned by Ellie. I think you and I probably have a lot in common." Pulling Maddie along and gesturing for me to follow, she pointed to a booth set up in the kitchen. "I cleared the V.I.P. section for you. That is unless you'd rather sit in the restaurant. I'm sure I could wrangle up a table—just take a few minutes."

"No, this is great," I insisted.

"Check it out," Maddie said, sliding into the booth and pointing to a huge glass wall to our left as soon as Joe shot off in the other direction to grab us some waters. The transparent partition separated the kitchen from the restaurant, which was clearly booming.

"Oh wow."

"Yeah, isn't it cool? It's because they do Molecular Gastronomy. Joe had the place designed this way so the guests could see into the kitchen."

"What's—whatever you just said?"

"Molecular Gastronomy? It's like food chemistry. It makes the dishes more unique—artsy. But if you're in the mood for something normal Joe will make it. She makes a mean burger."

"Actually, I think I would like to try something weird," I giggled.

Joe returned to the table with some water, then scooting in next to Maddie she folded her hands together over the red and black cloth. "You guys wanna order, or you want me to just bring whatever's clever?"

"Whatever's clever," Maddie said.

Joe raised a brow in my direction. "You cool with that?"

"Yeah," I returned, trying to sound a little cooler. Because that's what Joe was. She was cool. I could just tell.

She slapped the tabletop and stood. "Righteous. Give me a few."

Once she was gone, I dropped my head to my shoulder in observance of her character. "She seems really nice. Perfect for Ellie, actually."

Maddie had her phone in her hands again and was moving her thumbs around on it manically. "They'll get back together."

"You're so sure?"

"Yeah. They planned it before they even came here."

"Came here?"

"Into their lives."

I wrinkled my forehead. "What do you mean?" I knew exactly what she meant. When you grow up a witch, surrounded by other like-minded individuals, you get used to this sort of speak. Reincarnation, soul contracts—it was all perfectly normal to us. Maddie didn't usually talk that way, though.

She stopped typing for a heartbeat and looked like she'd slipped her foot into her mouth. After another second or two, she simply returned to her typing. "You know what I mean."

"Yes," I seconded, "I suppose I do."

Lunch was extravagant. Joe brought a 'grazing' for us. Between each dish was a spoonful of what looked like fish eggs, but they were in fact explosions of honey, lavender, and mint. We'd started with bruschetta, in the form of trimmed crusty bread, lying next to a whipped tomato concoction. Next was buttery steak over cauliflower rice, topped with a reddish foam that tasted of beets. After that we had a mouthwatering scallop ceviche surrounded by tiny purple flowers. Desert was a plate of spoons. I tasted everything from strawberry shortcake to s'mores, and a heavenly lemon tart.

When we were finishing up, I couldn't help myself. Speaking through the napkin I was using to dab at the corner of my lips, I said, "I think if I were Ellie, I would have forgiven Joe a long time ago, because if you can cook like that, then what is there to hate?"

Maddie jumped at the opportunity. "Dad is just as good—oh! Speak of the devil."

My heart instantly fell into my stomach. I froze solid as Maddie just sat there, nodding encouragingly. When I got up the nerve to turn around, I found two things I hadn't been expecting. One, that my husband was frozen in his tracks—a look of shock painted onto his face—and two, that he didn't look like my husband.

When I left, Tyler was nothing more than a miniature yeti. He would've fit the hipster vibe that all the kids were embracing these days; except back then it had been dorky, with his overgrown beard and old T-shirts over tight-fitting jeans. This man, though, this obviously dumbstruck prince, he was clean-shaven, and his clothes had been replaced by Banana Republic. He totally looked the part of a downtown Denver city dweller.

I gently laid down the napkin that was still crimped in my hand and stood up.

"Tyler."

His eyes fluttered from where they'd been in shock, into doubt, before growing instantly guarded.

"Where the hell have you guys been?" he asked gruffly.

I began to go numb, from my toes all the way up my body. "I—we went shopping. Maddie said she told you."

His lips pressed together for a brief second, before he

retorted sharply, "When she insisted that you bring her home, I was told it would be first thing this morning. Having it get pushed around is one thing, but then deciding that you can't deliver her after all—"

I shook my head. "No, that's not what happened." And although I wasn't done taking in every physical attribute of the man I was magically bound to, I still turned and looked questionably at my daughter. "Maddie?"

She'd sucked her lips into her mouth and was biting down. A wave of nausea rolled over me as I realized what was going on. She'd set this up. Tyler had been planning on avoiding me and she was trying to get us to see each other.

Looking past my shoulders towards our daughter, Tyler gave her a disgruntled look. "You told Joe not to worry about picking you up this morning because your mother was bringing you back. You know how busy I am; I don't have time for this right now, Maddie."

My face grew hotter and redder by the second. I tried not to pick up on the battered energy that was shooting out from every angle of his soul, but it was nearly impossible.

"I'm so sorry, Tyler. I didn't know—"

His gaze was so sharp it was cutting. He simply shook his head. "It's fine. Come on, Maddie. I've got a meeting at the restaurant and I needed to be there thirty minutes ago."

Maddie didn't move at first, instead she just sat there giving my husband one of the angriest, most hurt looks I'd ever seen, and I'd seen quite a few from her over the years.

"Maddie," I said quietly under my breath, "you should go with your father."

Her expression changed and she looked up at me in disbelief. "But don't you two want to talk?"

"No," Tyler said so quickly that it slashed my heart into quarters. Gesturing to Maddie, he turned back towards the door. "Come on, Mad." When she still hadn't budged, he repeated himself in a much gruffer voice. "Now."

Maddie scoffed before scooting out from the booth. Her face was beet red and she looked like she was going to cry.

"I'm sorry, Mom," was all she said on her way out the door. "I tried."

Those last two words of hers finished off the broken pieces of my heart.

"It's not your job to try," I whispered after they were gone.

I was so empty inside that it physically hurt, and with nowhere else to turn, I slumped into the booth and stared at the table. Within seconds I had tears streaming down my face. Normally I would've cared that there were perhaps a hundred people on the other side of that glass wall that had seen all that, that were watching as the strings holding me together came apart, but that was the last thing I cared about just then.

A second later a cold hand touched my shoulder, and I looked up out of my window of tears to find Joe. A sympathetic look covering her face.

"Come on."

I nodded and followed her into her office. It was dim, and her desk was cluttered with invoices and the usual business details. But it was quiet . . . and private.

"Have a seat." She pointed to a chair in the corner and handed me a box of Kleenex.

I couldn't speak, so I simply placed a hand over my running nose and graciously accepted the tissue. I blotted my eyes and nose, all the make-up I'd cased my face in that morning coming off in clumps. When I finally could speak, all I could say was, "He hates me."

Joe, who had taken a seat behind her desk, just nodded. It was the opposite reaction I'd hoped to get from her. Perhaps I'd been wishing for her to say something more along the lines of, 'He's just really busy,' or, 'We all have off days.' But what she ended up saying was a little more realistic.

"We fucked up, you and I."

A shadow moved across my chest. "We did, didn't we."

"Yep."

"I guess you were right, the two of us really aren't that different."

She laced her hands together over her stomach as she kicked back in her chair. "Nope. You deserted your family, and I did the same thing to Ellie by escaping into my own twisted world. Nobody deserves that shit."

"No, they don't." I wiped my nose again. "Maddie wanted us to talk."

"That little witch just wants her mom and dad to get back together."

I inhaled a ragged breath. She was right. That was all Maddie had ever wanted.

I sniffed. "She's not really a witch."

Joe lifted a brow. "Then how does she fly?"

"What?"

She chuckled, leaving my question unanswered as she readjusted herself in her chair, placing her hands over the desk.

Too caught up in the pain of what had just happened to even think about entertaining the strange banter, I simply looked at Joe and asked, "How do I fix it? How do I make him look at me as if I'm not some kind of monster?"

"Honey, if I had the answer to that I would be a zillionaire."

"Right."

"Hey. You just gotta be patient. I don't know your deal— whether you're just here for Arianna or if there's more to it. Maddie seems to think you're gonna hang out. I do know that you wrecked that man. He's not going to be ready to look at you for *a while*." My heart fell even more in my chest if that was possible. "Look, you should know that Tyler is fine. He's fine in the sense that he has managed to pull himself out from the shit hole he crawled into after he realized you weren't coming back. He had to clean himself up, figure out a way to live his life, because he had a daughter to take care of." Her attention veered to the corner of the room as she said the last part. "At least though, in Maddie, you will always have a piece of your husband—even if you can't ever have him back."

I blotted at the moisture over my cheeks, choking down the awful thought that I might never have the chance to make things right. As I satiated over Joe's opinions, I became struck with something else. A blaring confession that my sister's wife either intentionally or unintentionally had allowed to escape. "You want kids."

Her eyes twinkled in a way that led me to believe I'd just hit the nail on the head. "I want the chance to make things right. I want to be able to give someone the love I never received when I was growing up. It's like a need I have. When I saw Ellie's face for the first time, I saw the person I wanted to share that gift with." Her chin dipped and she said in a softer voice, "But some things just seem impossible, you know. Especially when Ellie looks at me the way Tyler just looked at you."

Another jab straight into my guts. "It definitely feels final, doesn't it?"

Her fingers, which had been tracing an invisible design over an area of her desk, untouched by clutter, made their way towards a small gift box that I hadn't noticed up until that point—the kind that might hold a ring inside it. It was wrapped in hot pink paper. Pushing it around with her fingertip, she said, "Hey, do me a favor?"

With my watery eyes glued to the box, I said, "What's that?"

She leaned forward and pushed the box across the table. "Give this to Ellie for me."

I stared at it for a second more before wiping my nose with the tissue. "Sure."

She gave me a toothless grin and a curt nod. "Thanks." Then tapping the top of the desk with her hand, she stood. "I gotta get back out there, but it was good to finally meet you."

"You too," I replied, taking a more in-depth study of her features as she made her way out. Suddenly I was aware that I'd seen her eyes before . . . but in someone else's person. Who though, I couldn't place.

Her hand on the doorknob, she paused before taking her exit. "Take as long as you need. And Olivia."

"Yeah?"

"I'm really glad you're back; she needs you more than you know. Not a day goes by where I don't blame myself for that coma she's locked herself into. It's time she returns to her life."

I nodded. "Don't worry, I won't rest until we get my mother to wake back up."

She shot me one final look before stepping out of her office. "I wasn't talking about Arianna."

OLIVIA

When I finally did return to Sage Brook that evening, the sun was setting and my father was asleep in his chair. I walked aimlessly around the house a couple times before settling for pouring myself a glass of Pinot Grigio and taking my new dress for a walk. I'd barely gotten halfway around the lake when I heard the sweet sound of Ellie's violin coming from her cabin.

Remembering that I had a gift to deliver from her wife, I headed back to my parent's house to retrieve the small box, then returned to Ellie's front door. I hesitated, letting the strings enchant the night, before swinging it open.

Inside, Delila was waiting for me, perched on top of Biscuit's head—a vision of the two familiars I hadn't seen since Ellie and I were kids. Ellie sat cross-legged on her kitchen table, her eyes closed, as she played. I sat down in the chair in the corner and listened as her magic filled the night with more stars, waiting to say anything until she was finished.

When she opened her eyes all she said was, "Hey."

"That was beautiful."

"Thanks," she said, laying down her instrument and eyeing my dress appreciatively. "You go shopping today?"

"Yeah, Maddie and I went to the city."

"You didn't buy any more of those goddamned awful head bands, did you?" she asked, forming her lips into a mischievous grin.

"No," I snickered. "But we did get lunch at Spiked." I could tell this information sparked some interest in my sister. I held out the box to her. "Joe wanted me to give this to you."

Ellie stared at it as if it might contain a bomb, but eventually she accepted it. I waited for her to open the wrapped box, but she simply set it next to her on the table.

"So, you met the wife, eh?"

"Yeah, I did. I really like her."

Her energy shifted, two winds colliding with one another, and she jumped off the table. "Yeah. Well, I don't want to make you drink alone." Gesturing to my near empty wine glass, she pulled out a bottle of red. "More?"

"Sure." I gulped down the last swig of white and held out my glass.

After filling it, Ellie pulled out a glass and poured one for herself. Just as she was climbing back up onto the table, Lillette appeared just inside the door, her pup running over towards Biscuit. Ellie followed my gaze as it followed the spirits, but she didn't say a word.

"So, what did you do today?" I asked, changing the subject.

"Fired my manager."

I practically spit out my next sip of wine. "You what?"

"He was being a dick. Mom's more important than a stupid tour."

"Yeah, but Ellie, what about your career?"

She waved an uncaring hand in the air. "Shit'll be all right. It always is."

Thinking over Joe's last words to me, I said carefully, "True . . . but you can't give up on who you are completely."

She shot a warning stare in my direction before retorting. "It'll be fine."

I hesitated, then nodded my head, because I didn't want to fight. I'd had enough bad vibes swimming around me that day to last a lifetime. "Right," I said, trying to look as sure of the world as she did just then. Searching for something else to say, my gaze fell to something resting on her table. Immediately goosebumps rose over every inch of my body. "Are those—are those my tarot cards?"

Ellie looked over at the lump wrapped up in the old scarf Tyler had given me when we'd first started dating. "Oh yeah. I just found them; thought you might want them back. Hey, we should do a reading!"

Lillette jumped up and down, clapping her hands together in anticipation. It was then that I noticed something about her, something so bizarre that it caused the sensation of a bolt of lightning to rush over me, and the words *no way* to course through my head.

"Actually," I said, reaching forward and taking my long-lost tools into my hands, "I think that's an excellent idea."

ELLIE

The lid of the little pink box had been removed and what was inside glared at me like a bleeding eye. A dry heave worked its way up my throat and I cupped a hand over my mouth as I shoved it away; I couldn't stand to look at it any longer.

Guilty. I don't think so. Guilt didn't even come close.

I was a monster. A fucking tool.

As soon as I recovered from the bile running down my throat, I kicked the side of my bed and picked up my phone, dialing Derek's number. I crossed my arms over my chest as my gaze fell to the contents of the box one more time. All I could do, as I waited for that prick to answer his phone, was hope that my new discovery wouldn't be the one truth that could dissolve her recovery.

V HAD SHOWN up two hours earlier. It had been a shit day, but I was managing to keep my cool. I'd even thrown a text Joe's way, now that my head had been just a little clearer, asking if we could meet up to discuss a few things. After the debacle I'd experienced with Derek, I was ready to start talking about putting the pieces of ourselves back together—all of course dependent on whether she had truly stopped drinking. I'd decided that it was best to leave out the part about Derek and me, permanently. What was the point of hurting her when I had decided it was something that would most definitely never happen again?

Nothing ever returns to us as it once was, though. Relationships included. And that couldn't be clearer from the moment V walked into my cabin, bringing with her more than the witch she'd used to be.

Tarot. It could be the beginning of all things, or the end.

She read the cards for *me*, even though I'd said we should do them for our mom. She was adamant that the cards were favoring *my* spirit.

She shuffled them in her hands, longer than she'd used to; but it had been a long time and I had a feeling that her hands had missed sorting through that deck. When she was finished, she handed them to me and said, "Cut them into thirds while you concentrate on your immediate future. Ask the cards what lies before you."

"Sure," I'd said, accepting the cards.

The second they were returned into her possession, something cold landed on my lap, and I looked up to find my sister smiling at me, her head cocked to the side.

"She likes you."

"Who?" I'd asked.

"Lillette. She's sitting in your lap."

"Oh, right. The spirit kid. Whatever—so how we gonna play this, yo?"

"I'm going to use the five-card spread," V replied, placing the cards face down.

"Cool." I took a sip from my wine and nodded for her to

start. She carefully flipped over the first card, which represented my present situation.

"Reversed Princess of Wands," I said. "Shit, I can't remember what that means." I didn't read tarot as often as V; I still had to cheat and look up the meanings most of the time.

Her eyes were closed, and her hand was plastered against the card. She once told me that her spirit guides spoke to her during her readings, translating the meanings of each card and how they applied for the person being read. Sometimes these messages came as whispers, other times as visions.

Before long, she spoke. "Journeys have been delayed by a relationship put on hold. Your energy is discombobulated from interruptions in your love life." She opened her eyes, they were apologetic. "And other relationships that may have been damaged in the past." When I said nothing, she added, "That's pretty spot on, right?"

"Sure."

"Next one then." She laid her hand over the second card, denoting my past, then flipped it over. "Another reversed one." She looked up and saw me cringe. "Don't worry, this is a good one to be reversed. Three of Swords. The conflict of the past has the ability to mend, but you need to take ownership of your own upsets." She studied me, and I could tell she was a little curious. I wished I could tell how much of my business she could see in those visions of hers. "Does that make sense?"

I jerked my head up and down. "Nobody's perfect. Joe isn't the only one who has made mistakes."

V continued to peer at me over the card in her hand. She was more than curious, she was suspicious.

"You want to talk about it?"

I set down my wine glass and scooted my hands under my butt. The words were on the tip of my tongue, that I'd slept with Derek—almost more than once—but I couldn't get them out.

Back in the day V would have been the first person I would have gone to the second I'd woken up next to him—regret strung around my shoulders like a messy bunch of flickering Christmas lights. Over the years I'd learned to hold things in. That's how my marriage had gotten so out of hand, because without my confidant I'd been too proud to admit to my family how bad things had gotten. Too honorable to concede that I'd married a woman who could down her weight in gin in less than an hour, and then proceed to change personalities just as quickly.

"No. It's not a big deal," I lied.

V nodded, laying down the Three of Swords and moving her fingers over to the one directly across from it.

She paused before flipping it over. "It's what lies before you. Your immediate future."

I gulped, and just as she was about to flip the card over, my hand slapped it back down.

"Maybe this isn't such a good idea," I said, my heart beating too quickly.

V wrinkled her forehead. "There's secrets in you, Sister."

My palm grew sweaty over her hand and I sucked in a quick breath. "What if it says Joe and I are over . . . that the rest of my love life will be cursed like yo—" I'd had to stop myself from finishing the sentence. Thankfully, V took no offense, and in the fashion of the sister I used to know, she had just the right thing to say.

"When it comes to love, our futures can't ever really be scribed. It may not say what you want it to say, but that just means you aren't ready for it to say the thing you desire. But I'll tell you this much, Elle, if you want it to say a certain thing, then you are more ready than you know, and you are closer than anything to being where you should be."

I waited a second, her words filtering into my mind. Finally, I very slowly pulled my hand away. "Okay . . . go on."

She held her hand over the card for another beat, as if it was the last page in the last book of a series that was rumored to end in disaster. As soon as I saw what it was, however, I let a heavy sigh of relief exit my hardened ribcage.

"The Lovers, that one I know."

"Looks like your heart is ready after all," was all she said, before methodically reaching for the next to last card. "And with that in mind, we can find out the meaning behind the reading. You ready?"

"Yes." My heart was happy, content. As far as I was concerned, we didn't even need the last two cards. I'd gotten my answer. Joe and I could have a future again—all bullshit set aside.

My next card was The Wheel. No big surprise. The Wheel was a cycle card. It could've meant many things, but since we'd asked about my immediate future, The Wheel was simply symbolizing an era. I was moving into a new phase of life.

Before V turned over the last card, the one that represented the entire reading, a final outcome, she stopped and stared down at the space between The Wheel and the next card. Very slowly, she lifted her head and looked up.

"Oh."

"Oh? What's that mean?" But she didn't say a single word back to me. "Yo V, what's going on?"

"Ellie?"

I was starting to feel a little nauseous, but I attributed the bile rising in my throat to my sister's foreboding lack of speech. "Spit it out."

"You and Joe . . . you've been separated for a while now, right?"

"Like six months."

"Uh huh, and have you guys been seeing other people? I mean, would either of you—"

"Look, whatever you're trying to say, just say it."

"Neither one of you has, like, you know—been with someone else? A man perhaps?"

I just sat there, something rancid continuing to bubble up from my gut.

V's shoulders rose as she took a deep breath. "Okay, let's just see what this says."

I reached over and slapped my hand over the card, causing her to look up at me again. "What are you seeing?"

"She has *her* eyes," she whispered. Then she pulled her hand away from mine and revealed the truth as foretold by the fifth card.

"Oh shit," I said, as the sting of the wine on my tongue became more and more apparent.

"So, is this possible?" She looked up at me, then down at the invisible child in my lap.

Pushing away what was left in my glass, I cursed. "Goddamn it. It sure the fuck is."

———

DEREK PICKED up after only three rings.

"What's goin' on?" His voice caused me to cringe.

I picked up the six-month AA token Joe had sent me and held it stiffly between my forefinger and thumb.

"Is this a good time to talk?"

"Yeah," he said. "You all right? You sound weird."

"No. Not okay. Not all right."

Joe was a full-fledged lesbian. She did *not* like boys in that way. I, on the other hand, had always been attracted to whoever I was attracted to. Gender was nothing but a thang. This was all on me.

"Is this about the other night?" Derek asked after a long pause. "Because I think we are best just leaving it, you know. I feel terrible about letting it happen at all, because I know more than anyone how hard Joe has been working—"

A nasty scowl found its way onto my face, and I gritted my teeth as I spat into the phone. "Derek, do me a favor and shut up."

There was silence on his end for a hard second.

"Ellie, what's going on?"

"I pulled The Lady."

"What?"

I raised my voice, causing Biscuit to whine. "The Lady, Derek. V read my cards and my ending card was The Lady."

Silence filled the other end of the line.

"Sooooooo, that means—"

"I'm pregnant, Derek! Pregnant with that fucking Lillette and she's yours!" Then, fueled by an intense rage, I hung up the phone, threw the coin, and screamed into a pillow.

OLIVIA

I couldn't believe I hadn't put the pieces together sooner. Lillette was Ellie's spirit child. She hadn't been in the mood to talk about it (once the realization of the last card hit her), but the explanation was written all over her face. She didn't have to tell me who the father was, because now all I could see when I looked at the little spirit girl was a little of Ellie, a little of Derek, and oddly enough, a little of Joe.

I had tried to remain passive, but Ellie's tantrum as soon as she realized the implications of the reading, had been enough to cause me to pack up my tarot and slip out the door. I trusted my little sister was doing all right, but an entire day had passed and she hadn't come out of her cabin. Still, we had a ghost to catch and a spell to deactivate. I only hoped she wasn't going to try and bail on our midnight swim.

I'd shown up at Lana's about an hour before I was supposed to get there, so the two of us had been wasting time sipping on iced tea and staring up at the stars.

"Goddess, it's humid," I said. "I don't remember it ever being this sticky here."

Lana made a clicking noise with her tongue and took a puff from the cigar in her hand.

"That's because it doesn't get humid here. It's your witch, she's brought the ocean with her."

My head cranked in her direction. "Rowena is the cause of this?"

Lana nodded. "You cursed her to stay in the wind of the past. Wherever she goes, she brings this with her. Can you not smell the salt in the morning air?"

As a matter of fact, I had, and I had thought that, too, was strange.

Footsteps stomping along the ground caused us both to turn and find Ellie, hurriedly making her way towards us. She ran up the porch steps and stopped short, just before dropping a white plastic stick onto the table.

"Tell me that is a wand and not a stick covered in urine," Lana said, her expression stern.

Ellie, ignoring her, threw her hands in the air and shouted, "It's official. I'm having Derek's goddamned baby!"

I set down my tea and carefully picked up the test, examining it; but seeing as she'd sported for the expensive electronic one that clearly read 'positive,' it seemed there was no denying the truth that my sister was pregnant.

She paced in front of us, biting her nails.

"When did this happen?" I asked.

"Just before you came here," Lana said in a calm voice, smoke exiting her nostrils.

"Seriously!" Ellie shook her hands up at the sky. "How could this have happened?"

"I think, Wichahpi, you already know the answer to that," Lana said. If I wasn't mistaken, there was the faintest outline of a smile on my aunt's face as though she thought this was amusing. "Don't worry, I am sure Josephine will forgive you.

You have, what do you kids say, a get out of jail free card. She did strangle you, after all."

Ellie stopped pacing and looked down at Lana; if looks could kill.

"At least we know I haven't lost my ability to read cards," I said, holding the stick up to the moonlight.

"Shut up," Ellie said, leaning down and taking the test back. "I have to figure out what I'm going to do."

"Okay, you girls," Lana said, throwing back whatever it was she was *really* drinking, because it was rarely ever just tea. "It's late and I think all the guests should be sleeping by now. Let's go swimming."

We'd had to let Ellie stomp around for a few more minutes, but even in her violent state she knew we had little time to waste when it came to saving our mother. *And* ourselves for that matter.

Lana escorted us to the dock. She was primarily with us for observation purposes, but I had an inkling she was hoping to see into the spell. I was unsure whether she could actually do that, but who knew—her abilities were always a mystery to me.

After getting to the dock and stripping down to our suits, Delila circled the cabins, returning to Ellie and me with a solemn nod that the coast was clear. Gesturing back to my familiar, I grabbed my sister's hand and counted to three, and just like the first time, we jumped into the lake.

"Be safe," Lana said, as our heads went under water. When we came back up, our necklaces were warm and glowing, and the moon took us away just as it had the time before.

———

AGAIN, I found myself in an envelope, some place between space and time. An observer rather than a player. It was night, but the setting was still the lost coast; except this time, I'd materialized a way down the shoreline, where the waves rolled over black sandy beaches. Had *she* not been there, an essence of death clinging to her now stringy hair, I may have found the quiet sloshing of the waves against the coast relaxing. Rowena's presence took away any lingering peace from the tranquil moonlit oceanside.

The sound of heavy fabric dragging along the ground broke the silence, and Rowena and I both turned to see the outlines of two women growing closer.

"Why are we coming here at night, Mama?" As Ellie, or Ella, came closer, the moonlight revealed more worry lines scribbled on her face than the last time I'd seen her, and her hair looked more ragged.

"Rowena asked us to?"

"Yes, because she is to kill us. We should be leaving now, not following her to our graves. There is nobody left in the village, she's killed everyone we care about."

My mother's soul bled inside the other woman's voice. "She is a witch, too. We must not leave her here."

"She's a murderer, Mama! This you cannot deny!"

The two women, who were physically closer to Rowena than they knew, came to a halt and our mother grabbed my sister's hands. "When Diana filled our hearts with her light, she made us all one. We must not desert Rowena, she needs us now more than ever."

"This is not wise. You are blinded by your heart," my sister said, shaking her head after they'd started to walk forward again. "You must see it! *That* is not Rowena, it is an impostor. I can tell you, this feels wrong."

"I am not as blind as you think me, but if she has been taken, then all we can do at this point is continue to speak to her. For she who sleeps, sleeps only of the body. Her soul will hear us . . . her soul will fight."

Ella's expression was severely crossed; however, she did not fight against these words.

As the two of them inched forward over the dark sand, my thoughts began to race. The words from my guide ringing through my head—*beware of imposters.*

They continued until they came upon Rowena, at which point my mother cleared her throat, announcing their arrival.

"You came," Rowena said, her back to them as she stared into the ocean. "I didn't think you would."

"We would never desert a sister in need," my mother said.

Without looking at the two of them, Rowena asked, "Have you thought about what I spoke to you about, Ella? Last time we saw one another?"

With her hands balled into fists, my sister lunged forward, but my mother pulled her back. "You mean the day you took Cora from me?" she said through clenched teeth.

"What you two were doing was sinful."

"She was my wife!"

Rowena spun around, her eyes completely black. "Two women shall never be married in the Lord's eyes!"

My sister spat at her feet, but the act didn't even seem to faze Rowena.

"I will give you one last chance to repent, to give away all your sins." The witch's voice grew deeper and shook with a violent excitement before she lowered it again. "Or I will take away your sins for you."

"Dearest Rowena," my mother said, "this is not you. Dig past the pain, I beg of you. Remember your heart."

The pale-faced witch took a step closer. "Your Rowena . . . she was weak."

My mother froze. A whisper fell from her mouth, but it was too soft to hear.

Rowena smiled sinisterly, then stood taller as she quoted a verse from a book she'd grown to know all too well. A book with passages that she'd taken into her own and twisted. "'But for the cowardly and unbelieving and abominable and murderers and immoral persons and sorcerers and idolaters and all liars, their part will be in the lake that burns with fire and brimstone, which is the second death.'"

Ella exploded. "That is a book written by several different hands—an interpretation! It is but a story, and not to be used as a weapon!"

My mother remained still; her lips pursed tightly together.

"Is it more fiction than the lies spun from your so-called sisters and brothers? Evil demons in disguise," Rowena muttered, her head jerking unnaturally to the side.

"No. You've been brainwashed by hatred. By men who fear what they cannot understand, who crave power and denounce love because of greed." My sister's chest was heaving as she spoke. "But what a hypocrite you are either way— you've turned into a murderer! What does your book say about that? You just said it was a sin!"

"I am a servant to the Lord. It is not murder, but a cleansing," she answered.

"Rowena was a descendant of the goddess Diana!"

Was? I thought.

"Stop," my mother said, putting herself between the two women. Looking at the maddened witch, she said, "Tell me, what is your plan? What will you do when we are all dead? Where will you go?"

"I will be rewarded by my savior."

"Lies! You've no savior! You are only out to gain more power for yourself!" Ella shouted.

Rowena said nothing back, instead she simply laced her fingers together in front of her stomach.

My mother looked down, and as she did, she asked very quietly, "Is she still in there?"

Ella was staring back and forth between the two women, her energy exuding nothing but fury.

Rowena narrowed her eyes at my mother but did not answer her question.

My mother stepped back in line with my sister and took Ella's hand once more. "Do your worst, so mote it be."

"Mama!"

"It's too late, Ella," my mother said. "It's made up its mind. Our sisters are but a space in time away—we will be home soon."

It . . .

Rowena, or this *thing* invoking her, was frozen, clearly befuddled by my mother's willingness to be sacrificed. "You will not repent?"

"No," my mother said, speaking for her and my sister.

"You will die for your evil lies?"

"There is no such thing as dying, only transitioning from one life to the next. It is my hope that seeing the last of us go will help the light push away the dark."

Rowena's gaze, twitchy and uncentered, moved in closer to my mother's. "Oh, dear witch, there is nothing that can push *me* away."

Ella cried out, but my mother stood strong and still as stone.

Finally, a fizzle broke the silence. It reminded me of a fire burning in the fireplace, one that had gotten so hot that the logs began to speak to one another as they crumbled from where they burned. Then, as though thunder was beginning to roll through the clouds in the distance, a low rumble sounded around the three witches.

Ella shrieked, and I realized she was unable to move. Rowena had sunken their legs into the sand so they couldn't run; and as Rowena began to chant, her feet slowly lifted from the ground.

"Fire burn, fire burn, sulfur rise into the air. Fire burn, fire burn, along the tips of the rolling tide, fire burn, fire burn . . ." As she spoke, her head rolling eerily from one side to the other, thick smoke rolled in over my sister and mother's heads, suffocating them.

"Rowena, can you hear me? Push against the darkness! You are stronger than this!" Ella choked, a tear running down her cheek.

The evil monster looked down at their two faces. "I am the ALMIGHTY!"

"You're mad!" Ella continued to cry, shaking her head as she coughed on the smoke.

My mother remained stiff, studying Rowena as though she was trying to unravel a riddle. It didn't look like she was breathing at all.

Behind them, the waves were rolling in faster and higher, and as they came up around Ella and my mother, soaking their dresses, a ring of yellowish, greenish fire encircled all three of them—a fire that could not be put out by the ocean tides.

Rowena continued to chant, "Fire to their second death, fill their lungs with smoke!" She lifted her arms to the sky, now floating a good eight feet off the ground. Her head rolled back as she continued to chant; the ocean now up to my mother and sister's chests with the enchanted ring of fire floating around them, and their lungs filling with more and more sulfuric smoke.

"Rowena!" my mother yelled over the rising tide and the evil witch's tantrum. "If you can hear me—we never left you!" She paused only to cough. "When you come out of this, know that we will still be here for you!"

She turned to Ella, who through the terror still managed to look at our mother like she was insane. Still, after a moment's deliberation, Ella looked up at Rowena and shouted, "Beast, look at me!"

The witch, delirious with power, dropped her chin and stared at Ella.

"Rowena my love, we are sisters of the light! I know you're there. I know there is still love in your heart—no matter what, I will still lov—"

But Ella never got to finish what she was saying. Neither did my mother, for that matter. As if suffocating them with sulfurous smoke wasn't enough, Rowena struck their heads under the water, laying their bodies down against the sandy beaches, under the unruly tide she'd angered. Their lifeless shells floated back up to the surface and as the light went out in their eyes the tides relaxed and fell back and away, leaving the bodies to rest, dead, on the beach. The fire went out, leaving only a black ring around their bodies.

When it was over and the wind had calmed and the scene was as quiet as I had first walked into it, Rowena's feet touched back to the ground. She leaned down to lay a hand over each of the dead witch's heads.

"I warned you," she whispered. "There is no room on this earth for sin."

Suddenly, inside my envelope, the spirit I was with cried out. *My* spirit from this past life—her rage and impatience flaring with the heat of the sun. I could hear her thoughts, *that she'd been glued to this window from the moment the foulness had taken her life, forced to watch those who she cared about being tortured and murdered.*

It was a sickness that started it all. Her thoughts reeled around and around. A sickness.

Whispering quickly under her breath, the transparent fold between this world and the next sparkled, showing her where the curtain could be pulled for her to step through.

Tiny bells clanked together, the same bells I'd heard strung around the ankles of the witches of Latharia. It startled the dark witch from where she knelt beside her victims. As the spirit I traveled with stepped defiantly onto the beach, feeling how cold the black sand felt between her bare toes, Rowena spun around and faced her.

She hissed. "How did you get out of there?"

"I put myself in there. I had the power to get out all along. I just forgot."

A sickening smile grew along the lines of Rowena's face. "You forgot? So very human of you."

"It was a mistake, one that I aim to correct." My spirit's gaze fell to an object sticking out of Rowena's dress pocket. Before the witch could snag it, a transparent hand reached out and the wand flew into it. Directing it at Rowena, my spirit said defiantly, "Now, *as for you*, your time is over."

Rowena's expression froze, but she wasn't given any time to plead or retaliate, for just then a light, so bright it was blinding, lit up between my spirit and Rowena as a parade of words poured from my spirit's mouth. It was a light so illuminating that everything went completely white, a colorless explosion.

The magic was fierce, but the sickness that had taken over Rowena's body was just as strong. Through the white noise, Rowena's body fell dead to the sand. But whatever had been in her body—*whoever* had been inside her—it wasn't dead.

"*You will pay for this,*" a familiar voice growled into my ears. "*From you I will take every son you have; destroy every loving relationship you find in every future life. I will hunt you down until you no longer feel anything but that of pain. And I won't stop until I'm strong enough to get my body back.*"

The voice faded into a seedy laughter. One that followed me from where I was residing inside my past self-spirit, into my current, physical body—to where I was nearly *drowning* in the lake.

I came back to with arms flapping, feet kicking, and unable to keep myself afloat. It was as though the lake was gulping me down. I had but a half second to realize what was happening. That Rowena—this demon—she or it was *in* the lake. The whispers filling my ears came from the same voice that had just spoken in the memory. Whatever this evil was, it wasn't just trying to frighten me this time. It was trying to kill me.

A fog lifted from the water and as it swarmed around me, I heard the voice of my enemy. *"Where is your mother now, witch?"*

Our mother's spell had taken us further into the past and Ellie and I were getting closer to the truth. The monster was threatened. I knew its game, that it was trying to frighten me into a state of irreversible weakness; but as the lake came alive around me, readying to swallow me up, I couldn't help the fear that trickled into my heart. I knew that to let down my guard was suicide, but at the same time, I was so vulnerable.

"Wachiwi!" Lana shouted from where her and Ellie were standing over the dock. My heart was racing and my teeth were chattering. I could only catch glimpses of them from where the water was sloshing madly around my head.

The fog dissipated, the waves silenced, and for a moment I thought it was over. However, I'd only been afforded about three seconds of sanity before a pair of hands swam up from the depths of the lake and pulled at my legs. As frozen fingers wrapped around my ankles, a sick laughter rang through my ears. The more I struggled, the stronger it pulled.

Oh god, I thought—struggling to keep my head above the water—*this is how it ends. This devil has gotten me right where it's wanted me all along, in the middle of a lake. It's going to drown me.*

As I fought against the relentless ghostly hold, I lifted my head into the air just long enough to witness a different supernatural occurrence.

"*As above, so below,*" the wind whispered into my ears. "*Don't allow yourself to be its reality . . . Go now. Swim away.*"

Then *the wind itself* dove into the water, causing a large wave to ripple out in all directions. Immediately my ankles were freed, and as I gasped for the air to fill my lungs, there was an eruption about fifty feet away from where I tread—two unseen forces coming together in one hell of a dispute.

There was no time for reflection, to think over the way the wind had spoken to me, or the recognition of its voice. I'd been saved just then; but if that *thing* got free, I was positive it wouldn't take its time drowning me a second time. So, with twice as much blood pumping through my veins, I focused on the dock and hammered for it—water sloshing back and forth behind me as though there was a shark fight ensuing.

Better late than never, for the dock was still quite a ways away, Delila swooped down and dropped my wand from her beak. As it landed in my hand it transformed into a broom and lifted me from the water, flying me straight to the dock and dropping me into the arms of my sister and aunt.

"What *was* that?" Ellie gasped, her arms around me in an instant.

Before I could answer, Lana crept up by our sides, her wand out before her as though it was a sword. "Keep your wands up, girls, this is not over. Your witch—she has not yet gone."

"That's no witch—" I started, but before I could finish my thought, Ellie and I turned to face the lake. The water had settled but the fog had not. In fact, it was moving towards us at a furious rate.

"GO!" I exclaimed, attempting to shove Ellie away. It didn't matter how quickly we moved. The fog was faster.

It rolled in under our feet, and as it did, I smelled it. Death . . . rot.

"What the fuck is that?" Ellie's voice was shaking as she

pointed down at the dock. A streak of wetness appearing from nowhere. The mark of Rowena's dress dragged across the surface, getting closer.

"Don't let it touch you," I warned, pulling my sister into me. I reached out to take hold of Lana, but my aunt was already frozen in her tracks. "Lana?"

She looked up at me, her eyes clouded over, and the foulest scent came from her tongue when she opened her mouth. "They will not always be there to save you, witch."

"They," Ellie questioned.

The thing inside my aunt sneered at my sister. "Olivia chooses to look away from both of them. Pieces of herself."

Maddened by the nerve of this horrible creature, I bared my teeth. "What do you want?"

It blinked thoughtfully. "What you did back then, it was a sin. You deserve all that becomes you."

Ellie stepped out from behind me, her wand held out before her. "I'm going to murder you, you sick twisted—"

Just as I was about to push her wand away, fearful that this was a trick to get us to kill our aunt, Lana's eyes returned to normal and her body nearly collapsed.

"Lana!" Ellie and I exclaimed together, reaching for her body as it teetered clumsily towards the edge of the dock.

She steadied herself, pushing us away. "I'm fine." She looked to the water, and then to the space directly around the three of us. "It has gone now. Come, let us get away from here. I think we have all had enough excitement for one night."

"I'd say so," I muttered, with the last of the breath saved in my lungs.

Once we were back inside the safety of Lana's house, bundled up and each with a cup of steaming hot tea in front of us, our aunt stated the obvious. "I think, perhaps, I speak on behalf of us all when I say this is far worse than I've imagined."

"That thing, like, tried to kill V," Ellie spat out in disbelief. "I thought it couldn't hurt us."

"It can do whatever it wants," I muttered. "Mom's spell can only do so much against something like that."

"Wachiwi," my aunt said quietly. The possession, though short-lived, had been powerful enough to drain her. "What did your necklace show you in this night's vision?"

Looking down into my tea, I said, "It wasn't Rowena doing the killing. It was her body, but it wasn't her. I don't know whether she was invaded or if she called on something, but whatever was inside her killed me in that past life and imprisoned me in some sort of fold, forcing me to watch her murder the rest of my family." I pressed into the sides of my cheeks with the pads of my fingers, unhinging my jaw over and over as I thought over the vision Ellie and I had just endured. "It was all a sick game to her," I muttered. "To this imposter."

"We are talking possession of a witch?" Lana clarified. I nodded. "The witch, Rowena, was she still in that body when it was killed?"

I looked to my sister. She was staring down into her tea with a blank look on her face. She'd said to me before we took that first plunge together into the lake that she had wondered if there were two ghosts. Good witch, bad witch.

"Original witch and possessor," I whispered. Then it hit me. "The true witch—it's Rowena. It's *her ghost* who haunts me . . ."

"Wachiwi." My aunt's hand touched mine. "What are you saying?"

"The imposter is the thing that possessed Rowena. It was this entity who filled my spirit with enough rage that I forced my way out from the fold." I thought back to the scene one more time, the way it had looked at me when I'd appeared on that beach. "It thought I was trapped, and when I walked out from that fold, I caught the entity off guard. I was so angry that I didn't just kill it—I cursed it." I clawed at my tangled, wet hair. "I don't understand why I would do such a thing. Why I would keep it around." It was just like Ellie's spell—if I'd burned it, it never would have taken my son. "I should have sent the entity away, but I didn't. It's like I was so angry, and I just wanted it to squeal, so I cursed it to forever live on in pain —to feel every day the pain it had inflicted on my soul." Lana sighed. "But that's not the worst of it. The curse backfired. This demon—it was stronger than I thought. It returned the curse back onto me. Onto our family."

"Great," Lana stated sarcastically. "So, we are dealing with a demon."

"Ish." Ellie said, refusing to look up from her tea. It was then I noticed that her necklace was still glowing, light flashing inside it like it was speaking silently into her soul. "It's hungry for the body it lost. With every death, with every lifetime is grows stronger . . . but it still needs the flesh. If it takes the light of even one more witch, its power could supersede our own, and if it takes the light of two, then we are really screwed; for it would have the strength to completely possess anyone, or anything without invitation." Daring a quick look in Lana's direction, she said, "It's already able to jump us." Finally, her gaze rested on mine. "You're right. Rowena's ghost, the true ghost, she hasn't been haunting you. V, she's been trying to show you."

"Show me what?" I questioned.

"It's feeding on Rowena. It shows itself in her skin to make you afraid of the real version, of the innocent ghost who's been lost in all this. To kill the imposter, we must find where the real Rowena is buried."

I furrowed my brow. "What? How do you—"

"That's all I can say," she said very quietly.

"All you can say?" I questioned, looking from her to my aunt, who had a very concerned look on her face.

When Ellie said nothing more, Lana suddenly transitioned, her expression satiating. She raised her chin, smacked her lips together, and sat back in her chair. Her gaze roamed from Ellie back to me, and she said in her most stony voice, "It is a message from Arianna. I am seeing the image of a mirror. I believe she is saying that it is time you begin scrying again, Olivia."

***

NOBODY SLEPT THAT NIGHT. But it wasn't because our thoughts were reeling over everything we'd just unraveled.

Ellie and I had been getting ready to leave our aunt's house when there was a call from The Dewdrop. One of the waitresses who had stayed late with Patrick was in hysterics. The three of us wasted no time getting to the shop, but once we arrived, I'd wished so much that we hadn't.

What we walked into was something I knew I would never be able to unsee, and the voice that eventually whispered into my ears—it would haunt me for the rest of my days. Even if I was able to end this curse.

"No." The word was spoken so soft, I'd barely heard it escape my aunt's lips. As her hands came up to her mouth, her knees collapsed to the ground.

"We were playing cards . . . We were just having a few drinks," Mona said, her voice so shaken it was hard to make out what she was trying to say. "And then it was like something grabbed him by the neck—and it—it lifted him up into the air." By now she was sobbing, her explanation of what had happened, choppy. "His eyes started *bleeding* and I knew he couldn't breathe. And then his body just fell to the floor . . ."

"NO!" Lana screamed, and for the first time in our lives Ellie and I saw our aunt begin to shake . . . and cry.

My fingers trembled over my mouth as I neared the body. He was stiff as a board, his eyes wide open, and tracks of blood trailing down his cheeks.

"I—I don't know what could've happened," Mona stuttered. "I've already called 911."

"They can't do anything about this," Ellie said shortly. She had tears welling up in the corners of her eyes, and her voice shook with rage as she spat out her next words. "That wretched bitch."

And that's when I heard it; the whisper meant only for my ears.

I told you the rules had changed. And when you fail, Olivia, his light will be mine. His light, along with all the others.

"Fuck off!" I screeched, far too distraught to even care about the other people in the room. "I will not fail!" My bottom lip quivered as I fell to my knees, cupping Patrick's lifeless hand in my own. "You're not getting him. Do you hear me, snake? You're not getting any of them!"

ELLIE

The following weeks were a shit show. We'd thought we'd been safe . . . that our mother's spell was enough to keep that imposter from slitting our throats, but our ignorance of how powerful the thing was that we were dealing with ended up biting us in the ass.

We set Patrick's body on fire and scattered his ashes over the river that my dad fished in. It was what he would have wanted. And when all was said and done, we deposited his wand into a box that sat over my parent's mantle. It was where they went after a witch in our family passed on.

Lana had been specific after that; she didn't want anyone mourning her son any longer.

"It's what it wants," she'd said as soon as his wand was placed in the box. Our entire family had been circled around the mantle as she spoke—including Joe, Derek, and Tyler. "You will do his spirit no good by allowing your hearts to stay broken. We must keep moving forward—we must end this curse. If even one of you refuses to let go, you are giving power to that which we cannot afford to give any more power to. Am I understood?"

We'd all nodded.

It wasn't going to be easy because it wasn't fair. Patrick's death wasn't fucking fair! But she was right. I knew that more than anyone because I alone had been shown in that message my mother had sent to me—just before we found our cousin dead—I'd been shown what we were up against. Even though my mother had been specific—that I wasn't supposed to tell V, because she was supposed to figure this out on her own—I knew this much: if we gave this piece of shit any more power, then we were screwed.

Other than Patrick's departure ceremony, I'd managed to avoid both Joe and Derek, which had been somewhat easy. They figured I needed space to deal with my loss. Even with all the crazy going on, I still had a baby bomb inside me, just waiting to go off and destroy what was left of my marriage; and because witches who were giving birth to other witches tended to grow faster and *glow* a few weeks into their first trimester, I was going to have to tell Joe soon.

Derek had been acting cool, and the band had continued to practice without me for a couple weeks, but I didn't have to be with him to know that he was impatient as hell. He needed to talk to me.

We hadn't spoken since the day I'd called to scream at him, and even though he'd been at Patrick's ceremony, he'd known better than to breach the subject during that time. But time was something I was running out of—not just with the Enrapture breathing down our necks, but we'd also just gotten word that Cindy Bernstein had moved her wedding date up. The band needed me to come back to practice. I could no longer hide.

I wasn't thrilled to talk to Derek about this pregnancy, but I *was* ready to get to the root of what exactly he was hiding from me. V had intercepted me a few days ago, and with some highly useful information regarding the spell ingredients I'd asked her about. Apparently, she'd done some research of her own.

She'd handed me a paper bag filled with 'supplies' and smirked. "Replace these with the real ones. I promise he won't know the difference until it's too late."

I'd cocked a brow at my sister. "How do you know it's a he?"

"Spirits talk," was all she'd said, fading away and heading back to wherever she'd come from that day. Most likely back to Lana's and back to her crystal ball.

Ever since Patrick's death, she'd been doing nothing more than staring into that thing. I just had to hope that she'd see it. It was right there . . . The question was, would she be able to see that it wasn't ever going to be *in* the ball, that it was going to be in the reflection? Only time would tell.

Presently, I'd escaped the retreat and was staring into Derek's opened garage from the safety of my car. I'd purposely arrived a good hour early for our last band practice. Before long he walked out from the kitchen, his eyes beating into mine. I nodded his way and reached for my bag, double checking that the glass jars I'd brought were still wrapped up. Reaching for my violin, I exited my vehicle and walked up to where he stood waiting, his arms crossed in front of his body.

"Hey," he said.

"Hey."

"How are you feeling?"

"Tired, stressed. I throw up at least three times a day."

His head bobbed up and down. "I was going to text you, like, a billion times, but with everything going on—"

"I wouldn't have answered," I said, point blank.

He readjusted his feet, moving his hands to his back pockets. "Have you told Joe?"

I shook my head, lowering my violin to the ground before reaching for the wand in my back pocket. "I will though. I feel like if you really love someone, like *really truly love them*, then you can't have secrets. That you wouldn't want that burden hanging over your shoulders." I dipped my chin and squinted up at him with one eye. "Don't you agree?"

He gulped. "What's this really about, Ellie? Do you have something you want to ask me? Because we don't really have time for bullshit anymore."

I petted my ebony stick gingerly between my fingers. "No, we don't. If I could know for sure that you were prepared to tell me the truth, then I'd say let's just have it out. But here's the thing—I can't know that. And at this point, I just need answers."

He furrowed his brow and began to retort, but before he could question me further, I flicked my wand at his nose, freezing him. "Sorry Der." Then taking a quick look over my shoulders, finding no one in sight, I quickly walked over to the kitchen door and closed the garage door.

I had no idea where Derek was keeping his ridiculous stash of bottled fog and E.O.C., but I had a little bit of time before Candy and Leo showed up. Ever since V had told me what these ingredients were for, I hadn't been able to stop thinking about them. According to her, if Derek had been changing the outlook of his soul, then he would have been doing it from the moment I met him. That just seemed like a really long time to pretend to be someone else.

"The E.O.C. is highly concentrated," she'd informed me recently, "so a little goes a long way. One can easily use one vial for many years. The issue being, of course, that the remedy must be taken daily, and as soon as it wears off, the spell is void."

She'd also said that the Chameleon Effect, as it is called, only takes on certain attributes of the soul being copied. Enough to overshadow his or her own soul. It wasn't like I was only attracted to whoever it was Derek was portraying—I still had a connection with *him*.

"Would it be enough to cover the fact that one is a witch?" I'd asked, piecing together my theories.

"Definitely," V had answered. "In fact, it's primarily why witches used it in the past. It helped us better keep to the shadows during a time of extreme persecution."

Derek and I had known one another for over fifteen years. Besides the fact that it was borderline serial killer to pose as someone else for that long a period, I couldn't figure out what in the name of Diana he would he be trying to keep from me? All four corners pointed to the obvious conclusion—that he was a witch. But again, why would he want to hide that from me?

As for the spell, V had been specific, there were two ways to work it. Both of them included gathering the breath or tears of the person into your wand, which is where the fog would come in and destroy their memory of it all. You could either crush up a strand of hair from the person you were impersonating with a mortar and mix a tiny drop of E.O.C. in with it before dropping the concoction onto your tongue—or for long time users, she relayed that most of them just simply snagged a piece of hair and added it directly into the vial of E.O.C. It was a timesaver and worked just the same. Obviously, if you were impersonating someone else's soul indefinitely, it would have to be the same person.

The first place I started to search out was the basement. It was small, but also as dark as an old, pickled heart, and there were plenty of odd hiding places. Standing in the middle of the unfinished cement floor, I licked the tip of my wand and held it up, whispering a spell I'd had to use a time or two. Because as far as witches go, I was a forgetful one.

"Oi be the one who loses her mind, oi be the one who has tooths to grind. I've got a bottle of fog you see, and a spell ingredient called E.O.C. Oh ye good spirits who hear me call, help me see through into the walls. For be it here or be it there, I cannot find these ingredients anywhere."

I pounded my right foot three times after the spell was spoken, awaiting the flutter of lights that usually flickered around the room after casting a lost and found charm. I waited patiently. I stood very still. Finally, a few seconds later I heard it. Three knocks. But they weren't coming from anywhere in the basement.

I lowered my wand to my side and quickly ran back up the stairs. I turned wildly from left to right. After seeing a few white lights fluttering in the living room, I ran inside and stood just before the television. Once more, I stomped my foot three times. Almost immediately the knocks were returned. This time, I could clearly hear where they were coming from. The bookshelf in the corner.

"What?" I questioned, nearing the shelf.

This was one of those things that hadn't changed since I'd lived in the house. It still contained the same three books, as well as an old camera, a couple pictures of Derek's grandmother, and his tacky beer mug collection.

"I hate to argue with you guys," I said aloud to my spirit helpers, "but I'm not so sure you got this one right."

A small flash of red light pierced my vision, a color denoting that the spirit aiding me with my plight was displeased. Soon after, the camera fell on its side and two mugs slid forward.

I raised my eyebrows. "Perhaps I spoke too soon. Sorry."

I reached for the mugs first. They were heavier than they should've been, and as soon as I looked inside, I heaved a sigh of relief. There they were—two glass jars filled with clouds.

Very carefully, retrieving the bottles of fog, I set them aside and pulled out two equally identical jars from my purse, placing them inside the mugs. Visibly they would appear to be the same thing, and according to my sister, who had a knack for this stuff, bottled calf gas had an eerily similar odor to enchanted fog. The difference being, obviously, in the desired effect. If Derek was using the fog to try and mess with someone's memory, then he was in for a rude awakening with this stuff.

Very carefully tucking the actual fog into my bag, I pulled out a small brown vile and moved on to the camera. I fondled the old Pentax for only about thirty seconds before figuring out the hiding place. Popping open the film compartment, I gleefully pulled out a small brown vile. Floating inside it—a single strand of hair.

"V, you twisted genius," I said, holding the two identical vials.

After making the switch, I held up my wand one last time. I'd already taken his stash, and since these spell ingredients were so rare, I was positive this was all he had, *but* I wasn't going to leave him with any extra actual components to his spell.

"Thank you spirit who I cannot see, you've helped me replace my ex's illegal ingredient with pee." I paused, snickering at my mischievousness. "But because you know I work for the greater good, I think you understand the meaning of should. My next question is this: s*hould* you tell me where the last component belonging to these finds is bared? I believe you know where it is I might be able to find a bit of hair."

The room was quiet. Too quiet. I began to worry that I'd pissed off my little helper. I'd already asked for too much—calling on this spirit to aid me in finding something that didn't belong to me. The only reason I could use this spell at all is because I'd used to live in this house.

Everyone knew it was the gnomes who helped you find your lost possessions, because gnomes, and the fey, loved *things*. It was essential to remember that as far as creatures went, gnomes had short tempers. For that very reason, Mom always said to be short and sweet when requesting services from gnomes or faeries.

I was just about to give up, or fall to my knees and beg, but just then a pair of small, stubby feet imprinted into the carpet. As I looked down, they disappeared—then reappeared, making tracks.

Without a moment's hesitation, I followed the invisible footsteps into the hallway to where they stopped at the bathroom. A second later the bottom drawer of the vanity slid open and an old hairbrush jumped out, like a fish out of water.

I reached for the old blue Goody brush, which contained only a very few sprigs of red hair. On that note, a bit of advice —don't ever let a witch get a piece of your hair. We can do nearly anything with it. It was, after all, how I'd gotten myself in this mess to begin with. If I'd never taken a strand of Joe's hair and attached it to that spoon from her restaurant and made a tracker, then I never would have spied on her that night and thought I'd seen her with another woman. I never would have called Derek in a violent rage, and slept with him, thus getting knocked the fuck up.

Damn this hair—whoever it was.

Very carefully, I skimmed away every single strand from that brush, until it was as bald as I imagined Derek would be after I was done with him. As I stuffed the last of it into a Ziploc baggie and threw it in my bag, I wondered—who was it I'd been drawn to in Derek all this time? Furthermore, what was *his* soul really like?

As soon as I was done, I thanked my helper with an offering of used tin cans—a gnome favorite—reopened the garage door and stood before Derek. There was still one thing I needed, and I had a hunch that if I just stuck my hand in his front pocket . . . yep. I grinned as I stared down at the bottle of mint drops that I'd never once seen him without. I flipped open the top and sniffed—definitely not peppermint.

I stuck the drops in my bag, pulled out one of the glass jars filled with enchanted fog, and dipped my wand into it as though it were ink. I then secured the jar once more and placed it back into my bag. A second later, I tapped Derek's head with the tip of my wand before lowering it down by my side.

He appeared a tad looney for a second; his memory of what had happened before I froze him, *foggy*. As I leaned down to pick up my violin, as if nothing had happened, he wiped a hand over his forehead and steadied himself with a hand against the garage wall.

"You okay?" I asked, apathetically.

"Uh . . . yeah. Just dizzy all the sudden. Um, I'm sorry—what were we talking about?"

"I was just telling you that I was going to tell Joe about the baby after this gig is over."

"Yeah . . . okay," Derek replied. "But we really shouldn't wait any longer than that. She deserves to know."

I brought my violin up under my chin and nodded. "Don't worry, I wouldn't ever intentionally try to hide something from someone I love."

I could feel his energy, his irregular heartbeats. "Right."

He knew I was getting warm.

OLIVIA

I'd been staring at the same spreadsheet displayed on my laptop screen for the past hour. I wasn't actually reading anything, just zoning out.

I'd just been informed that Willow Creek would be working with Spiked during the weddings from now on. That meant that Tyler had no choice but to start talking to me again at some point; in lieu of recent events, I'd decided to stay. Which meant that I'd accepted my job back as the wedding planner.

Patrick's death had definitely been a deciding factor in my final decision. The family and the retreat would need me more than ever; but besides all that, Maddie was in high school. She'd be graduating in just a couple years. It made sense to stay. And I *wanted* to stay.

It was my aunt's throat clearing that eventually brought me out of my funk and the blue light glaring back at me from the computer screen.

I lifted my chin but kept my eyes level as I waited for her to speak.

"You have a walk-in." My gaze slowly moved to hers. "She's waiting at the bar."

"I don't have time for that right now."

Lana made a fist and set it down before me. "No, you don't. You should be in front of your crystal ball, searching for Rowena, but you've chosen to be here. Therefore, you will do what needs to happen *here*."

I scowled. "You know very well that I've been doing nothing else. I've examined that damn ball for hours on end. There's nothing in there. No Rowena, and no body to be found." And no Patrick to be seen.

As the resident ghost whisperer, the load of searching him out had been placed over my shoulders. No one, not even Lana, had asked me to look for his spirit. It was possible he'd already returned home to Latharia, but our family's curse had changed during this lifetime, and what this nightmare entity sought was more than just a dead witch. It wanted our light . . . our souls. And it wanted all of them. If only I could just catch a glimpse of Patty, standing over the grill perhaps or trying to look down the shirt of an unsuspecting female guest —then my heartbeats could settle down just a little.

"There is plenty in there, Wachiwi."

"All I see when I stare into that ball is my own face looking back at me."

Lowering her voice, she stated firmly, and with urgency, "This is about more than you."

I stabbed the desk with a pencil, shattering its tip, before allowing my impatience to speak for me. "Don't you think I know that?"

I paused long enough to see the hurt wash over her—the stain she couldn't seem to get to go away, even though she'd been doing her damnedest to rub the pain from her heart. I set down the ruined pencil and stood up. "Look, this isn't easy for any of us, trying to pretend that his death hasn't ripped us apart. I haven't given up. I promise you, Lana, I will figure this out, and I will see whatever it is my mother wants me to see." Moving so that I was just inches from her, I clasped my hands around her shoulders. "I'm going to save his light, and my mother's, and I'm not going to let *her* take what's left of my son. I don't know how yet, but I'm going to make sure she burns."

Lana's stiff expression didn't budge as I lowered my arms and stepped aside, heading towards the door to go meet with my walk-in.

"It," she said, causing me to pause in my tracks.

I glanced over my shoulder to see that she hadn't moved.

"Don't call it he or she. That thing has never known what it is to be human. To *feel* what we *feel* while inside these bodies. *It* only knows destruction and it feeds from pain. Quit giving it an identity. It doesn't deserve that much."

Though she couldn't see me, I nodded. "You're absolutely right," I agreed, and then I made my way out from the office.

I was busy kneading my hands together as I made my way out into the bar area when I nearly walked directly into another female witch. I didn't notice her face at first—I was too startled by the near collision and distracted by her spiky purple hair.

"Oh my gosh, I'm so sorry," I immediately spat out. "Wait a minute—Cindy? Is that really you?"

The face of the girl I'd known once upon a time smiled, revealing two rows of extremely white teeth. "Yes, it's really me."

"Oh my goddess!" I leaned in for an embrace. "You're all grown up—I can't believe it! What—What are you doing here?"

Little Cindy Bernstein. She was one of those rare witches born into a non-magical family, but she was lucky; her loved ones had been more than accepting. Her mother had followed the rumors in her lady's circle—hairdressers and the like—and had brought her little girl to meet our mother.

I was present the day my mom opened the door to reveal a tiny toe-head of a witch. A white rat cowering at her feet, and her thin, pale arms clutching her mother's leg.

"Hi," her mother had said, looking a tiny bit frightened, but more so of rejection than of what our magic encompassed. "I hate to show up unannounced. I—I didn't know where else to go."

My mother simply looked down at the little witch, and the familiar next to her who was demonstrating both of their apprehensions. Then, with no more than a nod of the head she welcomed them into our house.

Cindy and Ellie were practically the same age, but I honestly don't think Ellie ever even knew our little apprentice existed. My sister was a whirlwind even back then and it was all my parents could do to get her to come down from the stars when it was time for dinner.

Cindy pulled away, while hanging on to my forearms, and as she continued to gaze at me, her smile faded. "I wanted to come say how very sorry I was to hear about Patrick. I can't imagine what you are all going through. Between that and Arianna."

"Yeah . . . it's been a little difficult, but we're coping."

She dropped my arms, then tightened her expression. "I don't suppose you've gotten any updates on your mom—on her condition?"

I shook my head. "She's still in a coma." Then, thinking it over for less than a second, I stated, "But between the goddess, you, and I, it's not really a coma. She's sort of gotten herself locked into a—"

"She's stuck in a spell," Cindy finished for me.

I wrinkled my forehead. "Yes. How'd you know that?"

"Because she told me."

I batted my eyes. "What?"

Cindy sighed, then held up her hand. She waved a finger, laced with a black diamond, in front of my eyes. "The wedding wasn't supposed to be for a few more weeks, and it was supposed to be just her and I and our families—we wanted to keep it simple. But your mother, well, she had other plans in mind." She sucked in a quick breath and gestured to an empty booth by the window. "Do you think we could sit down. This might take a while."

CINDY HAD LEFT two hours ago. Lana had gone off into the woods, and my father was fishing yet again. Ellie had been keeping to herself a lot lately, and I didn't want to disturb her. So, it was just me . . . and all my thoughts.

"Arianna has come to me," Cindy had said. "A circle inside a circle. On the night of the Enrapture I will wed under the tree, and from there you will see. This is what she showed me."

A procession of undefined clues, a puzzle spread out over a long table—none of the pieces seeming to fit together. I continued to pace before the black bowl of water in my parent's house, replaying Cindy's words and trying to figure out why my mother had chosen to reach out to her instead of me. Cindy had attributed it to a great debt. She'd always felt like she owed our family something since my mother had been there so much for her in her youth. A spell based on emotion . . . it was possible.

I centered myself over the scrying bowl, knowing there was one other soul who might know something. Someone who could potentially communicate with the ever-changing wind, who could help me see what I was, so far, blinded to. In attempt to focus, I pulled my hands away from where they were fitted against my skull and looked down.

My breath was shaky, as were my words, but still I whispered, "I know you're in there and I know you're here." I had been feeling his presence ever since that night in the lake. The night he saved me.

My throat tightened and my temples pulsated as the bowl of water remained still. My breath thickened through my nostrils and I refused to move.

"I am sorry. I—I . . . There is nothing I can say or do to undo what I have done." My voice cracked and a hot tear rolled down my cheek. "I shouldn't have left. I shouldn't have danced away. I shouldn't have believed you were gone. Please, Son, I need your help."

I wiped at the moisture on my face, unwilling to look away from the bowl. The room was far too still, too quiet. I was just beginning to believe that I'd given away all my chances when the water rippled.

A familiar scent, lost to me many moons ago, filled the air as a face began to manifest. It was a smell that nearly tore my heart in two. One of dirt, of morning dew, and of the river.

I held my breath, clasping my hands around my mouth. If anyone could direct me towards the path I was seeking, it would be this soul, because this was the soul who had once been inside me.

Just as the lines of the face were beginning to fill in—a reflection took over the water—of a dark cloud forming near the ceiling, and he was once more erased from me. My lips quivered as I stepped back. As the cloud fell, lightning filled the body of it, and I reformed my trembling expression into a fierce scowl. I raised my wand into the air because I couldn't show this thing fear anymore. Weakness meant more murder.

The same sick laughter I'd been hearing for weeks reverberated around my shoulders and the water within the bowl began rippling once more—the beast taking over.

Without a moment's deliberation, I shouted into the water, "What is your game? Who do you claim to be?"

The imposter faded away, replacing its image with a vision of Rowena, staring out over the lost coast. Into the ocean.

"You are *not* her! You cannot fool me any longer!"

A low gurgle mutated into a laugh, then oozed from all corners of the house. It seeped down to the floor and crawled up around my naked ankles until it completely surrounded me.

"It will be the tastiest . . . Your son's light."

Careful not to give the monster what it wanted, I balled my hands into fists. My wand tightening in my grip.

"You've taken your last witch and you will not have my son. He is too strong and too smart; you will never find him."

"You're wrong. I will have your mother's light, your cousin's, yours, and your son's; and when I'm through with all that, I will take all the light from all the remaining witches." As it spoke, the image of a candle burning took shape inside the bowl.

I refused to let this entity see my hesitance, my frustration. The candle depicted in the scene before me blew out, and the demon's laughter grew loud again as it whispered in my ear, *"He is mine."*

"No," I growled. After lifetimes of torture, my voice finally gained the strength it needed to be taken seriously. "NO! You sick, twisted creature—you will not take him away again!" Then I slapped the water bowl with so much force that it flew across the room, the water spilling all over the carpet.

The electricity made from the wretched spirit immediately dissipated, as did the laughter. I lingered, staring at the now upside-down bowl. My heart was racing, my teeth grinding. It wasn't until I moved, inching towards the bowl, that I said to *it*, wherever it was lurking, "All you've done is insure your demise. You've messed with the wrong family, the wrong witches."

273

I thought about leaving the bowl empty. I even thought about chucking it far into the woods, but it wasn't like getting rid of it would erase this darkness. After a few heated moments, I headed out from the house and towards the lake to fill it up once more. If anything, the healing waters would be able to cleanse any unnatural energy left behind.

I'd just sunken my bare toes into the lake, the new sundress I'd bought the other day gripped in my hand to keep it from getting too wet, and I was about to submerge the bowl in the water, purify it, when I heard someone walking up from behind.

From the shuffle, I thought perhaps it was my father, and turned, ready to explain why I was messing with my mother's bowl. When I searched over my shoulders, however, I found it wasn't my father at all. Although it was a male presence who had found me.

"Tyler," I said, backing my wet feet out of the lake and onto the soft grass. My toes were already dirty.

My husband, his hands resting in the pockets of his fitted pants, just stood there, his gaze rested over the surface of the lake.

"Are you here to work in the kitchen?" I asked.

He'd delayed his restaurant opening by about a month because of Patty's passing. Him and Joe and their employ had all stepped up, helping in the kitchen at The Dewdrop until we could find a permanent replacement. Though we all knew it would never be the same. The cinnamon rolls were already less sweet.

Tyler shook his head stiffly, refusing to look my way.

"Did you drop Maddie off? I didn't think she was working tonight, but—"

"You left us."

I exhaled a rickety breath, and fumbling with the bowl in my hands, I nodded. "I did do that. I wish I could undo it."

The color of his face was deepening. My own cheeks burned just looking at him.

"And now you've decided to stay?" His tone was stiff.

"Yes."

Finally, he moved his gaze onto mine. He spit out his next words as though they were nails. "I have spent years trying to hate you. For leaving, for ignoring *his* presence. For deserting our daughter. I have done nothing more than imagine seeing your face again and the words I would say to it."

The tears I had come to know all too well over the past month had returned, and my chin was trembling. "Tyler, I—"

Pointing a finger at my face, he cut me off with his sharp tongue. "No Olivia! It is *not* your turn, *not* yet!" He pursed his lips together, stuffing his hand back into his pocket and looking a bit like a package that was sealed far too tight. "All I want to do is hate you! Honestly, I wished for years it was you instead of him. And then I see you and I—" He zipped his mouth shut, cutting himself off. The pain radiating from him was palpable.

I stopped myself from saying anything, sealing the words against my tongue—that I was *so* sorry. That I still loved him and Maddie, and that I knew our son was still alive. That running was cowardly and all I wanted now was to stay here. Be with my family again. Lay on the couch with him and Maddie and eat shitty frozen pizza on Sunday nights. Instead, I stood there, crying and letting him vent his frustrations.

His face was now beginning to glisten with tears as he took a step back from where he'd been standing. Before he turned away and left me down by the edge of that lake in pieces, he whispered down to me, "You tore up my heart, Olivia. You wrecked me."

OLIVIA

I didn't know where else to go. I just needed to get away.

It was the first time I'd been to see my mother alone. I closed the door to her room and locked it the way Lana always did before making my way over to where she laid like a sleeping beauty. Except she was the witch instead of the princess. When I reached her body, I took her hand into mine, reaching over and brushing her unruly hair from her eyes.

"My mother the broom head."

I dropped my gaze down to the red charm hanging around her neck and automatically sent my hand to slip under it, holding it in my palm. It was warm. With my other hand I touched the one around my neck, it had also become warm. Unclasping my golden chain, I allowed the key to hover over my mother's lock. Sure, we'd already tried to unlock her heart twice and it had failed both times, but what was the harm in trying one last time.

"For when the sun shines on her cheeks, she glows," I whispered, repeating a line my mother used to whisper into my ears when I was a small child. And then, as though it was awakened, the charm began to swing in circles, much like a dowsing pendulum.

"Mother . . ." I whispered. A chill separated my heart beats as the little blue key charm inserted itself into her lock. "What do you want to show me?"

The door behind me swung open and I turned to the empty hallway. It had been bustling with nurses just moments ago. Right then, I knew something had changed, that the world on the other side of that opened door wasn't the same one I had just walked through a second ago.

I looked from the hall back to my mother. "You did this," I whispered.

She couldn't answer, but I was as sure of her magic as I was of the fact that there had to be answers waiting for me on the other side of that door. Leaving my necklace with hers, I reluctantly made my way back towards the doorway, which seemed more like a portal than anything now. I stuck my head out and found it unusually quiet; where there should have been the sound of monitors running and nurses making their rounds, it was as silent as a cemetery at midnight, and just as dead.

I walked through the door and over to the nurse's station. I'd already decided I was alone, an assumption that was proved false as soon as I took a few more steps. There was one other soul present, and as I grew closer to where she was sitting behind the desk, she lifted her head.

"Rowena." Her name came out as only a whisper.

She didn't answer me, instead she stood. Her expression was neutral, and I knew at once that this was the *real* Rowena. The true witch, not the imposter. The ghost, not the demon. As I continued to stand there, a tingling energy surging through me, she lifted a translucent arm and gestured to the elevator.

I turned and looked back at the hall, towards my mother's

room. It had faded to black. Returning my gaze to her, I stated, "You want me to follow you?"

She nodded.

"My mother . . . she brought me to you?"

Again, Rowena very slowly nodded her transparent head, then gestured to the lift. I did as I was instructed and followed her into the elevator, watching her every move as she pushed the button for the main floor. As we stood there together, I spied on the ghost out of the corner of my eye.

"How did this happen?" I questioned, hoping she might grant me some sort of answer. "Did something go wrong with your magic? To summon a demon at all is—"

"Shhhh," she said, turning my way only to place a transparent finger over my lips. A chill ran down my spine.

The doors opened and Rowena took only a second to look at me before walking out onto the main floor. I followed her through the empty hospital. The experience was eerily similar to the dreams I used to have when I use to sleepwalk . . . back when I was a child. It was as if the hospital had tilted on its side and emptied out everyone but Rowena and me.

I was on guard as we walked through fluorescent lit hallways, the ghost's dress soaked from the waves that killed my mother and sister, leaving streaks of moisture on the shiny floors.

"Rowena," I said, fighting to get her to communicate with me. "My sister has said that the demon who took you—that it has you buried some place. That to kill it we must find your body."

She glanced my way but said nothing. Instead she paused before a set of giant wooden doors that opened of their own accord. My heart sank when I peered into the room. It was the hospital's chapel.

"What is this?" I asked, staring at the witch whose demon had used religion as a weapon to kill.

Rowena said nothing. Instead, she walked inside and stopped before a giant bowl held up by a wooden stand. Her frame was still as ice. From there she looked down into the bowl and stated very softly, "Demons are born, Olivia. Energies are made."

My lips parted in awe of what she'd just said; and I felt, suddenly, as if I'd just gotten hit in the head by a giant rock. Energies . . .

"It isn't difficult for a witch to get rid of a demon, or a malevolent spirit. We simply encase them in spells, open a space void of life, then send them in to suffocate. But energies are different. To smother them, we must understand how they came to be. We must find what makes them tick and drain their source. Or in this case, set the life-force it is feeding from, free."

I remained planted, frozen, lost in thought.

"It's the water you've brought me to. You're here to show me how to kill it."

"I will show you as much as I can. The rest is up to you to uncover." As she spoke the water rippled. "In the pines, Olivia. In the pines."

A stabbing pain jolted my heart, and my senses were lit on fire as I studied her pale face. "What does that mean?"

"You will see." She pointed to the water.

I made my way very slowly towards the rippling water. My gift was divination . . . communication with the spirits. I was beginning to understand, more than ever, that nothing in life is accidental.

And then my thoughts were shut off as it all faded to black.

WHEN I CAME to voices were coming from all around me—clunky shoes running over wooden boards. There was a mustiness in the air, like that of wool, firewood, and dirt. If I'd had to guess, I would've said I'd been swallowed up by a black hole, shrouded in darkness; but somewhere, not far, I could hear the sweet sound of children laughing.

"Shhhh, I heard something over here," came a voice from the other side of wherever I was hidden. It was a little boy.

I was curled into a ball and as I pulled my arms around my legs tighter, I instinctively felt that I needed to stay hidden. Next to me was a child's ghost and she was trying not to laugh.

"I told you they would find us here," she was saying. "Next time we hide where I say we hide. And you know something, I think that boy, John, likes you."

"He pulls at my hair," I whispered back.

"Exactly," said the ghost.

"I hear breathing," a little girl's voice echoed from the other side of where we were hiding.

"Okay. One, two, three!"

A cabinet door flew open and light streamed in, along with an eruption of more childish laughter. Two pairs of tiny arms dove in and pulled me out. They moved so fast that I couldn't make out their faces.

"I told you! She's hidden herself in the food cabinet! Okay Rowena, you're it now. Close your eyes and count the stars!"

I stood, shuffling to my feet. As I did, my legs grew and the room I was standing in changed. Years had passed. My hand reached down and grabbed a lacy shawl from where it was lying over the table. There was a ghost spying on me from the corner. A different one this time.

"You look ravishing. I ask of you, witch girl, is it for love, or is it for lust?"

A knock came at the door and my legs moved automatically towards it, stopping only to check myself in the mirror hanging on the wall. Reflected to me was a young and beautiful Rowena, and she was ensuring that everything on her face was in order. My hearted fluttered at what I saw in the reflection. This must have been many years before she was turned into a foul murderer. Her irises were green and sparkly, like emeralds, and her skin was light but vibrant. Her long hair was halfway pulled back, and when she smiled, one could have easily accused her of being in love.

"You know very well the answer to that." Returning her attention to the ghost, she continued. "I've loved this man since I was seven-years-old."

The ghost giggled, then disappeared, leaving her to swing open the rickety old wooden door of the small, two-bedroom room house.

"Hello, John Wiley," she said as she greeted him. "What is it that you could possibly want at this hour of the day?"

The young man who stood before her had a blurry face, as if the memory was faded in parts.

"I've come to ask if I might escort you on a walk through the woods tonight?" His masculine voice was so thick with echoes that I couldn't place it, but I could feel the way it made Rowena's heart stir.

"Now now, John. What makes you think I would be interested in holding *your* hand under the moon?"

She was flirting.

"If it doesn't please Miss Rowena to be in my company, then I shall leave."

She reached out, touching his elbow as he stepped away. "Wait! I do believe I might enjoy a walk under the stars tonight. How about you pick me up as soon as my mother begins to glow."

"Your mother? I thought your mother and the rest of your family were out of the village until Sunday next."

"The moon, silly. My other mother."

"Is the moon not a man?"

Her smile grew. "No, John Wiley. The moon is a huntress."

Once again, the room changed. As it did, I saw glimpses of Rowena's mind, her memories: her and her John Wiley, arms linked, walking through the trees under the moonlight, night after night. Him pressing her against a tree, and the two of them undressing one another until their backs hit the ground.

"They call you witches," he'd said, through breaths as thick as worsted wool. Their naked bodies intertwined on the forest floor.

"That's because we are," she'd answered, gasping for air in between bursts of pleasure.

The visions hinged forward in time. Rowena squeezing a familiar hand as she screamed during childbirth—Ella's. Before long, out came a baby, a familiar witch glow to it as it was placed into its mother's arms.

The scenes were moving faster, swirling so quickly that I could barely see them. Amongst them was an image of Rowena and John marrying under a tree, light binding them together. Then one of a little boy running around in the yard, chasing a rabbit.

They lived in a small village just off a forest. There were many log wood homes and paths in between made of dirt. At some point, Rowena and her little boy walked through the town, a stone hitting her in the back of her head. She cursed before turning in the direction of where the rock had come flying. It was a teenage boy, surrounded by four other boys his age, and all I could hear in the muffled background noise was the word, "witch," as it flowed from his mouth.

I felt her discontent, but not as much as I felt her fear. Within seconds she was surrounded by the young men. She could not use her magic without consequence, and her husband was not there to keep her and her child safe. He'd gone with her father, to search out a new place for them to live. The people there were beginning to grow wary of who was living next to them. Their man of God had been preaching for years against the evils of sorcery. Most recently he had been spreading rumors that there were witches amongst them, sons and daughters of the devil. The villagers were growing superstitious, and like poisonous weeds, threats were beginning to grow around Rowena and her kind.

"We are only out to get my child his medicine," she said. "Please do back off."

"From where do you get this medicine?" the same teenager who'd thrown the stone asked. "The old hag who lives in the woods? Are you the devil's mistress?"

"Mama," said the little boy. He was wheezing.

"It's okay, son." I could sense it. She was actively trying not to use her goddess given gifts. There were too many witnesses. So many people of the village were looking in on this disturbance, yet no one was helping her.

"Rowena!" a strong female voice shouted, finally breaking the crowd away from where it was beginning to suffocate her. Bodies parted and air entered back into her chest as she looked out to see a familiar face. Ella. "Is there a problem here?" Ella shouted. She was as beautiful as she was in this lifetime, and just as radiant.

Rowena immediately pulled her son from the circle and walked towards her. "No no, just a little misunderstanding. Right boys?" she asked, still moving quickly, a quiver to her voice.

"It is no longer safe here," she whispered as soon as she was in step with Ella. "The minister has finally won. We are going to have to move. John and Father will be back soon, and from there we must make haste."

"I will spread the word," Ella whispered back, the three of them walking swiftly away from the town.

The memory shifted, but not that far into the future. The wind spoke, telling me that only a week or two had passed. The moon was full, and the air smelled of fire and sweat.

I was moving, or Rowena was moving, quickly; a merry go round made from a human chain. She was in a circle. We were dancing around a small fire, sage burning between us as we held hands and sang, bringing down our mother moon. Then the vision shifted forward, as we dispersed back into the village, preparing to gather our families and leave in the night . . . but we were too late.

There were Xs on most of our doors, and screams coming from the sisters and brothers who had already entered to find their homes empty. At that point everything began to spin. Rowena brought me with her. Into her empty home, and then as she ran, barefoot, through the town, until she stopped at a tree. From there a dark cloud descended over her shoulders. Two pairs of feet were dangling over her head . . . her husband and her son. They'd been murdered, along with whoever else hadn't gotten away in time.

A loud scream shook the earth as it bellowed from her lungs, then the earth met her knees as she dropped to the ground. Once more there were voices, too many to count or sift through.

"Come Rowena, there is nothing we can do for them now." They were the last words I heard before the sensation of hands grabbing under her arms and lifting her up took us away and into the next memory.

From there on out it was pain. The witches, and what was left of their families, had escaped to the west coast and built their own village. It was not a safe time, they decided, to mingle with those born without the light.

Visions flashed before me of Rowena running into the woods offshore, pounding her fists into the trees, cursing her light—tears so hot they were scalding, burning her face. There was so much screaming from these scenes, so much madness. Eventually a cyclone picked me up from where Rowena laid near death on the forest floor, but I didn't fly away until I heard her say, "Take me from here. I pray ye angels, take me from this body, take me from this pain."

Next, I was sitting on a rock out in the reef of the lost coast, and the all too familiar smell of salt water filled my nostrils.

Rowena's heart was cold and empty. There were colliding winds inside her, and they were harsh, like a storm brewing on the most frigid of winter's days. Her hands were clasped in her lap and she was staring out into the distance. Something was wrong though; I could have sworn there was no heartbeat in this body.

"You missed the circle last night," someone said from behind.

"I didn't feel like going."

"You've been keeping to yourself," the same voice echoed. I could not see who was speaking.

"I've been in hell."

A hand slid over her shoulder and ice trickled through her soul. "Rowena, my dearest, please look to me."

Rowena turned, and instead of viewing the scene from her eyes, I was an outsider looking in. I recognized my mother immediately, the concern radiating from her as she stared at this witch. The love and beauty I'd seen in the younger version of Rowena had completely fallen away and what was left was hard and angry. *She's already gone*, I thought to myself. But where had she gone? And what was inside her? Rowena's ghost had failed to show me the most important part.

"You claim to see into past worlds. You say we all held hands and brought down the goddess to fill us with light. What kind of goddess would make us endure this kind of pain? Can you tell me that?"

"She told us there would be struggles. She warned us that those born without witch light would not understand—"

"Or it was all simply a disgusting lie spun from the mind of a sinner?"

My mother, quiet but strong, placed a hand over Rowena's heart, then almost immediately flinched. I could tell, she knew something wasn't right.

"What reason would I have to lie to you, child? You are in pain; you mustn't let this emotion define you. It is what evil wants."

"Evil." The way Rowena's mouth moved as the negativity inside her spoke, one would have thought it was the name of its lover. "For years the villagers have called me evil. Perhaps I have only been brainwashed by witches into believing something untrue. Perhaps *I am* the devil's mistress."

"Rowena," my mother pleaded. "The truth is inside you; you mustn't cover it with lies. Listen to your heart. What does it say?"

For a moment, the entity living inside her body softened Rowena's eyes, and it took my mother's hand in its own. A full minute passed as the two shared in each other's silent company, but it was the creature who finally broke the silence when it dropped my mother's hand.

"I no longer have a heart," it said, Rowena's black dress dragging over the rocks of the reef as it walked away.

I remained there, in the memory of the lost coast, watching glimpses of Rowena's lost life. It was horrific. The negative energy possessing her body began to stalk the other witches, one by one, killing them—reading off lines from the Bible they'd heard the villagers use to curse them over the past years. I watched in agony as I was forced to see a replay of what Ellie and I had already been shown, of the beast inside Rowena killing my sister and mother right before my spirit walked out from her hiding spot and cursed the entity.

When it was over, I saw something that I hadn't been able to see the first time I witnessed this horrific scene. I saw Rowena's spirit step out from her body after she'd been killed.

As my own soul began to drift away, back into rotation, Rowena's ghost—the real Rowena—shouted up at me, "This is all wrong! The curse was turned. It's kept me here along with *it*!"

My spirit, beginning to fade against the night sky, shouted down to her, "In my next life, you will find me! We will fix this! Do not let it get to you!"

"You will not understand! All this will be forgotten!"

"I promise you—" But my words were lost as my spirit was taken back into the fold. Then, as it so often did at the end of a dream, it turned back to black.

When I reopened my eyes, I could once more hear the beeping and hustling outside my mother's opened hospital door. I sat up from where I'd shrunken down into the chair by her bedside, and when I looked up Lana was staring at me from the other side of my mother's bed.

"When did you get here?" I asked, blinking as I tried to sort out the present from the past.

"Just minutes ago."

There was a creak in my neck and I rubbed it out, sitting up. "What time is it?"

"Nearly five o' clock. Where have you been, Wachiwi?"

"With Rowena," I answered. My aunt raised her brow. "Not the imposter—the *actual* Rowena. Lana, we've had this all wrong."

Her expression softened as she examined my last response. "How do you mean?"

"I mean—I've completely misunderstood everything

287

about her. They hung the people she loved the most. They took away her love." I paused, the scenes Rowena had just shown me were still fresh, still moving around my head as though on a movie reel. "My mother used to tell me *not* to call them ghosts, for that is not what all of them are. Many of the souls I see are drifters, some are memories, and a majority are guides, but only a few are actually ghosts. Ghosts are lost. But Rowena isn't lost as the others are—she knows who she is. She's lost only in the sense, that just as us, she is cursed. Lana, Rowena didn't summon a demon—she—" It was on the tip of my tongue, the name of the creature.

I closed myself off from the hospital room, sinking into my mind and remembering a time from when I was little. When my mother had taken Ellie and I on a 'hunt' as she'd called it. Someone, a neighbor who knew what we were, had called on her for help. They had a ghost that needed redirecting, or at least that's what they thought. But it wasn't a ghost and it was definitely not a spirit. It was an energy that had been created by dead space and negativity, perhaps emotional pain even—and it was vengeful. She took us with her so that we could learn to kill these things.

"You mustn't ever show them fear, for it only gives them strength," she'd said, lighting the end of the sage stick in her hand with her mere breath. "When it comes to killing them, all you must do is stand firm, and undo the energy from which it first came."

"But how do you undo it?" I'd asked, Ellie's little hand cradled in mine.

"Simple. Tear open its heart with sage smoke or steel— they are also allergic to cedar—and ensure the rhythm of the hearts of the ones who created it return to their natural beats."

"What happens if you can't mend the hearts of the living who made it?" I'd asked.

The way she'd looked down at me, I should have known,

for it wasn't an answer she was giving me. It was a warning. "Then it will return over and over again, and it will get stronger each time."

Staring at my aunt, I said with unfettered certainty, "Rowena didn't summon a demon. She was taken by a Freddie."

Lana had slipped the tip of her finger between her teeth and was biting down. "Well," she stated, the shock I'd been presuming to see, lost on her, "that's unfortunate. Did Rowena tell you where she was buried?"

I shook my head. "She skipped over so many details. In fact, I never even saw her, or the Freddie, murdering me in that past life. All I know for sure is that the pain of losing her loved ones got the best of her and she allowed this thing to take over her heart." I paused, thinking over the last of it all. "When my spirit came out from where it was hiding and cursed that awful *thing,* it cursed me back, which has been the reason behind all the untimely deaths our family has experienced in every lifetime. It latched onto Rowena's soul as well, forcing her spirit to be left behind. Forcing her to become a ghost." I bit down over my thumb and stared over my shoulder. "It doesn't make sense . . . that shouldn't have happened. The curse should have stuck with me, but *her* soul should have been free to go."

"Normally, yes."

I looked up at my aunt, a tiny bit annoyed at how calm her demeanor was.

"Where then does this leave us, Wachiwi?"

I lowered my gaze and stared at my mother. "Truth?" I saw Lana nod out of the corner of my eye. "Other than we have a wedding to prepare for, I have no idea."

ELLIE

B rilliant. Cindy fucking Bernstein's wedding. Here . . . tonight. Same night as the Enrapture, and quite possibly the end of one or more witch's goddess given lights. Including my mother's. No, I wasn't freaking out. Not one bit.

At least Joe had been too busy with the food she was preparing to bend in and give me more than a peck on the cheek earlier. She hadn't had a chance to look up at me, therefore she hadn't noticed a thing out of the ordinary—like the fact that I was radiating light from every pore in my body. Her ignorance wasn't going to last for much longer, though, and neither was me being able to avoid her. Even if we were able to kill this asshole who was haunting our world, I was still going to find myself up against another obstacle.

"Nice glow, babe," Candy said, sauntering over and stealing a truffle fry from the plate of food I'd scored from my niece. Maddie was so wicked cute—all the servers were dressed in matching witch uniforms. She was so adorable that I could've shot rainbows out of my ass. It almost created a feeling inside . . . a sentiment, one could argue, of looking forward to watching my own kid grow up.

"Fuck off," I retorted, slapping Candy's hand away from my plate. "Get your own, I'm starving."

She chuckled and leaned back against an amp. "So, what's that mean—the glow? That you're definitely having a little witch."

I chewed on my last bite like a cow eating grass. "Yes."

Then, just as if he'd been cued in by the god of everything shitty, Derek wandered onto the stage, coming towards us with one of the most frazzled looks I'd ever seen painted on his face. His mere existence pissed me off, but still, I was jittery with excitement because he'd had to have come across my booby trap already. There was no question about it.

"What up?" Candy asked. "We about ready?"

"Uh . . . yeah," he said, looking anywhere but at me.

"You see this shit?" Candy pointed at me. "You see what you did? She's like a goddamned light bulb."

Derek attempted to shake it off, his hands tucking stiffly into his tight black jeans. "Yeah. Hey Elle—" He lifted his chin up in my direction but was careful not to look me in the eyes. "Have you had a chance to talk to Joe yet?"

"About the me being pregnant thing?" I questioned, plucking one of my fries from Candy's hands.

"No. I mean—I'm assuming you're still waiting to tell her after tonight. I just mean—"

"Spit it out, Der," Candy said.

"Never mind." His head lowered down as if in shame and he walked away.

Candy and I scrutinized his behavior as he made his way over to the mic to test it out.

"Why's he being all weird?" she asked.

I continued to feed my little fetus beast as a sly smirk curled into my lips. "Beats me." But I was pretty sure that it had something to do with a few lost ingredients, and a bit of truth that I would see if he would just look up at me. Everyone knew that the eyes were the window to the soul, and since I'd stolen his chemistry set, he no longer had the elixir he needed to hide his true identity.

The party got started pretty quickly after that. Leo sat behind his drums, Candy took her guitar and stood behind the mic, and Derek stood up front—holding both his guitar and my violin. Other than a few years and a couple giant life changes, it could've been 2005 and in a dive bar. I couldn't wait to play with these weirdos. I hadn't realized until recently how much I missed our band.

Just before he kicked it off, Derek got into his band persona—caressing the souls of the audience in a way that only he knew how to do. He had this thing about unwinding stupid little stories about each song as if they were balls of yarn that needed detangling.

"I know it's a wedding, witches—" As soon as he said the word *witches,* the audience exploded. Wands and broomsticks raised in the air, and they all hooted and hollered. Then there was me, standing back with my arms crossed, a grin on my face that I could no longer contain. "I thought we'd start out the night with one of the first songs I ever wrote, *The Sound of Souls Parting.* Maybe you think it's sad and all that bullshit, but the thing about souls drifting apart is that they always come back together." He paused, his cheek turning just enough my way that I knew the glance was meant for me. "It's not really a sad song, you see. In fact," --he tapped his foot three times on the ground, signaling for Candy and Leo to start picking up the beat— "if you're lucky enough to have someone to share your soul with, then you shouldn't ever be unhappy, because even if you can't live beside them in whatever life or universe you live in, you're never truly alone, and you're never apart forever."

I'd never heard him talk about that song before. To be honest, I couldn't remember the last time we'd played it. We definitely hadn't practiced it in his garage over the past few weeks. He was just lucky Candy and Leo remembered all the notes.

Candy's fingers gently strummed the beginning melody as Leo set the pace, then Derek moved in on the mic and started unfolding the lyrics that had always somehow haunted me.

"*The rip, the tear, we've been here before . . . The fall, the break, the last look on your face . . . But you never hear it, not even for a pace . . . I am left standing, alone in this empty case . . . The sound of souls parting, echoing all over the place . . .*"

I was so lost in the song that I barely took notice when the tempo picked up and Derek lunged forward, chucking my violin far up into the air. Ignorant of my daydreaming, he grabbed his guitar from around his belly and strummed away alongside Candy.

"Ellie—go!" one of the backstage persons yelled at me, jolting me upright and causing me to gather my footing as I took my cue.

I ran from where I was hiding backstage and lifted into the air just in time to grasp the violin handle in my hand and tuck the instrument under my chin. The wand in my other hand transformed into a bow, and I slowly fell back down to the stage as I began to play. Derek's voice streamed out into the crowd, and something in my gut told me to listen to his song. Like, really listen.

OLIVIA

The forest as we knew it had been rearranged—the scene set for Cindy Bernstein's wedding. I had never seen so many witches in one place in all my life. The air was sparkling with magic, and the laughter of the fey was in the ears of every living, breathing soul.

Appetizers were being flown around by witches on broomsticks and The Wicked Incantations were kicking it off. Derek had just chucked Ellie's violin up into the air, and even with her recent glow, my sister didn't hesitate to fly up and catch it just as she always did. Everything was running smoothly. Just as Cindy had requested, we were having the reception first and would be heading off to the marrying tree as soon as the moon appeared . . . only an hour before the Enrapture.

Cindy had been specific the day she'd come to me. My mother had sent to her a vision of her wedding night under the stars, or under the meteor shower to be exact. She would bring witches a plenty and together they would join around our family as we drew my mother back down to our circle. Since I hadn't had any real clear revelations between that last day at the hospital and now, I could only hope that at some point in the next couple hours, I would gain the confidence I would need to face whatever was lying inside those magical circles Cindy had seen in her head.

In the end, this was all up to me. I was the one who had cursed that Freddie—an energy that had grown so strong that it would take all these witches to help me kill it. I was the only one out of us all who could truly stab this creature in its heart.

Exhausted from the long day I'd already had, I lowered my clipboard. All my assignments as wedding director had been checked off. The sun was beginning to set and since my job was done, I decided to take a walk.

I removed my shoes and I crept along the creek, the grass brushing through my naked toes. Before long I came upon Lana, who was camped out next to the trickling water, drinking a tea laced with whiskey and braiding together a handful of sage.

"Hey there," I said, taking a seat next to her. "Did you get some food?" Outwardly, she'd been standing strong since Patty's death, but her clothes were starting to look a bit looser.

"I did," she answered, handing me a bundle of sage. Taking in my appearance, she stated, "My goodness, you look beautiful, Niece."

"Thanks," I replied. It was a black shimmery dress I'd bought while with Maddie the other day. She'd said it made me look powerful and I could use as much of that as I could muster.

I separated the plant Lana had handed to me and was preparing to braid it together, when I noticed she'd held out her drink and was waiting for me to take it.

"Oh. No, thank you," I said.

"Don't give me that. You used to drink plenty of whiskey by my side. I think you may need it tonight more than ever."

I stared at her for a full minute before caving. "Fine. To

Patrick," I said, lifting it into the air. I took a sip and immediately winced, coughing as I lowered it into my lap. "Goddess, how do you drink this stuff and continue to stand up straight?"

Lana smiled and pulled out her wand.

"Right. Sobering spells."

I took another swig before handing it back to her. "Too bad Joe isn't a witch. Maybe if she could've spelled herself sober after a few drinks then she wouldn't have had a problem."

"Naw." Lana shook her head as she finished with one smudge stick and went on to the next. "It still requires restraint to stop and spell oneself sober. We may have goddess light, Wachiwi, but we are still somewhat human. Even we have ailments." She stopped what she was doing and gave me her full attention. "Are you ready for tonight, little witch? Do you know what it is you must do?"

To be honest, the only thing keeping me going was Lana's fearless nature. Even in the way she posed the question, she made it seem as if my answer didn't mean life or death.

I looked up into her stone cold, black eyes. "Truth?"

She remained still.

"I've no goddamned idea."

She pursed her lips tighter together and nodded her head. "You will be fine."

I studied the way she held herself—the way she still managed to hold her head up and carry herself around with those steel bones of hers. "You know already, what's going to happen. Don't you?"

I could almost feel her inside me, searching through my soul. Finally, she gathered the pile of smudge sticks she'd made into her lap and stood, the ice in her glass clinking. "The future is uncertain." She gestured to the sage in my hands. "Continue to wrap them, it will clear your energy." She winked as she said the next part. "Perhaps even show you how to open a door or three."

I watched her as she walked away. Those words were familiar . . .

As her speech echoed in the back of my head, my surroundings begin to spin, and the world tilted on its side. "What the—" I started, but cut myself off, suddenly caught in an unwelcome epiphany.

I lifted the herbs she'd handed me to my nostrils and sniffed at them. Immediately I recoiled, dropping the leaves to the ground as though I'd just realized the herbs were covered in maggots.

"Foul enchantress!" I cursed, snapping my head in the direction my aunt had just taken leave. But she was already gone, and the world was already beginning to fade in and out —the colors bleeding into one another as though it were all a work of oil splashed with paint thinner. "Lana—no!" I exclaimed, but no one could hear me. She'd made damn sure of that. "This is not the time or place!"

When we were children, Lana and my mother used to argue about our aunt rubbing a bit of what we called flying ointment on our skin. Witches used to use it to open their third eyes, to see beyond the veil directly before them. It was trippy. Lana had insisted it was a rite of passage for every young witch, to see clearly into the other world; but our mother hated the stuff. She thought it was a barbaric practice, as well as dangerous. However, that hadn't stopped Lana from using it on both Ellie and I once upon a time.

Taking our little arms into her hands, she'd rubbed a very small amount into our skin, all the while saying, "And from this you will see . . . perhaps even open a door or three."

Very carefully, pulling the herbs up by the stems, I inspected them. She'd fooled me, causing me to see it as sage, but it was not that. It was instead a small bouquet of plants, namely mandrake and belladonna—poisonous and known for their hallucinogenic properties. Cunning as she was, she'd rubbed them in flying ointment and ensured I handled them well.

I clenched my teeth together and threw the plant down to the ground, springing up to my feet—but as I rose, I couldn't stop, and before I could gather what was happening, feathers sprung out from my skin and my arms lifted into the air—my body shrinking.

"No," I whimpered. "Not the owl."

It had happened the last time as well. I'd turned into an owl and Ellie had been a wolf. Just like our spirit helpers.

Gaining speed, I spotted Lana down below. She was making her way towards the food tents where Joe and Tyler were working relentlessly to keep the witches fed. I swooped down by her and prepared to shout at her, but all that erupted from my mouth were a series of hoots.

She smirked, glancing at me. "You gave me no choice; time is not on our side. I've had to ask someone else to help you lift that veil from over your eyes—someone I wasn't quite sure you would allow yourself to see otherwise. Now off you go, little witch. Search out your truths."

Truths! I prepared to counter, but my fierce argument remained as owl speak.

I was furious, but what could I do now? I'd been transformed by Lana's magic and lost in a world of delusion. As the paint continued to swirl and drip, my aunt's face changed from her own into Rowena's; but it wasn't the ghost I was looking at—this poor soul who was stuck in a separate dimension because of the Freddie's curse. No, it was instead the beautiful young woman I had seen getting ready to open the door and greet her future love in the memory she'd shown me back at the hospital.

"Oh! there you are, Lilly Pad," she said, looking up at me. "I've been searching for you."

Her arm reached out as mine often did for Delila to take her perch, but I just continued to stare down at her while flapping my feathered wings out to the side.

"Come on now, don't be silly." Rowena smiled—a large toothy, happy smile.

I took a moment to adjust as the edges of the world straightened out. I was still an owl, and as I cocked my round, feathered head to the side, I saw that everything that had been there a second ago was gone. It was just Rowena and I and an empty retreat. Because of the wedding everything had been shifted around, the cabins magicked into the woods, but in this moment, everything was back in place—and as far as I could tell we were the only souls in sight.

My aunt's speech reverberated through my head. It didn't take me long to realize that I needed to follow whatever path was directly in front of me, because it was only down one road that I was going to find my truth. So, reaching for Rowena's arm with my talons, I lowered my wings, consenting for her to take us wherever she intended to go.

"It's pretty here, isn't it, Lilly? Enchanted is this place . . . magical. I am unsure of how we slipped into this fold, but I suppose all that matters is that we return before the moon rises back at home."

Fold . . . Rowena understood about the folds? I tried to speak, but still all that came out were hoots.

Rowena turned to me, her footsteps leading us inward of the forest. "What are you trying to say, Lilly? Are you afraid? Please don't be. We will be back to our time very soon. It appears we've wandered sometime in the years that lay before us. It is very strange."

She led us into the forest, her black boots crunching over pinecones and sticks—and that's when one scene ended another began. The wind changed, sweeping across my face. I stood as myself once more, in the black dress that made me look like a witch and watched as Rowena and her owl began to disappear into thin air.

"Wait . . ." The word balanced over my tongue. I could've sworn she glanced back over her shoulder, but whether she saw me it didn't matter—she was already transitioning back into her time.

I was just beginning to sort out why I'd been given such a strange and jolted experience—the sounds of the wedding party wafting back into this part of this forest, bringing with it my sister's violin against Derek's voice—when something happened that caused my heart to stand still.

His voice seeped out from the trees, and as it did, I was overcome by the feeling of a thousand needles poking from every inch of my skin; and my tongue, still laced with whiskey, felt swollen. Though it had aged since last I'd heard it, it was a voice I would know on any given day. And it was no longer a whisper in the wind.

"She actually did that—Rowena. She walked through time, following ghosts as they traveled here and there. What was it you used to say? That it was like an envelope? That you could bend your fingers into the folds of what was inside and reach for different dimensions. Rowena felt the same way, except she actually walked through those curtains from time to time."

Shame washed over me—I was *afraid* to turn around and face him. "You're not real . . . None of this is. It's part of the delusion."

"What is delusion really?" he questioned, sounding just like Tyler. "But that's not what this is."

My blood froze in my veins. "This is the Freddie messing with me. It wants me weak."

There was a small rustle of leaves, as though someone was

readjusting themselves over the forest floor. "Now that part is where you are wrong, Mom. Right now, the Freddie is nowhere in sight. It's allergic to cedar, remember. It is why Grandma chose this patch of land for your work tonight, for there is not only pine trees, but cedar. The Freddie cannot stay in the trees for very long."

A very soft heated breath exited my parted lips and I turned. He sat on a fallen tree; a stick made of beechwood lying over his lap. He wasn't the young child the Freddie had robbed me of. He was now a young man.

"Thaden." His name was shaky as it exited my mouth, and my throat tightened as tears sprung into production.

"We don't have much time," he said calmly.

His comment barely registered as I worked on moving my feet out from the cement they seemed to be encased in. As I neared him, my hand reached out to touch his. My chin quivered as I muttered the only word I could find. "How?"

He grasped my hand, the rest of his body unmoving from the log. I could feel the blood pumping in his palm, the magic I'd passed down to him. He gazed up to the tops of the trees towering over our heads. "I pulled from it—the extra magic in the forest. I don't think there has ever been this many witches gathered in one place other than the planet where we were born." Returning his attention to me, he pulled me down so that I was sitting next to him. "I have watched you struggle. Watched *it* play with you as it played with me."

My heart sunk. "I know it was the Freddie who took you."

"No. It was the Freddie who persuaded me to take myself."

I tried to stifle it, but I couldn't. A cry escaped my mouth. I just couldn't believe I was really looking at my son. I shook my head as I said, "This is some kind of evil joke. You're not here. It's—it's not real. It's the poison—"

"The poison has worn off. Lana only gave you a sparse

amount; enough to relax you, to help you let go of disbelief. I am here, Mother, as I always am. It's just that now you can see me."

He squeezed my hand. In his touch the strings of my heart came undone, and my lungs suddenly filled with the breath of the wind. My chest lifted, and he said very softly, "It's okay. You can let go of it all. That's what all this is about." Dipping his chin and looking up at me with a pair of eyes that haunted me every time I looked in the mirror, he said, "You can do this, Mom."

"*Do what?* What am I supposed to do? What am I supposed to let go of?"

Still squeezing my hand in his, he said, "The pain of the past." When I didn't reply, he continued, "Your Freddie is highly intelligent, you cannot go into that circle without the truth."

I shook my head. "What truth?"

Thaden looked down at our entangled hands and took a beat before responding. "You know, I didn't realize that my ghostly little friend was an imposter until it was much too late. Before the day she insisted that I recite Ellie's spell, she was gaining my trust by showing me how to use the gifts I inherited from you." My heart fell slightly in my chest. "She helped me see that I could unfold the curtains and look between them." He pointed the wand in his lap towards the space where we'd just seen Rowena and her owl disappear. "Like your ghost used to do while she was alive, the Freddie showed me how to do the same. To time travel."

"Time travel? Wait—so you—you can travel through the folds? Even as you are? Forever banned to the elements?"

He nodded. "So can you. In fact, you have been doing just that through Grandma's spell. That's all she did. She pulled away the folds for you and Ellie to sink back into that past life."

I stared at him in disbelief. "I never knew I could do that."

"Correction. You never knew you could do that in *this* life."

I lowered a single brow.

Changing gears, backing up, he said after a moment had passed us, "The Freddie showed itself to me as a little girl, and there was no way you would've sensed her. She hid whenever Maddie or you were around."

"Why would it need to hide from Maddie? Maddie can't see ghosts or Freddies."

"Maddie can see everything."

"What do you mean by that?"

He didn't answer me. Instead, he chose to leave it, the corners of his mouth curling up. As I considered his expression, Joe's words from the other day suddenly rang through my head—*then how can she fly?*

"We don't have a lot of time," Thaden repeated, redirecting my attention. "We were given this moment for a reason, and before I have to go—"

"Wait—no! You can't leave, you just got here!"

He shook his head. "I'm only here at all because you still refuse to see it, and I may be the only one who can shake the truth out of you."

A small fire ignited in my chest. "Why does everyone keep speaking of *my truth*? I've seen what happened—I cursed a Freddie!"

"Yes, you did, but there's more to it than that."

"And why do you think you're the one who can help me see past this fog?"

Without missing a beat, he replied, "Because I am like Rowena."

A thick line appeared between my brows.

A small sigh escaped his lips. "I have been with you every day since I was taken into the elements. It was your pain that overshadowed my presence, that separated you from me. I was always there—in the wind, in the ocean, in the flame of every candle you lit. I wanted you to see me, just like your ghost wanted you to acknowledge her. The shadows over your heart, put there by the Freddie when you weren't looking, they were so dark you couldn't see through them. You couldn't see either of us."

With my eyes closed, a tear escaped as I whispered, "What does this have to do with my truth?"

"Your truth is what is left after you shake away the shadows. Once you push aside the barricade that the Freddie has been holding in place. Then you will see the origins of this pain and where the evil originated."

I reopened my eyes to find him staring directly at me.

"I've been trying to find where the evil originated and where Rowena's body is buried. I've been doing nothing else!"

"You've been scrying."

"Yes!"

"You've been gazing into your ball because that's what Lana said to do, but she was never told that you needed to scry."

Puzzled, I retorted, "Yes she was. She said that my mother was trying to communicate with her, that she was given the image of a mirror."

Thaden looked down into his lap, to the beechwood still within his grasp. "You've been scrying your whole life, so of course you would immediately associate that image with divination; but I'm afraid that's never what Grandma meant." His gaze raising back up, centering over the charm hanging from my neck, he said, "There is one door you have yet to unlock. One that has been waiting hundreds of years to be found and opened. The evil one who watches over you has done its job well, keeping you shrouded in emotional pain through every life—posing as someone you threw away. The answer, Mom—your truth—it lies in what you see in the mirror."

"I told you—I see nothing—"

He jerked his head from side to side. "It's not inside the reflection. It is the reflection itself." He paused briefly. "Who is it that the Freddie tried to make you fear when this all began?"

I thought about it for only a moment. "Rowena."

Thaden nodded. "And it makes sense that this is the form it took. It didn't take on Rowena's form because hers was the last body it wore, it did that because it *knew*."

"Knew what?"

"Who is it we often fear more than anyone else?"

I shook my head. "I don't—"

"Come on, Mom, I know you know. Deep down, there is a reason you never saw yourself in those past scenes Grandma opened for you. There is a reason."

My mouth was quivering, my next line nothing more than a quibble. "I couldn't see myself because I was a spirit."

"And how did your spirit get there?"

"I—I don't know. Rowena or the Freddie—it killed me."

"No, pain killed you."

An explosion went off in my head. I couldn't quite see what was waiting for me in the distance, but it was beginning to take shape. As it did, something heavy lifted from over my shoulders.

My lips began moving, but my words were a little late to the party. Whatever was readying to come out of me never made it, for all the sudden Thaden's form fluttered between an image of himself and someone else's.

I dropped his hand and reached for his shoulders, trying to hold him still—to keep him with me. "Wait! Thaden, what's happening?"

He looked up through the trees, at the darkness falling over our shoulders. "My time is running out. I've got to go."

"NO!" Pulling at his arms, pulling him into me, I continued to shout, "You can't go! You've only just arrived!"

The gentleness that I'd seen in him when he was just a little boy was still there as he returned his gaze to mine. "Don't be sad for me. Ellie's intention has come through in this spell. It *is* a dance that never ends. It's a beautiful life."

"It's a curse! You are as good as gone!"

He laid a finger over my lips. "You know that I am not. And I know that you know that. For now, promise me that you will embrace the ones you have before you instead of dancing away. Remember, the Freddie feeds on your pain; do not give it reason to do so. Do not show it fear, do not let it win. Tell me you forgive this curse. Tell me you will let it go. And instead of feeling pain for me, feel me in the wind."

Choking on the tears running down my throat, I struggled to get my words out. "It's just—if I can't see you how am I supposed to know that you're okay?"

Cupping his hands around my head, my son answered while pressing his forehead into mine. "I am in every tear you cry; in every creek or river you pass by. When you light a candle, I am the flame that dances in the dark. I am the whisper in the wind, and I'm with you always."

"How do I know?" I repeated.

"You will know. You always have."

I closed my eyes and bit down over my lip.

"Okay," I whispered. "I believe you . . . I will let go of this curse, of the pain. I will let it go."

When I lifted my eyelids, I found myself in the company of my other child. She was dressed in her waitress's uniform from the wedding. A witch's hat on her head, and in her hand the same wand that Thaden had been holding.

"Maddie?" I questioned, blinking away thick droplets of moisture. "Oh my god . . . it *was* a dream. And I'm still hallucinating."

Her typical dry look fastened securely into place, and she answered simply, "No, *Mom*, it wasn't."

"What?"

She jumped off the log before offering me a hand to get to my feet. "Come on, we've got stuff to do."

It wasn't until then that I realized it was a lot darker outside than it had been just moments ago. Somewhere, not too far away, were the many footsteps of witches entering into the forest. The music had changed from the band to wooden flutes. A ceremonial march; one our kind often did on our way to a celebration.

"I don't understand," I said, looking up at my daughter, still too dazed to move from the log. "Was he real?"

Maddie popped her hip out and shot me an annoyed look. "Of course he was. Now come on, the ceremony is about to start, then after that we have circle."

I stared stupidly at the wand in her hand. It was charged . . . I could tell. Suddenly, I spit out an array of discombobulated words. "What? But it can't be. You're not a—*are you*? No. How?"

Maddie rolled her eyes, then pulled me to my feet. "Come on, we have to go."

"Does it work?" I asked of the beechwood.

Maddie sighed, then flicked her new wand at a pinecone, turning it into a tiny house fit for a faery or a very small gnome. "Thaden activated it for me."

"Thaden turned that into a wand for you?"

She nodded.

"But the person using it has to have magic too."

"Yeah. So?"

"Maddie Jean, what aren't you telling me?"

She spun the wand in her hand and clicked her tongue. "We're not the same, but that doesn't mean we didn't come from the same place. Now come on, we have to go."

"Wait—so Thaden used your body to show himself to me?"

She grabbed my elbow and led me towards the commotion of witches pouring into the woods. "It takes a lot of energy for him to do so. He could only do it because there was enough magic in the forest tonight. You know, with all the added witches. It was Lana's idea."

"Right," I muttered. "The witches."

"Yeah," Maddie chirped, an impish quality peeking through the glint in her eyes. "It was important for him to see you, so I'm glad we could make it work."

"You sound as if you and he have been communicating. Have you?"

Maddie shot me a funny look. "Of course we have, Mom."

"Since when?"

"Since forever. Anyway, did he get to say everything he wanted to? I couldn't really hear."

"I—I don't know. I think so." My thoughts were deviating in about four different directions.

"Good, I'm glad," was all she said.

I don't know whether it was a residual effect from the flying ointment, but I could have sworn just then, in the beginnings of the moonlight, that I saw a pair of translucent wings flutter out from behind my daughter's back.

ELLIE

V had been specific; the band was to play until the moon winked at us from the pale blue sky. The Enrapture was scheduled for some time after nine o'clock, so for things to line up perfectly, *and they had to be perfect*, Cindy's wedding ceremony needed to happen around eight. That would allow us time to form into circle afterwards, and to complete my mother's spell. She'd also said to meet her behind the stage as soon as my bow turned back into a wand, but it had been fifteen minutes since that time, and she was still nowhere to be found.

I'd reached out for Derek after the show only to have him jet off in the other direction. Between that and having my stomach prodded by at least twenty witches, 'tickled to death' by the light streaming from my skin, I was *so* not in the mood for my sister to be late.

Finally, I saw a break in the stream of witches making their way into the woods, and from the gap I caught sight of Lana. I tucked my violin into my side and jogged after her.

"Yo, Lana, where's V?"

Without even glancing my way, she continued through the

brush. "On her way to the marrying tree, I suspect. Same as us."

"She was supposed to meet me."

Lana shrugged. "Perhaps she got sidetracked."

"Seriously? You're not at all worried? What if she freaked and took off—it wouldn't be the first time."

"Do not worry, Wichahpi. Your sister will be there."

I began to retort, but before I could, Lana nodded in the direction of a male witch hovering on the handle of a thick broomstick, then ran over and jumped on as if it was a motorcycle. She disappeared into the thick of witches, leaving me to fend for myself as crazy magical folk with wooden flutes continued to pat my stomach as they marched onward.

"Dammit Lana." I cursed her name all the way into the clearing where the ceremony was getting ready to unfold—the tree of life strewn with flowers and faery lights. It was pretty fucking magical, too bad I was too distraught to appreciate it.

"Ellie!"

I looked around, searching for whoever was calling out my name. After about three rotations I found Tyler and Joe clumped together, off to the side of where everyone else was finding seating.

"Hey," I said, slipping between the crowd.

As I walked up, Joe pulled me in for a short embrace, chancing a quick peck on my cheek for the second time that day. I couldn't even put into words how much I missed her . . . how terrible I felt about what I would have to tell her when this was all over.

"You sounded great up there," she said.

"Thanks." My gaze collapsed around my wife's slender form, and I had to hold back the urge to cradle myself against her. Damn if it wasn't this pregnancy, or maybe it was just because it had been so long, but I could barely breathe in her presence. I wanted to feel her skin against mine so badly. "You, uh, you look really good, Joe. Healthy." The way she'd looked when I first met her.

With her tongue resting gently between her teeth, she smiled at me, and I knew she felt the same. "So do you. Except . . . wait. What's this about? You're, like, glowing."

"Holy shit," Tyler said, popping his big dumb head into our personal space. "I didn't know you were—ouch! What the hell, Ellie?"

"Oops," I said, lowering my wand. "Didn't mean to buzz ya."

Tyler rubbed at his forehead where I'd shocked him, and I mouthed the words 'shut the fuck up.'

"Uh—right. No—No problem," Tyler stuttered. Then, working to fix the disturbance he'd initiated, he said, "I forgot, you get like that when you use that much magic, don't you?"

"Yeah, I do," I retorted, nodding a little too fast. "Plus, I was, like, flying a lot, and stuff."

"Yeah, and with circle after this it probably won't fade out right away, huh?" he asked, playing along.

"No, probably not," I agreed. This time I mouthed a thank you.

Joe, meanwhile, had twisted her lips over to one side and was looking back and forth between Tyler and me. "Seriously? I've never seen her glow like—"

"*So*, you ready for this?" I asked, cutting her off from finishing her interrogation.

"For what?" she asked.

"Circle."

Joe and Tyler weren't witches, but they, along with any other non-magical family and friends, were going to be expected to hold hands and stand with the rest of us alongside the inner circle. We needed all the energy we could muster— blessed by the Goddess Diana or not.

"I guess so," she muttered. "So hey, what happens after this is all over?"

The question had layers.

"I guess," I said, trying for an easy answer, "we all go home. Either way, this will all be over. And as long as the Freddie doesn't crush my goddess light, I guess we see if we can put things back together. You and I, that is. I mean, something good's gotta come from all this bullshit, right?"

And just like that, Joe was encased in her own glow. All I could hope for was that it would stay there.

Lana's cutting voice was the bowling ball that came crashing through our glass encased moment. I turned to find her by the marrying tree, next to a purple-haired witch who I now understood to be Cindy Bernstein. I signaled to her to let her know I would be there in a second, before turning back to Joe.

"Looks like we're about ready to start."

"Wait a sec," she said.

"What's up?" I asked, hesitantly.

Pulling me aside, she spoke quietly into my ear. "I need to ask you something."

"What's that?"

"It's about Derek."

The inclination of my voice stilled. "Oh?"

"He's been acting *really* strange today."

I waited a beat or two to reply. "How so?"

"First of all, he insisted that I ride here with him, even though I tried to tell him like a zillion times that it was just easier to go with Tyler and Maddie in the catering van. So, then we got into his car, which by the way reeked like ass, and he started doing this crazy chanting thing, and, like, staring me down. Then the motherfucker plucked a piece of my hair!"

I squared my shoulders with her, standing up a little straighter. "Did he now?"

I squinted in his direction; he was seated right next to my father. That son of a bitch.

"It's super weird, right?" she asked.

"Really weird."

So, he wasn't just avoiding me because I'd messed with his spell. He knew very well that any second I would put together the pieces. And here I had it all wrong. I thought that catching Derek's prey would be a lot harder.

"Yeah. I was just wondering if he seemed all right to you. I know the two of you have been hanging out a little more this summer and I was just—I don't know—worried about him. As long as I've known him I've never seen him this way. And I've known him—"

"Since you guys were little kids."

"Yeah." She dropped one of her shoulders down as she stuffed a hand into her pocket.

"Right." My jaw clenched together as I stared at Joe's spiked black hair. Except it wasn't really black, was it? It was red, just like the strands I'd pulled from that little blue brush I'd found at Derek's house. I'd had so much going on that I hadn't been able to investigate those red hairs, but the answer had always been right in front of me.

What a douche bag. He'd been using her soul as a beard all this time.

"Wichahpi!"

I flinched at my aunt's piercing tone and faced her just in time to find her impatiently gesturing for me to head over to the marrying tree. I signaled to her that I would be there in a moment, then turned back to Joe.

"I really wouldn't worry about it. He was probably just stressed out about performing for the first time in forever."

"You think?"

"Yeah." I reached for her shoulder and gave it a reassuring squeeze. "I have to go, but we'll pick this up later, okay?"

She relaxed her shoulders and grinned softly. "Yeah." It wasn't until I started walking away that I heard her say to my backside, "And here I was beginning to worry that I'd lost you to the same guy I stole you from."

I couldn't help but freeze, but I just as quickly forced myself to regroup before she could get suspicious. Turning my cheek to her, I said, "You know that's a whole lotta crazy, Josephine Redvine." Then, hugging my violin to my chest, I made a quick break for the marrying tree.

"Good," Lana said as soon as I arrived by her side. "Get ready to start. I need to go double check on the other bride."

"Wait, you're leaving?" I glanced around Lana's shoulder to where Cindy was standing.

"Yes. I'll be right back. Is everything all right?"

"Uh. I'm fine—it's nothing."

I just didn't want to be left alone with Cindy, that was all. She'd been shooting me nothing but odd looks all day, like she was in on a joke I wasn't aware of. I only knew who she was because she was only one of two people wearing white. Ugh.

"Okay. I'll be right back."

"Great," I chirped, with notes of sarcasm dripping from the ends.

Attempting to play it off, I shuffled myself around the witch of honor, dipping my head as a token of being nice, or whatever.

"Nice glow," Cindy said, winking at me.

"Thanks," I muttered.

"Wife doesn't know, does she?"

She seemed highly amused.

In an attempt to set her straight, I replied, "As you are about to find out, being married to a woman is much harder than being married to a man."

"How would you know?" she asked, her arms clasped

314

before her in an irritatingly calm demeanor, as she stood there in her white fitted suit.

"Because I nearly married a man, and I was with him long enough to know the difference. Females are more complicated as a species. But hey, at least my wife's not also a witch. Have fun with that, Cinderstyx."

Cindy chuckled, shaking her head softly to herself. "So, you *do* you remember me."

I shot her a strange look. "What?" Truly, I still couldn't place her.

"That's what they called me in high school." She gauged my reaction, then rolled her eyes when she could see that I had no recollection. "Never mind, you must've just gotten it off my soul." She licked her lips and dug a hand inside her front pocket. "I was a total nerd and you were the opposite. They called me that because I played the drums in marching band and had an unfortunate overbite until I learned how to fix it with my trusty aspen handle. It didn't surprise me when you didn't pay attention to me in school, though. We were in different classes, and you were never around when your mom was tutoring me. But that doesn't mean I didn't follow your music career."

Just as Lana reappeared and made her way towards us, Cindy pulled out a card and handed it to me. "I didn't ask your band to play because I knew I'd be getting married here. To be honest, I didn't even know the wedding was going to be at Sage Brook until a few days ago. I wanted you guys to play at my wedding because I loved your sound."

I looked down at the card in my hand. "Enchantress?"

"I'm starting my own label. And . . . I want to sign The Wicked Incantations. Although, we are going to have to work on that name."

I raised my eyebrows. "You know, we aren't really a band anymore."

"And *you* really aren't signed anymore." She paused for effect.

"How'd you know that? I literally just fired my manager."

"Word travels fast where I eat. And by the way, I didn't get fired from my label. I quit."

"You quit your job? But you were, like, with a stellar label."

"So were you." She tapped the card. "I just think, Ellie, that we could do great things together. You and your band, that is. Don't get me wrong, your solo act is awesome, but the sound coming from the whole of all parts—it's straight wicked."

Lana, now back by Cindy's side, gestured for me to back away. "We're ready," she announced. "Time to start making the strings sing, Wichahpi."

"Right." Stuffing the card into my bra, I nodded to Cindy. "It's something to think about."

I started to play, and as I did, a little flower girl on a broom flew down between the many seats made of tree stumps, dropping seeds to the ground which immediately grew into flowers. When she reached Cindy, she jumped off the broom and walked a couple spaces to the left. Next was the other bride, a beautiful Latina witch who traveled on foot. Unlike Cindy she was dressed in a traditional wedding dress, with a train as long as the aisle. As soon as she reached Cindy and Lana, the two brides held hands and the flower girl dropped the broom by their feet.

When all was said and done, Lana lifted her hand to the sky and brought down a bit of moonlight magic. Next, a strip of white light bound itself into a knot around Cindy and her bride's clasped hands. Lastly, they jumped over the ceremonial broom. Then and only then was it time to bring down our goddess. To stab that piece of shit Freddie in the heart, and to rescue my family once and for all.

Just as Lana had speculated, as we began to form into our circles—my family making up the smaller ring in the center of the much larger one encircling us—V turned up with Maddie attached to her side.

"Where have you been?" I whispered haughtily, as she took my hand in hers.

"Sorry," she returned. "Got caught up. I'll explain later."

"Whatever. I'm just glad you're here."

"Ellie."

I looked to her.

"These past lives of ours . . . you could hear your thoughts while you were in the memory, right?"

"Yeah."

"I was just wondering, because you said after that first dive into our past that you remembered thinking your sister had died, and now your lover."

"Right . . ."

"So, you remember me being dead, then? While Rowena, or the thing posing as her, was still alive? You remember her murdering me?"

I pressed my lips together, exhaling a breath through my nose before answering her. "What I meant was that I remember thinking my sister as I knew her was dead."

V just looked at me. "I see."

She looked away, leaving me to stare at her cheek. There were gray stripes running down her skin as though she'd been crying and her mascara had bled.

"Hey," I whispered. She glanced at me. "Are you ready to go back there one last time?"

"Yeah, I think I am. I'm ready to let go . . . of all this."

I squeezed her hand harder. "You got this, Sis. Mom thought everything through. Once we begin, that thing will get sucked into our circles and trapped—and because we are surrounded by cedar trees, it will be weaker."

317

"Right, I got this," she repeated.

As V continued to train herself to remember her strength, I worked on my breath. In through my nose and out through my mouth. As I did, I found myself staring across our circle, directly at Tyler. He had a look on his face that I only got when I had raging diarrhea, and he was looking anywhere but at my sister.

"Shit," I whispered.

"It'll be fine," V said quietly. I turned and looked at her, her eyes were closed in concentration. "The cards have already been dealt. I've got this."

"Yes," I said, and looked back at her husband, "you do."

She was right, the cards were dealt; it's just that we'd been working so hard on trying to get my sister to acknowledge the piece of herself she'd always run away from, that we'd forgotten that in nearly every life she'd been bound to another soul. It wasn't just V who needed to forgive herself. Tyler and V shared a bond. For things to work, to kill this Freddie, all working parts needed to be mended.

As my thoughts continued to stir, the witches surrounding us began to chant, moving counterclockwise. Soon after, our own little circle followed suit. Before long, pieces of white light fell from the sky, piecing together over our circles like two giant gold chains. As the circles continued to move, readying to undo a spell inside of a spell, the bands of light grew stronger, and as the chanting grew louder, my necklace began to burn.

I turned my head in V's direction and my chest rose as the charm hanging from her neck glowed even brighter. Then, just as the times before, my sister and I were pulled away.

ELLIE

We were back in Rowena and Ella's lifetime. It was beginning to feel like watching the same rerun over again and again. Like a bad hangover that wouldn't go away.

It was the same as all the other times; I was a guest along for the ride and I couldn't manipulate this body's speech or movement. As I sat there, I listened to myself speak to the other girl in the room, in this small house with wooden floors covered in dirt. Her back was to me, and she was stirring something over a burning cauldron . . . it smelled of chocolate.

I picked up my skirt and studied it, then let it drop to the ground. "This is the ugliest color. I don't see why I can't make it purple; it is not my fault that these people we live amongst can't do the same thing."

The girl turned around to face me. It was Rowena, but a much younger version than the one who killed me and my mother. It occurred to me that this was a much earlier glimpse. If I had to guess, I would say that she was fourteen and I, twelve.

"It is not wise to show off, you know that. We can make

this village home. It's the longest we've ever lived somewhere amongst nonmagical people."

"I don't really care. I can dance anywhere I want."

Rowena stepped away, throwing a piece of hair behind her shoulders like a vain schoolgirl. "Well *I* care. I intend to marry that boy."

"Who? John Wiley?"

"Yes, as a matter of fact."

"Oh really?" I said in a snotty tone. "And what makes you say that?"

"Because I love him, and because my rune stones said I would marry him."

"Oh Rowena, your silly runes also said that you'd turn into a monster." I giggled. "And we both know that's impossible. Although when you don't braid your hair before you go to bed, you kind of look like someone who came from the ground when you wake the next morning."

Horrorstruck, she scrunched up her face, before pulling out her wand and striking me with a blue light.

"Hey you!" I yelled, my hair frizzing out on either side of my head. Excitement welled up inside Ella's body, and she grabbed for her own wand—a purple spark shooting out from the end.

"Toad's curse!" I shouted, and immediately a big hairy mole grew out of Rowena's nose.

She screeched, laughing all the same and pointing her wand at me again, about to strike me with another curse. But just as she was about to, there was a knock at the door.

"Shhhh," Rowena said, both of us jumping at the interruption.

"The chocolate," I whispered.

She turned and pointed her wand at the pot over the small fire and whispered something. Instantly the hot cocoa transformed into what looked like potato and onion soup. We turned to one another and undid our curses; then, smoothing out the wrinkles of my dress, I backed away into the chair I'd been sitting in as Rowena opened the door.

"Oh, hello minister."

My heart was beating faster, and the wand I was holding under my dress was being gripped tighter. I could hear Ella's thoughts: our families had reason to believe this man was dangerous. He claimed to be a man of god, but there was nothing but hatred lurking in the shadows of his heart; it was an unnatural energy. As I stared at the man, I heard it—the echoes in Ella's heart. I followed the reverberations, and as I did, I found something I hadn't seen before while in this body. A truth. The man had not always been a threat; it happened after he'd tried to get Ella's mother alone with him, and when she had refused, he'd grown indignant.

So, there it was, I thought as I sat in Ella's body, *because our mother wouldn't sleep with him, he turned his people against theirs. What a sick, vile creature.*

But there was more, so much more. His rejection turned into hatred . . . and it festered and festered and festered. Until it broke free. And that is where it began.

Goddamn, I thought. It had all started with the same old story. A man, weakened from a woman's refusal to have sex with him, who then lashed out the only way he knew how— by making women appear evil. I wanted so badly to shake my head, but I wasn't in control of this body.

I had no choice but to return my attention back to what was happening in the room.

The man was dressed in a heavy black suit and was carrying a black, leather-bound book.

"Is it that I smelled something strange walking by this house?" he asked.

Rowena innocently looked from the man back to me, and then stepped away, allowing him to walk inside.

"Ella and I were just practicing making dinner, Minister Frederick. I'm afraid we aren't very good cooks, and since we are getting older, we thought it would be best to learn how to make a wonderful soup, so that when we marry we can feed our men happily."

I was trying like hell to stifle a laugh, as I could clearly see that Rowena was mocking the roles of women openly. The minister seemed blind to all of it.

The man stepped inside, searching, it seemed, for clues as to our being up to no good.

"I would not be lying if I said I did smell something strange. Sweet, mouthwatering almost."

Rowena tied her hands together behind her back and put on her best impression of innocence. "I'm so sorry, minister, for if we had such a wonderful thing as you just described I would love to share it with you."

Ella snickered and the minister's attention moved so that it was on her. He opened his mouth as if to question her, but then decided against it.

"Would you like to try some of our soup?" Rowena added, a sinister quality glistening around her soul.

"Well, I—you know it does smell lovely. It is bitter cold outside. It would be nice to warm up with a bowl."

"That is wonderful," Rowena said, clasping her hands together and signaling for Ella to help her. She winked at me as I stood.

"Papa and Mother went to the forest, hunting. They should be hungry when they get back, so you can tell us whether this is fit for our providers."

She grabbed a wooden bowl and ladled a decent portion into it. "Give this to the good minister, won't you, Ella."

I raised my eyebrows, but Rowena just nodded mischievously.

I turned and handed the bowl and wooden spoon to the

clergyman. He'd taken a seat at the kitchen table; his book, which I could clearly now see was a Bible, was off to the side. I narrowed my eyes at it. There was a strange dark quality living inside that leather binding. *Is it breathing?* Ella thought to herself.

The minister thanked me and said a prayer over the food. Before digging into the mystery stew Rowena had conjured, he placed a hand over his book and said directly to Ella, "What do you think of God, young lady?"

I moved my gaze to Rowena, as if asking for guidance.

"I am a very spiritual being, sir," I said after a short period of silence.

"And do you believe in good and evil?"

"Yes."

"I've heard rumors, young Ella. Jacob Monroe's daughter and you have been seen holding hands, walking out from the forest together."

Rowena's back stiffened and she looked as if she was holding herself back from pouncing. "They are young girls, minister." She forced a smile. "Young girls hold hands and play."

He lifted his spoon and prepared to scoop up some broth. "Yes, but we must be careful that innocence does not bleed into carelessness. There are some things that are unnatural and lead to temptation of evil."

Ella had backed away. There were two winds coming together inside her body—fear and anger. Her gaze drifted back down to the book.

"Now then," the minister said, lifting the spoon to his mouth and taking a hearty bite. However, as soon as the liquid was against his taste buds it became apparent that the last thing he wanted to do was swallow.

"Is it good, minister?" Rowena asked, her tone much like that of a naughty pixie delivering a poisoned peach to an elder.

The man choked a little before finally swallowing. "It's quite different, isn't it?"

"Oh please, do eat it all. I would just feel sad if you didn't," Rowena continued.

The minister studied the giant bowl of soup and then looked up at the two of us. "But of course, I will," he said, a bit of disagreement in his voice.

I sat back down in my chair and crossed my hands over my lap, while Rowena took a seat opposite the minister.

"Aren't the two of you going to have some?" he said, trying to muster up the courage to take another bite.

"Oh no, we've eaten plenty while preparing it. We are quite full, aren't we, Ella?"

I nodded my head.

The minister begrudgingly ate his soup, starting with small bites before deciding it might be easier to take larger ones to get it over with faster. At some point he took a break and looked up at us.

"Why is it, might I ask, that I never see your families in church?"

I waited for Rowena to reply. She was older, she was the one to manage this sort of talk.

"Our people do worship, but since our families all moved to this village together, we prefer to do so amongst ourselves."

"It's strange to us, you must realize this. Five or more families move into our village. They build homes faster than any of us have ever seen—almost as if the structures went up overnight. These families are part of the community in every way, for what has it been now, at least five years. *Your families* are part of us in every way, except for worship. You know, some of the villagers say they've even seen your families coming out from the woods during very early morning. It's curious."

The young version of Rowena crossed her hands over the

table and leaned in. "Well minister, how else do we go mushroom hunting? I believe I've seen you at my aunt's grocery on more than one occasion, purchasing vegetables from our gardens. And if it wasn't for my mother's apothecary shop, would your son have managed to overcome that infection he received last fall?"

The minister was quiet. At some point he'd given up on trying to finish the soup, although he'd gotten pretty far with it. Scooting his chair away from the table, he stood.

"I believe I've overstayed my welcome. Marina shall be wondering where it is I've gone off to. Thank you so much for the soup, perhaps with a little practice you two girls will have an award-winning recipe on your hands." He was still struggling to get the taste out of his mouth, we could tell by the way his tongue was thrusting around inside it.

Rowena stood as well. As the minister reached for the door, she called out, his Bible in her hands, "Oh Mr. Frederick, you've forgotten your book."

He glanced back at her. "Keep it. For I have many more, and something tells me you may learn to enjoy it in your future years, Miss Rowena."

There was something foreboding in his words, and more than a little haunting about his energy.

"No. You should take it. We have our own here in this household."

The minister burped, covering his mouth.

"I insist," he said, before turning back towards the door and exiting our space, jumping at the sight of a wolf a few feet away with an owl perched on its head.

"Don't worry," Ella's little voice said. "Those are our friends; they won't hurt you."

The minister looked back at Ella in a most threatening way, and then keeping a wary eye on the animals, he put one foot out the door.

"Perhaps less spice in your next batch, ladies." And then he was gone.

As soon as the door shut, we burst out laughing. I stood and ran over to the pot of stew.

"What is it?" I asked.

Rowena, looking proud of herself, listed off the ingredients. "Plenty of lemon, a pint of salt, dragon's breath, burnt chili powder, and faery's piss."

I scowled. "That's absolutely revolting!" Just the smell was enough to make me want to wretch up everything in my stomach. Ella backed away from it, staring at the door. "He was digging."

"He was planting fear, the worst kind of magic. Mother was more than right about him. He's repulsive."

"He knows we aren't like the rest of them. He knows *I'm* not like the rest of them."

Rowena took my arm. "Don't give him any mind. Love doesn't care what gender you pick. We live in a biased world and must stick to the shadows, but there will come a day where we will not have to hide. There will come a time when people will see that these prejudices are nothing more than delusions created from fear of what they don't understand. It is a beautiful thing to be different, Ella. It is a beautiful thing to love at all."

Ella looked from Rowena down to the book in her hand. A vision flashed before her, of a pale-faced woman with unruly hair. Eyes like the devil. She shivered.

"Promise me you'll remember those words."

Rowena cupped Ella's hand. "My dearest Ella, why would you say that to me?"

Her head shook and her cheeks burned. "Just promise."

OLIVIA

A wind came and swept me away from young Ella and Rowena. For a short time, I forgot we were inside my mother's spell, and took pleasure in the way the wind zipped through my hair and against my cheeks. Eventually, it evaporated, dropping me into the woods. When next I came to, I was back in Rowena's shell, this time lying in the dirt.

Sickness was immanent, and it was enveloping this soul; there was a sinking, poisonous sensation in Rowena's gut. Our surroundings smelled of sea air . . . and pine. Winged spirits were floating above—and that's when I placed it. I was in the memory Rowena herself had shown me; of the time she'd prayed for the angels to take her from her body. At this time her son and husband had already been taken from her and she was through with life.

"Rowena! Rowena, what are you doing?"

"Go away from me!" The words streamed from her mouth. Her pain and her sadness were overwhelming; it was as if someone had scraped out her heart.

"We've been searching for you all day!" It was Ella.

"I just want to be left alone."

"You are hurt! Mama, she's over here!"

The rustling of feet, and the swirl of energy quickly surrounded us.

"Pick her up," said a male voice. "Carefully though."

Rowena was scratching at her skin, pounding her fists into her stomach. "Let me die! Leave me!"

Ella's lips lowered so they were against her ear. "I know you lost the baby, but John would not want you to die like this."

She was pregnant?

"The baby was *his* familiar—Hayden's! Don't you see? She died inside me as soon as his neck was broken!"

Ella's hands gripped Rowena's harder. "I know this is more than anyone should be able to take, but sister please, you still have us. When this life is over, you will see them all again."

"I don't want to hear it! Just let me die. I want to go to them now! I do not want this life anymore!" She was shrieking, and she continued to do so as her body was lifted and carried out of the forest.

She was placed in a bed and surrounded by flowers and herbs. The woman who was my mother in this life walked around her, chanting softly under her breath as she pointed at Rowena with a wand made from the branch of an apple tree.

Rowena was forced to rest, her eyelids too heavy to keep open. When she woke, the pain was still there. The emptiness. I was with her one hundred percent, just like the dread that began to grow as she slowly got out of bed and realized that all the wounds she'd inflicted upon herself were now healed.

"All that is left is the pain inside . . ." she said to herself, looking down at her hands, now clean of any blood.

She regarded the circle of herbs and flowers, picking up a handful of cedar and letting it fall through her fingers. She stood still for so long that fatigue found her legs.

Finally, my mother reappeared. The lines of her face were as gentle as always, but I could still sense that she was worried.

"Rowena."

The witch's gaze darted in her direction. "If you knew how badly it hurt, you would've let me die."

My mother's hand came to Rowena's cheek. I longed to be able to reach up and touch her back, but I couldn't. I was at the mercy of the memory.

"We've been here before, Rowena. We've done this many times. We have to learn to overcome our struggles—"

"I don't want to hear it!" An unearthly anger flashed through her, and the flowers surrounding her bed wilted instantly.

My mother looked down at them, saddened. Squeezing Rowena's arm, she looked away. "I will leave you alone. You need some time to yourself." And then she let go, walking out of the bedroom door.

Don't go away, Mom, I wanted to say, but I was a prisoner inside someone who had let melancholy overshadow her soul.

Rowena, stiff as clay in hot sun, finally moved over to a long box resting on the windowsill. Carefully opening it, she removed a wand. It was made of willow.

"Rowena." A small voice coming from the hallway made her turn.

It was Ella. She looked so scared; a trait I wasn't used to seeing in my sister in any life.

"What is it?"

"Do you remember that day when Mr. Frederick came to our house?"

"Ella, I am tired. I do not feel like reminiscing just now."

"I will leave you, but first I need to say something."

"What is it?" Rowena's impatience was coming to the surface.

"You never answered me that day."

She crossed her brows. "What are you speaking of?"

"When I asked you to promise me that you would remember the things you were saying—you smiled and hugged me, but you never promised."

A frown deepened across Rowena's face, and she held her wand carefully in both hands. "Is that fear I sense in you, sister?"

Ella backed away.

"I thought you said I could never be a monster."

A tear ran down my sister's face, but instead of saying anything more, she ran off.

Rowena walked over to the door and shut it, closing her eyes as she leaned against it. When she reopened them, she struck the cedar and deadened flowers into dust with one flick of her wand before she lunged towards the chest sitting before her bed and opened it. Shoving blankets and spell ingredients out of the way, she pulled out a heavy blue bag pulled together by a drawstring and held it before her face. Cupping a hand under its weight, she seemed to be examining the energy of whatever was inside. *Runes*, I thought, *those were her runes*. Other than seeing spirits, her specialty was divination . . . the same as mine.

"What can my future tell me other than I have lessons to understand?" she said heatedly to herself. "I am tired of lessons."

She looked on them no more, pitching them to the ground. A heavy thump as they landed on the wooden floor. Still wrestling with the contents of her chest, she dug into a corner where her fingers wrapped themselves around an old book. She pulled it from the chest and stared down at it. It was the Bible the minister had left with her when she was a child.

You kept it? I thought.

In the previous memory she had felt that the book carried with it a voice. She'd been curious, but too young to distinguish between the heaviness in the book and the foul energy that was inside it.

She held it in her hands, like a burglar might when coming across something unknown. She was dissecting it, attempting to sort out whether this tool could be valuable, or whether it could be the end of all things.

"What say you? I know you are in there." Rowena opened the book's cover, a crack sounding from the binding as she did so.

She leaned back as the pages of the book fluttered, and as they did, a voice I knew all too well spoke back to her.

"*Rowena . . .*"

Inside her, I flinched. The way it said her name, it was like a snake tasting the air around its prey. It was the same voice who had been taunting me for weeks.

"Traveler," Rowena said into the pages. "I am so sorry I buried you, but you frightened me so. I fear now, though," she paused, stifling a cry, "you may be the only one who will allow me to feel my pain."

"*You have prayed for your death.*"

"The pain has gotten the best of me."

"*A piece of your light for what it is I have to offer.*"

Rowena bit down over her lip, considering the offer. "Why, traveler, would you need a bit of me?"

"*I am weak. I have not the strength to aid you in your journey. But if you were to help me, then I could ensure this heartache of yours will be no more.*"

Rowena was still, her hardened gaze set into the pages of the Bible given to her by a false man. A prisoner meant to watch her own execution, my spirit tightened. Rowena was tapped out. Weak, tired, and hopeless. This thing inside this book, a bit of the minister's fear and hatred that had clung to his most valuable possession, this voice—it preyed on these emotions; and just as I suspected, it began to tell her exactly what she needed to hear.

"*It was the humans who took everything from you . . . hung the same blood which runs in your veins by his tiny little neck. I heard the snap, like chicken bones. His own father couldn't save him from their nooses, from their stakes. Your pain is their victory, your baby's death just another trophy to hang on their wall. Give me a tear Rowena, a tear so full of light, and I will take vengeance on those who most deserve it.*"

NO! I screeched inside of Rowena's skull. *It is lying! Telling you what you desire to hear! It is fake!*

But of course, she could not hear me. I wasn't really there. *I* was the real traveler. That thing in the book was nothing more than evil, an entity which Rowena had confused for a lost soul attached to an old item, when in fact the book was purposefully left behind by a man driven by this sinister energy's persuasions. It was the greatest of misfortunate events.

Rowena looked up at the light streaming in through her window. "You will make this go away?"

"*Yes . . .*"

"Then so be it," she whispered. As she did a single tear fell from her eye; and as it fell from her face to the opened book, a bit of her witch light twinkled inside it.

As soon as it hit the scripture there was a fizzle. The book glowed and her heart stilled, her thoughts reeling around the consideration that she may have made a mistake. It wasn't until her body locked up and an illuminated claw reached out from the book, that real fear stirred within her.

"*Now you're mine.*"

Rowena tried to say something, but the hand clenched stiffly around her throat, and the book fell from her lap as an unseen force pulled her up to standing.

"This is all wrong. I—I refuse you," she hammered out through a tight jaw.

A lunatic laughter filled Rowena's room and from it a voice replied, *"This body is mine now. Your refusal means nothing, witch."*

Rowena's body, so obviously already not her own, flinched unnaturally as the entity from the book took hold of its new shell. Rowena, catching sight of her bit of willow branch that lie forgotten on the floor, squeezed her eyes shut, and with the last of her strength, pushed past the piece of the minister's stolen energy and called for her wand.

It immediately flew into her hand, causing her to gasp in relief; but her time was limited and there was no time for celebration.

"You—can't—have—me—" Rowena stammered, tapping at the nearest wall and drawing up what looked like a funnel. It was a fold. Just like Thaden had described.

"You dare . . ."

Ignoring the demonic seething filling her room like twisted vines—a wicked energy eager for something to suffocate—Rowena lifted her wand and pointed it at her head like a gun. "Oh, ye Light of Exodus, take thee from my flesh, from my bones—"

"You wouldn't. It is forbidden, this spell."

"Take my light and place it away, leave this body to rot and decay!"

A stream of light shot from her wand into her head, and in an instant, I was staring at her likeness—at the body she'd just jumped from—from inside the fold she'd conjured. It took me a moment to realize what had happened, that she'd essentially tried to kill herself by removing her spirit from her body. As I stared out from the curtain she'd opened, I realized she'd made one dire mistake.

Her body was still very much alive on the other side of the fold, and as she stared at it, the Freddie smirked. "But all your light was not your own, for you gave to me a piece of yourself. It wasn't much, but lucky for me I know how to add to it." Waving a finger at the fold, it said, "Foolish girl, oh how foolish." Rowena's body, now powered by that of a Freddie, moved over to where the book had been left and picked it up. "Now now, where shall we start. Oh yes, here we are—fitting name, I would say. Exodus 22:18. 'You shall not permit a sorceress to live.'"

Rowena's soul clenched up, and her fists pounded against the wall that she'd procured. She screamed at the top of her lungs, "NOOOOO!"

It was too late. Once we are out of our bodies we rarely get back in, but that wasn't even the darkest of it all. She had thought by using the Light of Exodus, by killing herself, that she would thus be setting fire to the sickness that had taken over her body. Unfortunately, the Freddie had been right, she'd given a bit of her light away. The entity had already possessed her body and her magic was enough to keep it alive. From what we'd already learned of this entity, it grew stronger with every magical life it took.

Distance grew between me and the scene. At first, I fought it—there was so much more I needed to see. But then I heard a soft female voice speaking to me. The same one, in fact, that I'd heard in my crystal ball nearly a month ago, when I'd first arrived back home.

"Do you see now? Do you understand?"

I turned to find the spirit of a beautiful woman. A pair of transparent, golden wings fluttering out from behind her back.

"Who are you?" I asked.

"Your guide." She pointed to where my past life spirit was standing inside the fold. "Look child." I followed her lead. "Remember, in these bodies, we are only half of ourselves. We leave the other part in Latharia, so that when it is time, we can find our way back home."

I stood in observance, as the other half of Rowena's spirit came to retrieve her—to take her home—because without her physical body she belonged in Latharia; but Rowena simply shook her head, refusing to go.

"We must stay until we can fix this," she stated, her gaze plastered to the other side of the fold, to where the Freddie was becoming comfortable in its new shell.

Her other half did not argue, instead the two spirits merged into one, and Rowena was left with the scent of the tide of Latharia in her hair. Her ankles were still strewn with flowers and bells, but the soles of those feet would not return to touch the sands of her homeland for a very long time. For now, she would stay there, watching through her veil as the monster inside her body would kill every last person she loved.

"Can she see us?" I asked my guide.

"No, she is a memory. Come." The woman held out a hand for me to take, and as I accepted her invitation, a wind embraced our shoulders as she moved us from this place, towards yet another destination.

Visions of Rowena, or of the imposter, blurred together— scenes I'd already witnessed. Including the last one where I'd been forced to watch my mother and sister drown. My mother realized in those last moments of her life, that her daughter, had been taken by something more than evil.

She'd muttered a word just before her death; she'd spoken something directly to the darkness inside Rowena. I hadn't been able to hear it the first time, but as I witnessed the scene again, I watched as her mouth moved, forming her lips around a name. Frederick.

"The minister," I said to my guide. "She knew that's who this energy came from. That's why my mother calls them

Freddies. Did the clergyman plant that energy in the book intentionally?"

"I do not think Frederick had the intelligence to do such a thing, but we both know that fear is its own entity, and he was possessed by this. His anger and his fear planted itself in that book; it leeched itself onto his most valuable possession, becoming the worst of the scripture, and it found a way to get next to the brightest of lights. Its next great achievement."

"Then Rowena, she stupidly—*I* stupidly invited it into my body." My son's words to me—who do we fear the most? Ourselves. I'd always referred to Rowena as my ghost. I'd just never realized how literal that statement was. "How did I not see it before?" I questioned. "She—*I* never meant for this to happen." I turned to the winged spirit. Something about the way her eyes sparkled, the golden quality found inside them, made me curious. "Tell me, spirit, who are you?"

"I told you, I am your guide."

"But I know you."

She curled her translucent lips up at the ends and bowed her head. "We leave a piece of ourselves in the spirit world as well, taking on the form requested by our witch while on the earth. You know me as this." She lifted an arm, brown and white spotted feathers erupting out from her skin.

"Delila?"

The swirling wind we floated inside of stilled, and she nodded. "Yes." Her feathers disappeared and her wings fluttered softly behind her back. "We are our own magic. We are with you even through the worst of it all."

"You are your own magic." The words I'd already heard spoken a time or two before sparked a brand-new realization.

"Yes. We come in many forms." It was as if she was answering a question I didn't quite know how to ask.

As much as I wanted to stay on that subject, to keep the window of information open, the memories were still unfolding all around us. I was forced to watch yet again as the imposter murdered the past version of my mother and Ellie, and as my spirit found the strength to push through the fold she was encased in and take vengeance on the Freddie.

"It lashed out," I observed, finally piecing together the jagged edges of this story. "After I separated it from the body and the body died, it cursed me right back." Suddenly I was hit with a new understanding. "It *split* my soul back up, leaving part of me in the past, and the other part of me to be reborn without the ability to return home, to Latharia, between lives."

Delila nodded. "This is truth. In that Freddie lives the pieces of light from endless witches it has murdered over the years. It is how it grows stronger with every life it takes. But as long as steel pierces its heart, magic will find its way home— the pieces of their souls that have been snipped away over time will be returned to the witches of Latharia."

My fingers traced the outline of my lips. "This is so much heavier than I ever thought. How in the world I am supposed to reverse this?"

Delila wrapped her hands together and lifted her chin. "What are the origins of this curse, child? What did the Freddie promise Rowena in the very beginning?"

"It promised to end her pain."

"And now we know that it was always pain it intended to keep with her, for it feeds on her bleeding heart. I ask of you, where was it you've seen her bleed the most? Where is it you've felt drawn to in every life, even this one? A place you find inescapable, a place that keeps you far from those you love?"

A chill ran through my body. In the pines . . . "Oh my god! It's been playing with me all this time!" It was leading me to the beginning of the end with its song. Rowena laid in a forest of pine trees, fighting against her soul in agony—the pines that no longer existed in this life because my beach house sat upon their graveyard.

"The coast," I muttered. Delila simply blinked and maneuvered her chin to the side. "The curse lives on in my pain."

"You know how to find her. You take away the pain, you take away the Freddie's lifeline. It will not matter how powerful it has become if it does not have something to feed from."

I looked up at my guide, my familiar, and just as I realized what I had to do, the smell of salt water flooded my nostrils, as well as the all too familiar sound of waves crashing over the rocks of the uneven reef.

Everything fell away. Delila, the memories, all of it. For all I knew I had awakened back into a time before any of this. Before my necklace had turned blue and before I'd returned home. I was back on the rock I commonly took in the reef of the lost coast, watching the waves crash. The foam settle.

And then she came to me. Rowena's ghost. My ghost.

As she stood before me, I muttered the only words I could think of in that moment. "I'm sorry." She stood very still, drenched in the waves that had surrounded her body seconds before the Freddie was taken from her physical shell. "I never meant for you to become a prisoner; I was only trying to fix it."

Her eyes—tired, I realized—blinked slowly. "We are rooted."

She raised a finger and pointed into the direction where my house would've been in this life, but what I was looking at were the woods that had taken up that lot back when Rowena had been living.

Climbing out of the reef, I followed my ghost as she led me into the trees. As we got closer, I could hear the sobs, the retching, and I knew what I was about to see.

Rowena and I halted before the image of the girl we both used to know. Burning tears scarring her face, fists clenched tightly together down by her sides, her body flinching. She was begging for the light to be pulled from her body.

"This is where we left our self," Rowena stated plainly. "We never truly came away from here."

I stared from the ghost down to the portrait of unedited pain.

"This whole time?" I managed to ask.

Rowena nodded.

Pushing myself forward, I knelt beside the woman wrenching in pain. Carefully, I laid a hand over her forehead.

"Rowena," I said carefully.

She flinched.

Repeating the words my son had said to me just hours ago, I said, "It's okay to let it go."

She shook her head violently.

"I promise," I said. I ran my hand over her head, untangling her hair from the twigs that had gotten messed into her frizzy locks. "It's okay. Letting them go doesn't mean you don't love them anymore."

She jerked her head to the sides yet again, screaming.

"I know it hurts, that watching those you love being taken away from you because of your magic is the most painful thing. That it is easier to sink away rather than face it, but it doesn't make it go away. And the fact is, they haven't left you."

She cried out against me and I pulled back.

Looking up at my other ghost, who was just standing there, waiting, I pleaded with her. "She will not see reason—she's too far gone."

"Make her understand." She touched her heart. "The ones we've loved who we've lost, they've always been in here. You must make her see."

I blinked away a tear and reached up to wipe it away. Ever

so slowly, staring back down at the other part of me, the raw part of me, I sniffed and bit down over my lip before trying to reach her once again.

"They never left you. Not really. They are but whispers in the wind, Rowena, and they stay with you until you are able to join them in the night sky." She stopped shaking her head long enough to look up at me. I could *feel* her heart bleeding out. "When you swim, they guide you through the water. When you write in the dark, they are right there with you, burning in the candlelight, and even when it seems a nearly impossible thing for them to do—they forgive you." I bent down so that my cheek was on her cheek. "Please Rowena, can we let the blood wash away?"

For a moment I thought she was ready to listen. Her energy softened and it was as if she was welcoming my presence, but the occurrence only lasted for a fleeting second.

In the moment it took me to inhale, her body became stiff and she cringed as though a knife had been stabbed between her ribs. "But *he* doesn't forgive—he holds the grudge of a thousand men!"

"Who? Who doesn't forgive?"

"He who our heart is bound to! I cannot give up the pain, for he has yet to do so himself!" Her words drifted away as she recoiled from my touch.

I lifted away from her, speechless. Tyler.

I stood, balling my hands into fists. This was *my* curse, *my* pain. The fact that this evil piece of shit had infiltrated my husband, had me ready to cut this beast's throat.

"Where are you?" I growled, taunting the vile energy. Its teeth had punctured not only my heart but that of my mate's. I turned in circles, staring out into the woods. "I won't let you win!" I shouted to wherever it was lurking. Because it *was* here —our circles had made sure of that.

The Freddie refused to show itself. Instead it stayed

hidden, a low gurgle coming from the trees. From the pines. It was enjoying the show because it had thought it had found a loophole. We'd been working so hard on me this whole time, none of us had thought to diffuse Tyler of his pent-up emotions.

Still, I couldn't let it win—not this time. If I did, it would take all our souls, and goddess only knew how far it would get then.

"Hey, V."

I flinched. *Was there someone else here?* There were only two people in this world who called me that.

"Over here, kid."

My veins pulsed with electricity as I turned around to find the person who belonged to that voice.

"Patty?" I couldn't believe what I was looking at. "Is that really you?"

He dipped his chin and laid a hand over his chest. "Of course it's me. Did you really think I was going to let my cuz get stuck in here while that fucking twat of a Freddie gets set loose? Fuck that shit, man. No."

My heartbeats slowed their pace just a little. This really was Patrick. No one, not even the cunning Freddie could play his character that well.

"Come on," he said, gesturing for me to follow him. "It's over here."

"What's over where?"

A swish of wind picked up nearby, along with a growl, and I suspected that the Freddie—who had been watching and waiting for me to fail—was growing uneasy.

Patrick, dressed in the same clothes we'd found him in, jeans and his chef's jacket, reached for my forearm as he led me further into the pines. "The door, dude." He glanced at me, gauging my reaction. "Come on, V. Weren't you listening when your kid told you that the key around your neck had one more door to unlock?"

"That was literal?"

Patty shook his head. "You are so lucky that thing killed me." He brought us around the trunk of probably the biggest pine tree in the forest, revealing an actual door. It was blue . . . the same color as my key.

"I—I don't understand. How did that get here?"

He shrugged. "It's magic, yo. Can't always explain it. I mean, shit, I've been stuck in this lame ass forest since that thing choked the life out of me. I've got no explanation for that."

"That's because the Freddie brought you here, and when I failed it was going to eat you."

He crossed his arms over his chest. "Yo, that shit ain't cool."

"Yeah," I said. "I know." My hand lifted and grasped the key around my neck, yanking it away. With my gaze centered over the bronze lock, I asked my cousin, "I just unlock it?"

"Seems like it."

"Okay. Then what?"

Again, he brought his shoulders up by his ears. "I don't know, man. This is your pile of shit."

"Right." And then, knowing full well a clock was ticking somewhere outside of this fold, I stuck my little key into the little lock in the magical blue door.

Just before I entered, Patrick hollered at me, "Try not to fuck it up—whatever's in there. I really don't want to be Freddie food, 'kay cuz."

"You won't be," I answered, then slipped inside.

Immediately I recognized my surroundings. I was back to the very beginning of all this. I was inside a circle inside a circle.

I looked around at all the faces of my family members.

Their eyes closed, their mouths moving in unison—possessed by our goddess and my mother's magic. I didn't hesitate to find my target. Tyler.

Speak to him, my Olivia. He will hear you.

I gasped. "Mom? Are you here? *Mom?*"

The answer was in the silence that followed. I knew just then that this door standing alone in the woods, that it was all just part of my mother's very carefully constructed spell. She'd prepared for everything. Even my husband's thwarted spirit.

As I came upon Tyler, I whispered to him, "You can't just repeat these words. They mean nothing unless you believe them."

As he continued to chant, I thought over our last conversation. How broken he was—*still*. I wasn't sure how to put the pieces back together, but in the end all I could do was try. As soon as I began speaking, my throat tightened and I tasted tears all over again.

"Tyler, my only heart, my only love, I beg of you to hear me." I waited for some sort of recognition. When there wasn't any, I decided to continue anyway. "I know I've written us a story you can't read. That warm nights inside our home may never happen for us again. That our little family will never be what it once was, and that we will most likely never see our son again in his physical body. But Tyler, Thaden is *happy*. He hasn't forgotten to love, in fact, love is all he is now. My wish for us is only to know what he knows. Not resentment or regret. I wish only for us to enjoy the dance—what is left of it in this lifetime. For there will be more lives, that is inevitable, but they won't be like this one. I won't be the me I am now, and you won't be you."

I paused. He was still chanting, and other than my mother's insistence that he could hear me, I had no way of knowing whether my message was getting through to him. No way to tell if this was all some sort of lost cause.

I swallowed hard and released a ragged breath. "A very long time ago, a little girl fell in love with a little boy. She knew he was her husband, that one day they would marry and have a beautiful baby boy. What she didn't know was that all that love was going to be stripped from her, a test of her strength. She failed miserably when that day came . . . she let pain get the best of her. What she never intended for, though, was that her pain would infiltrate those who she loved the most. That her curse would become theirs as well. Please Tyler, if nothing else, do not let my curse be yours."

Suddenly the glow surrounding these circles grew brighter, and the chanting got louder. The Freddie, it was near. It was fighting against the magic, against me. Without hesitation, I did the only thing I could think to do and placed my hand over my husband's heart—he inhaled sharply. He could feel me.

"Tyler, *my love*. I am sorry. In the end, there is only one thing left for me to do. If my mother could do her worst to undo a curse than so can I. I will make it easier for you." I choked down a sob as I saw a vision of the memory Rowena had shown me, of her younger, happier self, answering the door—the face of the man who she had loved for years on the other side. It had been fuzzy the first I'd seen it, but now I saw it clearly. It was Tyler. "When this is all over, I will make a deal with the goddess. I will ask her to unbind the magic that has held us together. I know there will be consequences, but they'll find me and not you, because you don't deserve to spend a life cursed from love just because you married someone who was too blind to see she was the curse all along. I love you. Just, please, do your best to forgive me—to let go of the pain I've caused you. If not for me, then for our son."

I dropped my hand down to meet his, and let my head fall backwards. "You said he could hear me, Mom. I've done all that I know to do."

Just as I was about to step away, to walk back through that door and face whatever nightmare was waiting for me on the other side, I heard him mutter very softly, "Forever and always."

A second later, a bit of white light dropped down from the sky. My mouth parted as it wrapped itself around our hands, just the same as it had on our wedding day. The goddess herself was both officiating and giving us her blessing. As we'd already married once in this life, this was a double binding. A reassurance that our union was meant to be.

I gasped, and my husband opened his eyes. There was no way to know whether it was the spell, or if what I was looking at was real, but I knew just then that regardless of the situation he had heard me. With our hands still tied together, a white light escaped his parted lips and floated near my own. When next I inhaled, I took in the light, and immediately felt the tears in my heart—those which had been opened from all the sadness in this lifetime—suture themselves back together.

"Forever and always," I whispered back.

Tyler blinked, his eyes filling up with the reflection of our mother moon, and then they were closed and he was chanting again.

Not even a second later, I was pulled back through the door and into the forest with Patrick, as well as the two ghostly apparitions of my past self. And then all hell broke loose as the silence inside the pines was ripped to shreds.

When it happened, it sounded like the shattering of a thousand glass walls, followed directly by a wail that could only have been made of someone, or some*thing* that had caught on fire.

I knew at once what was happening. Tyler had forgiven me, and that was enough to shake the Freddie. It was ready to run. My mother's spell had it trapped inside a magical circle inside another circle. It had nowhere to flee but towards its own death, and now that I was addressing *all* my pain—and in the process depleting its lifeline—the words being spun from the witches who it had burned many times in many lives, were now burning its soul alive.

"Its strength is faltering," Patrick said, standing across from me, his gaze scanning the woods.

"Yes, but it's not over. I still need to kill it." Staring down at the forest floor, searching for sage, I replied, "Even if I could find what I need, smoke would not be enough to kill this creature."

The chanting coming from the circles was so loud now that we could hear it in this fold. As the witches and our family continued to stand firm, the Freddie continued to shriek. At some point it tried to plead with me, its voice echoing through my ears, "*I will be thy traveler—I will be thy friend.*"

When it was too weak to hide or even scream anymore, it appeared before me. It manifested as a cloud of smoke, trying to take the form of a human; but without its strength, all it managed was the shadowy outline of a person.

"*Mercy . . .*" it pleaded.

My face contorted, sickened by its request. And as I spoke, my fingers curled around something that had been placed into my hand. I looked down to find an athame tucked into my fist. The same magical tool that had always taken up residence a top the altar that stood in my mother's bedroom. The steel blade was dripping with cedar water.

I matched my gaze with Patrick's, and in an instant, we were both grinning from ear to ear.

"Never one to disappoint, that Arianna," he said.

"Never." I returned my attention back to the vile thing that had infiltrated my world time and time again. "Mercy? You dare ask for this thing when you have taken all that you could possibly take from me?"

"I will be thy friend."

I gritted my teeth and shook my head. "You are no friend of mine. I may have been weak once, but that is a sickness I have recovered from." Then before the mist could even attempt to move away, I lunged forward and slashed through it. As soon as the blade hit its foul energy, there was a long-drawn-out screech, and a fizzle as it fell to ash before a wind came and blew it away.

Overcome with a sudden fatigue, I dropped the athame and I fell to my knees, just next to the version of Rowena who had been chained to these pines for years. Her eyes opened, then landed on me. They were still for the first time since I had seen this version of myself.

"You," she said. "I dreamed of you."

I heaved a sigh and squeezed her hand into mine. "You're free now, Rowena."

Her soul quieted and her expression softened. "Is that the wind I hear? What is it saying?"

Patrick had taken a step closer to us. He had a hand up in the air, as if he was feeling it speak into his fingers.

I couldn't help but laugh as relief flooded my entire being. "It is calling you home, Rowena. After all this time, it is inviting you back to where you belong."

Her gaze shifted to where our ghost was standing over us. There was a glow around her that hadn't ever been there before, and as I stared past her, I could see that she was surrounded by what looked like an endless circle of witches. We were looking through a window into Latharia. They had come to take them home—the other halves of my soul, and of course, my cousin as well.

"Who is that?" she asked, looking at her future ghost-like self.

"She's a part of us," I answered. "And she's going to take you with her."

The ghostly Rowena held out her hand, and the one on the ground took it. They stared at one another for only a second before becoming one—before transforming into the version that belonged to all of us—the girl with saltwater in her hair and bells strung around her ankles. The part of us who stayed in Latharia.

"Soooo, that was pretty rad," Patrick said.

I very carefully came up to my feet, reaching up and putting my hands around his shoulders. "It's time for you to go too, Patty."

"Yeah, I guess it is."

I laid into him, my cheek against the warmth of his chest. "I'm so sorry things turned out this way. You weren't supposed to go like this."

"Shit V, you always were a stubborn ass. I think this is exactly how things were supposed to end up. Now go on and get the hell out of here, and tell my mom I love her, okay. That I'll see her in her dreams. Oh, and that I stashed a bottle of Barrell Bourbon behind some chips in my pantry at home. I meant to give it to her on her birthday. She'll want that." He smirked.

"Yeah . . . I'm sure she will."

The scene from Latharia opened enough for Patrick and the other half of my soul to walk inside. The bells jingled as a piece of me disappeared, but just as Patrick started to wave good-bye, the transition began to glow and fade, cutting him off from escaping back into the birthplace of his witchy soul.

And then there was nothing more than falling stars. Nothing but the pines. And the two of us.

That is until the wind came.

It swept around our shoulders, and as it did, Patrick looked to me, concerned. "What went wrong? I thought I was supposed to go home."

"Me too," I said, looking down to see that we were floating

in darkness. There wasn't time for speculation, however, because before long, the black hole we seemed to be blowing around in sparkled with colors. The Enrapture.

I blinked, and it was all gone.

I RETURNED to solid ground as if I'd just woken from a dream. I was chained into the circle, my legs moving along with my companions in a clockwise motion. We were now taking the energy forward, in closing.

As soon as our feet stopped moving, I let out a very ragged breath and my eyes popped open, searching for Patty.

Before I could utter a single question or word, Ellie's arms wrapped around me and she hugged me tighter than a boa constrictor. "You did it," she whispered, pulling away just enough to shake my shoulders. "I can't believe you actually fucking did it."

"Patrick? Where's Patrick?"

Her expression quickly turned to concern. "V . . . he's dead. Remember? He was killed."

"No." I tore away from our circle, ignoring all the eyes on me, all the happy embraces going around both circles. They hadn't seen what happened . . . they hadn't seen Patrick get locked out. "He couldn't get back. I—I—"

"V?" Ellie squared her shoulders with mine. "What are you saying?"

Snow fell over our shoulders. Snow, in the summer. I looked up at the branches of both pine and cedar and ignored my Aunt Lana's exclamation that it was the signal of the end of my mother's spell. Instead, I broke away from all the reaching hands coming in my direction and I ran out of that forest as if the devil himself was after me.

I'd gone deaf to what was behind me, the voices of all the

witches, all my family. I just ran, and I didn't stop until I got to The Dewdrop. When I reached the old café, I didn't hesitate to swing open the front door—because I just knew, somehow, that we'd been sent a gift.

And I was right.

Standing there, in his chef's jacket, just as he'd been moments ago while we'd been fighting for our lives in the pines, was Patrick. He was still in shock, staring down at his hands as if he wasn't quite sure whether they were real. I walked up and touched his arm.

"They let me come back," he said, finally looking back at me. "The witches and the goddess, they decided I could return."

A rocky breath left my chest, but before I could say another word, the door behind us flew open and our inner circle surrounded us all over again. After that, everything sort of happened all at once. Lana pulled me away from her son so she could take his face in her hands and make sure he was real. Ellie and Joe embraced off to the side and Maddie reached down to pick up Mr. Jackel. And then there was Tyler, who didn't hesitate for a second to take my hand as soon as he was within touching distance.

"How?" he asked, without making eye contact.

I shook my head. "I have no idea. Magic . . . it cannot always be explained."

"Mom."

I looked over to where Maddie was standing with fresh tears in her eyes. I unclasped my hand from Tyler's and reached for her. "Maddie, baby, what's wrong?"

She looked down at the cat in her arms, then back at me, and then she shook her head. It was then I realized that the cat had closed its eyes, and it was no longer breathing.

A shudder of a breath left my lips as I cupped a hand over my mouth. "No," I whimpered.

Maddie bit down over her lip and nodded her head. "He's gone, Mom. Which means . . ."

"I know, Maddie," I said, reaching for her and pulling her body into my own. I held her tight as those around us took notice of the occurrence, shifting their awareness from the miracle of Patrick's resurgence, into the tragedy of someone else we loved dearly. "I know," I repeated.

Magic. It couldn't always be explained. And it wasn't always fair.

ELLIE

I lost my mother before telling her that I was becoming a mother myself. I lost my mother . . . before I could tell her that I was becoming a mother myself. I lost my mother. I lost her.

My sister always said to me that even the hardest surfaces are worthy of a good crack; what I had in me now was a ravine.

The night that we laid our family's curse to rest and welcomed Patrick home, our mother returned to hers. I don't know when the wedding party left, but at some point, they did. All that remained of us when Lana and my father went to the hospital to confirm what we all already knew, was Joe, Derek, Tyler, Patrick, V, Maddie, and me. While they were gone, no one hardly said a word. We sat at the tables in the café, sipping on the drinks that Derek poured for us.

"It was a trade," Lana said shortly after they returned. Her expression was stony, but anyone could feel it, witch or no, that she was immersed in pain. "We all knew what she did was mess with a curse, and that is something that cannot be done without consequence."

"It's because of me, isn't it?" Patrick had asked. "It was me or her."

"No, son," Lana had said, her eyes beating down into his. "This was always how it was going to end. I think Arianna knew that from the beginning."

"She did know," my father whispered.

I cried myself to sleep that night. Derek and Joe took turns holding me. I didn't fight them. Later that week we had a ceremony, similar to what we'd done for Patrick, which ended with placing my mother's wand in the box above the mantel.

When all was said and done, we still had a family business to run, so even though we were all grieving, things had to start going back to normal. V was back now, and even though shit wasn't straightened out in her marriage, it seemed her and Tyler had started talking again, so that was good. She moved out of our parent's . . . or our dad's house, and in with Lana. Our dad needed space and Lana didn't. It worked out. As for me, I had decisions to make, but unfortunately, I couldn't get out of my bed to make them.

They let me stay there for five days, my family that is, before calling in the soldiers. It was Joe who came to me first and sat on the edge of my bed. It was Joe who petted Biscuit's tail while pulling the pink hair out of my face.

"You need to get up, Elle. This isn't good for you, and it's not good for the baby."

I turned my cheek towards her from where I'd been trying to bury my face in my pillow. "You know?"

She smiled, as much as someone *can* smile when faced with the kind of pain I was throwing out into the universe. "I may be without magical blood, but I'm not ignorant. You're still glowing, and I know your appetite got spoiled after your mom died, but I don't think grief causes people to throw up three to four times a day." I sat up very slowly. As I did, she reached for my hand. I let her. "It's Derek's, right?"

I gulped. "Yes."

Her chin met her chest and she nodded. "I figured."

"I never meant to hurt you, Joe. I just—I thought you cheated on me, so I did what I do best—I got even." I licked my lips, which were cracked and dry, then bit down over them as I studied her. "It was a mistake—"

"No." She shook her head, then looked up at me with glossy eyes. "Don't say that. This baby is a gift, you know. I mean, all that's happened—all this death. Through it all, *you* were able to bring in life."

Again, I was crying. I'd been crying all week. This time it felt different though, almost like it was a relief. "Are you saying you don't hate me?"

"Of course not! Ellie, I'm happy for you."

I pulled my hand out from where she'd taken it and took hers in mine instead. I squeezed it tight as I spoke. "Happy for me or happy for us?"

"Is there still an us?"

More tears fell down my cheeks. "I want there to be."

"I just thought that maybe you and Derek—"

"No. I will always love him—but Joe, I won't ever love him like I love you. Not in this life. We've been through so much shit together in and out of this lifetime; it can't have been all for nothing. And this baby, she's yours as much as his." I wiped the moisture out from under my eyes and took both her hands in mine. "I know this doesn't make sense, but V has seen her . . . she has your eyes."

Joe didn't say anything back, she didn't need to. Her eyes, her lips, her tears, they all spoke for her, as did her arms as they wrapped around me and held me tight. "I'm so sorry about everything, Ellie. I love you more than anything."

"I know. I'm sorry I can be such an asshole. I hope Winter takes after V more than me."

Joe pulled away just enough to look at me. "Winter?"

"Yeah, do you like it? It's cause she's going to be born when there are snowflakes on the ground."

She looked at me just then the same way she had the first time we met. Like someone had just dropped off the one thing she knew she needed but had forgotten she wanted. "Hey, let's get married again. Under the tree. After the baby's born. We can call it a renewing of vows and a christening all at once. Hell, fucking Derek needs to be involved somehow, so we're going to have to do a christening or witch's initiation anyway. And, uh, V's back—so, you know, she could be there this time."

I bit my tongue as I studied her. Still buried under our grappled hands, Biscuit sneezed. We took our turns rubbing her stomach and laughing at the old girl, and eventually I returned my attention to Joe. "Yeah. Let's do it."

"Yeah?"

"Yeah."

"Cool, but uh, there's something you need to do first."

I raised a brow. "What's that?"

She signaled to the door, and I, ever so slowly, crawled out from my sad little nest and went over to have a look. Derek was out there, standing against his car.

"What's this?" I asked, turning back around to face Joe.

"He's got some shit he needs to say, and you need some fresh air."

Derek's weird little secret had gone from the top of my list to the bottom over the course of several days. After the loss of my mother, it just hadn't seemed very important anymore. "Did he tell you, about what he—"

"Yeah." She stood and placed her hands in her pockets. "And if I decided not to get mad about it, then I think maybe you should hear him out and maybe cut him some slack too. He did what he did because he loves you, Elle. I can't blame the guy for that. Plus" --she managed a chuckle— "he's going to be in our lives forever now, so you might as well try to forgive him."

I bit my lip again before answering her. "Right. I guess you've got a point there." Not to mention that all he'd been since my mother's death was supportive. Lana had told me a day ago when she'd come in to check on me that he had come by every day to help at the café. He was a shady little shit, but he was family.

"Here," Joe said, picking up a pair of pants from the floor and tossing them to me. "Get dressed and go. I'll hang back and start packing for you."

"Packing?"

"Yeah," she said firmly. "There's no reason for you to stay here and Lana said they need the cabin back for guests. Besides, our house is ready."

"Our what?"

Joe smirked. "Tyler decided V belongs here in the forest—he doesn't ever see her living as far away as the house he built—"

"Wait a second, what are you talking about? V and Tyler aren't back together."

"No. Not yet, but there's hope, and that's enough for him. He wants to help at the café for a while so he can be around Olivia more. In the meantime, I'll take over Willow Creek; it'll still be there when he's ready to come back to it. He signed over the house to us this morning, and I signed over our loft to him."

For the first time in my life, I was speechless. "What?" I said, when I could finally speak. "What about Spiked?"

"I'm hiring another head chef. It's all getting worked out, Ellie. I don't want you to worry about shit, all right. Except maybe getting the *you* back in you." Her eyes darted to my violin case. "For someone so selfish, you can really suck at doing what's best for you, you know that." She walked over and pulled a card out from her back pocket, sticking it in my bra. It was the card Cindy gave me. "I found that on the floor in here the night Derek and I brought you back, the night your mom died. Cindy wants to sign you, doesn't she?"

The words almost got stuck in my throat, but I found them. "Y—Yes—well, the band. She wants to sign the band."

Joe looked a little shocked for a moment, but then she smiled. She smiled big. "Wow, that's pretty fuckin' rad."

"Yeah," I said, realizing that for the first time that week I was feeling something other than sadness. "Yeah, I guess it is."

WHEN I MET HIM OUTSIDE, I decided that Derek was like a scolded child who had already had plenty of time to figure out that what he did was wrong.

"Wanna go for a ride?" he asked.

"Sure," I replied, letting him open the passenger side door for me. There was a strawberry milkshake waiting for me inside.

"I made sure to get it right this time," he said, as he got in.

"Thanks." I picked it up and started drinking it. As soon as it hit my stomach, some of my nausea started to lift.

"V said ice-cream always helped her when she was sick with the twins." He drove out of Sage Brook and turned onto the road. "We were all starting to get a little worried because you haven't been eating."

"My glow hasn't dimmed."

"I know, but still. It's just been a shit week, and it's hard on everyone. You, especially, don't need the added stress."

I set down the shake after I'd sucked about half of it down. "Look Der, I know you can see into our past like . . . like my mother could. I know you're a witch."

"Yeah, the secret's out. Lana already has me putting

together spell ingredients for the gift shop. Apparently, she was *wowed* by my skills."

I turned and looked at him. "So, everyone knows."

He glanced at me briefly before pulling over near a hiking trail off the road. Once the car was in park, he rolled down the windows and turned it off—then he pulled a pencil from his dash and shook it out until it became his wand. "I never wanted to hide from you, Ellie, and I didn't want it to end like this—you being the last person I confess it all to."

"I already know why you did it," I said, as moisture found my eyes again. So much fucking crying, I was going to dry completely out. I laid a hand over his leg. "I knew the second you sang that song when we were performing last week. I don't know why I never paid attention to the lyrics before. It was all laid out for me. I guess I just don't understand. Why did you hide it—why did you hide who you were?"

He was my counterpart. Not everyone had one; it was actually kind of a special fucking thing. We each had our own spirits, our own identities, but we would always be drawn to one another—our souls a reflection of each other's.

"I never meant to lie to you," he began.

"You're my soul mate. It's—It's why Biscuit loves you so much. She's your familiar, too." It was the only time two witches could share the same familiar.

"I thought I could trick you."

"Why?" I was as raw as I ever could be in this life.

"It was stupid, okay. I realize now that no one, not even I could change how fate was supposed to unfold. It's just, I was in so deep that I didn't know how to come out of what I'd started."

"Derek . . ."

He took a deep breath. "You're right, I can remember the lives we've lived. I've seen you and Joe end up together repeatedly, trying to fix a relationship that was broken ages ago. A marriage that will continue to be formed until what is meant to be is played out. It is heartbreaking to watch the two of you fail repeatedly—to watch the other half of my heart break again and again."

"Oh Derek," I whispered, but he held up a hand.

"I just—I thought if I could just have this one life with you—that we could be happy together. So, when I met the soul early on who I recognized as your lover in the past, I took a piece of her and held onto it. I used the spell I remembered using in previous lives to hide our identities and laced the truth of who I was with her."

"What were you thinking would happen? That I would confuse you for she who fate intended me to be with?"

"I *wasn't* thinking . . . not clearly anyway. Ellie, I was just a kid—a stupid one at that. I was moving on impulse."

"So, you what? You prepared a potion and waited until the day you first saw me?"

"As crazy as it sounds—yeah. I thought if you recognized Joe's soul, you would latch onto me and your spirit wouldn't seek her out anymore. In the past, even though you knew I was your soul mate, you always left me for her."

I bit down over my fingernail. "But Derek, you were the one who introduced me to Joe. Why in the world would you do that, knowing full well that I would be drawn to her?"

He took a deep breath and sat back in his seat. "Partly because I was forced to watch as my friend fell into a drunken stupor, because she *still was* my friend. She always will be. It wasn't until she was hospitalized for nearly drinking herself to death that I realized the one person who could help her was the one I was holding hostage. The other reason was that I could tell, your soul was still reaching for her. I may have blinded you, but somewhere inside, you knew there was someone waiting for you."

"So, you introduced me to her knowing that it would be the end of us?"

"Ellie, I was the one who convinced her to move back to Denver after her treatment, to open up her restaurant."

"But you never stopped loving me . . ."

"I never will."

"Christ."

"Look Elle, I know how weird it is, what I did, but I *really was* trying to figure out a way to tell you before all this happened. Whatever happens, we're going to be in each other's lives for a while now. I want our relationship to be built on something other than lies."

I stared out the windshield into the bright, sunny day. The sun felt different now that my mom was gone; it felt like it was trying too hard. "It's probably best it came out this way," I admitted. "I might have killed you had you told me without any warning."

Tossing his head from side to side, he replied, "You're probably right." Then reaching for my hand, he said, "I really am sorry."

"I know. I could never hate you, though." I chuckled. "It would be like hating myself."

"There is that," he agreed. "So, what happens now?"

I thought about it for a minute, then told him about what Joe and I had discussed. After he'd cleaned up his pansy assed tears—even though I secretly loved that the idea of us renewing our vows and having a family blessing with all three of us and the baby made him cry—I pulled out the card Cindy had given me. "Oh, and I propose we get the band back together."

He plucked the card from my fingers and stared at it. "What?"

"We, uh, we sort of got picked up after we played at the wedding."

"No shit," he mused.

"We'd have to square it away with Candy and Leo, but I was thinking—"

"We're gonna play again," Derek said.

"Yeah," I seconded. "I think we are."

ARIANNA

I raised my girls in such a way that I hoped they would not call them ghosts—the spirits who could be found amongst the living. However, Ellie didn't care about them either way, and my Olivia, well, she ended up calling them all ghosts anyway. I assure you, though, witches, as I say this to you, I have a smile on my face.

It is a difficult thing, for the living, to understand the afterlife. I knew when I created that spell and messed with our family's curse that it would be the end of my life as Arianna. I also knew that it would be the last time I would return to Earth. That problem was solved; there were other places that needed me now, other souls. Therefore, I found it fitting that I should haunt my last life. Besides, what was the point of having a daughter who could see spirits if I couldn't take advantage of it once I was one myself?

I knew they were grieving. Ron had already spoken to me about it when I met him in the river earlier that day. He couldn't see me, but I was the love of his life and he was mine —he knew when I was with him. He told me Ellie had finally gotten out of bed and that her and Joe were moving into their first real home together. He chuckled as he said that he hoped the country life would settle Ellie down, and in the same breath he said that he knew that would never happen.

"Her light won't ever let her settle down, Arri. But hell, you did good with that one—she's gonna be a good mom." I'd rested my head on his shoulder as he pretended as though his eyes weren't wet and recast his line into the river. "And Olivia, well, I reckon you are gonna go see her next, aren't ya?"

"Yes," I'd answered. "I love you so, my heart."

"I love ya, too, Arri."

The sun was setting when I left my husband to find our daughter. I didn't have far to look, for she was right where I knew she would be. Both my girls had always been water babies, and whenever it got above eighty-three degrees, even after Labor Day, you could bet that at least one of them could be found by the lake.

"Sit down, Mother," she said, as soon as I walked up behind her. And so I did, sticking my toes into the lake, just beside her own. I reached over and traced the outline of a new tattoo on her shoulder.

"What's the feather for?" I asked.

"Letting go. Patrick did it for me."

"A tribute?" I asked.

"And a reminder," she answered.

I nodded my head. I was so very proud of her.

We sat amongst the tranquility for a while, enjoying one another's company—listening to the fish jump out of the water, and the creatures of the forest as they hunted and frolicked. It had been a long time since we'd been able to share a summer's night together.

She was the one to first break the silence. "That was risky, what you did, Mother. I could have failed and it all would have been for nothing."

"But you didn't."

"Why not just tell me to confront the Freddie out right?"

I gingerly took my daughter's hand and held it in my lap, studying the way the wrinkles in her palm went in all directions. Yes, we could feel one another's touch.

"Because, my little witch, you never would have understood it, not without living it." She was silent. "Am I wrong?"

"No," she said softly.

A soft breeze tickled our shoulders as it swooped down into the lake, causing a ripple effect that no ordinary wind could. My grandson was with us.

"How are you and Lana faring as roommates?"

Olivia chuckled. "Good. As long as I don't make too much noise in the morning and she doesn't get too rowdy at night. But it's good."

"And Tyler, how are things with him?"

I turned to see her cheeks coloring like a teenage girl in love. "It's going. You know, Mom, I think I'm going to marry that John Wiley someday."

I smirked.

There was a catch in her throat as she said her next words. "I've had to work so hard to forgive myself for—well everything. But if there's one thing I've learned, it's that letting go is necessary. Except, I don't know if—" She hinged forward and sobbed softly into her hands. I laid my hand over her back. "I don't know if I can forgive you for leaving us. I just—I love you so much, and Ellie—"

"Ellie will be just fine. So will you, and so will your dad. And of course, Lana is a brick. But I promise you, my Olivia, everything will be just fine. I was never going to live forever."

She wiped her nose and looked up at me. "Ellie is pregnant."

I smiled. "I know. And you can tell her that whenever she

needs me, I will be there. I will be there for anyone who needs me. I am but a whisper away."

She laid a hand over my leg. "Thank you, Mom. And thanks for bringing me back home. I am sorry it took you sacrificing your life for me to finally see the truth."

"It was just one life, and one life well spent."

She covered our entangled hands with her free one. "Stay for just a little longer?"

"As long as you want, my Olivia." I watched her as she stared into the lake, the sun was casting a beautiful orange and pink hue against her skin. "For when the sun shines on her cheeks, she glows," I said, a warm smile finding its way onto my face.

I turned and faced the water, seeing what she was seeing. A dancing ripple swimming through the lake. My grandson was showing off.

"Did you ever find his familiar?" I asked.

"I did, actually. She was here along."

Again, something I'd had to let my daughter figure out on her own.

"But more importantly, Mother, I found him. And I think that's all that really matters."

"Ah, yes. To that be true."

As the years would go on, the Straight Wickeds would earn themselves a gold record, topping the charts more times than anyone could count. Tyler and Olivia would build a new home around the lake at Sage Brook and fill it with new memories, and Tyler and Joe would end up opening eight restaurants in total, every one of them a huge success. The best food was still found in the shop by the road, and with Patrick's life gifted back to him, the cinnamon rolls were just as sweet as ever. My granddaughters would inherit my and Ron's home as well as the retreat once everyone had passed—the wands retired into the wooden box over the mantle. Maddie and Winter would raise their own families, continuing all our traditions in the forest.

Maddie would end up outliving every witch she gave birth to, and she accepted this as her fate. Until the day that Winter would pass, and on that day, she would whisper into the little black bowl she kept filled under the skylight—just where I'd left it upon my own passing. She would tell her brother that it had been a magical life, and that she knew that he could dance forever, but that she was tired and was ready to go home. And from there, the two of them would return to Latharia.

You see, everyone has the ability to reach the goddess and to become filled with her light. Humans speak of eternity, a life without end. In some respect they are right, because as you see, our spirits are immortal. Continuously moving on toward the light they initially came from. Still, there will always be conflicts to overcome, ghosts to deal with, so that light just keeps getting further away. All we can really do is keep moving forward. Keep love in our hearts.

Magic is nothing more than energy, as is the emotion of love. So, my advice to you, witches, and those who claim to be otherwise, is to keep your love grounded. Don't be afraid of it, and above all else, believe. The ancients knew this, and if you listen hard you can still hear them repeating these truths. Just go into the forest and open your ears. The whispers are there, as they have always been, in the pines.

COMING SOON!

The Lost Erwain
Y9ung Adult Fantasy
May 2024

The Hall of Shadows
Horror
November 2024

ACKNOWLEDGMENTS

Firstly, thank you Jean Lowd and CJM, for taking a chance on *In the Pines*. This book has come a long way from where it first began. Which brings me to the second shout out that I must make or forever be cursed. To my dearest members of the Pink Curler Chronicles, you know who you are, and you know that *In the Pines* may never have come to light if I hadn't realized that even witches have bad hair days.

Thank you to everyone who has colored in the lines of my strange and somewhat interesting life. From college professors, friends, and family (my parents—thank you for allowing me to be weird), and the old crew from Cheyenne Meadows. Izzy and Titus, you're in there too. All my dog familiars, whether you're physically still here or not. I love you more than hot chocolate.

A very special cheers to every magical being who I've been fortunate enough to bend my energy around, especially those who helped me realize I was living inside a closet full of brooms. And to you, my early readers. I appreciate every beta reader I've used over the years, particularly you, Courtney! You didn't just give me meaningful feedback; you gave me hope. Every unpublished writer needs that.

Finally, a heavy thank you to my husband. It isn't easy being married to a writer, but you've always supported me. You've not only given me the ability to dedicate more time to my craft, but you also gave me my daughter. I love you for that. And Liviana, thank you for being my muse.

ABOUT THE AUTHOR

Mariah Stillbrook, originally from Iowa, lives in Colorado with her white german shepherd, husband, and little girl.

She graduated from the University of Colorado at Colorado Springs. She spends most of her days writing, reading, and enjoying the occasional hike.

In her late twenties she realized that her writing was missing something, magic. She now focuses her writing on horror and urban fantasy in both adult and young adult genres.

Printed in the USA
CPSIA information can be obtained
at www.ICGtesting.com
LVHW040404270924
792228LV00004B/392